The Rise
of the
Red Shadow

Joseph R. Lallo

DEDICATION

This book is dedicated to the readers of the Book of Deacon series. *The Rise of the Red Shadow* exists because of you. You provided the money, the motivation, and the inspiration to make it happen. I wrote *The Book of Deacon Trilogy* for me. I wrote *The Rise of the Red Shadow* for you.

Table of Contents

ACKNOWLEDGMENTS

I would like to acknowledge:

Nick Deligaris once again for his brilliant artwork.

Anna Genoese and Claudette Cruz for their help cleaning up my grammar.

Sean, Cary, Pete, Lily, Katie, Brandy, and all of the other people who have read my stories and given me advice on how to make them better.

Prologue

Heroes come in all forms. Some are born with righteousness in their heart. Others are forged into a tool for good. And some . . . some become heroes in spite of themselves. The tale you shall now read is one that was nearly lost to history. All knowledge comes at a price, and none has been more costly than the details of this precious record, but to prevent this story from going untold I would gladly pay it ten times over. It is the tale of the rocky road traveled by the least likely hero of the Chosen. By some he was called Leo. By more, he was called Lain.

Most knew him as the Red Shadow—though, in truth, few knew him at all.

His story begins in a nameless forest in the land of Tressor . . .

Chapter 1

The deep south of Tressor was not a land known for its forests. Most of the kingdom was made up of vast plains. Those plains near to rivers and lakes were fruitful, some of the best farmland in the world. Those far from water were dry and barren, giving way to two vast deserts. Farther north was the Great Western Forest, and quite a few respectable forests could be found toward the border with the northern kingdoms, but trees in the far south were scattered and sparse. Where a handful of them stood together in what could be charitably called a grove, hunting was usually poor.

Of course, that depended on what one was hunting for.

In the stifling heat of a night in the deep south, a pair of men moved with slow care, stepping lightly to keep the crunch of dry grass from betraying their approach.

"This way. I saw prints. He can't be far," hissed the first of the men. He was short and wiry, and whereas most of the people of Tressor shaded themselves from the searing burn of the sun by wearing broad-brimmed hats, this fellow had taken a much older route. Every inch of his exposed skin had been smeared with red-brown mud. It had since dried into a crust that blocked the sun nicely, but left him looking as though he'd staggered out of a swamp that morning. From between his teeth jutted a stem of a plant called sugar-stalk, a weed popular among the nomads for the sweet, syrupy pulp that it produced when chewed. His hair was cropped short, and he wore clothes of a billowy, sand-colored cloth. The sleeves of the shirt and legs of the trousers had been rolled up to provide relief against the heat.

"How do they always manage to make it this far south?" moaned the second man quietly. He was taller and stouter, with the same short hair and billowy clothes, though he'd allowed the sun to bake his exposed skin to a leathery hide. He was also weighed down with ropes and sacks, and was swatting irritably at a cloud of flies that seemed dedicated exploring his nose and ears.

"I don't ask questions. I just bring them back. You do the same and maybe you won't need me to come along with you next time," replied the smaller man.

The Rise of the Red Shadow

The many farms of Tressor needed workers. Most of the smaller ones were run by families and communities, with workers drawing a wage, selling their goods, or simply living off of what they grew. The larger plantations, however, tended to work their land on the strength of forced laborers. Slaves could come from any number of sources. Captured soldiers from the increasingly common skirmishes in the north and clashes with disloyal tribes to the south and east made up most of the workers. Others were brought back on ships from far-off lands. Some were simply slaves because their parents had been. The only thing they had in common was that, at some point in their lives, they would look beyond the walls and yearn for their freedom.

If they decided to act, to flee their enslavement, there were men who made their livings by hunting them down and bringing them back. One would be hard-pressed to find two more typical examples than the pair wading through the bushes that night.

They stalked toward a tight cluster of four trees, the ground between obscured by a clump of short, prickly bushes. Boot prints led into the stand of trees. A quick search revealed that there were no prints leaving it. The men communicated with short, sharp hand gestures, indicating what each should do and where each should be. When the thin man was satisfied that each was in position, he drew a short, curved blade from his belt, crouched, and launched himself with a bellow over the bushes. There was a bizarre, high-pitched squeal and a rustle of bushes, then silence. No shout of anger or fear, no fleeing fugitive, just the constant drone of flitting insects in the shaded moonlight. The thin man looked over the ground and grimaced in frustration.

"Never mind, Latak," he grumbled. "He's dead."

"What? Dead? What do you mean he's dead, Dihsaad? How?" replied his heftier partner, Latak.

"You won't believe it. See for yourself."

Latak thumped toward the bushes, no longer worried about being heard and angry that he wouldn't be earning his bounty. When he reached the point where his thin partner was standing, he grimaced. "Augh. Is that a malthrope?"

"Can you think of anything else that looks like that?" remarked Dihsaad.

On the ground, covered with wounds and dried blood, was a creature. It looked as though it was a cross between a human and a fox,

3

with the beast's head and fur applied to an otherwise human form. This one was a female. It was dressed in rags and, judging from the looks of the injuries, it had been dead for a few hours. The slave they had been hunting was a short distance away. His face, neck, and arms were striped with the slashes of claws and peppered with the punctures of teeth. In his hand was a crude club, little more than a branch.

"Looks like he stumbled onto a hiding place that was already taken and they did each other in," Latak reasoned. "But what made that noise?"

His partner made a sound of disgust. "This is why I'm the one who ends up doing all of the tracking."

He slowly crouched, one hand out, and when he came near enough, darted it into the shadow of the nearest bush. More earsplitting squeals rang out as he pulled free a struggling blur of red fur and tattered cloth.

"Enough! Quiet!" he growled, shaking the little creature until it lost the will to struggle.

It was a young malthrope, barely a toddler, dangling pathetically by its tail. The little beast was more animal in appearance than the adult, with spindly limbs and stubby, almost paw-like hands and feet. Its eyes were locked on the motionless form of the female on the ground. Quietly, it made a sound somewhere between weeping and whining.

"This is probably why our bounty got killed. The females are extra vicious when there's a fresh litter to protect," he said.

"How do you know that?" Latak asked.

"I used to hunt these things with my father, back when there were enough of them to make a living at it. I still do, from time to time." With the toe of his boot, he rolled the dead creature to its side, prompting another agonized squeal from the struggling beast in his hand. "Someone got to it already. No tail."

"Well," said Latak, "At least we won't leave empty handed. I hear they pay upwards of seventy entus for a baby malthrope."

It was widely felt that malthropes were a menace. Stories told of them carrying off children and raiding livestock. The creatures were the villains of more than their share of bedtime stories, and were always a safe thing to blame for your problems if you weren't happy with your lot in life. One of the few things that the north and south halves of the continent could agree upon was that wiping the creatures out would be an improvement. Thus, a price had been put on their heads—or, more accurately, their tails. Slicing the tail off an adult and handing it in to the authorities would net you a small fortune in entus, the silver coins that lined the pockets of the more well-off Tressons.

For *young* malthropes, though, the rules were different.

Latak fetched a sack. "I just wish I knew why we have to turn the babies in alive."

"Oh, you didn't hear? A fellow up in Delti was turning the things in, oh, two or three times a week? People got suspicious and took a closer look. Turns out he was just catching foxes and dressing 'em up a bit. Since then, they don't pay unless you can stand 'em up on their hind legs."

"Figures some scoundrel would ruin it for honest folk," he said, taking the struggling thing from his partner and shoving it in the sack.

#

Far north of Tressor, in the very northernmost city in the kingdom formerly known as Vulcrest, sat a cold and meticulous man. The city was known as Verril, and the man was known as Bagu. He was dressed as a noble—clothes exquisite and expensive, face as flawless and emotionless as a sculpture. In very short order, he had risen from a simple member of the Vulcrest military to one of the most powerful and influential of the king's advisers. He now held the rank of general, and already it was said that the vast armies of the newly formed Northern Alliance did not make a move without his direction. He was second only to the king.

In a room adjacent to the entry hall of Castle Verril, its walls littered with maps and its shelves heavy with parchment and books, he waited. His eyes drifted to a sand timer standing in the corner of the room. It was tall and narrow, framed in an ancient black wood carved with symbols that seemed to have no place in this world. Rather than a steady stream of cascading sand, the timer seemed almost frozen. Now and again, a single grain would tumble through the pinched glass and add to the thin dusting in the lower half. At such a rate, it would take decades, perhaps centuries for the timer to run its course.

The click of heels on polished stone echoed through the halls beyond his chamber; moments later, the heavy door was pushed open. In stepped a woman with features very much like his own. She was tall and slender, skin pale and milky, with dark lips and narrow, sharp features. She was beautiful, but in a disconcerting way, as though her beauty came not from nature but from careful study and dedicated

Joseph R. Lallo

attention to detail. Her face as immaculate as his own, but flavored by emotion that made her seem brittle of confidence and short of patience. Her clothes were heavy and layered, caked with fresh snow that was beginning to melt in the relative warmth of the castle.

"You needed me, General Bagu?" she asked.

"Shut the door," he instructed, eyes not even turning to her.

She did as she was told and began to pull the leather gloves from her hands.

"Leave them, you will not be here long."

"Have you a task for me?" Her voice had the restrained energy of someone bursting with eagerness but well aware that to show it would be undignified.

"Of sorts. Our associate Epidime has finished . . . *consulting* with the seers of this place. He has compiled what he believes to be the most accurate of their visions and prophecies. We are now confident in a number of things. Foremost, as we suspected, one of our targets is to be one of the malthrope creatures. Three of the five we seek appear to have already been born or created, and he is quite likely among them. To the best of our detection, he is somewhere south of the front."

"Shall I kill him?" she offered. Her enthusiasm was somewhat more poorly disguised this time.

Bagu closed his eyes and breathed a slow, irritated breath through his nose. "I realize that you are the least experienced among us, Teht, but I am certain I have explained this on more than one occasion. The rules of discourse are quite clear. If we take no direct act of violence against them, they cannot unite against us. You must not—*must not*— kill him. Nor any of the others. If action must be taken, it must be taken through surrogates, and of their own volition. All that I require is for you to locate and secure him. Fortunately, he is a malthrope. They hunt them as vigorously in Tressor as they do here. You should have little difficulty finding him—or, at the very least, little difficulty in finding aid."

"That is all? An errand? I am a mystic specialist, Bagu. I feel as though I should be doing more than acting as tutor for that blasted necromancer and dashing to Tressor whenever the need arises."

"You are the least senior of the generals, Teht. You will do as you are instructed."

"My skills are being wasted!" She was bordering on petulant now, a bratty scowl working its way into her expression.

6

"How your skills should be put to use is my decision alone. Do not question my orders any longer, Teht."

Bagu's final words were delivered no more forcefully than any of the others, but as he spoke, there was a subtle shudder, and around him the papers and shelves rustled and creaked as though under great strain. Her brittle confidence shattered, the boldness and defiance dropping swiftly to subservience. It was as though he had pulled a knife from his desk and explained, in detail, how he intended to use it if she did not fall into line.

"Yes, General Bagu. Of course. It is an honor to serve!" she said hastily. She pulled open the door and marched out.

He leaned back in his chair, eyes turning to the timer once more as the tension faded from his mind. "If she does not learn her place, that woman will come to a very unpleasant end."

Chapter 2

In the dusty fields of Tressor, a short night and a long day had passed. Dihsaad and Latak had trudged back into their camp, reaching it as the sun was setting. It was a typical camp for slavers, a cluster of low, lashed-down tents set up in a circle around a large bonfire. Every aspect was designed to be set up and taken down quickly, and to be easy to lock down and defend. In all, it had the feel of a prison combined with a traveling market. Carriages fortified with bars—little more than rolling cages—were crowded with their valuable cargo, recently acquired workers. Most were members of scattered nomadic tribes, but not all. Mixed among them was a pair of fair-skinned elves from the land across the sea to the east, a place called South Crescent. There was a short, stout dwarf from deep in the mountains as well. Each had been taken far from their home, and all but the newest of them had been stripped of their will to struggle by time and the lash of a whip. Now they sat with empty eyes, waiting.

"Latak! Dihsaad! You had better have a good reason for getting here so late!" growled a voice nearly as grizzled as the man it belonged to. He was the slave master, a man named Grahl, and his leathery skin was a veritable road map of scars from years of encounters with men and women unwilling to become his prize without a fight. "Where is the man I sent you after?"

"Jackal food, by now," Dihsaad remarked.

"You killed him!" the head slaver roared.

"He got *himself* killed. Ran afoul of a malthrope vixen protecting her young," he explained.

The slave master grumbled a few creative profanities under his breath as he wiped away the sweat beading on his brow. "Did you at least get its tail?"

"Someone got it first. But we got the kit," he said, holding his hand out for Latak to supply the bag.

Grahl snatched it away, prompting a few weak growls of complaint. He untied the bag and glanced inside, grimacing slightly at the sight of the occupant. The little creature, barely conscious after the rough trip and intense heat, stared up through dry, red eyes.

8

"Gah. They really *do* look like drowned rats. And the *smell*," he muttered, handing the bag away. "Someone dump some water on this thing. If we want the bounty for it, the ugly little monster is going to have to be alive. And we're probably going to need that money."

"Something got you on edge, boss?"

"On edge? Do you want to know what's got me on edge?" he replied with a sneer. "Look over there. Do you see that dust cloud to the north? Do you know what that is? That's a plantation owner. He's coming to buy a dozen peak-condition slaves. Do you know what I have? Eleven. You were supposed to bring me the twelfth!"

"So they take the eleven and we pick up a spare in the next raid."

"Our reputation is pitiful, idiot. This will be what? Eight, nine times we over-committed? He won't be back, and he'll spread the word that we can't fill our orders. We can't take another stain on our record. We'll be finished!"

"Well, why do you keep selling more than we have?"

"Because people *want* more than I have on hand. When I found out this plantation was looking for my whole stock of single-stripe slaves, I foolishly trusted my best men to bring back the runaway *alive!*"

"Perhaps he will accept a discount."

"He paid already. I convinced him we needed the money to pay for transport."

"Well then perhaps he will take a refund."

"I *spent* the money already, Dihsaad! Gods . . . this will ruin us!"

As the distant carriage trundled ever closer, Grahl alternated between berating anyone within earshot for their laziness and ineptitude and attempting to miraculously identify a twelfth slave that was worth selling. Most of his latter efforts went as far as repeatedly counting the occupants of the carriages, as though it was possible he'd merely overlooked someone during the previous twenty counts. Eventually, time ran out and the prospective customer was stepping out of the sturdy carriage.

The man who stomped his boots to the sandy earth of the slave camp was instantly recognizable as a lifelong farmer. He was getting on in years, but those years had tempered him like steel, leaving him with a shock of silver in his otherwise black hair and beard. He was every bit as sun-broiled as the slavers, as was the case for most everyone in the land of Tressor. His build was lined with dense, gristly muscle. It had been earned years ago, the product of decades of back-

9

breaking labor, and even now that the hardest of the tasks fell to his workers, the wiry muscle was slow to fade.

Everything else one might need to know about the man could be gleaned from the expression on his face. The set of his jaw and the hardness of his gaze spoke volumes of the determination and effort he poured into every enterprise he put his hand to. A slight sneer of disgust twisted his mouth, the sights, sounds, and smells of his surroundings nearly turning his stomach. Nevertheless, this was a purchase important to his business, and thus important to *him,* and he would not leave it to underlings, no matter how trusted.

Out of his rugged and practical carriage stepped two servants, the sort of burly men one tended to bring along when doing business that might go wrong. A third servant remained in the carriage, reins in hand.

Grahl marched up to the newcomers, a practiced look of hospitality hastily locked onto his face in place of panicked anger. The seller and the buyer approached each other, and each slapped his left hand on the right shoulder of the other, a gesture which in another culture would have been a handshake.

"Jarrad! This late in the day I feared you would not make it!" Grahl said.

"I keep to my schedule, Grahl. Are these my men?"

"Yes, yes, ready for inspection!" he said with a brittle grin. "As you can see, some fine ones here. All of them unbranded or single-stripe, as requested. You'll get many good years out of each of them. Worth every entu."

"Mmm," Jarrad grunted.

"Look, here. You see? We've managed to find a pair of elves. Not much muscle on them, but renowned for their stamina. Should be able to do the work of two humans each."

"Mmm," came another grunt, this one more irritated.

"And we've even got a dwarf. Good strong mountain stock. He ought to do the work of *three* men, easily."

"I count eleven slaves here. Where is the last?" Jarrad rumbled.

"I . . . ah . . ." Grahl began, realizing too late that he should have set a few minutes aside from his angry screaming to craft a convincing lie. "Disease, I'm afraid. It came upon him quickly. We separated him from the rest, but he died. Had to bury him deep. Couldn't be helped."

"I need twelve."

"But the elves! And the dwarf! They—"

"I don't care how hard they work, Grahl. This is about numbers. I paid you for twelve healthy men because I have twelve jobs that need doing. Either I leave here with twelve single-stripe slaves, or I'll take back my money and find someone who can provide them."

"I assure you, I am the only slaver in ten territories who deals exclusively in quality slaves. You won't find another slave to match these for twice the price."

"Fill my order as requested or I will take my money and go elsewhere," he said with the slow, deliberate tone of a man on the brink of violence. Responding to the unspoken threat, his hefty servants formed up on either side of Grahl, causing a stir among the more loyal of the slaver's men.

"Of course, of course. Just one moment," he said bowing and stepping back while snapping his fingers insistently for Dihsaad.

"What do you want, Grahl?" asked the far from enthusiastic underling.

"Bring me Ben," the head slaver muttered quietly.

"You don't honestly expect—"

"I wasn't asking for your opinion, Dihsaad," he growled, "Just get Ben!" Turning his attention back to his unsatisfied customer, he displayed his incomplete, yellowing smile. "Now, I may not be able to provide you with a replacement of the same level of quality on such short notice, but I assure you this man will be an asset to you, as he has been to me and my men for quite some time."

After a moment or two of anxious silence, a man was led from within one of the tents. In a camp such as this, it wasn't uncommon to see someone being led. Thanks in large part to the fact that all but the slavers themselves were in heavy restraints, nearly everyone had to be led, if only to keep them from attempting to escape. There was no threat of such a thing in this case, and only minimal restraints, but he still had better reasons than most to require aid in finding his prospective buyer.

For one, he was old. Old enough to be a grandfather. While in actuality he wasn't very much older than Jarrad, by slave standards he was ancient. He was also better dressed than the other slaves. Rather than the torn and filthy remnants of the last clothes he'd worn as a free man, he was wearing a long-sleeved tan robe, caked with dust. The waist was tied inexpertly closed with a length of rope, and the front was open enough to reveal a tunic and trousers of a matching color. A scraggly wreath of gray hair wrapped around the back of an otherwise bald head, and a wild mass of whiskers had claimed most of his face. Most notable, though, was a strip of cloth tied in place as a blindfold and explaining the main reason for the guiding hand.

"A blind man!? You had better be joking, Grahl," Jarrad barked. "You, slave. Show me your arm!"

"Are you talking to me, sir?" asked the blind man with a crisp, precise manner of speech that seemed out of place in a place like a slaver camp.

"Of course I am!"

"Well, there are a number of slaves about, sir. If a man can't make eye contact with you, you really need to be more specific than that," he replied, rolling up his right sleeve to reveal three deep scars, short lines arranged like the rungs of a ladder. The first was ancient and faded with time, the second somewhat more recent, and the last fresher still. The rest of his arm was littered with no fewer than six marks, ranging from letters of two different alphabets to simple insignias. The arm told a story, as was its purpose. The symbols told of past owners. The lines spoke of value. It was never a good sign to see too many of either.

"You would offer me a triple-stripe slave in place of a single-stripe?" Jarrad growled.

"What I am offering you is experience, Jarrad. This man has had half a dozen owners, yes, but he learned everything the first three had to teach, and taught the second three all they knew. You've got good strong backs, but Blind Ben here will keep their equipment in good repair, and teach them tricks that will make them work harder and faster than you'd believe. You and I both know a man doesn't end up with six slaver's marks on his arm unless there have been six bright and wealthy men interested in his service."

"Six marks also means five bright and wealthy men felt he was beyond his usefulness," Jarrad countered.

"Six, sir, seeing as how I'm back on the market, so to speak," corrected Ben.

"You would speak to your master that way?"

"You haven't bought me yet, sir. Grahl is my master," he said evenly. "But since you ask, yes, I would speak to my master that way. I'm too old to be worrying about who hears what."

Grahl's fists tightened, his muscles tensed, and another moment would have brought a strap across the slave's back, but a wry grin came to Jarrad's face.

"Right. I'll take him, but he's still not a single-stripe. I want the difference in silver," Jarrad said.

Grahl twitched. "Yes, that . . . that is perfectly fair. I . . . I can have your silver for you in—"

"Today."

"I . . . I have something better," Grahl proclaimed, hissing again to Dihsaad, "The bag! The bag!"

The weakly struggling bag was thrust into his hand, and he held it out to the dissatisfied customer.

"In this bag is a malthrope. A baby," Grahl said.

"What good does that do me?" ask Jarrad, recoiling from the sack.

"You know as well as I do that a live baby malthrope fetches no less than seventy entus. That should go a long way to making up the difference. And turning one of these in is a civic service. People will respect you for bringing this in."

"Where did you *get* this thing?"

Grahl opened his mouth, but shut it again quickly before the truth tumbled out. He couldn't very well say that his men had found it while hunting for the slave he'd just said died of an illness. After taking a moment to remember to plan out his webs of deceit with a bit more care in the future, he wove the best one he could manage on short notice.

"My brother found it . . . with its mother. The creature had died giving birth. We managed to keep the little pest alive so we could claim the bounty."

"This hardly looks like a newborn," Jarrad said, tugging open the bag and peering inside.

"Look, that doesn't matter, does it? What matters is you'll gain standing with your community if they know you're taking the time to help rid the area of these little monsters, *and* you'll have the money you're missing."

Jarrad looked long and hard at the man holding the bag.

"I'll throw in food and water enough to keep the thing alive until you get home."

The customer's jaw tightened and he snatched the bag away. "Very well, since it is clear you don't have my money anymore. Load up the blind man and the food, and for heaven's sake, don't say another word. This deal has gotten twisted enough."

13

Blind Ben was led to the barred carriage, and when there were enough armed men on hand to make those already inside think twice about escape, the door was opened and he was helped in. Before the door closed, Jarrad upended the bag onto the floor of the carriage, causing the ragged ball of red fur to tumble out. The breath of fresh air and shock of the fall had brought its senses back and it made a mad scramble for the door, but the bars were slammed hard enough to knock the beast to the center of the carriage floor. A few halfhearted kicks and shoves sent it scurrying for cover, the same way one might treat a rat that had been dropped into a crowded room, and the same way the rat might behave.

Ben had wearily taken a seat on one of the plank benches that lined each side of the carriage, and was too tired to grope for the creature when it wedged itself underneath. When it became clear that the thing wasn't going to climb out, the other slaves left it cowering and trembling behind the blind man's legs, its eyes wide and its heart pounding.

#

For a slave, the origin and destination of a trip have profound implications. When on the way to a slave trader, the journey was a perilous one. They were forced into ships, hundreds traveling in space intended for dozens, or into long and poorly equipped caravans of carriages and wagons. As the captives were tossed by the seas or burnt by the sun, those who could laughably be called their caretakers take little notice when a handful fewer arrive than had departed. There were simply so many, and each was so cheap, that it wasn't worth the effort to take any real interest in their well-being. *Some* of them always survived.

When on the way *from* the slaver, however, things were different. Now they were few, a precise number, purchased for a tidy sum and intended for a specific purpose. Very few plantation or mine owners could afford to buy more than they need, so every one of the workers was looked after for the duration of the trip, so that they would be strong, healthy, and ready to work when they arrived. It was astounding how much the value of a living, breathing creature could change based solely upon where it was headed, and how many coins had been exchanged for it.

Regardless of the philosophical ramifications, it was this monetary value that had been one of the two things that had allowed the little malthrope to survive his journey. Jarrad was no fool, and the slaves he had purchased were far more than a simple purchase of workers. They represented his next harvest, and those for years to come. They were the tools that would allow him to grow more crops on his farm, and, in turn, would allow his farm to grow larger, and more successful. So he gave them food, and he gave them water, more than enough of each. He even provided a pair of buckets; one to wash with, and one for . . . other necessities. Though the red-furred creature was not destined to be a worker, it did represent a respectable quantity of silver when the time came—but only if it was alive. Thus it was only sound business sense to see to it that it received a share of the food and water.

That was enough to keep it from wasting away, but for a helpless and reviled creature among a dozen frustrated slaves seeking a target for their hostility, there were greater dangers than starvation. The carriage had barely been on the road for more than a few minutes when the tribal and racial lines began to be drawn. Of the twelve slaves in the wagon, three were from Tanoa, an island off the western coast. Five more were nomads, two from Nattal tribe and three from the Wendo tribe. Each of these tribes was in on again/off again conflict with the others, and both were at war the Tanoans.

The two elves quickly became the targets of their combined hostility, as well. Initially it was for the simple fact that they weren't human, but this was soon overshadowed by the fact that they were just tall and graceful enough to look down their noses at the rest of the group. That left the dwarf, who had no particular gripe with any in attendance, but was eager for a fight just to break up the monotony. Twice the various combinations of allies and adversaries came to blows, and twice the hired hands supervising them had to lay down the law before they would settle for trading increasingly creative obscenities and eying each other distrustfully.

The only passenger who seemed to be exempt from the posturing and prejudice was Ben, the blind man. Though none could explain precisely why, no one felt particularly inclined to involve him. He merely sat on the edge of the bench and slouched forward, swaying side to side as the carriage jostled along the poorly kept roads. Perhaps it was because he was blind. If he couldn't see *them*, it seemed only fair that they treat him as though they could not see *him*. Or perhaps it was because he was so old that he had earned a measure of respect and reverence simply for having survived so long in so wretched a life.

Whatever the reason, the blind man was left alone, as though he emitted an aura of solitude. Huddled beneath Ben's seat, the malthrope was mercifully afforded the same luxury.

It was a very long journey from the slaver camp to Jarrad's fields. True, Tressor was a vast land, but most of the trip was spent attempting to maneuver an overloaded carriage over poorly maintained roads. That much time trundling along in the hot sun was enough to take the fight from even the feisty dwarf. As each of the men slipped into his own tight cycle of anger, frustration, boredom, and hopelessness, the creature among them drifted through its own sequence of emotions.

First was fear. The carriage shook and rattled all around him, assaulting his keen ears and turning his stomach. And then there were the others. The little beast had seen and smelled things like those that surrounded him before, but only from afar. Worse, whenever he did, he saw and felt an anxiety in his mother that he quickly learned to adopt. If she was afraid of something, then it was certainly something to be feared. Now, for reasons he had no way of understanding, he was trapped with them.

Worse than the fear, though, was the sadness. As he huddled in the corner, his deft paws hugging his gangly legs and his prized tail wrapped around his feet, he thought of the place he called home, a forest that was already farther away than he could even imagine, and growing more distant by the moment. He thought of his mother, too. Motionless on the dusty ground . . .

The image burned hot in his mind. What burned his mind more was the slow realization that both his home and his mother were lost to him forever. He thought of these things, and quiet, bitter sobs shook him.

Grief is like any other kind of pain. No matter how intense or how constant it is, time takes the edge from it. It may not fade, but it loses its sharpness. It becomes the new normal, and eventually steps aside and makes room in the mind for other things.

When his mind had numbed to the sorrow, and for the moment there were no more tears left to cry, the little fox felt the parts of himself that had been buried by the tragedy creep to the surface. Chief among them was curiosity. As frightening as all of this was, it was new, and something inside of him wanted to know more. He inched out from his hiding place, stretching to get a better look and retreating when he was noticed and a foot or fist swatted in his direction. The attacks didn't make him less curious, just more cautious, teaching him to watch where they were looking and picking his inspections accordingly. He sniffed and tugged at boots and cuffs, generally making a nuisance of himself until a particularly quick kick sent him scurrying back to his corner.

The food, when it was offered, was another curiosity. Once each day, a bowl for each of the slaves was slid through a rectangular slit along the bottom of the carriage door. When he received his share the first time, he didn't know what to make of it. The stuff was wet and mushy, and it didn't have any flavor to it, but it took the hunger away. It also gave him a bowl to play with until they were able to get it away from him. With a carriage of slaves to deal with, the servants couldn't very well climb inside and chase him around. As a result, they were forced to loosen the chain securing the door enough to fit an arm through and try to snatch the bowl away. Since it was the slave-keepers who were trying to take the bowl back, the longer he was able to hold onto it, the more entertained the other slaves were. It quickly became a game, and the little creature became very good at it, particularly since it was the only time he was able to scamper around the entire floor of the carriage without dodging feet.

Eventually they just let him keep the bowl rather than fight with him. When a new one came at the next meal time, he would grab the new and they would take the old.

When the current bowl became tiresome, he would look out between the bars of the carriage. There were many unfamiliar sights. Until the horrible day that his mother was killed, the malthrope's world had been little more than thin forests and the occasional sprint through the sandy fields between. The nearest he'd ever had to a house was a simple hut composed of twisted branches, mud, and thatch. It was a place he only dimly remembered, because they had been forced to abandon it one night and never returned. Now he saw homes built of wood or stone, and there were so many of them. Sometimes they were far enough apart that he could only see one of them from one horizon to the next. Other times they were close enough that they were nearly touching. The closer the houses, the more people there were, and the busier they seemed to be. The busier they were, the more they spoke.

To sharp ears honed to pick out the rustle of a single tuft of grass half a field away, the sound of so many different voices speaking was simultaneously the most terrible and the most wonderful thing he had ever heard. It was a chorus of complex sounds and unfamiliar voices. Sometimes he let the sounds blend together, washing over him. Other times he tried to single them out, scanning the crowds and attempting to match the mouths to the words. Some of the sounds had a familiar shape to them, things he had heard his mother say on one of the rare occasions that she spoke.

Once he tried to form some of the sounds himself. The high-pitched, squeaky attempt at speech must have caught the attention of some of the townsfolk, because eyes turned to him, voices raised, and he learned a few new words that stung him with their tone. From that time onward he huddled in the shadow of the bench and kept quiet when people were near. There were some words he knew he never wanted to hear again.

Chapter 3

The parched land and near-desert were long behind the carriage now, replaced by the lush green fields and rich brown soil of the heart of Tressor. The gray stone of the road traced a long, meandering line down the center of sprawling plantations on either side. Each was preparing for the long growing season ahead. The little malthrope tucked himself deeper into shadow as the sound of voices began to grow louder. It wasn't a city this time, but a crossroad. A noisy wagon loaded with hay, tools, and workers rattled by, taking the more worrying sounds with it. In the carriage ahead, he heard the man who always told the others what to do raise his voice above the rest. This caused his ears to perk up, as this was typically what happened right before one of the large men handed out food.

"Blast it. They still haven't fixed that road to the bounty office," Jarrad spat angrily as he stepped from his carriage and eyed a rocky trail with at least three fallen trees across it. "I am not going to risk snapping another axle trying to get a carriage down there to cash in that malthrope." He turned to one of his men. "You, fetch the beast and walk it down to the office to get our silver. Shouldn't take you more than an hour."

The young creature spotted one of the servants headed his way and mischievously snatched the bowl up, ready for another round of keep-away. The lock on the barred door to the slave carriage was undone and the chain holding it shut was loosened, the servant's arm reaching inside. A quick yank pulled the bowl easily out of reach, but the man wasn't after it. Instead, he grabbed the beast's tail and hauled him out. Before he knew what was happening he was dangling from the servant's fist, yelping and flailing about as the man struggled to get a sack open to drop him inside.

"Hmph," came a grunt. "I've been purchased by a fool."

All eyes turned to the blind man. Aside from requesting food or one of the buckets, it was the first sound he'd made since they had loaded him into the carriage. The sharp looks he received from Jarrad and his men made it a pretty safe bet that it would be the last sound he'd be making for a while if they had anything to say about it.

19

The servant not currently grappling with an unruly rascal stepped menacingly toward the blind man, a stiff leather strap in his hand. Though it hadn't been put to use yet, there was little doubt that it was a favored disciplinary tool. He folded it over and gave it a vicious slap across his palm to give the sightless man a sense of what was about to come. Before he could reach the door to wrench it open, though, Jarrad stopped him with a hand to the shoulder.

"Blind man. Ben, is it? Your former master claimed you were a man of wisdom and experience. Talk like that suggests it was another of his lies. Explain yourself."

"Are you a farmer?"

"I am."

"And do you sell your seeds, or do you wait and harvest them when they are full grown?"

"What sort of a question is that?"

"An apt one. You're about to hand over a seedling."

Jarrad looked to the creature just as it was finally wrestled into a sack. "You aren't suggesting I let that thing grow up?"

"I'm saying that a grown male malthrope's tail is worth a hell of a lot more than a brat like that. Certainly enough to make for a good return on a little bit of waiting and a few scraps of food."

A look of disgust curled his lip again as the plantation owner looked to the struggling bag. It was a distasteful suggestion . . . but, then, such was so often the case in business these days. The last he'd heard, the bounty on an adult was at least two hundred entus, and it changed daily. Sometimes it climbed to over five hundred. Strictly speaking, it wasn't permissible to harbor a malthrope, but his land was tucked away at the tail-end of nowhere. The chances of the local watch ever finding out were pretty slim, and after the trouble they gave him when he was attempting to buy the new fields these men were to work, the thought of defying them a bit was enticing. Yes, he would have to feed it, but the skinny thing couldn't eat much more than one of his hunting hounds . . .

With a shrug, the little beast's life was spared—at least for a few years.

"Throw it back with the rest of them," Jarrad instructed the servant with the sack.

#

Jarrad marched out before the assembled slaves, flanked as always

20

by his burly servants. Neither had yet had his name spoken, but names weren't really necessary in their line of work. Their purpose was to be a force of nature, a physical weight applied to their master's words. They did their jobs very well. Each held a leather strap, wrist-width and arm-length, in one hand. The other hand held the harness of one of the master's dogs.

Unlike the men who held them, the dogs were sleek and thin. They had the short hair and mottled coat shared by most of the hunting dogs of Tressor, and to the untrained eye they were not terribly threatening. To one who had been chased by one, the cold, measuring look in their eyes as they stood at the ready stirred chilling memories and caused old scars to ache.

Their owner turned and scanned his own gaze across the new workers, as a general might review a group of new recruits. When he'd determined whatever it was he'd been seeking to determine, he spoke. His voice was strong, and carried to the far reaches of his land with little effort.

"By now you've seen your quarters, and you've seen the land. It is paradise by no means, but you can be damn sure that there are worse places to be. There are farmers, many of them, who think the best way to get a day's work out of a slave is to beat it out of him. They think the best way to earn a pile of gold is to scrimp in the bowls of their workers. I'm not one of them. I know that if I want a hard day's labor done well, then I need my slaves healthy and strong. On this plantation, life will be as good as you allow me to make it. If you work hard today, the harvest will be strong, and there will be more than enough food to fill your bellies, and more than enough silver left to keep roofs over your heads and clothes on your backs tomorrow. Slack today and you will feel it tomorrow. Your meals will be meager, your clothes will be ragged, and the holes in your walls will not be patched, because you will not have given me the means to provide anything better. I don't punish you for a poor day's work—you do.

"Now, do not think for a moment that this means there will not be punishment if it is earned. You'll notice my men carry straps. Some of you have already felt their lash. I cannot abide disobedience or disrespect. If you attempt to steal from me, if you speak ill of myself or my family, or if you do not do as you are told, punishment will be swift and severe. Is that understood?"

There was a grudging murmur of acknowledgment.

"*Is that understood!*" he growled, the nameless enforcers advancing a step.

"Understood!" the slaves replied quickly.

"Good! Now, as your first week on my land and under my ownership, this is brand week. Many of you are familiar with what that entails, but for the rest, listen closely."

Jarrad turned and motioned to one of his men, who paced toward a shed near the edge of the field.

"You are slaves in the kingdom of Tressor. That means that your right arm must bear two things. The first is your set of stripes. You will bear one, two, or three depending on how valuable you are. The strongest among you will receive a single stripe. This signifies that you are able to work the hardest and the longest. This also means that you will have the best food, the best quarters, and the most privileges. Those who cannot or will not work to that level will not receive the same level of treatment, and will bear two stripes. Men and women too weak or old, or otherwise useless in the fields, will be given three stripes and very little else. If you want a happy life, you will fight hard to avoid those extra stripes."

As he finished this first speech, the man he'd sent away returned. Rather than the strap, his free hand now clutched a short iron shaft with a twist on its end. Even in the bright sun, it was clearly glowing cherry-red.

"Aside from the stripes, you will be branded with this mark, the letter J. It labels you as my property, and in the event you escape and someone tracks you down, it will tell them who you should be returned to. You should know that, to this day, no slave has ever been brought back to me. Most have never tried to escape. Those who have didn't make it far before Keenock and Ebu here got their teeth into them."

At the sound of their names, each dog perked up and turned to its master. He walked over and scratched each of them behind the ears.

"You try to run away more than once, and these little devils will make sure that the second time will be with a limp. Understood?"

"*Understood!*" the slaves hastily replied.

"You learn quickly. Good to see. Now, obviously I don't know for certain how hard each of you can work, so most of you won't get your stripes until one week from today. You have that much time to prove your worth, and I suggest you use it wisely. One of you, however, already bears his third stripe, and thus has nothing to prove. He is also the only one of you who has been foolish enough to speak to me improperly. Thus, he is the volunteer to show each of you what you've got to look forward to. Blind man, step forward and roll up your right sleeve."

With the resigned sigh of a man who had done it too many times before, Ben took three steps toward the voice. Jarrad took the harnesses of his guard dogs as his men approached. One manhandled the old man's arm, steadying it while his partner raised the cooling brand. With a swift, efficient roll and a sickening sizzle, the tool was applied. Ben gritted his teeth, his legs deciding without his consent that they no longer wished to support his weight. He was lowered to the ground as he heroically resisted the urge to scream.

The plantation owner looked up, his face blank and unfeeling. "Let that be one final motivation to work hard this week. One less stripe is one less branding. Get him on his feet and take him to my personal workshop. I'm going to put the dogs back in their pen. The rest of you, line up. Today you get a brand and some rest. Tomorrow you start earning your keep."

Chapter 4

"Inside," growled Jarrad, forcing the sturdy wooden door of the workshop open.

Ben placed his hand on the door frame, then slid it to the door and glided his fingers along its surface to guide himself inside. Were he able to see, Ben would likely have been very concerned indeed by the contents of the room. Woodworking tools of every type hung from pegs on the walls: axes, hammers, saws, and a dozen more implements with red-brown stains that could be rust, or could be something else. Most of the walls were wood, and most of the floor earth, but at the far side of the room was a stone slab and brick wall. The slab was scrupulously clean. At its center was an anvil and assorted smithing tools. Against the wall was a furnace, its door open and the fire inside slowly dying. There were many, many things that could be put to torturous use if punishment was the aim of this visit.

Even without his sight, the old man was able to learn more than enough to make him nervous. From the feel of the door, it was a rough, thick construction; heavy enough to withstand an awful lot of punishment . . . and dense enough to keep virtually any noise from filtering through. From the crunch beneath his sandals, the floor was nothing but dirt and sawdust, the kind of floor that didn't show stains when blood was spilled. When he was far enough inside to no longer feel the sun beating on his back, Ben's new owner stepped inside and slammed the door, bolting it behind him. A rough grip on the blind man's shoulder maneuvered him forward a few steps, then aside.

"Sit," growled Jarrad.

After feeling around behind him to be certain there was a bench waiting, Ben obeyed. A creak signaled his master doing the same. After he sat, Jarrad released a long, meaningful sigh. It was the sort of sound one makes after placing down a heavy load, the body's expression of bone-weariness. He mopped his face and threw down the strap on a work table, silently staring into the middle distance.

"I want to ask you some questions, blind man," Jarrad said with weariness in his voice.

"Do you? I'd imagined you'd brought me here to put one of those straps you kept talking about to good use," Ben remarked.

Jarrad looked to the loop of leather, then to Ben. "In my experience, when a man reaches your age, he's set enough in his ways that a few lashes aren't going to change anything."

"There's truth to that."

"The slavers tell me you are a man of many skills."

"There's truth to that as well. Through six different owners, I've put my hand to just about any task that might need to be done. I've spent time in a mine, I've pumped bellows, plowed fields, worked a loom . . ."

"Fine, fine. We grow rakka here. Familiar with it?"

"Tricky stuff."

Calling it tricky was an understatement. Known variously as rakka berry, rakka fruit, red-seed fruit, and long-life fruit, rakka was infamously finicky. It would only grow in certain types of soil, needed a very specific climate, and couldn't survive without just the right amount of water. It grew in dense bushes with cruel thorns, and didn't even have the decency to ripen the way other fruits and vegetables did. The berries grew in clusters of a few dozen, and in a single cluster there could be fruits at every level of ripeness, from green to nearly fermented. Worst of all, the plant sapped the life from the soil. If you were foolish enough to grow it for more than a season or two on the same field, the land would be barren for years.

It was a crop that had ruined more than its share of farmers, but if you had the dedication and resources to cultivate it properly and seek out properly ripened berries day after day throughout the growing season, it was bar none the most valuable thing a farmer could produce. Properly dried and roasted, the seeds from within the berries could last for years without spoiling. Ground and boiled, they produced a tea that was the only known treatment for a withering disease that the locals called bone-rot. Soaked and mixed into soup, porridge, or stew, they fortified even the most meager ration enough to keep a man alive for days. Indeed, they were largely responsible for the Tresson army's well-earned reputation of having seemingly endless stamina. The berries themselves had all of the usual uses one might have for a sour fruit, the vines made for decent rope, and even the thorns had their uses. Growing it was a gamble, but one with a tremendous reward when it could be coaxed to pay out.

"How much experience have you had with it?"

"Two owners ago I worked on a rakka plantation on the east coast. I was there for six years."

"So you know how to process it?"

"I do."

"Explain."

"Well, every day you go out and track down the ripe berries . . ."

"Describe a ripe berry."

Ben raised one hand and touched his thumb to his ring finger, then pinched the meat of his thumb with the other hand. "That ripe."

"You do it by feel?"

"I don't have many other options, master. Though I've heard you pick them when they are as pink as the inside of your cheek."

"Right, go on."

"You squeeze the seeds out, then set aside the fruit for wine or preserves or whatnot. The seeds get a soak in oak ashes mixed with water for a few days, three at least. Then they get dried in trays, then roasted until they smell right . . ."

"And how long is that?"

"*Until they smell right*," Ben repeated with irritation, "I know it when I smell it. You set me down in the roasting house and I'll tell you when."

Jarrad grinned in satisfaction. "Continue."

"Then you cool it, dump it into a sack, and sell it."

The owner leaned back in his chair and breathed another sigh. "Well, Grahl wasn't lying about you, at least. You'll be helping to train the others. From the sound of it, you can teach my existing workers a thing or two as well. The question is, what do I do with you after you're through teaching them?"

"The slavers had me fixing their equipment."

"What sort of equipment?"

"Whatever they gave me."

Jarrad grunted. "We'll see what you can do in that area later. Tell me. What motivated you to speak up about the malthrope?"

"You were about to throw away an opportunity. That's something I hate to see," he replied, adding with a shrug, "So to speak."

"Mmm. Well, listen closely, because there are a few things you need to learn about me. I'm not so hard-headed that I'll ignore a good idea simply because of who suggested it, but I absolutely will *not* tolerate disrespect. You crossed the line with your remarks. As I said, I don't see how beating you will do any good, but those three stripes on your arm afford you very little, and until I feel like you've atoned for your mistake, you will get even less, because every morsel I feed that malthrope comes out of your share, and every problem the beast causes, you solve. Understood?"

"Yes, master."

"Good. Now go clean up that brand of yours," Jarrad said, making his way to the door and unbolting it. His servants were waiting on the other side. "Take him to get cleaned up, then take him to the bunk house."

Chapter 5

That first week on the plantation—brand week, as Jarrad had called it—was a revealing one. Even to the newcomers, it was clear that the plantation had just undergone a massive change. The land was arranged into three long, narrow fields, but a novice could see that only the first of them had ever been worked. The other two were a match for the surrounding countryside; rolling, wild grassland with the occasional tree or bush. A newly built fence, new enough that the wood was still green in places, loosely separated each field from the next, and a more imposing one ran the perimeter of the plantation.

Like the fences, the slave quarters were brand new, to the point that three of them hadn't yet been completed. Each was little more than a shack; three solid walls made from rough planks were topped with a roof that sloped upward to a fourth wall featuring a door and a window, each covered with a woven-grass mat. Inside, there was enough room for a bed and a table with two chairs, with a bit of floor space to spare.

At least, such was the case for the single-stripe slaves. Double-stripe slaves packed two beds into the same space, and until they proved otherwise, all of the new slaves were given this treatment. As for triple-stripe slaves, it turned out that Ben was the first of them to work on the plantation long enough to require lodging, so it was decided it was fitting to quarter him in one of the unfinished shacks until a more appropriate dwelling could be prepared. As expected, seeing the better treatment a hard day's labor could buy them and the punishment that awaited them for laziness was a remarkably effective motivator.

As the week wore on, the slaves slowly allowed the lines between their factions erode. The Nattal and Wendo tribesman were the first to give up their rivalry after each realized that they could not remember the precise reason their tribes were fighting. The elves and the dwarf agreed that they ought to ally themselves together, since they were the non-humans of the group, and the alliance lasted until the dwarf remembered how smug the pair of fair-folk were and decided he preferred the humans after all. He alternately joined the Tanoans and the tribesmen in their various tasks, mostly because he had a hard time telling them apart, and eventually the elves caved and pitched in with the rest.

Briefly, the newcomers attempted to draw a line in the sand between themselves and Jarrad's original slaves, but by the final day of brand week, everyone had come to the conclusion that formalizing their prejudices was more trouble than it was worth. Life was hard enough without having to remember whether you were supposed to hate the man working beside you.

Each day that week was spent plowing, tilling, dividing, and marking the new stretches of land. Each night, a fire was built to dispose of the weeds, shrubs, and other waste that had been pulled free during the day. The slaves would gather around the flames, eat their evening meal, and recover from their day. As they did, they spoke to one another. It was in this way that the newcomers learned that Jarrad had managed to squeeze from the land an exceptional crop the previous year, and had used the profit to buy the two plots of land beside his own, with the remaining money going to the purchase the slaves to work the land. Thus, a single-plot farm with half a dozen slaves was now triple the size, with eighteen men to work it. It explained why there was so much hard work to be done, and promised a back-breaking season ahead, because their new owner had sunk every last coin he had into this gamble.

That meant he would squeeze every drop of effort out of the slaves to make sure it would pay off.

#

On the last night of brand week, as the sun set and the fire smoldered, the inevitable subject arose. It was a topic that eventually made the rounds in every prison or labor camp, regardless of location or culture. How did you get here?

As the stories began to flow, a sad fact once again came to light. For those unfortunate enough to have been a part of more than one such discussion, it became clear that there were only a handful of ways one became a slave. Most were taken by raiding parties, groups of ruthless men and women who made their living snatching up fresh workers. Some were taken because they had no means to defend themselves from the usually heavily-armed and heavily-armored raiders.

This was the case for the Nattal tribesman. The Nattal were a loose group of desert nomads who traveled together from oasis to oasis. The

Joseph R. Lallo

unlucky pair now sitting around the fire had been separated from their caravan. Before two days had passed, slavers snatched them up like cows too slow to stay with the herd. Others were in the wrong place at the wrong time, caught trespassing on Tresson land or in Tresson waters . . . or at least near enough to Tresson land or waters for the raiders to claim they were trespassing. The Tanoans and the Wendo tribesman had been captured in that way. The Tanoans grudgingly admitted they were fishing in Tresson waters. The Wendos had attempted to squat a piece of land that they thought a local lord had abandoned. The lord felt differently, of course.

"So, what about you, Blondie? How did you end up here?" asked Gurruk the dwarf as he shoveled thin stew into his mouth. The comment was directed at one of the two elves.

"My name is Borohnirr, not Blondie! I already told you!" the elf replied. "I was the *first* one you asked."

"Well, how am I supposed to tell you elves apart? You can't even grow a decent beard! And I can't remember what you said, anyway. Means you're a bad storyteller."

"Or *you're* a bad listener," Borohnirr groaned. "For the last time. I was aboard a ship. It was a diplomatic mission. I was attacked, quite unprovoked, off the east coast. I fought valiantly, but I was subdued, and ended up working in a saltern. Imagine me, a *prince*, raking salt on the shore of this blasted continent."

"Oh, right. A *prince*. What about you, Goldie? A prince as well?" Gurruk asked, pointing a grimy finger at the other elf.

"Not Goldie, Glinilos! And if you must know, I was a . . . well, you wouldn't understand my native term, but I was what *you* would call a duke," replied the other fair-haired fellow. "I was planning on buying a tannery, and the blasted raiders decided to put me to work there instead."

"Uh-huh." Gurruk nodded. "Thought so. You know something? In my life I've met an awful lot of elves, and I've never met one that didn't claim to be one kind of royalty or another. Either South Crescent is absolutely lousy with nobles, or you folk can't be bothered to come up with an original lie."

"Believe what you choose," remarked Blondie. "I suppose you've got a better story, Gurruk?"

"Me? Well, I'd been drinking a bit too much—" he began.

"Why do I get the idea most of your stories are going to start that way?" Goldie jabbed.

"Because I'm not a hoity-toity elf who needs to make up grand tales. Anyway. I got drunk, and I woke up on the wrong side of a border. Simple as that."

"Ha! Simple as that, eh?" snapped one of the Tanoans.

He was the youngest and scrawniest of the Tanoan trio, a boy still in his teens that the others called Nac. He was the only one of the newcomers who seemed to be in danger of falling short of single-stripe status when the time came to apply the brands. It was partially due to the fact that he simply didn't have the strength to work as hard as the others. Mostly, though, it was due to a spark of spirit that hadn't yet been extinguished.

"Something wrong, Nac?" asked Gurruk.

"Something wrong?" he raved, glancing about before lowering his voice to an insistent whisper. "We are *slaves*. We are being held against our will. How can you all just sit around the fire, chatting as though there is nothing wrong?"

"What's the alternative?" said one of his fellow Tanoans wearily. "We knew that this was a risk when we set foot on that ship. The rest of the crew had enough money, or rich enough relatives, to buy back their freedom. We didn't. Take your fate like a man."

"A man doesn't just accept a yoke around his neck like a wild horse that's been tamed."

"Have you ever seen a wild horse tamed, Nac?" asked Blondie. "There are a handful of outcomes. Sometimes they give up quickly. Sometimes they fight valiantly and must be worn down. Sometimes they fight so hard they break a leg and are no good to anyone."

Nac scowled, his voice growing a bit louder. "I guarantee you I could be over that wall and half a day away before anyone even knew I was gone."

"I can give you five good reasons why you're wrong, son," came a voice from the other side of the fire. It was a man named Menri, the unofficial leader of Jarrad's original six slaves. He was older than the rest, but was as well muscled and able-bodied as any of the group. On his face was a crudely trimmed beard and mustache, and the march of time had left his head nearly bare. The right sleeve of his slave tunic was raised, displaying his brand and stripe with the same pride a soldier might show his rank. Despite his advancing years, he'd yet to be given his second stripe.

"Oh, yeah? And just what are they?"

"One, you see these scars?" he asked, pulling up his trouser leg to show a knot of skin that looked to have been the result of a pitchfork attack. "Old Jarrad wasn't joking about those hounds of his. These are from his old ones, but the new ones are just as mean, believe me. Two, let's pretend you get away from those demons. All the farmers in this area know each other, and they know a slave tunic when they see one. Even if you can get to the next farm without a horse, one look at that outfit and you'll be knocked down, tied up, and dragged back.

"Three, let's pretend you stole yourself a set of clothes and made it to a town. You've still got that brand on your arm. Think back to every time you've crossed a Tresson border or used a port. They ever forget to check your arm? Knocked down, tied up, dragged back. Four, let's say you manage to find a smuggler to get you over the border. Half of those guys will just sell you back to the raiders, and then it's knocked down, tied up, dragged back again. Mainly though, there's five."

"What's five?"

"Whisperin' only makes 'em listen harder."

Nac's eyes shot open, and he turned just in time to receive a punishing backhand across the face from one of Jarrad's men. While he was still reeling, he was snatched up and dragged away. The others watched as he was pulled aside and the punishment was administered for the cardinal sin of the plantation: plotting escape. No words were exchanged between those remaining around the fire, but the same thoughts churned in each of their heads. It was a well-known fact that once you'd been captured by the Tressons for one of the right reasons and had been held long enough to be sold, there wasn't much hope for you.

Slavery was like a rare disease with an even rarer cure. You never imagined you'd catch it, but once you did, there was little sense in fighting. The real question that burned at the minds of this freshest group of slaves, though, was the more troubling realization: the fact that they had probably breathed their final breaths as free men, or the fact that they had accepted the fate so quickly. A small piece of them wished they'd still had the fire in their heart to feel as Nac had.

As the first lashes of his punishment began to pierce the air, that voice within them was quickly silenced.

#

With the weight of their thoughts dragging their spirits down, each of the slaves tried to find some manner of distraction. A flicker of motion and a gleam of eyes at the edge of the fire's light provided it. Menri saw it first, and for an instant he felt the flutter of fear in his stomach as memories of his encounter with Jarrad's dogs flashed. A moment's thought brushed the feelings away, and dark grin came to his face.

"Ho, blind man! Your shadow is back!" he said with a grin, pointing.

The other slaves squinted in the indicated direction. First they saw Blind Ben, then the yellow gleam of beastly eyes—the malthrope. Ben had been sitting a bit farther from the fire than the others, quietly eating his meal until Menri's comment. Now his spoon was still and his head was cocked. If he'd still had his sight, he would be looking around. Instead, he was listening. When the little creature took another step closer, crunching a tuft of grass as he did, the old man sneered.

"I don't know how that blasted thing keeps getting out!" he grumbled.

While the slaves had found their niches with relative ease—and, in any case, had jobs to do, the malthrope was another matter entirely. It was all well and good to imagine the pile of silver his tail would fetch when it was long enough, but until the day it could be sold, Jarrad had made Ben responsible for dealing with the body it was attached to. It was far more complicated than anyone had imagined. The first plan had been to lock it up with Jarrad's dogs, but that idea turned out to be problematic in a number of ways. Initially the hounds backed the little creature into the corner, barking and growling to the point that there was concern they would tear the little investment to bits. After the cowering beast dropped to the ground, exposed its belly, and generally bowed to their dominance though, the dogs backed off. Later that day they somehow got loose, then twice more the next day. Finally, it was revealed that the malthrope had learned how to work the latch, reaching his cunning little hand through to open the gate to the pen. Over the course of the two days that followed he was placed in the equipment shed, the seed shack, and any other building that had sturdy door, but the little escape artist always managed to slip out.

"Where were they keeping it this time?" asked Gurruk.

"The master had us build a pen next to the dog pen for it. A little one with a roof. We got the slats so close together you can't hardly fit a whisker, though," Menri said, leaning aside slowly to scoop up a stone to pitch at the creature. The gleaming eyes darted aside, easily dodging the projectile.

"First we put a latch, but he got it open. Then we tied it shut, but he managed to gnaw through it. This time it was barred from the outside and the blighter *still* got out," Ben muttered.

"Why do you suppose it doesn't simply run away?" asked Goldie.

That was the most curious part of the little beast's repeated escapes. Without fail, every time he defeated the latest attempt at captivity he was discovered lingering somewhere near the workers or Jarrad's residence. As far as anyone could tell, he had never once tried to escape the plantation, or even find a secluded place to hide. This was doubly confounding considering the excellent motivation the slaves and servants had given him to stay out of sight.

Remembering the "game" from the carriage ride, he had first made it a point to pester the servants. Though it did seem to get the same level of encouragement from the slaves as the bowl game had, a moment of distraction had earned a strap to the face that convinced him to leave the servants alone. If he tried to approach the slaves, on the other hand, a swinging rake or a thrown stone inevitably sent him scurrying. Slowly, the realization dawned that there was one slave who never took a swing at him: Blind Ben. Once this discovery was made, the creature began following the blind man around, staying as close as he dared. It didn't take long for the other slaves to start joking that Ben had acquired himself a little red shadow.

"It is a mally. There's no 'why' to the things it does. It just does them. Like a rock rolling down a hill," Menri stated.

"Maybe when they are little, but I hear they're pretty devious when they grow up. My granny used to tell me about a malthrope in the Great Forest who would turn signposts and hide paths until people got good and lost, then he'd get them to trade him their first-born in exchange for leading them out," remarked Gurruk.

"That's nothing. There is a malthrope back in Qualia, on the South Crescent, who sneaks into bedrooms and whispers into the ears of sleeping women to make them unfaithful," Blondie countered. "And any child born of the infidelity is *born* as a malthrope."

A few of the others nodded appreciatively. The story was a rare new addition to their already extensive knowledge of malthrope lore.

"Maybe that's what they do in your parts, but where I come from all they do is steal anything that doesn't move and kill and eat anything that does," Menri said with a shrug, snatching up another stone and narrowly missing the creature. "Look at it. The stupid beast doesn't even know enough to stay clear when folks are throwing stones at it."

The malthrope trembled slightly, anxiously anticipating another attack. One or two more halfhearted attempts to strike him were made before the workers lost interest as they always did.

Their attention elsewhere, he crept just a bit closer, locked his eyes on Ben, and opened his senses. He listened to their words, smelled their scent. After his first escape, whether the slaves realized it or not, the little creature *had* tried to run. He'd scrambled over the fence and through a fair amount of countryside without being noticed, but when the panicked urge for freedom began to subside, he realized that he was out in the open. There were foreign smells, strange new sights . . .

When he'd been behind the bars of the carriage the new sensations were exciting and fascinating. Now he remembered how dutifully his mother had avoided lingering in the open fields, how carefully she'd kept to the shadows. He felt exposed, small, and frightened. He felt alone, and when he was alone there was nothing to keep the feeling of loss from creeping up again. Painful images took root in his mind, and the tears began to flow. The others didn't like him, but when they were near, it kept him from feeling the emptiness. They might not be his family and it might not be his home, but he had no one else and nowhere else to go. And so he went back. Anything was better than being alone.

Every few minutes he would creep just a bit closer to the blindfolded man, the one who didn't chase him. In a world where everyone else actively despised him, having someone who ignored him was almost like having a friend. He was huddled in the shadow of the man's bench, nearly close enough to touch him, when the old man released an irritated sigh and placed his bowl on the ground. The creature sniffed the air and stretched to get a peek at the contents. It looked like the mushy stuff they'd given him in the carriage, but a bit wetter, and with a meaty smell to it. Casting a wary look up at Ben, he reached his hand out into the flickering firelight. When his fingers fumbled at the edge of the bowl, the blind man's hand darted down and closed around his wrist. It was a dizzying motion, fast as a serpent's strike.

"Got you, you little devil," Ben remarked triumphantly, raising the struggling creature up and holding it aside with a bit of difficulty.

35

"Ugh," said Gurruk in disgust. "I don't think I'll ever get used to seeing that thing. Here, look at that in its chest. Master Jarrad got a defective one."

"What is it?" Ben asked.

"Some sort of black patch on its chest. A squiggle with a blotch over it, right over its heart," the dwarf remarked. "I didn't know monsters could have blemishes."

"I'm sure we will have plenty of time to ponder it later, when I'm not hungry and weary," Ben said. "Come on. Back to the pen with you. Maybe you'll spend the whole night there for once."

The malthrope tugged and pulled, trying to twist free or pry open his captor's fingers, but the grip was like a vise. He squeaked and yelped his beastly little protests, and when it became clear he wasn't going to get free, he huffed out a breath in frustration and defeat. What he did not do was scratch or bite. The one time he'd used his teeth, it had been on one of the servants. The beating he'd earned for it had left bruises that would linger for weeks. It wasn't a lesson he was eager to learn a second time. Instead, once Ben had leaned down to fetch his walking stick, the malthrope dangled his feet until he could just about reach the ground, and tried to walk along beside the human. Before long, fatigue forced the human to relax his arm enough for the beast to walk more easily.

Ben counted out the final three paces from the fire to the path and smiled as he felt the coarser gravel crunch beneath his feet. While the others had spent the week working, he'd spent the week helping them to learn their tasks, and having them lead him from place to place. After a few days of pacing the grounds, tapping the path ahead with the end of a stout length of pole, he'd managed to pull together the beginnings of a map in his mind. It would be a while before he knew the plantation inside and out, but for now he could get where he needed to go, and the walking stick kept him from stumbling over any new obstacles. Two hundred-fifteen paces to the next turn in the path, then eighty more to the turn for the little monster's pen.

The pen was small, a bit less than waist-height and perhaps three feet on a side. The walls were slats of wood nailed to stout wooden posts, scraps from one of the many lingering construction projects that were scattered throughout the plantation. Ben set aside the stick and felt along the top of the roof of the pen until he found the hatch. A grin came to his face when he realized it wouldn't open.

"The thing is still barred," he muttered, impressed in spite of himself. "Clever little thing, aren't you? What did you do? Bar it again when you got out? Or did you find another way?"

He slid aside the brace for the hatch and opened it, tossing the malthrope into the pen and announcing, "In you go! And this time you better *stay* in."

Once the hatch was secured again, he paced around the edge of the enclosure, feeling at the dirt until he came to a shallow little hollow beneath the slats of one wall. It was just barely large enough for the malthrope to slip through.

"Ah-ha! Found it," Ben said. He kicked some loose dirt into the hole and stamped it down good. "You're going to have to do better than that. Tomorrow we'll drive some stakes down along the edge of the wall. I can't wait to find out how you'll get past that one."

The little creature twisted his head and pressed an eye as best he could against one of the wider gaps in the wall, watching the blind man go. Once even his sharp night vision couldn't make out Ben's form, he sniffed around the inside of the pen. A moment's search turned up a reasonably soft patch of dirt, and he began digging again.

#

The following morning, the slaves were lined up and assembled before their master. Joining him was an official of the local lord, on hand to record the number and worth of the slaves so that his annual tribute could be duly adjusted.

Jarrad marched out and peered across the land spread out around them. The speech he'd delivered upon their arrival had done its job, because the slaves had certainly done theirs. Where just days ago had been two roughly roped-off stretches of untamed land, now there were two fields of supple, plowed earth ready to accept seed. The rest of the slave quarters had been completed, and the framework of what would eventually be a sturdier fence had been laid. Another week like the last one and the land would be ready to begin earning back the fortune Jarrad had paid for it. He nodded and turned to his workers.

"You did well, men. And when you do well by me, I make it a point to do well by you. And so I shall, with two exceptions. Nac, step forward."

All eyes turned to the youngest of their group. He took two unsteady steps forward. A vicious red welt ran across the back of his neck, and another graced his cheek. From the way he moved, there

37

were plenty more hidden beneath his tunic. He tried to muster a defiant look, but much of the fire was gone from his eyes.

"You could have worked harder, but you are young and that can be forgiven. What is not so easily set aside is your talk of escape. You'll have two stripes, and until I'm satisfied that you've learned the error of your ways, I've instructed my men that you are to be treated as though you have three. Go to the tool shed. The brand is waiting for you," he decreed.

Nac silently obeyed, the servants and slaves alike watching as he walked.

"As for the rest of you, the new slaves have demonstrated that they deserve a single stripe each, and I've seen nothing to suggest that I should add a stripe to any of the veteran workers. In a moment, those earning their first stripe will follow young Nac to the tool shed. Before you go, I want you to know what that stripe gets you. Each of you will have your own hut. The land behind your hut is yours to work for your own purposes. Food, recreation, whatever you like. You will be given three meals a day, one with meat. Plenty of you couldn't hope for half as good back where you came from.

"Now—to the shed, and after that you've got the day to rest. Tomorrow the planting begins. Dismissed," he decreed. As the slaves shuffled back toward their quarters, Jarrad added, "Ben, you stay behind."

The blind man remained as the others departed.

"To my great surprise, you've given me reason to believe that you will be as useful as your previous owners suggested. You've got a good head on your shoulders," Jarrad said.

"Thank you, master."

"And then there is the matter of the malthrope . . .

Ben slouched slightly and cleared his throat. "Yes, it has proven to be somewhat more difficult to handle than I had anticipated."

"That's putting it lightly. Unless I'm wrong, the beast has spent more time outside of its pen than in."

"That is likely, master."

"I made the thing your responsibility."

"And I take the responsibility very seriously. I do believe the creature has not done any damage."

"No, but it is a distraction and a disruption, and I won't put up with it for very much longer. Handle it, blind man."

"Yes, master."

The master and his servants paced back to the residence. Those slaves who did not require a fresh brand retired quickly to their quarters, and those earning their first stripe reluctantly made their way to the tool shed. It left Ben alone at the edge of the fields. After a few moments, he was just barely able to hear the quiet crunch of tiny feet. Ben didn't need eyes to know that it was the malthrope taking the lack of witnesses as an opportunity to slip from his hiding spot and take a few steps closer to his "friend."

The old man sighed heavily. "You aren't going to make this easy, are you?"

#

The next few weeks were extraordinarily taxing, but in different ways for different people. Most of the slaves faced long hours of hard labor, starting before the sun had finished peeking over the horizon and ending sometimes long after it had dropped below it.

One field was planted with precious rakka seeds. As was the case with every other aspect of the delicate crop, planting had to be done with great care to have even a chance at a healthy crop. A measuring stick was supplied to each slave to push into the soil to a precise depth. A seed was then dropped in, covered, and the soil was moistened until it was just the right texture. Experienced slaves took the lead, demonstrating the proper methods.

The first three weeks were so crucial that three slaves were designated "blackfeet." They would march the fields during the height of the broiling Tresson midday, their feet bare and watering can in hand. If the earth began to feel a bit too dry, it was watered to perfection. Those newcomers who learned quickly were trusted to remain on the rakka field, while even a single mistake banished them to the second field, now being planted with lentils. As a crop, they were far less fussy, but no less important, because the harvest from that field would provide the bulk of their meals for the year to follow. The third field, formerly Jarrad's only piece of land, was left to lie fallow.

During the day, Ben spent most of his time as a "blackfeet," a job to which he was uniquely well suited. When the hottest hours had passed, though, the time inevitably came to deal with his far more challenging assignment: catching and controlling the little malthrope. Realistically, he shouldn't have even had a chance to catch the little thing, but for some reason the malthrope didn't have the good sense to stay away. All Ben ever had to do was hold still or pretend to be distracted while no one else was around and the beast would come out from whatever dark corner he had found and gradually work his way toward Ben.

At first, the rascal would come near enough to practically touch his playmate, but after getting snagged once too often, bait was necessary to entice the thing near enough to be caught. Fortunately, he didn't seem to be very picky. Food was the obvious one, and it continued to work at least once a day. Failing that, a bit of rope with a knot in it, a strangely-shaped stone, or virtually anything else Ben held briefly in his hand was enough to get the creature to tiptoe into range and investigate. Once the blind man felt the pest was near enough, he would reach down, grab a handful of pelt, and hoist the malthrope from the ground. By the third time he had been caught, the creature didn't even struggle. This had simply become the new game, and getting caught was just the end of the first round.

The second round began once Ben deposited the beast into the latest attempt at captivity. For the first few days, Ben continued to try to make the pen a suitable prison. Stakes were driven into the ground surrounding it. Boards were added to the floor, more nails, more slats, a better latch. After each improvement was made and each flaw corrected, Ben would proclaim "In you go!" with escalating frustration and slam the hatch.

Seldom would more than a few hours pass before his shadow was back behind him.

When it became clear that the pen was a losing endeavor, Ben sought out alternatives. One of the only doors with a legitimate lock on it was the grain storehouse, so he managed to get permission to lock the pest inside, if only to see if he would be able to get out. It was an educational experience to say the least. At first, it seemed that they had struck upon a solution, since the malthrope didn't seem to show up in any of his usual haunts for nearly a day. Noon the next day, though, the blind man heard the familiar echo of footsteps along with his own.

Though the old man would have to take their word for it, the other slaves claimed that the little creature was practically waddling, stomach bloated and face the very picture of contentment. Ben rushed to the grain house to find the door still locked. When he managed to have it unlocked, he did his best to inventory the sacks of grain, but none seemed to have been emptied, or even opened. He shrugged his shoulders, crossed the storehouse off the list of potential enclosures, and received a vicious dressing down from Jarrad for the fiasco. It wasn't until days later that he finally learned where the beast had gotten his meal.

Ever since the incident, Ben had been losing track of the little devil for about an hour each day, and he had a strong suspicion that the creature had been sneaking back to the storehouse. Sure enough, on one such occasion, the blind man made his way back to the sturdy, locked door of the communal pantry and pressed his ear against it. Inside he heard the scrabbling of claws and the squeaking of a mouse. The squeaking came to a swift and sudden end, and a moment later something dropped down from an upper window, then down to the ground, licking its chops all the while.

"Well . . . if nothing else, you'll keep the mouse problem under control," Ben grumbled. "Come on. Let's see where you'll be escaping from next."

He paced back to the fields, his shadow faithfully in tow.

Chapter 6

"You, blind man!" came Jarrad's bellowing voice from across the fields.

Ben had been busy marching in measured steps along the fence line, part of a daily regimen to complete his mental map of the plantation grounds. When he heard the call, he turned to its source, mostly because he'd long ago learned that people still expected him to look at them when he spoke, even if it didn't do him a lick of good.

"Yes, master! How may I help you today?"

"In the workshop—now!" Jarrad replied. He didn't sound angry—or, at least, no more angry than he usually did. He rarely addressed his workers individually, and when he did, it was with the same force and manner that he used when addressing the group as a whole. All in all, it painted a picture of a man who exclusively spoke at the top of his lungs.

"Yes, master!" Ben quickly replied, pivoting his feet and beginning to trace a path to Jarrad's workshop.

In short order, he reached the door and was ushered inside.

"What is it that you require?" Ben asked.

"There's a chair in front of you. Sit down," Jarrad said.

He extended his waking stick until it clicked against one of the legs, then stepped forward and sat.

"Planting season's over," Jarrad said.

"It is."

"Nine in ten of the rakka seeds sprouted. Best year so far. You did a good job teaching the new slaves, and you taught *my* men a thing or two."

"I'm happy to have succeeded in my tasks."

"Mmm. *Most* of your tasks."

"Yes, master," Ben said with a sag of his head, "most."

"Mmm," Jarrad repeated, "and the most sensitive part of the year is behind us now. The other slaves know their roles, there's no more need for blackfeet. Your good service of the past isn't enough. This is not a charity. I can't afford to be putting food in the mouths of workers with no work to do. Not *this* season. So there are two things to be done. You need to get that rat that follows you around sorted out, and you need to find some way to make yourself useful until the rakka starts to bear fruit, or I am going to have to start cutting your share of meals down."

His words were not delivered with anger or reprimand. They were frank, steady, and matter-of-fact. He was simply explaining the reality of things, with the confidence of a man who knew that for this patch of land, reality was his to sculpt.

"That is understandable."

"So, have you got any other skills that might be helpful?"

"I am something of a repository of skills, master. What needs to be done?"

Jarrad took a seat and drummed his fingers on the table, eyes wandering in thought for a few moments. "Many of the tools are in a state of disrepair. For the last few seasons, I have been paying a tinkerer to visit from time to time to mend them. You indicated in the past that you could do this job. Are you confident you still can?"

"Quite confident, if a few requirements are met. Will I be doing my work here?"

"No. There is a small shack at the far end of the fallow field. That should be sufficient."

"Very well. I presume that I will be the only one using the shack."

"My men use the equipment there from time to time."

"That will have to stop, I'm afraid."

Jarrad shot Ben a hard look. Realizing that the withering gaze would do little to intimidate a man who couldn't see it, he growled. "You do not give *me* orders."

"I would not presume, master. But if I am to use the tools, I must be the only one. I cannot simply look for the appropriate tool. It must be precisely where I expect it to be or it will take me hours to find it."

"I will instruct my men to put things back where they found them."

"That won't do. You see this?" Ben asked, extending his hand. Across one palm was a vicious scar. "When last I shared a workshop, the man I worked with put a saw back where he found it. The blade was facing the wrong way."

Jarrad looked at the ancient wound thoughtfully, then reclined in his chair and quietly considered the situation. At the creak of his master's chair, Ben closed his hand around the walking stick and waited patiently. In his experience, slave masters did not typically respond well to logic when it conflicted with their whims, but he was well beyond the age of worrying about such things. They would do what they pleased regardless.

Jarrad leveled his smoldering gaze again.

"You have three stripes, blind man."

"I do."

"You are the only one in your quarters."

"I am."

"That is a right reserved for single-stripe slaves."

"It is."

"The workshop shall be yours, exclusively, but you will no longer be permitted your own quarters. Your cot will be moved into the workshop. Is that understood?" Jarrad asked.

The final words were a dagger-sharp dare for further objection. Ben wisely did not challenge him.

"It is," replied the blind man, nodding in deference.

"So be it," Jarrad said, rising and opening the door. "Have one of the others move your cot for you, and instruct them to bring any tools in disrepair to your new quarters. I shall inspect the results personally. For your sake, you had better hope your skills are sufficient."

"I am confident that they will be adequate," Ben said, standing. The master slapped a hand hard onto the old man's shoulder and pushed him back to his seat.

"One last thing to remember. I don't care if you fix every tool on this plantation better than the day it was made. If you don't get that little demon of yours under control, I *will* find a way to make you pay for it."

Ben nodded and was allowed to stand and leave. When he was clear, the door slammed behind him. Not three steps later, his footsteps were joined by the light padding of his little shadow. He stopped, and the creature stopped with him. He shuddered, then headed off in the direction of nearest activity in order in enlist aid in setting up shop.

#

Preparing the workshop was little trouble for Ben. It was a task he'd done many times in his life. The shack that would now serve as his workspace and residence wasn't nearly large enough to serve either purpose properly, but he'd hardly expected any better. Whereas the housing for the slaves was simple but solid, the shack was a flimsy excuse for a building, constructed less to keep the elements from leaking in and more to keep the tools from walking away. Putting equipment in the hands of a slave was unavoidable during the course of their labors, but letting them hang onto the more versatile tools during their off hours was an excellent way to lay the groundwork for an escape or an uprising. Thus, Ben's new home was drafty as an open robe, but it had a sturdy door with a key lock. Rather than entrusting the key to him however, Jarrad supplemented it with a brace on the inside, instructing his men only to lock the door when Ben was not inside.

Every inch of floor was utterly littered with scraps of wood, rope, and leather, as well as hammers, saws, vises, pliers, and a dozen other tools. For the better part of a day, Ben painstakingly inventoried, sorted, organized, and stowed each item he found. When he was through he'd managed to unearth a passable worktable and enough floor to place his cot and a chair. Thus prepared, he opened the door and began his new task. Rakes with loose or bent tines were straightened and tightened. A nearly-bald broom had its bristles replaced and lashed securely in place. Shovels were sharpened, splintered hoe-handles were mended or replaced. One by one, each tool was efficiently restored, and, one by one, the slave owner inspected the results. Most were good as new. Many were better.

Satisfied, Ben's new task was left to him without further comment. Unfortunately, there was still the matter of his other task.

In the days to follow, any moment not spent sleeping, eating, or mending was spent devising new methods to capture and secure the malthrope. The procedure was always the same. Ben would find some corner of the plantation away from prying eyes, at which point the little thing would be bold enough to approach him. Then he would pull out what he came to think of as "the prize." Lately he'd been piecing together any odd assortment of scraps from the workshop into a haphazard bundle. As soon as it was revealed, the beast would fairly scamper up to him for a closer look and a chance to snatch it away. In what was no doubt the most entertaining part for anyone who caught a glimpse of it, the blind man would then try to pounce on a creature a fraction of his size and a multiple of his agility. Each day, the malthrope got his hands on the prize a bit sooner, and Ben got his hands on the malthrope a bit later.

Strangely, he always seemed to catch the creature eventually.

Next, it was into this pen or that, each time with some new attempt at security, and each time with an eventual escape that would bring the whole process to full circle. After a week, Jarrad made good on his threat and cut Ben's meals in half, which added a level of frustrated urgency to the next round, but did little to increase its success.

Near the end of one particularly hot day, a week before the rakka plants would be showing their first ripe berries, he took his usual position near the far end of the fallow field and fished out a knot of leather and feathers that would serve as the day's prize. No sooner had it been drawn from the pocket of his tunic than it was snatched from his fingers, scrabbling paws retreating beyond arm's reach to inspect the trophy.

"Blast you, you little devil," growled the blind man in frustration, swinging his walking stick and attempting to lunge at the sound of footsteps.

A clump of earth caught the man's sandal and he lost his footing, tumbling to the ground and sending his walking stick clattering across the ground and well out of reach. It was the last straw, and for a few moments he allowed himself to spew long sequence of remarkably colorful profanities. When he'd managed to regain a bit of composure, he raised himself stiffly to his hands and knees and began feeling along the ground in the direction he'd last heard the rattle of his lost stick.

"Little blighter," he muttered angrily to himself. The footsteps tapped closer. "Yes, yes. I hear you. You can go back to making a fool out of me soon enough. I've just got to get my walking stick back. I tell you, if I could feel that thing thump you good and hard on the head just once, I could die happy."

As the blind man continued to mutter angrily, the malthrope watched him, head cocked to the side. This was the first time the old man had ever done this. It wasn't part of the game. Not the one he was used to playing, anyway. He watched and tried to figure out the purpose of it. The man clearly wouldn't catch him crawling around like that. As fun as the keep-away part was, getting led to someplace new—the "in you go" part—was his favorite. It always gave him something to figure out. They'd never get to that part with him crawling around on the ground. It took a few more moments of watching and wondering, but he figured out what the old man was after.

Ben heard the feet suddenly scamper ahead, then the unmistakable sound of his walking stick being dragged along the ground, then snatched up.

"No, no, no. You little monster, you give that—" he began to object, reaching his hand out. His exclamation caught in his throat, interrupted by something it took him a moment to comprehend. The stick had been pressed into his palm. Slowly the old man realized what had happened. "You . . . you've been doing this on purpose the whole time. You *like* doing this."

The only sound in reply was the tap-tap-tap of the malthrope's feet as he fairly danced in anticipation of the next part of the game.

"Well, I'm through. No more," Ben grumbled, using the walking stick to climb to his feet. "My stomach hasn't been full in days because of you. If I'm going to go hungry, I might as well save my energy rather than keeping you entertained."

Ben made his way forward in the direction he was reasonably certain led to his workshop. The tumble had forced him to lose his bearings somewhat. The malthrope scampered along behind him, then beside him, impatiently waiting for the old man to make his next grab. When none came, the creature ventured closer. Usually, the old man turned in his direction when he made a noise, so experimentally the creature hopped about, thumping and stomping the ground to get his playmate's attention. When that didn't work, he placed his stolen toy in his mouth and stalked closer on all fours, gingerly tapped Ben, then sprang away.

"Enough. I told you, I'm through," he muttered at the creature, which he could plainly hear pacing in frustration. "I'm finished with this game. Why should I waste my time finding new ways to catch you and lock you in a pen when I know you have no intention of staying in?"

The creature's eyes lit up and his ears twitched at the final word. Opening his mouth, he took a deep breath and released it in a squeaky, not-quite-human yelp. "Ih!"

Ben stopped. "What?" he said slowly.

"Ih?" the beast attempted again.

"In?"

"In!" the thing said, excitedly. "In y . . . In yuh . . ."

"So you can talk, now, can you?"

"You! In you guh . . . In you *guh* . . ." the malthrope attempted, as though saying the first words forcefully enough would give the next enough of a push to cause it to spill out of his mouth.

47

"Go," Ben supplied.

"In you go!" it piped insistently, springing about, nodding vigorously. "In you go! In you go!"

The blind man took a slow breath and stiffly crouched, extending a hand. His little shadow crept up, looking at the hand.

"In you go?"

"Yes, in you go," Ben said flatly. The creature placed his wrist in Ben's hand. The old man dropped his head and sighed in frustration at the lost hours. "I've been going about this the wrong way. Come on, you clever devil. Let's see if we can find a better game."

#

"All right," Ben said, when he reached the pen that despite all attempts had not been able to keep the creature locked away for more than a few hours at a time. "In you go."

When he failed to hear any sounds to suggest he had been obeyed, he pointed and repeated himself. "In you go."

His shadow glanced up at the hand, then climbed to the roof of the pen, pulled open the hatch, and dropped inside. Ben grinned.

"Now, the sun is going down, there," he said, pointing to the west. "It will be dark. You stay in until the sun comes up, there." He pointed to the east. "Understand?"

"In?" it asked from within the pen.

"In. All night."

"In," it replied resolutely.

"Good. I will be back when it is light. If you are still *in,* I will give you something."

"In," it repeated with vigorous nods.

"Right. You had better be inside when I come back tomorrow," Ben said, closing the hatch and bracing it.

The malthrope watched him go, then sat on the floor of the pen and waited. For a time, the half-understood promise of reward and the simple joy of another creature acknowledging him with something beyond casual cruelty was enough to keep the dark memories at bay.

Nights are long, though, and loneliness is an emotion that will not easily be pushed aside. Sleep was slow to come and quick to depart. Each time he jolted awake, the creature cast a hopeful glance to the eastern sky for some hint of light. Each time, he saw only stars, and, finally, not even that. The beast's sharp eyes squinted in confusion at the field of black where the familiar points of light should be. The wind was howling and gusting, rattling at the slats of his pen and whipping at the crops. Then, as if they had been waiting for him to wake up, the skies opened and rain came pouring down.

One of the things that made this region so lush and green, the key to making it home to so many farms and villages, was the rain. In other places, rain could come down in any number of ways. Fat, hammering drops. Fine, settling mists. Torrential downpours or irregular sprinkles. Here, it almost always came as a gentle, constant shower. It was as though the heavens wished to be sure that every patch of ground got its fair share, so they provided a steady and even flow without relent, and it would persist for hours. Rain poured between the slats of the pen and doused the little creature to the bone. No amount of scampering about the roughly built shelter/prison was able to yield a dry patch to curl up and ride out the storm. Drenched and miserable, he looked to the east again, and let out a moan of dismay.

#

In his shack, Ben woke to the sound of rain. He was pleased to discover that, though they may have cared little about the wind, the owners of the plantation knew enough to keep the rain off of their tools. The roof was perhaps the only fully intact part of the entire structure. At least he would be dry. For the most part, anyway. Here and there a gust of wind forced itself through the drafty walls and brought a spritz of water with it. Rather than wake up with a damp blanket, and no doubt catch his death of cold, the old man reluctantly climbed from his cot to shuffle it a bit farther from the wall.

"First thing in the morning, I see where the wind is getting in, and see what I can do to fix it," he muttered to himself.

Once he was satisfied that he was out of reach of even the most motivated leaks, he rolled himself onto the canvas of the cot and lay his head upon the bundle of cloth that served as a pillow. The instant sleep began to claim him though, a scratch at his door shook him from his doze. For a moment, he dismissed the noise, assuming it was a bit of bramble or an errant tree branch broken free by the wind. When it turned to an insistent hammering on the door, Ben groggily hoisted himself to his feet again.

"What is it? Whoever it is, haven't you got the sense to stay out of the rain?" he grumbled, removing the brace from the door and easing it open a crack.

Even the whisper of an opening brought a veritable stream of water spattering to the ground by the door. It also brought a sudden pressure as something heaved itself desperately at the opening and scrabbled to get through.

"What in blazes?"

"In! *In!*" the malthrope squealed, trying his very best to wedge his head through the tiny opening.

"No, no, no! Out you go!" Ben growled, nudging the thing's nose with his foot as he forced the door shut.

"In you go! *In* you go!" the creature whined from the other side of the door, ramming against the solid planks with all of the force his spindly frame could muster.

The creature may not have been very large, but he was determined. The rattling had dislodged the brace from where Ben had left it, and as the blind man leaned low to reach for it, one last clash shook the door just enough to rob him of his balance. The old man tumbled down, the door flew open, and the malthrope exploded into the shed. By the time Ben managed to get the door shut and braced again, he was soaked and muttering a fresh batch of profanities from his seemingly bottomless supply of them.

"Where are you, you little devil!?" he hissed.

Ben held still and tried to listen past the rattle of the walls and patter of the rain. There hadn't been the clatter of tools when the thing had burst inside. Thanks to the need to use every last morsel of space within the shed for storage, the only place a beast might be able to hide without disturbing a crate of tools or a pile of materials was a cramped little corner beneath the old man's cot. He crept a bit closer and crouched low, listening. Sure enough, there was panting breath and the drumming of a panicked heart. Working out as best he could where the creature's tail ought to be, he raked his fingers across the earth and managed to grab it near its base. With the beast firmly in hand, he hauled him out into the open. The creature didn't even struggle.

If Ben had his vision, the old man would have been treated to a truly pathetic sight. The little thing was drenched from head to toe, robbing him of his fluffiness and revealing how scrawny and gangly he really was. His paw-like hands were caked with mud from his escape, and more of the stuff smudged his rags and matted his fur. The beast twisted his head and looked up at Ben miserably, water dripping in a continuous stream and pooling on the floor. Even without seeing, Ben could feel that the little thing was chilled to the bone and shivering. He found himself feeling a dash of pity in spite of himself.

"We've had very little luck keeping you in that pen of yours," Ben reasoned out loud. "And we've had very little luck keeping you out of the grain storehouse. If I toss you out, you'll just burrow your way into this place, or pry up a piece of the roof, or some other destructive bit of ingenuity, and then I'm stuck fixing it . . . so, tonight . . . if you don't make a nuisance of yourself . . . and you don't touch *anything* . . . I'll let you stay in here."

"In?" the creature said hopefully.

The old man lowered his unwelcome guest to the ground, but as soon as the malthrope's paws touched the damp floor, he tried to bolt for the cot again.

"No!" Ben scolded, yanking the tail. "You stay *here*! Out in the open. Where I don't have to crawl around to get you. You understand? Right *here*!"

Each time he said the word "here," it was punctuated by a sharp downward point of the free hand. The malthrope watched his finger.

"Here?" his guest asked, head cocked to the side once more.

"Stay here," Ben said with a nod.

"Shtay here," the malthrope attempted, mimicking the motion more successfully than the phrase.

"Yes," Ben said. "And you do not touch anything. No games, no snatching things away. No touching."

"No-touching." The phrase was spoken as a single word.

Ben slowly loosened his grip. The creature didn't run, instead crouching on the ground and lightly shaking away some of the water still clinging to him.

"Good. Now don't make me regret this decision too badly," he remarked, easing himself back into the cot.

The creature watched, tail swishing back and forth, as the old man drifted to sleep again. Then the little thing curled up and released a contented sigh through his nose, falling asleep for the first time in too long without the blackness of solitude heavy in his chest.

Chapter 7

A wise man once said that if one does a job well enough, one will be doomed to do it forever. Ben had more than justified his room and board with the quality of his repairs. So much so that once the rakka berries were beginning to ripen and his skills were once again needed in the fields for training, each night he found hours of work awaiting him. Farm equipment, clothes, and all manner of other things were heaped at the door of his shack, each in need of repair. The toll was a high one. Days spent baking in the sun, teaching the new slaves the finer points of finding, fetching, and processing berries, followed by evenings working his fingers raw mending things would have taxed the heartiest of workers. And Ben was not a young man.

Worse, there was still the matter of the malthrope.

The little thing, mercifully, had learned to stay out of the way at the very least. As feared, once allowed into Ben's shack, the blasted thing refused to spend nights anywhere else. During the day, though, the old man had finally coaxed his ward into remaining in, or at least *near*, the pen they had built. Once or twice daily, the beast would make a stealthy trip to the grain storehouse to supplement his diet with a few rodents, but Jarrad and his men were willing to look the other way on this particular infraction. They didn't care one way or the other if the beast ever got to eat his fill, but if ignoring him helped to keep the mouse and rat problem under control, a blind eye was worth turning.

This meant that the creature was able to go through his days relatively unharassed, so long as none of the day's labors brought some of the crueler slaves or slave-keepers near enough to jab at him. It also meant that while Ben was being run ragged, his nightly ward had little to fill his days.

To stave off boredom and loneliness, the creature first spent his time dismantling pieces of the pen, eventually dislodging enough slats to give himself an unobstructed view here and there. When further renovation started to earn him cruel looks and the occasional strike with a strap, he decided to train his keen eyes and ears on whatever group of workers were nearest to the pen, trying to match actions to words, and imitating them both. When the sun began to dip, he would eagerly watch the pathway toward Ben's shack. The instant the old man began the slow trudge home, his shadow would slip from the pen and take up his rightful place in the old man's footsteps. From there he would watch as Ben worked his way through whatever had been left for him outside his door. Then came a night of well-deserved sleep, the malthrope curled in the center of the floor.

One night, after nodding off a third time while trying to lash together the tines of a wooden rake, Ben decided to leave the task until morning. It was more than enough to pique the interest of his guest. The old man had never left work undone before, and anything new was a source of endless fascination for the creature. He glanced at the sleeping man and stood, leaving his designated patch of floor and venturing nearer to the half-finished rake. Each step was taken tentatively, and with a long, careful look in Ben's direction, as though the rake may have been the bait in an elaborate trap.

Once he reached the work table, the beast stretched up and peered over the edge, looking first to the ball of twine, then the half-lashed rake, then the sleeping old man. Finally, he gingerly plucked the twine from the table . . .

#

Birdsong rang out, stirring Ben from sleep. On a normal day, there would be a bit more time before the slave-keepers roused the workers for the day's toil, but he'd let his age get the better of him the previous night. There was work to be finished. He stood, took a measured step to the side, and pivoted to take a seat at the work table. A practiced motion brought his hand down where the ball of twine ought to be, instead it struck empty table. It only took a moment for him to realize what had happened. He forced himself to calmly place his palms on the worktable.

"It was bound to happen," he stated. "I'm frankly astounded you'd managed to behave until now."

The first words startled his tenant awake. As the creature shook away the grogginess, he listened. The tone of stifled anger in his caretaker's voice was unmistakable, even if the statements were not wholly understood. The creature sifted through the words that he knew, trying to work out what was wrong.

"I was willing to put up with you, so long as you didn't interfere with my work. But now I'm going to have to throw you out."

"Out!?" he piped in dismay. "In. Shtay here!"

53

"If you wanted to stay here, you should have listened when I said no touching," Ben fumed, jabbing the table with his finger.

"No-touching!"

The words seemed to come with a burst of realization, as the little beast scrambled across the floor, between the old man's legs and gathered up something it found there.

"No, stop that. Whatever you're doing, I assure you, you're making things worse for yourself."

"Here!" the malthrope said, darting out from beneath the work table and slapping a half-used tangle of twine down where it had been the night before.

"Ah . . . well . . ." Ben remarked, clearly unprepared for anything resembling an appropriate response to his scolding, "Where is the rest? And what else did you touch?"

The malthrope slinked nervously to the rake that had been set aside the night before and nudged it toward Ben's hand.

"No, blast it, tell me you weren't playing with—what . . . what is this?"

Ben's fingers slid across the business end of the rake. Where he expected to find the barely attached bundle of wooden tines he'd left the night before—or worse, a gnawed or piddled upon mess—he found instead something quite different. The point where the tines attached to the handle was a veritable bird's nest of improperly tightened loops and poorly aligned lashings. It was held together not so much with knots as with twine so twisted and tangled that it wasn't able to unravel, but it *was* held together. Yes, it was an atrocious job and would have to be almost entirely redone, but it was clearly the work of something that knew what needed to be done and roughly how it ought to be done. It was a pale imitation of Ben's own repairs, but an earnest attempt.

It didn't make sense. Until this moment, Ben would have imagined that the malthrope's intelligence fell just barely beyond that of a dog. It could parrot a few words, and it could obey a few commands, but it was still a *creature*. The confounding ability to escape from the pen was one thing, but this was quite another. This was something that a child might have done. A *human* child.

"You did this by yourself?" Ben asked, pointing first his guest, then at the attempted repair.

The malthrope looked to the rake, then back to Ben and nodded.

"Did you do this? Did you learn to do this by watching me?" the blind man repeated.

The creature nodded more vigorously.

"Where are you?" Ben said irritably, reaching toward where he imagined the creature to be.

The beast first darted away, then crept back and raised his arm to place his wrist in the old man's hand, as he did when the time came to be led to the pen for the day. Ben lifted the little thing into the air and plopped him down beside the chair, letting go of his wrist and placing his own hand on the thing's head.

"Did *you*," he said, pointing at the beast with his free hand, "do *this?*" His final word was accompanied by a jab at the rake.

Another nod, this time taking the old man's hand along for the ride. He groaned and pinched the bridge of his nose.

"Listen. I am blind. Unless you can nod that head of yours hard enough to rattle your brains, it isn't going to do me any good. So pay attention. *No*," he said with an exaggerated shake of his head.

"No," the beast said, imitating the motion.

"*Yes*," Ben said, now with a nod.

"Yesh."

"Now, once more. Did you do this?"

"Yesh," came the mush-mouthed reply.

"Good enough for now," Ben said, absentmindedly patting the creature's head. "Now, let me get this fixed before the sun finishes rising. Watch closely. You might learn something."

#

As the sun began to slip from the sky at the end of another long day, Ben made his way to the equipment shed, as he had weekly since he'd been made the official tinkerer for the slaves. A routine quickly formed between himself and whatever servant of Jarrad was currently playing the role of assistant to the supply chief. Supply chief was a position staffed by one of the paid slave-keepers, but if a slave had done a particularly good job or been on particularly good behavior, then as a respite from field labor, the easier task of transporting materials was granted as a reward. Today Gurruk had that honor.

"Blind Ben!" he declared brightly, tipping a wheelbarrow onto its wheels. "The usual, I imagine?"

"Mostly," the old man replied. "But first something off the list. I need a cot."

"Something happen to yours?" he asked with a wink. There was a looseness to his speech and a slight waver to his posture that suggested he'd been taken advantage of the lighter duty by indulging in the fruits of his leisure time labors. The fact that he'd winked at a blind man was a fairly strong indicator that he wasn't quite sober.

Each single-stripe slave was permitted a small patch of land behind their quarters to do with what they wished. Most wisely used the land to grow additional food. Gurruk used a bit of it as a garden as well, mostly to grow herbs and other ingredients to be dumped into the primary resident of his piece of land: his still. The thing was a triumph of ingenuity and misappropriation, assembled out of spare parts, scraps, and items traded for or outright stolen. It was truly astonishing how quickly he had put it together. Into its boiler would go any overripe or otherwise inedible rakka that came out of the fields, along with stems, botched seed batches, and anything else that the masters intended to throw away. What it produced was an evil-smelling concoction that the elves called pomace brandy. Everyone else called it rotgut. By rights, the stuff should have been weak as water based on the ingredients, but one should never underestimate the ingenuity of a thirsty dwarf. Somehow, he managed to produce a spirit strong enough to bring the hardiest of drinkers to the brink of blindness. Gurruk drank it straight.

"I need it for the malthrope," Ben stated.

Gurruk flinched at the statement. In general conversation, "malthrope" was less the name of a creature and more a slanderous insult to hurl at an enemy. Most slaves hadn't become comfortable with one of the beasts being near enough to warrant a mention, so the word had yet to lose its edge.

"You mean that shadow of yours? Err . . . supply chief?" the dwarf asked, turning to the scrawny clerk in charge of the equipment and materials, "Do monsters get beds now?"

"The mally sleeps on the ground. No cot," came the reply.

"Yes, that's the problem. He sleeps on the ground. He's always underfoot. I can't tell you how many times I've stepped on the confounded thing. At least with a cot, I'll know where the blasted thing is when he's asleep."

"The monster does not get a cot," repeated the clerk. "Ask again and I'll have yours taken away."

"As you wish. To do the day's repairs, I'll need three lengths of pole, six medium planks, a hank of twine, two spools of thread, a needle, and a half-bolt of canvas," Ben listed.

"A bit more than last time," the clerk remarked, waving Gurruk into the shed to fetch the appropriate supplies.

"The men have been working hard, wearing through things."

"Mmm," replied the clerk without truly listening. He marked off the contents of the barrow as it was loaded to ensure nothing extra was taken, then waved Gurruk on his way.

The dwarf easily raised the barrow and set off toward Ben's shack, the old man in tow. With nearly the length of the plantation to walk, and more than enough rotgut in his belly to make him feel particularly social, he decided conversation was in order.

"So. That little monster *has* been spending the night in your shack," he said.

"He has."

"How can you stand it?"

"Haven't much choice in the matter. He gets into and out of whatever he pleases. At least with him spending the nights on my floor, I haven't gotten an earful from the master lately."

"But the stories . . . you know what those things can do. It might steal your soul . . . or curse you . . . or something like that."

"Thus far, the creature hasn't done anything worthy of campfire tales."

"Not yet, maybe. I'd keep an eye on it, if I were you."

"If you were me, I can assure you that you would not."

"Eh? Oh, yeah," Gurruk nodded, glancing at the blindfold. "What's it like being blind?"

"Close your eyes. It is a bit like that, only more so. What is it like being a dwarf?"

"Eh. It's life."

"You seem to have taken to slavery a bit more easily than the others."

"Yeah, well. A free dwarf spends his time working in a mine until he's exhausted, then his nights drinking until he passes out. Only difference between that and being a slave is a bit more fresh air and a bit less strong drink." He pulled a leather flask from his belt, something he'd had Ben make for him, and took a long swig from it. "Now there's little difference at all. What about you? Why are you such a model slave? What's your history?"

"I don't have a history. I just appeared one day, old and blind, with

57

a job to do," he said, flatly.

"Mmm. I hear you. Best not to think about things in the past. Or, better yet, do what you can to blot them out." Gurruk took another swig.

The slaves reached Ben's quarters and unloaded the barrow, at which point Gurruk drained the rest of his flask and stumbled vaguely in the direction of his still to refill it. The dwarf hadn't made it more than a dozen unsteady paces away when the light crunch of paws signaled the arrival of the little creature.

"Right," Ben said, opening the door. "In you go."

His guest hardly needed to be told, scampering inside before the door had finished swinging open.

"I've got a lot of work tonight," the blind man continued, taking a seat at his work table. "But this first bit I want you to watch closely."

"Watch," his ward stated with a nod.

"Yes. Because I am going to show you how to build a cot . . ."

Chapter 8

The days that followed brought many things. Already deep into the growing season, the lentils and rakka alike were growing in leaps and bounds. For the berries, this meant twice daily stripping away the ripe berries for processing and the overripe ones to make room for the next batch. The cruel thorns and long hours combined to produce the need to constantly mend equipment and workers alike. During the cool nights, the malthrope earned many a lesson watching Ben do his work until even the beast's sharp eyes couldn't make out his motions in the darkness.

Before long, the little thing began to take on some of the simpler steps himself. He was an eager learner, quick to pick up the broad strokes but slow to master the intricacies. Nonetheless, he clearly enjoyed the chance to be with someone, and to be engaged in some way. In fact, each day he grew a bit bolder, venturing out of his pen earlier and sticking close to Ben even when other slaves were around. It did not go unnoticed.

"Blind man!" growled a voice from the edge of the rakka field as the slaves were leaving for their midday meal.

"Yes, Master Jarrad."

"Your shadow is back," said the owner, eying the malthrope as the creature peered nervously from behind a clump of rakka bushes.

"He is, master."

"For a time I thought you'd managed to keep that thing in check. I was almost ready to restore your rations. I do not enjoy repeating myself."

"Nor should you, master."

"Then would you care to explain why you do not even appear to be interested in catching it?"

Ben paused. The honest answer was that he had become accustomed to the thing constantly at his side. That was an unacceptable reply for any number of reasons. Fortunately, a reply that was marginally less likely to lead to harsh punishment presented itself. "Because I am beginning to think that keeping the beast locked up is nearly as great a waste as it would have been to slaughter him as you'd intended when you first received him."

"You're questioning your master's judgment?" Jarrad fumed.

"I am suggesting that you did not know, nor did any of us, that the beast could be useful. Right now he is nothing to you but a mouser and a tail awaiting harvest. Until that day comes, surely any work you can wring out of him only adds to the return on your wise investment."

"And what good can the beast be in a rakka field besides upsetting the other workers?"

"Let us see," Ben said.

He took a few measured steps toward the field, his mind working feverishly to produce something resembling a useful job for the beast . . . of course. He was a beast! He was used to foraging and the like. That was all that harvesting was, after all. Tapping about with his walking stick, Ben found a few of the baskets holding the morning's harvest. They were sturdy reed baskets, stained with the berry juice of half a dozen seasons. Around the rims hung a dozen or so burlap slings, worn by the workers to carry the harvested berries before being added to the bushel basket. He leaned down and sampled the contents. A bit of squeezing identified one basket of ripe fruit, and another filled with discarded overripe berries.

"Right, come here, you little devil," he said, snapping his fingers.

Locking his eyes on Jarrad, the malthrope slipped from his hiding place a few steps at a time, skittering a bit on all fours before stopping to sit up and assure himself that the master wasn't going to pull out a strap to swing or a stone to throw. When he reached Ben, he stood and finally shifted his gaze to the nearest thing he had to a caretaker.

"Here. This is ripe. This is what we want. This goes in here, with the rest," Ben demonstrated, amid many exaggerated gestures. "These are overripe. You put them here, with these. The rest are not ripe. You leave them be. Don't break any branches. Don't pull any leaves. Go, find some ripe ones."

The instructions thus handed out, Ben handed down a sling and paced slowly back to Jarrad's side. His apprentice watched him go with a curious look, then peeked over the edge of a basket and sniffed at the contents.

"It clearly doesn't understand a word you say," Jarrad muttered, "Look at it. And besides, that row has already been worked, I checked it myself. There isn't anything but under-ripe berries left."

"Well, then anything the beast might find would certainly have been lost otherwise."

The two men watched as the beast took one final look at the ripe berries before darting into the bushes. Jarrad wore a stern look on his face as he watched the bushes rustle.

"If that thing harms so much as a single rakka bush, I claim the bounty today and you are on half-rations for the next year," the plantation owner rumbled.

Ben responded with a nod. To his surprise, he found that he was almost anxious for the little monster. Realistically, with that thing gone his life would be immeasurably easier. No more having to keep the creature occupied, no more wrangling him or warning him away from the slaves more vigorously hateful toward him. Half-rations were a small price to pay . . .

And yet he found himself hopeful that his ward would come through this, and a shade guilty that if the beast did not, the little thing's death would be the result of a hastily composed plan to avoid further punishment on his own behalf. He listened as bushes rustled up and down the row, and finally as his apprentice emerged and padded toward the baskets. A telltale tap and bounce of falling fruit as the creature walked made it clear even to Ben that the foraging had not been in vain.

"Have it bring them here," Jarrod ordered.

"Bring them here," Ben repeated.

At the sound of the blind man's request, the malthrope approached, putting as much distance as possible between himself and Jarrad as he did so.

"Here," the creature said, managing to shuffle the berries about enough to free a hand. He pulled down Ben's free hand and filled it with berries.

What had been two heaping paws full was just enough to fill the human's hand. Jarrad inspected. The deep pink color of the fruit declared them to be perfectly ripe.

"The beast found a dozen or so berries. Hardly worth the trouble of having it loose during—" Jarrad began.

"Here!" the creature interrupted.

Jarrad glanced down to see the malthrope looking up to Ben, hands outstretched with the sling that had previously been slung out of sight behind his back. The rough cloth of the sling was bulging with berries, each one just as ripe as those in the blind man's hand. The plantation

61

owner reached out to take the bag, but the little creature pulled it away and retreated a bit, eying the other human suspiciously before attempting to present his hard work to Ben again.

"Fine. I want that thing with you in the fields. Each time the others finish harvesting a row, have it do a pass as well. It clearly hasn't got the sense to stay clear of the thorns, so it can reach the berries the others can't. At the end of a week, if there has been no damage to the crop, and it continues to turn up berries, then you are back on full rations. But keep it on a short leash, Ben. I won't tolerate *any* problems."

"Understood, master."

Ben listened as the heavy, plodding steps of his master retreated into the distance. When enough distance was between them, the blind man's protégé took a few more steps forward and hung the well-filled sling over the end of Ben's walking stick. The old man sighed and shook his head.

"I do not know if I've done you a tremendous favor or a grave disservice, but one thing is now clear, my little red shadow. From this day forward, we are in this together whether we like it or not."

"Together," the creature nodded.

Ben paced to the baskets and managed to dump the berries into the appropriate one, the beast skittering behind and collecting the stray berries that spilled to the ground along the way. He dusted off his hands, stood up straight, and declared. "I suppose we may as well have ourselves a meal."

#

The creature did his job admirably, for the required week and each one after. Through the whole of the growing season he solidified his reputation as the old man's shadow, perpetually a few steps behind his keeper. Now that the malthrope had an official job to do, the slaves were forced to endure his presence, an affront that had a mixed effect on them. The elves had already been behaving with carefully cultivated disdain for their fellow workers, so heaping a bit more on this latest one was hardly any trouble. Gurruk, typically in one state of inebriation or another, never seemed more than vaguely aware of the beast. The rest, though, either avoided the malthrope, or gave him a very good reason to avoid *them.*

Of all of the slaves and servants, by far the most thoroughly hateful was Menri. When stones were thrown at the little thing, his were the largest and the sharpest. When others muttered vile words at the beast, Menri spat on him. The elder slave would tug rakka branches as the creature rustled between them, raking the thing with thorns. More than once Menri had "accidentally" struck the malthrope with a shovel while widening an irrigation ditch. The creature never lingered near Menri if he could help it, and other times always made certain to keep Ben as a buffer between them.

Ben himself faced a bit of a struggle as well. Though Jarrad was no longer after him to corral the beast, the stubborn plantation owner was *very* slow to warm to the idea of keeping a triple-stripe slave. The blind man was constantly forced to find new ways to contribute. Fortunately, his long life of service had afforded him an impressively diverse set of skills. On any given day, he could be found coaching slaves in the rakka fields on the best way to find and select berries, or perhaps in a slave's quarters treating this injury or that ailment, or else in his shop-cum-abode repairing or improving any equipment that required his attention. Regardless of the task, his shadow was always there, watching and mimicking.

On this day, the last of the growing season, Ben and his protégé were toiling away at what was easily the most miserable task on the plantation—seed roasting. Inside a shack just slightly larger than the one Ben called home, there was a large metal drum. Beneath it, a fire was built using any scraps and trimmings that came off of the field. Heaping baskets of rakka seed would be dumped into the drum, which had to be kept rotating at a constant, steady speed. All the while, the tumbling seeds were monitored by color, scent, and taste. When the seeds were just right, they would be dumped and quickly cooled. On the coolest of days, the air within the shack was stifling, and the powerful odor of the roasting seeds mixed with the smoke of the scrap-fueled fire to make the air nearly unbreathable.

Most days it was a trio of the veteran slaves manning the roaster, but on the final harvest day—a day when both the rakka and lentil fields needed to be stripped clean—every able body was needed on the fields. That left Ben to supply the muscle to rotate the drum and issue orders. All other tasks were performed by the malthrope. Thanks to the well-trained nose of the blind man and the sensitive nose of his apprentice, there was no need for looking or tasting, and thus little use for a third man. Even with only two slaves on the job, much of the time was spent waiting, with the occasional request for another bundle of dried scraps to be thrown on the fire.

"Smells close," wheezed Ben, cranking industriously at the drum. Once or twice, he had experimented with allowing the creature to man the crank, but that idea had been abandoned fairly quickly. The little beast invariably cranked a bit too enthusiastically, as though turning the crank faster would roast the seeds faster.

"More," remarked his shadow, sampling the air for the smoky, spicy scent. "More . . . more . . . no more!"

Ben halted the drum and stepped down on a foot lever, which, through a series of interlinks, managed to hoist the far end of the drum toward the roof of the shack, dumping the seeds into a carefully placed basket. When every last seed had tumbled into the basket, the malthrope shoved and heaved at it until he'd managed to maneuver it out the door, where it could be dumped into a wooden tray and spread thin to cool.

"Quickly, load the next batch," Ben managed to order between coughs.

"No next batch," the malthrope said.

"We've actually gotten ahead of the shuckers?" Ben asked, referring to the slaves performing the only marginally less laborious task of removing the single seed from the center of each rakka berry, dropping it into a vat to soak, and collecting the seeds from three days prior to be toasted. "Thank heaven for small favors."

"Thank heaven," came the parroted reply, accompanied by a nod.

To keep the drum from overheating while it awaited its next load, Ben wedged his chair over the foot lever. He then stiffly made his way to the outside, where a second chair had been set up for these rare opportunities to get some fresh air into his lungs. The chair hadn't even finished creaking when he heard the creature plop down beside him. From the sound of it, the beast was tinkering with something.

"What have you got?" he asked.

"Wait. Not done," his shadow replied.

Ben grinned at the response. The weeks since their arrival had seen a veritable transformation in the little creature. For one thing, he had grown like a weed. He was nearly a head taller than when he had been found, and his hair had grown into a wild and unruly mop that dangled in front of his eyes. He had also become a veritable chatterbox, at least when the two of them were alone. Once he had learned that gestures and nods didn't get a response, he had quickly learned which words would do the job instead, and his vocabulary had soared, even though his grammar needed work. It was difficult to believe that something so young could have developed so much over the course of a single growing season—but, then, no one truly knew enough about malthropes to venture a guess at how young the creature really *was.*

One thing was certain, however: if this beast was typical, then malthropes seemed to develop much faster than their human counterparts. It stood to reason. They tended to live such short and harried lives, the species wouldn't exist if it couldn't learn the ins and outs of survival quickly.

"Fetch some water," Ben said.

"Uh-huh," his ward replied, jumping up and trotting off.

A moment later, the apprentice returned with a wooden pail and a dipper. Ben let a mouthful of cool water scour away the layer of soot and grime that seemed to have coated his tongue, then spat it on the ground and took a long, badly needed drink. By the time he'd had enough water to convince himself he wouldn't shrivel up and turn to dust, the tinkering sounds had stopped.

"Here. Done," the malthrope said.

A hand tool, a trowel, was placed in Ben's hand. With the sheer quantity of secondary tasks that the old man had been forced to take on, he'd begun handing down the simpler tasks to the malthrope to do alone. The results were typically lackluster, but they left Ben with far less work to do to bring them to a proper state of repair. He turned the latest test of his apprentice's skill over in his hands and felt the joints, testing the strength and feeling the edge.

"It could be better. The grip is a bit rough, and the edge could use sharpening," Ben critiqued, handing it back.

"But . . . but good enough, right?" his shadow defended.

"If it can be better, then it isn't good enough."

"But it . . . I have to give it to Menri."

"What difference does that make?"

"I don't *like* Menri."

"What difference does that make?" Ben repeated, a stern edge to his voice this time.

"I don't want him to have a good tool. Not anything good."

"Well, that's too bad. The purpose of the task, *your* purpose, was to fix the tool. When you have a purpose, you don't always have the luxury of choosing who it benefits."

"Then I don't want one."

"Don't want one what?"

"A pur . . . a thing like that."

"A purpose."

"Uh-huh."

Ben smirked. He'd long had a feeling that the creature actually knew a great deal more words than he used. The broken and awkward manner of speech seemed motivated by his desire to avoid certain sounds. Now was as good a time as any to test the theory.

"Say purpose."

"Purposhe," the beast slurred.

"Still haven't learned to speak correctly, I see."

"It'sh hard! My mouth ishn't like yoursh. The shound shpillsh out the shide when I shay shome shoundsh," it sputtered.

"One would imagine that it is difficult to say anything at all in a human tongue, considering you don't *have* a human tongue."

"Uh-huh."

"Well then, if it is so difficult to speak at all, then you may as well put in the last bit of effort and speak properly."

"Uh-huh," it pouted.

"Now what don't you want?"

"A purpos-s-s-se," it managed, emphasizing the S partially as an act of rebellion and partially to be sure it sounded correct.

"That's your second mistake. There is nothing, *nothing,* more important than having a purpose. A purpose is the whole reason you exist. Some people have grand purposes, others have simple ones, but they are all important, and to be given a purpose, to know what your purpose is, is a gift. It doesn't matter what your purpose is, once you have one, you must perform it to the best of your ability."

"But why?"

"Why? Because a sharp trowel cuts the earth more easily, and a smooth grip is easier on the hand. A proper tool makes work easier. It lets you do more work. That means more rakka, which means more money, which means better treatment. It means more lentils, which means more food for everyone. But, more important than that, easier work means a better life. And I think you'll agree that life is hard enough for everyone, and anything that can make it better is worth doing. Most of all, having a purpose is what gives life meaning. Without it, there would be no reason for you to wake up every morning. Nothing to work toward. Life would be empty. Understand?

"No."

"Well, one day you will. Until then," he said, handing down the trowel, "do it because I said so."

"Okay . . ." moped the little beast, taking the tool back.

"But later. It sounds like the next load of seed is ready . . ."

Chapter 9

That first year had been a good one. Jarrad's gamble with the new land and larger rakka production had paid off, and his plantation flourished as a result. True to his word, he did much to reward his workers. Wooden tools were largely replaced with metal, and gloves and boots thick enough to withstand the vicious rakka thorns were provided to all. Even Ben felt the benefits, as the new tools required him to take on metal working, requiring an anvil and furnace. That meant a new room added to his shack, which, in turn, gave the creature a place to sleep without getting in the way any longer.

Of course, while a blind man can do a great many things by hand and by ear, one cannot hope to shape hot metal without sight. Perhaps predictably, in the early days, it was Gurruk who worked the steel. When he first took on the task, the flaring flame and pounding hammer terrified the little malthrope, sending him scurrying into the workshop for protection from Ben.

"Calm yourself," the blind man said irritably. He was at work sharpening the teeth of a saw. It was a slow and tedious process, and having a trembling beast clutching at one's legs wasn't terribly helpful.

"Why is he doing that? Why doesn't he stop?" the creature whispered urgently.

"He's doing that because that is how metal is shaped."

"But . . . metal is hard. How can you shape something that's so hard?"

"You shape it in the same way that you shape anything else. With something harder. You can't make something harder, or sharper, or better, without testing it against something stronger. It's the same way with anything else."

"Anything?"

"Anything. Iron sharpens iron. That goes for men as well as metal."

"Men? How?"

"Ask the people heading into the Cave of the Beast."

"What?"

Ben sighed and set the task aside for a moment, scolding himself

68

for mentioning the place. It was a fine story, and as such the little beast surely wouldn't let him finish his job without hearing it from beginning to end.

"In the north, in the Nameless Empire . . ." Ben began.

Gurruk stopped hammering and spat on the ground at the mention of the land to the north. The malthrope ducked a little lower behind Ben's chair.

"Why did he do that?" he asked.

"Because we are at war with the Nameless Empire."

"Why?"

"One story at a time, you little devil. Now, in the land to the north, as far east as you can go, there are mountains. At the foot of these mountains there is a very thick forest. At the very deepest part of the forest, where the trees and the mountains meet, there is a cave. They call it the Cave of the Beast. It is called that because there is a creature that lives inside. None have seen the beast and returned to tell the tale, but sometimes if you listen closely you can hear it roar with a force that makes the very mountain tremble. Those warriors who fancy themselves the best in the world make their way to this cave, with hopes of besting the beast."

"You said no one has come back."

"That's right."

"So they all die?"

"One must assume."

"Why would they do it?"

"Well, it is said that the man who defeats the beast will be hailed the world over as the greatest warrior who ever lived. There have been rewards offered, but most of those who test themselves against the beast do it for the glory. They say that killing the beast is proof of greatness, that no one but the strongest and most skilled of warriors could strike down the monster."

"Do you think that?"

Ben sat for a moment. "You can't fight someone without learning something. Every clash with every foe leaves each a bit stronger and a bit wiser. This creature, if it exists, has faced hundreds and hundreds of the best the world had. And it has bested them all. Imagine what it has learned in that time. And imagine what one might learn by facing it."

A sudden startling hiss erupted from the other room as Gurruk quenched the horseshoe he had been shaping in a bucket of water. The sound launched the malthrope into a run, scurrying out the door.

"That's all for today, old man," he said, setting down the hammer. "The fourth shoe can wait until tomorrow."

"Very well. Put the hammer back where it belongs," Ben said.

Gurruk rolled his eyes and slid the hammer into the other room. "You talk to that thing like it is a proper child," the dwarf remarked.

"Perhaps if I treat it like a proper child, it will grow into a proper adult."

Gurruk grunted and wandered out the door. A moment later, Ben heard the malthrope scurry back in. As he went back to work on the saw, he heard the hammer slide across the ground and, amid much pattering of feet and huffing in effort, hung on the proper hook.

Chapter 10

Life as a slave is nothing if not consistent. Barring major disaster, the year is divided into a series of seasons, and each season is the same as it was the year before. First comes a short planting season, filled with tilling and hoeing, sprinkling seeds and watering seedlings. Then comes the long growing season, filled with tending and picking, seed roasting and wine making. Then came the short harvest, when the food for the next year is stowed. During cool, dry off-season, the rakka plants are pulled from the ground, sorted, dried, and turned into stout rope or rough cloth. After that, the cycle began again with a new planting season.

The new workers worked well, and the farm thrived, affording them each more to eat and greater privileges. Just as life began to improve for the others, though, it became steadily worse for the beast. He was growing quickly, and with each new inch, the attitude of the other slaves soured all the more.

When he was small, he was harmless, practically a mascot for the plantation. Now, each day he was a step further from that tiny thing so easily kicked aside and a step closer to the monsters of their myths and fables. In response, efforts to put him in his place grew more and more intense. The casual acts of cruelty became frequent, and the slightest infraction earned him a savage punishment from the servants. He was perpetually bruised and battered, and his skittish attitude evolved into one of bitter and hunted anxiety. When anyone but Ben was in sight or earshot, he was utterly silent: head low, ears sagging, eyes to the ground. Any motion in his direction was enough to make him jump and scurry for the shadows. He endeavored to stay out of sight as much as possible, and became very good at it in short order.

Despite this, as his body grew, so too did his skills. After a year his pudgy, paw-like hands began to become more slender and dexterous. Repairs that had previously been too tricky or fine for him to perform slowly became simple. By the third year, he was the size of an eight or nine-year-old boy, and able to take on some of the more labor-intensive tasks, like turning the earth or toting and spreading manure. He would work the bellows of Ben's furnace, or hammer out hot metal

71

when Gurruk was too tired or sore. He grew stronger.

Most importantly, he grew smarter as well. Though it had taken time, the creature had come to embrace his mentor's advice about finding a purpose. He worked diligently at any task he could. The quality of his repairs never seemed to match those of Ben or the tinkerer on Jarrad's payroll, but it came a bit closer each day. When he was sent to a row of rakka to give it a second pass, it never needed a third, because his sensitive nose and diligent fingers found every berry worth picking.

While everyone noticed that the malthrope was getting larger, only three residents of the plantation seemed to notice that he was getting better at his jobs. One was Ben, who had come to treat the creature almost as an extension of himself, serving as a spare set of hands when his own were busy, or a set of eyes when he needed them. Another was Jarrad, who watched quietly as his little investment paid larger and larger dividends with each season. The last was Menri.

The elder slave's hatred for the creature had always burned the hottest. No one knew why, or cared to ask, but it couldn't be clearer. In the earliest days, it was simply a general distrust for the species that seemed to fuel his anger, but as the years rolled on, a new reason began to stoke the flames. Menri was getting older. Each year he had to fight harder to keep from having a second stripe added to his arm. No one worked harder than he did, not even the handful of fresh slaves that were purchased each year. No one got more done, no one did a better job, and no one got the privileges and respect that he did. It was a matter of pride, of identity. But when he saw the malthrope in the fields, he saw a creature that could do things he couldn't. It already worked tirelessly, and whereas each season robbed Menri of a bit more of his strength and stamina, the blasted monster got stronger by the day.

#

"Master," called out Menri.

The plantation owner halted on his way out for his customary inspection of the day's work and looked to his hardest worker. It was the end of a long day of labor. Most of the slaves had eagerly retired to their meager quarters to recover, and even if they hadn't, it was rare for any of them to address him. Rarer still for Menri to do so. In all of the time that Jarrad had been working the sturdy old slave, he'd not once had more to say than the answer to a question or the acknowledgment of an order. Now he was approaching, purpose in his eye . . . and a

72

length of rope in his hand. A pair of slave-keepers, never far from their employer, emerged from the shadows and lurked ominously as a warning should Menri have undesirable ideas for the rope.

"What is it, Menri?" he answered, eyes squinted against the setting sun.

"It is about the beast."

"What about it?" Jarrad replied gruffly.

"Nac knows a thing or two about their bounty. His father tracked them. He says the full bounty is paid when the tail is this long."

Menri held out the length of rope and let it roll out to its full length. It was about the length of a man's leg. If the beast's tail wasn't already a match for the length, it would be by season's end.

"Your crop's just about ready for harvest, I'd say. Good news, eh?" Menri said, handing over the rope. "No more having to watch that thing lurking about the fields. Eating the same food as us. Doing the same jobs as us. By the time we're gathering up the last of the rakka, you'll have your bag of silver, and we'll have the plantation free of that devil."

"Your aid in this matter has been noted," Jarrad said, coiling the rope and stuffing it into the pocket of his tunic. "Back to your quarters with you."

"Yes, master," Menri said with a crooked grin.

The slave paced the path back to his hut, leaving his master behind to roll out the rope again. He looked at it thoughtfully, then turned his eyes to the fields. Ben was plodding toward the repair shack that he called home. Behind him, as always, was the beast. The thing was carrying an armload of uncut wooden poles, each no doubt destined to be a tool handle. The pile was almost too much for the creature to handle. He struggled every few steps to tip the load this way or that, wrangling stray lengths of wood with a raised knee or hastily moved hand, then scurrying to catch up to his mentor.

"Ho! Blind Ben!" Jarrad called out. "Come here! Bring the mally!"

Silently, the blind slave shifted his path, his shadow stumbling along behind. When the duo arrived, Ben motioned for the creature to set down his load.

"Ben, are you familiar with the length a tail must be to fetch a full bounty on a malthrope?" Jarrad rumbled.

"Thirteen hands," Ben answered without hesitation.

Jarrad grinned slightly and shook his head. "It seems you know just about everything we need you to."

"One must find a way to stay useful."

"Would you say that this rope is thirteen hands long?" Jarrad asked, passing the length of rope into the blind man's hands.

Ben slid the rope through his fingers, ending with a nod. "A few fingers shy, perhaps, but roughly."

"And would you say that the creature's tail has reached that length?"

"I couldn't venture a guess. I have seldom found the need to run my hands along the beast's tail."

"Beast, present your tail," Jarrad barked.

The creature quickly turned and straightened his tail. Jarrad stretched the rope beside it. The tail was a bit longer.

"It seems that it is time to harvest," Jarrad stated.

"It seems so, master," Ben replied steadily.

"Send the beast away," Jarrad ordered, pocketing the creature's death sentence.

"Go. Take the supplies to the shack," Ben said.

Jarrad watched as his investment faithfully obeyed. The creature gathered up the ungainly load and made his way toward his home. The owner's hand was wrapped tightly around the coiled rope in his pocket. He drew in a breath and exhaled through his nose in what might have been a sigh if not for the edge of anger and frustration it carried with it.

"Something troubling you, master?"

The plantation owner paused, watching the beast retreat into the distance a bit longer before answering. "Decisions are simple things, Ben. Others may fret and fuss over them, but they are truly simple things. When given two choices, one is better, one is worse. Choose the one that does the most good. If no good can come, then choose the one that does the least harm. That is the correct choice. That is the only choice . . ."

"An admirable way to live one's life, master."

"I can't think of more than a handful of times I've been faced with a decision that I've second-guessed, or one that wasn't diamond clear. And lately, you seem to be at the root of them all. When that beast was foisted upon me, the choice was clear. Kill it. Get the silver. Balance the scales. It was useless otherwise. As you pointed out, however, keeping it alive *could* make sense, as it would be worth more in the long run. So, a new option: keep it until it was ripe, then harvest it as any other crop. Now . . . the creature has been useful, no question. We've been harvesting easily an extra bushel a day since he's been working the rows. And that nose of his has sniffed out seeds roasted to a level of perfection that we've seldom managed without him—him. Listen to me, I'm speaking of the blasted thing as though it were a man!"

"One would imagine that the choice would still be a simple one. Is his continued service more valuable to you than his bounty?"

"You are doing it, too, old man. *He* isn't a he. There would be nothing to discuss if he was. You don't sell a good man who still has good years in him and a job to do. He would remain here. But that thing is not a man. It is a monster. Fortunately, there haven't been many who have noticed it on the land, or I would be facing the local lord's wrath for harboring it. Is he useful enough to risk the consequences of keeping him? Or do I lop off the head, slit the throat, and squander a perfectly good worker for a mound of silver that he might one day have earned back three times over? And how do I know that the beast will even continue to cooperate? What if I spare it, and in a year it grows into its reputation? I'll have been harboring a killer, and there will be no one to blame but myself."

"I can understand your difficulty, master. Perhaps, in time, the answer will become clear."

"Time? No. Time muddies things. Invites second guesses. I'll do as I always do. Set a date to decide by. Whatever decision I make, I stand by. The end of the month is brand week. I'll send word, see to it that the official on site is a bounty officer. I'll have the answer by then."

"Wise."

"Mmm. Dismissed, Ben," Jarrad stated, turning on his heel and heading toward his manor.

Ben paced off toward his shack. If his mind was affected at all by the implications of the days ahead, it didn't show. He wore the same impassive, stoic expression that seemed never to leave his face. When he reached his shack, his apprentice was already inside. The sound of a blade scraping against wood rang out from the smithing room that had been added.

"Preparing the handles already?" Ben asked.

"We've got a dozen shovels and six hoes to build. Not much time to get that done," the beast replied. "What did the master need you for?"

Joseph R. Lallo

"He needed to think. Sometimes it helps to do so out loud."

"What was that about . . . about a bounty? And my tail?" he asked, a dash of anxiety in his voice.

Ben drew in a deep breath and let it out slowly. The beast had never been told. It was hardly a surprise that the other slaves hadn't. Most of them would rather die than be seen even appearing to have anything less than profanities and slurs to say to the thing. But Ben hadn't told him either. What good would it have done? Tell a boy that those keeping him are doing so only until he is old enough to be killed and his life will be naught but anger and fear and sorrow. Tell a creature whose life is already filled to the brim with such things? There was no telling what would have happened. So he was kept in the dark.

And now? What good would it do now? Tell this creature here, today, that in a month his fate would be decided by whether his life was more valuable than his death? There was no doubt what would happen. But still, he deserved *some* answer. Even the lowest of creatures deserves a glimpse of the truth before the end.

"There is a bounty on you. On all malthropes."

"But . . . I didn't do anything."

"It doesn't matter; you're a malthrope."

"Why are people all so angry about malthropes? Angry enough to put a price on them, just for being what they are?"

"They aren't angry—they are afraid."

"Afraid? It sure doesn't feel like fear. Not when they catch me off-guard with a shovel to the back."

"They're afraid of what you'll become. And working with you all of these years, it isn't hard to understand where that fear comes from."

"What . . . what's that supposed to mean?"

"Really now. Look at yourself sometime. You're nearly as tall as I am. You've been here five years. That makes you, what? Six, *perhaps* seven years old? You're the size of a teenager, and you're thinking like a young man. You've got more stamina than a human, more speed, sharper senses, sharper teeth. Man wasn't always what it is now. Cities? Plantations? Societies? There was a time before all of that, when man was still huddling in the darkness. Good heavens . . . something like you? It must have been a nightmare. The same teeth, the same claws, all of the worst features of those things that preyed on man, and a mind to match his own. And now I learn that your kind are full-grown in a

76

decade? More than reason enough for a fear to last generations."

"Well . . . that still doesn't explain why he's so interested in my tail."

Again, Ben paused before answering. "I've told you many times that there is nothing more important than having a purpose."

"Yes."

"That to be useful, to do what is needed, is the only reason to wake in the morning. That without a purpose, there can be no worth."

"Yes. I know."

"Well . . . never, *never*, has that been more true than now. You must prove that what you are, that what you have become, is more than the beast they brought here all of those years ago."

"What if I can't? What if I don't?"

"Then you'll learn why the master is so interested in your tail."

"But I *want* to know."

"No, I assure you, you do not."

#

In the days that followed, the malthrope became distinctly aware of a few things. For the most part, the slaves and plantation were as they always were at this time of year. The hottest days of the season were still weeks away. The hardest work was still days away. Slave and slave handler alike were making the best of a few days with little to do before the rush of the planting season began in earnest.

Despite the inactivity elsewhere, Ben was stretched thin, his many skill in higher demand now than any other time of year. He spent hours tutoring the ever-increasing population of slaves so that they would be ready for the season, and hours more were spent seeing to it that all equipment was in peak condition. Wherever possible, the beast was there with him, acting as the blind man's eyes and spare hands. All of this was normal. What was new, however, was the constant feeling that he was being observed.

The malthrope had long ago developed a sensitivity to being watched. When you live your life among people who would sooner strike you than look at you, how to remain unseen is a lesson quickly learned, and *being* seen is a tangible sensation. Even with his eyes closed or his back turned, when eyes were turned in his direction he could feel it as a point of pressure, like a ghostly finger pressing on his skin. The feeling grew with time, until it smoldered in the back of his mind, gnawing at his thoughts and fueling his anxiety. Since the mysterious talk of his bounty, it had been constant and maddening.

More worrisome than the knowledge that he was being watched was the realization of who was watching him. The first was the plantation's owner. In truth, there was nothing new about that. Jarrad was endlessly watching his workers. For years, though, the beast may as well have been invisible. In watching his workers, the master's eyes would flit toward and away from the malthrope as quickly as they might from a stone or a bush. Now Jarrad seemed to watch no one else.

Worse, though, was the second set of eyes: Menri.

Of all the slaves, Menri's hatred had always burned hottest, and the years had done nothing to stifle the flames. His hatred, even his abuse, had become such a constant presence in the creature's life that it had simply become another part of the day to day struggle. Now it had stopped—but what replaced it was, in a way, far worse. He too was simply watching, the permanent scowl of his face twisted by the slightest whisper of a smile. There was a chilling quality to his gaze as he watched, as though he knew something terrible was in store, and he refused to look away for even a moment, lest he miss it.

The constant observation made the beast feel small and frightened again, as though he was still cowering under the seat of the carriage on the way to the plantation. He wanted nothing more than to scurry off, to find some dark corner and curl up inside until he was forgotten—but those days were gone. There were jobs to be done now. It was clear that Ben wasn't simply humoring him by assigning him these tasks. The old man truly needed his help, and even if there wasn't a single other resident of the plantation, slave or keeper, who valued him or his role here, Ben was reason enough to endure the torturous scrutiny. He owed the man that much—and more.

A month crawled by, and finally the last day of brand week was coming to a close. The day had been unseasonably warm, making the last minor preparations a test of endurance. It seemed an eternity before the sun mercifully slipped below the horizon and the cool of night drifted over the fields. The day had taken its toll on everyone, but it was clear as he trudged back to the shack that Ben had fared far worse than the rest. His breathing was heavy and labored, and his steps slow. His walking stick creaked under his weight as he thumped it to the ground with each step. If not for the stout stick, and more aid from his apprentice than he normally allowed, the old man may not have made it to his shack at all. Once inside, he stumbled to the cot and fairly crumbled into a heap upon it.

"Here, there's some water here," the malthrope said, plunging a dipper into a bucket of cool water beside the cot and guiding his ailing keeper's hand to it.

"Good, yes," Ben muttered hoarsely, draining the dipper and handing it back.

"It was warmer today than usual. You shouldn't have spent so much time on your feet."

Ben released a few weak chuckles. "Is it *you* who teaches *me* now? I didn't think you'd come *that* far."

"Do you need more water?" the creature said, concern knotting his brow.

"No, no. Just sleep. I did too much today."

"You can't sleep yet. Remember? The master needs your help with the carriage."

"Blast it, that's right . . ." Ben said with a grimace. He leaned his head back on the bundle of cloth that served as a pillow for a moment and thought. "I can't. Not tonight."

"Then you'll have to tell him. Or get someone to tell him."

The old man heaved an irritated sigh. "Do a job well enough and you are cursed to do it forever . . . You'll have to do it."

The beast shuddered. "If you need me to, I'll try to get someone to deliver the message for you."

"No, you do it."

"I don't think the master would like it if I tried to speak to him," he said, tipping his head and briefly allowing confusion to replace the concern on his face.

"No. You help with the carriage. It is just a few broken spokes, a bit of grease to be added, a bit of work to be done on the axle. You've done all of it before."

His apprentice stepped back, eyes wide, as though a lit torch had been waved in his face. "I can't do work for the master. He . . . I . . . he doesn't even allow other *slaves* to work so near to his home without special permission."

"There's a job to be done, shadow. If I tried to do it in my state, I doubt I could finish, and the results would be unacceptable in any case. Go. He hates to be kept waiting."

"But I—"

"Go! Grease, spokes, axle!"

Joseph R. Lallo

The apprentice stood and quietly assembled the things he would need, a mixture of nerves and anger tying his tongue. A pot of grease, a brush, and a few hand tools were thrown into a satchel, and a few lengths of the appropriate wood were slid from the pile beside the door as he left. The sound of his departure brought a slow grin to Ben's face. With no apparent difficulty, he sat up on the cot and listened to the creature march toward his master.

Despite years on the plantation, the beast had never been inside the master's residence, or any of the outlying buildings. The place had begun as a modest home: a bedroom for each of his three children, one for himself and his wife, and a large kitchen and dining room. As the plantation grew, and his family grew, the home had grown as well. It was now a proper mansion: two floors, a dozen rooms, and all of the pointless but beautiful details that tended to accumulate on any sufficiently wealthy home. A porch wrapped around the building's base, with chairs and tables for enjoying the nightly breeze. The railings had lathed balusters, the windows had carved shutters, and the shingles had been painted a warm cream color. Strangely, with each addition Jarrad himself seemed to spend less time there.

The one new feature that he seemed to use was a stable. With the purchase of the new fields, more oxen were needed to pull more plows, and thus a dedicated stable had been built beside his personal workshop to house the horses responsible for pulling his carriage. In a way, it was the last *practical* addition to the home, and thus the last one that made sense to a dyed-in-the-wool farmer like himself. Between his time spent marching the land watching his workers, and the time spent working or tinkering in his stable or workshop, the only times Jarrad seemed to step inside his own lush estate were meal time and bed time.

He was standing beside a lit lantern with his arms crossed, two of his house servants lingering on either side of the stable's doors, when the sound of footsteps could be heard along the gravel walkway around the corner of the stable.

"Get back! This is the master's residence. Back!" growled one of the servants suddenly.

"Who is it?" Jarrad asked, pacing toward the commotion.

"That beast."

Jarrad grumbled. "Ben! I thought I told you to leave that thing behind when you come here. Get one of the other slaves to haul things

80

for you. My wife doesn't like to look through her blasted *curtains* and see a monster."

When the owner arrived, he glanced around to find the malthrope standing rigidly in place, tools and equipment set carefully at his feet. There was no sign of Ben.

"Go get the blind man," Jarrad ordered one of the servants, turning to return to the stable's entrance.

"He . . . he won't be . . . he isn't coming, master," the beast said shakily. Speaking in the presence of anyone but Ben tended to end poorly, so he tried to avoid it. With no other option, he murmured with his eyes turned dutifully toward the ground, head bowed and ears turned down. "He feels ill. From the heat. He said I should help."

Jarrad stopped, turning back with a dubious expression. "You? Do *you* know how to repair a carriage?"

"I . . . Ben. He repairs carts. Wagons. I watch. I do it sometimes, when he is busy."

Jarrad cast a long, hard look at the creature. "Come. The blasted wheel is ruined anyway. It isn't as though it can be made any worse." He turned to his men. "You and you. I want you near the door. Closer eye than usual on this one."

The servants turned back to the malthrope and watched with an intensity that made the month of observation feel pale by comparison. He gathered his equipment with slow, deliberate motions. Anything sudden would earn him a strap across the face, a lesson that still lingered with him from his earliest days in this place. He was escorted around to the stable's entrance, where Jarrad directed him to the damaged wheel of the carriage. It was indeed in terrible shape. Seven of the dozen spokes were either splintered or outright broken. The axle was still whole, but one of its supports was split, and the iron hub had been warped and twisted by the irregular load. A stack of crates was holding the damaged corner of the carriage off the ground.

"There. Work quickly. I may need it in the morning."

Jarrad watched as his investment went to work. It laid out the parts and tools, then began to work the hub off of the wheel. There was a care and precision behind its motions, as though they were the result of long practice and endless repetition. He'd seen the thing work before— for the last month he'd done little else—but in the fields it was always simple work. The creature would dig holes, pluck berries, and carry tools. There was nothing he'd seen it do that couldn't be done just as

81

easily by even a triple-stripe slave. He'd seen little to convince him that the thing was anything more than a creature that had been taught a few impressive tricks. This was different. Something less than human should have greater difficulty with so fine a task. There was no sign of that.

"How many times have you done this, beast?"

"Many, master. Smaller wheels," he replied, levering out one of the undamaged spokes and laying it out beside a length of wood. He marked off the length and slowly lifted the saw from its place beside him, the motion causing a menacing stir from the servants.

"Let it work," Jarrad instructed his men.

The saw was put to work cutting replacement spokes to length.

"You've been helping Ben for some time now," the owner remarked.

"I have."

"Why?"

"It is important to have a purpose, master."

"Mmm. Your kind. Malthropes. They say they are all thieves and killers."

The creature paused in its work, one hand hovering over a hammer. With a deep breath, he grasped the tool and answered, not looking up from his task. "Yes, master. They say that." He began to hammer the warped hub back into shape.

"Is it true?"

"I do not know, master. I have never met one," he answered between blows.

One by one, replacement spokes were lined up, and with hammer in one hand and chisel in the other, the creature set about shaping the ends. Jarrad watched as each step was performed. The beast was not fast, and he was not terribly efficient, but he was thorough. Slow, deliberate motions and endless checking and rechecking ensured that no mistakes were made, and gradually the replacement parts began to take shape. After an hour, the spokes were ready, and the tedious task of fitting them in place could begin. After a second hour, the crunch of steps on the path heralded a new visitor.

"Father, *tell me* you've got that carriage fixed," came a young voice.

When he reached the doorway, the visitor turned out to be a young man, barely out of his teens, but with the tone of voice and general attitude of a privileged child. In the face he was the spitting image of his father: dark hair, hard jaw. A single glance was all that it took to reveal that the resemblance stopped at the surface. He was thin, skin practically pale from lack of sun. His hands were smooth and unmarked by labor, and he wore an attitude of smugness and superiority like a crown. There were princes less overtly enthralled by their own power and position. When he saw the beast working at the wheel, he sneered and stepped back.

"Honestly," Jarrad's son scoffed, "You let that *thing* this close to the house? I simply will *not* ride in anything that has been touched by *that!*"

"You are not in a position to choose, Marret. It is our only carriage," Jarrad rumbled.

"Exactly, Father! It is a crime that we haven't got two carriages. Or three! I really ought to have my own by now. I'm the heir to this plantation!"

"Marret, we've been through this. We do not need it. I will not stand for another coin being wasted on pointless status and show when it could be invested back into this land!"

Marret scoffed again, dismissively turning to march back to the manor. "Fine, Father. Toil away in the dirt. When *I'm* in charge, things will be different."

Jarrad released a hissing sigh, like steam rushing from Gurruk's still, and clenched his fists tightly enough to crackle the knuckles.

"You two, go!" he barked at the servants by the door. "I can handle the beast."

With a reluctant nod, the men departed, leaving Jarrad alone with the malthrope. The owner stalked around the stable, jaw tight and teeth bared. Finally, his anger got the better of him and he unleashed it, grabbing a bucket and bashing it against the wall. His men came running back, no doubt expecting to see the creature at their employer's throat. Instead, they found the creature crouched on the ground, head covered and trembling as the owner seethed in the middle of the floor.

"Sir?" ventured the braver of the two. "Is there something wrong?"

"Did you hear me call you back?" he barked. "Get out! I'll call you if I need you."

The men scurried away once more, leaving Jarrad to simmer in anger again.

"Get back to work," he said, pacing back and forth.

The malthrope nervously picked up the hammer and began tapping apart the wheel so that the fresh spokes could be inserted.

"Money. Money is the problem. It ruined that boy," Jarrad began. "Look at him! He's never had a speck of dirt on those hands. The sun has barely touched his brow. Five years . . . five *years* is all it took. One day, he's a little boy, it is all you can do to keep him out of the fields, keep him from doing something to get himself hurt. The next day, the first big rakka harvest is sold and he thinks he's royalty. It is like you said. Purpose. A man *needs* purpose. That boy looks at this land and he sees the money it can make him. He doesn't understand that you only get out of it what you put into it. This land has got to feed more than two dozen mouths. And it *has*, faithfully, but only because I gave it what it needed. And one day it will all belong to that boy.

"I swear, if either of my girls had even the slightest interest in this place I'd leave it to them. But the oldest, she's got her own family now, and the youngest . . . well, she's nearly as bad as him. She knows a thing or two about how to run things, but it is still all about the money for her, and she'll get her claws into some damn fool like me before she decides she wants to do something on her own. If that boy doesn't open his eyes and start to understand where all of those fine clothes and expensive habits are paid for, this land will collapse once he gets his hands on it."

Jarrad took a deep breath and looked to the creature. The beast had been quietly working. He had managed to insert each of the spokes loosely into the hub. The thin bits of wood were all angled upward, holding aloft the hub of the wheel like the peak of a tent. He was standing, circling the wheel. The plantation owner crossed his arms and leaned against the door, curious how his investment intended to force the hub flat to notch the spokes into place and finish the wheel. Such a thing was normally achieved as the wheel was being built. Doing it without disassembling the wheel seemed unlikely.

Nearly a minute of watching the malthrope pace around the wheel had nearly sapped Jarrad's patience when the beast finally stopped. He crouched slowly and reached out to straighten the hub, then in a flash of dizzying motion, sprang into the air. The powerful leap was nearly enough to brush the points of his foxy ears against the high roof of the stable. At the peak of the jump, he pulled his legs up, and as he came down upon the wheel he straightened them, fast and hard, driving both

84

heels into the hub. With a creaking pop, the hub snapped flat to the floor, all spokes firmly seated.

"You didn't learn that from watching an old blind man," Jarrad remarked.,

"No, master. Ben usually gets a few of the heavier slaves to stand on the hub."

"Well, why didn't you get a few slaves in here to finish it?"

"They are resting, master. Tomorrow is brand day, and then comes the harvest. Much work to be done. And I was told to help you. This was my job to do." The creature stated each sentence as simple fact, as though it was strange that he had even been asked. "I'll get the wheel back on and fix the support now."

The owner nodded and watched as the simpler tasks were done. A broken strut was pried loose, a fresh one fitted. A coating of grease here, a wheel twisted on there. In no time at all, the wagon was ready to be pushed free of its support, rolling steady and true on its repaired wheel. If not for the freshness of the wood on the replaced pieces and the dings left from hammering at the hub, one would scarcely know it had ever been broken.

By the time Jarrad was finished admiring the job, the beast had collected the tools and scraps and was heading out the door.

"Ho, beast," he said, stopping it in the doorway.

"Yes, master?"

"Good work."

"Thank you, master."

#

"Up, up!" Ben said, nudging his sleeping apprentice.

"Why? It is brand day. Until the master decides to add any new stripes, there isn't any work to be done. You don't need me there," the creature answered, sitting reluctantly up in his cot.

"This time you'll need to come along."

"Why?"

"Because you will. Now come," Ben said, giving the beast a motivating thump on the back with his stick.

The duo marched out into the rays of the rising sun and made their way to the north end of the middle field, the traditional meeting place for the annual appraisal of skills and worth that was brand day. Most of the other slaves were already there, arranged into a handful of clusters of individuals who got along, and here and there a few hard stares from individuals who didn't. Menri was at the head of the remaining original slaves, a wide grin crossing his face when he saw the malthrope approaching. The other slaves adopted less jovial expressions when they noticed their unexpected guest, but the arrival of their master forced them to come to order before anything beyond a few harsh words could be hurled in the beast's direction.

Jarrad was joined by a thin, well-dressed, well-armed gentleman that none on hand had seen before. The newcomer had a short sword in an expensive leather sheath on one side of his belt, balanced by a pair of daggers on the opposite side. His clothes were of a thin and tailored tan fabric, and he carried a messenger's bag with a few scrolls and a quill peeking out from inside. He had a tightly cropped beard, a sculpted mustache that tapered along its length, and short hair covered with a formerly white kerchief that was tightly tied and had absorbed more than its share of sweat.

"All right, everyone, we've done this all before, and there is a long season ahead. We'll do it quickly and you can get back to your quarters," Jarrad stated, as he had each year prior. "This is Mr. Straab; he will be marking down how many slaves of what type I have. I'm happy to say that only two of you will be gaining stripes today. Goldie, step up!"

"What!? But master, I have worked just as hard this year as any other. I haven't—" objected the elf.

"You *know* why you're getting a stripe . . ." he said darkly. "If you *weren't* such a good worker, I'd be giving you two, or taking your nose."

There was an exchange of knowing glances among slaves and servants alike. There had long been a rumor that Goldie and Jarrad's youngest daughter had been involved in the past. It would appear that the rumors were true.

A barrow filled with glowing coals was carted up to the line of slaves as Goldie was muscled forward. Slowly, eyes turned to the familiar and dreaded bit of equipment. The stripe brand was among the coals, as it always was . . . but the second brand, the one bearing the owner's mark, was there as well, and laying among the coals was the curved blade of a sickle. When in the best case a barrow contains objects intended to sear one's flesh, those who may potentially be at the receiving end of such implements tend to be keenly aware of anything out of the ordinary. The symbol brand indicated a new slave would be joining them. A murmur among the slaves was unable to confirm what exactly a sickle might mean.

The only one who seemed to know anything was Menri, and his only response was to smile a bit wider.

A bit of coaxing from a trio of servants eventually dislodged Goldie from his place among the other slaves while a fourth servant raised the stripe brand. It was applied, bringing with it a distinctive smell and a cry of pain that reached a pitch high enough to prompt a snicker from those slaves still standing at attention.

"Patch him up and arrange new quarters for him," Jarrad instructed the servants, adding with a vicious tone, "Make sure they are *far* from my residence."

Straab drew a lidded pot of ink from his bag, dabbed a quill in it, and shook a few stray drops from the end while deftly replacing the lid, stowing the bottle, and fetching a scroll with his remaining hand. A short symbol was sketched onto the page, denoting a slave dropping from single to double-stripe status. When he was through, he nodded to Jarrad.

"Beast, step forward," ordered the owner.

All eyes turned to the creature. Instantly he felt hunted, cornered, stricken with the same panicked reflex to run from the light that drives any creature beneath a lifted rock. He turned to Ben.

"He doesn't like to be kept waiting," Ben said quietly when he failed to hear footsteps. Stepping close, he added quietly. "Whatever happens, hold still. It will be better for everyone."

The beast drew in a breath and stepped forward. Straab's hand smoothly shifted to the hilt of his sword, but when the creature stopped and stood awaiting instruction, he raised an eyebrow.

"I must say," remarked the official, "I've never seen one so obedient before."

"Is this what you would consider a full grown malthrope?" Jarrad asked.

Straab looked over the beast before him, tipping his head to the side a bit. "As large as I care to see them get, yes."

"Worthy of the full bounty?"

"Five hundred entus upon the rendering of a tail as proof that an adult malthrope has been eliminated from the population," Straab recited.

At the sound of the words, the creature shuddered, his instincts screaming to run. With the full force of his will, he managed to keep from sprinting for the fields, Ben's words echoing in his head. Every ounce of trust that the blind man had earned in their years together was being put to the test. It was just enough.

"Mmm," Jarrad remarked. He looked to the malthrope with a steady gaze, his expression betraying no hint of his thought or intention. Finally he gestured to his men. "Hold the beast."

The statement was the last straw, instinct finally overruling reason, but it was too late. Servants on each side grasped and immobilized his arms. Another quickly looped a strap around his muzzle, locking his jaws shut. Panic brought strength, but despite a valiant effort the wiry little beast could not wrestle himself free. His eyes widened in terror as Jarrad took a thick leather glove from one of his men and slipped it on.

"On the ground," he instructed.

His servants kicked the legs out from beneath the malthrope and forced him to his stomach. One on each side held him down by his arms and shoulders, another held both legs, and a fourth placed a boot on his back to hold him still. He couldn't move at all. Jarrad took the sickle from the fire. The blade was glowing. Horrified squeals and whines, muffled by the strap, filled the air. He watched Jarrad stalk closer, but when he tried to turn his head, the strap around his mouth yanked his head straight. There was a tight grip near the base of his tail, a firm tug, and then . . .

Nothing.

The creature heard the sizzle, he smelled the burnt hair and flesh, but beyond a short flash of heat there was nothing else: no pain, no sensation. The weight of what happened didn't strike until he saw Jarrad pacing back toward Straab. In the master's hand was the beast's tail, fiery orange and tipped in creamy white, still twitching slightly. The sheer disorientation of seeing something that had moments before been a part of his body was momentarily enough to wash away the emotion of the moment, leaving awe and disbelief to fill the void. It was surreal, too much for his mind to grasp at once, like walking down the road one day and meeting oneself. It simply shouldn't happen. There wasn't even much blood, the hot blade closing the wound as quickly as it had opened.

The moment of respite from his emotions ended with a vengeance when he saw Jarrad hand the stolen tail to Straab. A potent bewildering mix of fear, anger, betrayal, and hate shook the beast as a growl rattled in his chest and tears filled his eyes.

"You've got your tail," Jarrad said to Straab. He tossed the sickle into the barrow, sending a cloud of embers into the air. "I'll take the silver the next time you pass through."

The official nodded, tying a bit of twine to the base of the tail and hanging it from his belt in a practiced manner. "I'd prefer to see it killed before I go."

"I won't be killing it."

The statement brought the slaves, servants, and officials to a sudden, confused silence.

"The reward is for killing the beast."

"That beast is a good worker. It has not left this plantation since I acquired it, and it will not leave this plantation alive. I've never had a slave escape, and I don't mean to. I've gotten years of good work out of it, and I mean to have years more."

"It is a menace. It is your duty to eliminate it."

"Three of my slaves are criminals who were sentenced to slavery rather than execution. Their lives ended the day they came here. That creature is not alive. It is property. It is *my* property, and I will not have it damaged until I've gotten my use out of it."

"What could it possibly do for you?"

"That isn't your concern. You have the tail, and you have my word that this beast has breathed its last free breath. By my account, I've earned that bounty."

Straab scowled. He rummaged through the bag and pulled out a few scrolls, sweeping over them with his eyes. After tapping his foot in irritation for a moment, he looked down at the still-immobilized malthrope. The creature had stopped struggling and his eyes were squeezed shut, tears running down his face. Another glance at the scroll seemed to make the official's decision for him.

"I don't like it, but let us not fool each other. I don't know how long that thing has been on this farm, but it is a wonder it is still alive, and I doubt very much it will remain that way for long. You'll have the bounty, but you also have my word that if that thing ever escapes, any crimes it commits will be on your head. And since there isn't any way to know that it is *your* malthrope that would commit these crimes, any murders, any thefts, anything by any malthrope is on your head until you can prove that *your* malthrope is dead."

"If I allow it to escape, I will deserve it."

"So be it. But so long as we are following the letter of the law rather than its spirit, that *thing* is, by my measure, an adult working on this plantation. That means it goes on the count, and you pay."

"As I should. And by the letter of the law, stripes denote value, and this is a slave I can never sell," Jarrad said. "That means three stripes."

Straab nodded, preparing the quill again.

Jarrad turned to his men. "Get it on its feet."

The handlers hauled the creature to his feet. It was clear that the pain he had been spared by speed of the tail's removal was slowly building, and the emotion was raging in his eyes. Jarrad stepped close.

"Look at me," he hissed under his breath. The beast locked his anguished eyes on the master's. "If you are half as clever as you seemed to be yesterday, you know that what I did today has kept you alive. Once these marks are on your arm, you are one of my workers. I take good care of my workers. If you ever, *ever*, make me regret this, you know what will happen. Do you understand?"

It took some time for the creature to wrestle back enough of his wits to respond, but finally he gave a stiff nod.

"Release the strap. Brand him, three stripes," Jarrad ordered his men.

The handler securing his mouth released it and wisely backed away, but beyond an involuntary twitch of a lip, baring cruel and clenched teeth, the beast did not react. The effort necessary to keep his screaming instincts from having their way was plain to see. His body was quivering with tension, like a stretched bow string. His breath came and left in short, severe bursts. He watched as a handler removed the symbol brand from the coals. A quick efficient roll of the iron hissed at his arm. He just shuddered once, eyes still locked on Jarrad. The stripe brand was applied, and again. By the third time, it prompted no reaction at all, not even a blink.

Jarrad stared down the beast that had for years been an investment, and now was a gamble. "Release it."

With no small amount of caution, the handlers on each arm let go. The creature stumbled and fell, knees not ready or willing to support his weight. The slaves and handlers watched and waited, but all that greeted them was the sight of a creature recovering from an ordeal. Straab shook his head and marked down one additional triple-stripe slave.

"The bounty will be delivered in a few days. Good luck keeping that thing in check," the official remarked, marching away from the fields and toward his awaiting carriage.

"That is all for today. Return to your quarters. Tomorrow begins the planting season. I want you rested," Jarrad instructed.

The slaves and handlers slowly spread out across the plantation, each tending to his own business. Only three lingered. One was the beast, the trauma of mind and body making the process of climbing to his feet an uphill battle. Another was Ben, who stepped slowly to the sounds of struggle and offered a hand, then a shoulder to the beast.

The last was Menri. He did nothing, said nothing. He simply stood, disgust and hatred plastered in his expression and fury smoldering beneath the surface.

#

Ben and his apprentice finally reached their shack. Getting from place to place as a blind man is difficult, but it can be mastered. Getting from place to place as a blind man supporting an unsteady creature is another challenge all together, and had the beast not recovered enough to walk on his own, it might have taken them until nightfall before they'd reached home. Once inside, Ben took a seat at the chair in front of the worktable. His apprentice leaned against the wall and slid shakily to the floor.

For a time there was silence, but silence of a very specific sort. This was not the quiet of two individuals with nothing to say. This was the void left by words unspoken. It was potent, dense, and oppressive. When it was finally broken, it was with a single word.

"Why?" the malthrope said.

"What are you asking?"

"Why did they take it? Why did they cut off my tail?"

"The bounty, remember?"

"You knew that they would do this? All this time you knew what they had planned?"

"I did. Everyone did."

"Why didn't you tell me?"

"What good would it have done? 'Come here, you little scamp. See that tail of yours? They mean to cut it off when it is long enough. And they'll likely cut your throat along with it.' What would you have done?"

"I . . . I could have run away."

"No doubt you could have. But you were a whelp when you first

91

came here. Jarrad had been given a reason to keep you alive. I convinced him it would be worth the wait to turn in the tail when you were grown. It is why you are still alive. No one out there would have waited longer than the next visit to a man like Straab."

"And what about after that? What about once I could take care of myself?"

Ben gave a short, bitter laugh. "You think you can take care of yourself? That Straab character might think you're full-grown, but you have no idea what you'll find outside those walls. You aren't ready. Not yet."

"Well . . . maybe it is time I learned for myself. That fence might stop you and the others, but not me, and those dogs like me better than they like Jarrad."

"Mmm. And what about Jarrad? You heard what they said. He put his neck on the line. You leave this place and he feels the consequences."

"*He cut off my tail!*" the beast hissed.

"He *also* spared your life. He could have drawn that blade across your throat and been better off, but he didn't."

"He just wants more work out of me."

"What does it matter? He wants you alive. He was given the choice of killing you and sparing you and he spared you. How many others would have done the same, regardless of the reason? What he has for you may not be trust, but it isn't far from it. Running now would only prove to him that he was wrong."

"Why you, then? Why did you convince him in the first place?"

"I just knew you would be worth more as an adult, and I thought that you wouldn't be much trouble. I didn't want them to waste an opportunity."

"And when you learned how much trouble I was?"

"I still didn't want to waste an opportunity. Listen I didn't know much about malthropes before you came along. Now I know far less."

"Less?"

"Indeed. Before, malthropes were mindless monsters. They were murderers and thieves implicitly. Now I find that is not true. Now I know nothing except what I've observed. And what I've observed is a creature who seems able to do anything asked of him. Great potential. A great opportunity. And I cannot stand idle while an opportunity is wasted."

The beast fidgeted painfully, dense silence creeping back. He looked to the ground beside him, to the place where his tail should have been. It was as though it was still there. He could feel it, the sensation of it moving when he tried to curl it, but it was gone. Now his eyes turned to Ben. The one person, the one *thing* that he had trusted. The trust should be gone as well . . . but, like the tail, he could still feel it. His mind churned over the last few weeks. Ben's insistence that he demonstrate his worth. His sudden illness that forced a few hours alone with Jarrad . . .

Maybe trust wasn't like an arm or a leg. Maybe, even if you couldn't see it, it was still there if you could feel it.

"And what if I stay? What happens then?"

"Now you are one of us. All of these people share a common goal. The same goal. To do what they must, to make things better, to live their lives, and to serve their purpose. You share that goal, and that means that these are your people. You bear his mark, the same as anyone else."

The creature scoffed. "The same? They certainly won't *treat* me the same."

"Behave as though you are equal and they will treat you as such. Follow orders not just from me but from the master and his servants. Work with the other slaves . . ."

"And they will treat me as one of them?"

"In time."

"And if they don't? Why should I behave properly if they don't treat me properly?"

"Because all good things must start somewhere, and all bad things must end somewhere."

The creature was silent for a time. Then, painfully, he made his way to his feet.

"Where are you off to?" Ben asked.

"Tomorrow the new rakka field gets readied. I've still got half a dozen trowels to look over," the beast said, pacing off to the second room.

The blind man listened as the scrape of a sharpening stone, the sound of a job being done, replaced the silence. A smile came to his face.

#

The next day was the beginning of the growing season, just a bit

93

more than five years to the day since Ben and the malthrope had arrived. The day's task was to prepare a field for rakka. Rows had to be heaped to a precise height, with just the right mix of compost and manure. The plant's food had to be carted along in a barrow, or hefted on one's shoulders. Each seed needed to be placed at a precise distance from the last, such that each row had the same number of plants. Though with enough time it could be done by the most novice of slaves, doing it quickly and well was, in short, one of the most skilled pieces of labor to be performed in a given year. A single error at any point would result in a crowded row that was difficult to harvest, or else a sparse one that wasted precious land. Redoing a row was a phenomenal waste of time and resources, as the mixed soil would need to be dug up and replaced lest the temperamental rakka plants refuse to sprout.

Yet despite all of this, to Menri's fury, the blind man and his blasted malthrope had been put on the field beside the *real* workers to prepare the final row. It was a stomach-turning sight.

"Ho, blind man," growled Menri. "Get the mally off the fields. You can't let a mally lay a rakka field!"

At the sound of the man's voice, the creature lowered his head and shuffled aside a bit. Despite his size, shoulder-height to Ben, he looked much smaller: perpetually slouched and thin as a rail. For the first time he was dressed as the other slaves, a shirt and trousers made from the rough cloth produced from the dried rakka vine and colored the same distinctive hue. It was the first time he was considered one of the workers, and thus was assigned one of their uniforms. The coarse cloth weighed down the fluffy red fur that covered the beast, making him seem thinner still, and a cascade of tangled hair that had never seen a blade flowed from his head and into a ponytail.

"Jarrad's orders, Menri," Ben replied. "You wouldn't second-guess the master's orders, would you?"

Menri scowled, glancing at one of Jarrad's paid servants at the edge of the field. A word against the master would have consequences. He clenched his teeth and squeezed the handle of his spade, eyes turned to the earth. At his feet was a smooth, fist-sized stone. He plucked it up and turned to the malthrope. The beast was crouched at the beginning of his row, knocking free the dirt that was caked on the bottom of a pair of buckets and making ready to begin his task. Menri hefted the stone . . . then turned a bit more to see the blind man leaning on his walking stick and giving instruction to the monster. A fiendish grin twisted the elder slave's lips.

The beast's ears flicked and his eyes darted to the sky. A stone didn't make very much noise as it flew through the air, but a malthrope's ears were very sensitive and years of dodging thrown stones had inspired him to develop a keen awareness of the near-silent whistle. He spotted the stone and traced its path. It would miss him by quite a bit. In fact, it was heading toward the blind man.

The old man's shadow sprinted to him, shoving Ben aside the instant before the stone would have struck him.

"What was that all about?" Ben grunted, taking a few steps back to steady himself.

"He threw it at you, Ben. He threw a stone at *you*," his apprentice answered.

Ben heard something in his protégé's voice as the creature spoke the words. There was the tremor of anger, the spark of violence.

The wicked grin on Menri's face widened. "Sorry, Ben. I was trying to hit that pet of yours. Considering how long you've been keeping it so close, I'm surprised this hasn't happened before. I wouldn't be surprised if that starts happening more often, old man."

The creature's lips pulled back, revealing vicious, needle-sharp teeth. His eyes narrowed, the intelligence behind them draining away to be replaced by raw, animal instinct. Ears twisted back. Fur bristled. A low growl, unheard by any but Ben, rattled in his throat. The beast took one step forward.

"Don't," Ben stated.

"But he—"

"Don't," Ben repeated, his hand finding its way to the creature's shoulder. He began to speak, his voice kept low enough so that only the beast could hear. "It is what he wants. No good can come of what you want to do. If you let that part of you take over, you'll prove them right. You'll be what they always expected you to be. Understand? You want to hurt him? There are other ways. Better ways."

"What do you mean?"

Ben took a deep, steady breath. "You've got a job to do. Get it done."

"But—"

"Get. The job. Done," Ben repeated with finality.

The apprentice took a deep breath of his own and snatched up one of the buckets in his shaking hands. His eyes turned to Menri and watched for a moment. The senior slave laughed a greasy laugh and lifted the end of a barrow, beginning his row. The beast had watched him do this job before. Menri always worked it the same way. He would load up a barrow with the compost and manure, all that he would need for the entire row. As he prepared the row, he would edge it forward, mounding the earth with his wide spade, then portion out the contents of the barrow. No one else carried the barrow from the beginning. All of the other slaves used a smaller barrow, and a smaller spade, and made many trips. Menri's strength and his skill with the spade meant that he always finished his row first. The beast's eyes narrowed again. Not this time.

He took off at a sprint, one bucket in each hand and a trowel tucked into the rope that took the place of a belt. The creature didn't have a barrow at all, and wouldn't have had the strength to move one the size of Menri's beyond a snail's pace if he did. The buckets that took its place each held barely enough of their given ingredient to feed a single planting site. That meant that each mound would require a long trip to the opposite end of the field and back, but that didn't matter. The beast was fast. He streaked across the field, wind whistling in his ears until he slid to a stop to load the buckets. Manure and compost were heaped inside, eight scoops of one, five of the other, and the beast was on his way back. The planting site was mounded and sculpted, fed and marked, and the trip began again.

Menri had made his first five stops before he'd even noticed that the beast had begun working, and when he did, it was with no small amount of satisfaction that he observed that the thing had only managed one.

The rakka fields on Jarrad's plantation were large by any standard. There were twenty-eight rows, and each had room enough for three hundred bushes. The average slave could do a bit more than one row in twelve hours. Menri had made a name for himself by managing the same feat in seven—and, on one notable occasion, had managed two rows in the same day. After the first hour, he checked his competition. The beast was trailing far behind, but there was something worrying about it. His opponent hadn't slowed down. A blur of red was streaking along the row, loading up buckets, ferrying them back, and crafting the contents into a well-formed mound, then back along the row.

Another hour passed. Menri's row progressed steadily, and each time he paused to check the progress of the creature, his lead had grown by a bit more. The thing had been doing a passable job at preparing the row, and even seemed to spend quite a bit less time at each mound than Menri did, but the long run to fetch more supplies was causing him to fall further and further behind. He had barely lost a step, but Menri convinced himself there was nothing to worry about. After the third hour, though, something happened. The creature had managed to match his pace. An hour later, Menri was half-finished with his row, but the creature had begun to close the gap.

Slowly, it dawned on the brawny slave that each trip back and forth for the beast added another plant to the row, which meant that each trip was shorter than the last. The thing couldn't possibly keep this pace much longer, but if he did, he *might* catch up. Menri heaved the significantly lightened barrow from the ground and shoved it forward. It would be a cold day in hell when a malthrope could out-work *him.*

Another hour rolled forward, and the word of what was happening was spreading. Slaves working elsewhere found reasons to linger near the rakka fields. The work on the other rows slowed as more eyes turned to the spectacle. The sun was beating down on the fields now as the hottest part of the day approached, but neither man nor beast had stopped for water in more than an hour. Even the slave handlers had begun to gather now. Six hours since work had started; there were fewer than a dozen planting sites left to be done, and the creature was only a few steps behind Menri.

The beast was panting heavily, his tongue lolling from his mouth. Every inch of him was smeared with mud, compost, and fertilizer. His lungs, legs, and eyes were burning terribly, but he willed himself forward, refusing to slow. Before long, Menri was unwilling to spare even a moment to see how close the monster had come. He was tired and cramped, but his barrow had been nearly emptied, and thus took little effort to move.

Just a half-dozen more mounds to form. All work on the rest of the plantation had stopped now. A few moments later there were only three more mounds. Out of the corner of his sweat-burned eye, Menri spotted Jarrad looking on. A few moments more and he was on his last mound. He dumped the soil into place, heaped it with the spade, and raised his hands triumphantly.

"Finished! Finished!" he bellowed, wiping sweat and dirt from his eyes.

Menri's heart was pounding in his ears, but he'd expected to hear the boisterous hoots and hollers of his fellow slaves as he put the little monster in its place. There was silence. He looked first to the malthrope's row. It was finished. He looked next to the gathering of slaves. Mouths were agape, heads were shaking, eyes were wide with disbelief. His eyes then turned to the figure before him. It was the malthrope, nearly doubled over with exhaustion, trying to catch his breath. When the thing saw that Menri was looking, he forced himself to straighten, rising to his full height and for the first time looking the older slave square in the eye.

"I wouldn't be surprised," the malthrope croaked through his parched throat, "if that starts happening more often, old man."

The creature limped painfully toward the shack it called home. A combination of awe, disbelief, and even a sprinkling of respect was enough to leave the beast unharassed as it marched.

#

From that day, things changed on the plantation. None of the slaves ever behaved quite the same way. Most steadily shifted from general disgust toward the malthrope to a hardened, targeted hostility. Having to cope with a monster sheepishly taking orders and ducking out of sight at first hard look was bad, but tolerable. Being told that the same monster was to work the same jobs *and* be given the same privileges as a person? That was more than most of the other workers would willingly bear. More and more often, the slave handlers were having to break up fights, as old slaves and new attempted to put the inhuman monster in his place once and for all. Jarrad had no patience for anything that might injure his slaves, and thus the first few fights were harshly punished. It was enough to convince the less dedicated slaves to back off. For the others, it simply taught them to select their arenas more carefully, and to find the handlers who were willing to look the other way.

This forced the malthrope to learn a few lessons of his own.

No teeth, no claws. That was the first and most important thing. The strap across the face he'd received years ago was reason enough, but now there was a better one. Quite simply, the other slaves didn't *have* claws, and they didn't have teeth like his. If a slave showed himself to a handler with something as distinctive as a slash of claws or a few teeth marks, there was only one way he could have gotten them. The fact that they were delivered in self-defense was not relevant. Those same handlers who would ignore a few fists in the beast's ribs were only too willing to make an example of him if given half a reason. Using fists and feet to defend himself, on the other hand, was almost a sure way to avoid being blamed for an injury, because no one who hadn't seen it with his own eyes seemed willing to believe that any animal with teeth and claws would ever fight without using them.

By necessity, and as a result of far more practice than he would have liked, the creature became quite adept at dodging blows, batting attacks away, and returning them with enough force to ward off attackers both larger and more numerous than he.

The creature steadily began to slice his day into two parts. While working, he stayed in the open, in full view of a handler at all times. As much as it bothered the beast to be exposed, it was better than risking a beating. At night, his dyed-in-the-wool instinct to stay out of sight was honed to a razor's edge. When the sun went down and the work day was done, the beast may as well have ceased to exist. Shadows, tall crops, gulleys, the roofs of shacks and huts, anywhere a casual glance wouldn't catch him, that's where the creature was.

He had been called a shadow before, but the name had never been more fitting. Slaves frustrated by their inability to vent their hatred upon the beast briefly attempted to target Ben instead. It was a decision each made only once. As unpleasant as it was to fight the malthrope when he was defending himself, it was downright nightmarish to fight him when he was defending Ben.

By the end of the growing season the slaves were beginning to lose their enthusiasm for picking a fight with the beast.

Some lost their taste for combat faster than others. Goldie, Blondie, and Gurruk never seemed to share the same eagerness for "putting the beast in its place" as the other slaves. This was likely because as the only other non-humans, that "place" was uncomfortably near to their own in the humans' eyes. A few of the older slaves backed off before long if only because they were too tired and sore to be taking the lumps they inevitably received in return for the ones they gave. Only the young bucks with something to prove came after him with any regularity.

And, of course, Menri. The show the malthrope had put on lit a fire under the slave's already raging hatred. For a time, targeting the beast was more important to him than working. He would linger near the beast, arrange to be given matching tasks, and at every opportunity lash out viciously. The other slaves just wanted to hurt Ben's apprentice, backing off after a bit of blood was spilled or some bruises were given. Not once did Menri stop until handlers or other slaves hauled him off. Only the threat of adding a stripe was enough to get his mind back on his labor.

Months passed, and eventually things became stable. The malthrope remained a favored target, but vigilance could counter that. Each time a new slave was added to the ranks, he felt the need to prove with his fists that while they may both be property of the same man, a malthrope was *not* his equal. It seldom lasted much longer than a few scuffles. As happens in even the worst conditions, the trials and tribulations of existence became familiar, tolerable, and normal. And so they remained for a number of years.

Chapter 11

A bit more than four long years had passed since the malthrope had lost his tail. The plantation had grown steadily in the intervening years. Rakka harvests had remained strong, and the three fields had grown to seven, worked by nearly fifty slaves. The farm had flourished.

Not so for the farmer. Jarrad's health had declined sharply over the previous year. He was not a young man, and despite increasing scale of the task of running the plantation, he insisted in doing it himself— overseeing the work, negotiating prices, managing workers, and a thousand other little tasks. The plantation was simply too important to him to be left to anyone else.

One day, when screaming at one of the carriage drivers responsible for transporting a harvest to market, the old farmer collapsed. He never truly recovered. Healers of every sort were brought to him. Even a mystic was found, casting spells that seemed to bring him back to health, but it didn't last. No treatment seamed to last. There were whispers, inevitably, that somehow the malthrope was to blame, but all agreed that if the monster were to target a single human it would be Menri, not Jarrad.

Eleven months later, he was gone.

The night of his funeral, in accordance with his wishes and Tresson tradition dating back longer than history records, he was to be burned in a pyre with the three things that signified his worth in this world so that he would be duly honored in the next. A shovel, the very one that had broken the ground on the first day that the land had been his, rested on his chest as the flames crackled. To one side there was a rakka bush, the finest of the harvest. To the other side, a painting of himself with his wife and children, a rare extravagance he'd allowed himself, commissioned on Marret's first birthday. Both of his daughters, each now married, each with children of her own, stood tearfully by the fire with their mother. A few steps closer stood Marret, his only son, hand-in-hand with his wife.

The slaves had been given the day to mourn, but most had little love for their owner. Only Ben and Menri had chosen to pay their respects by witnessing the lighting of the pyre, though someone who knew where to look might have spotted the telltale gleam of foxy eyes as the malthrope watched from afar. Tradition called for those who would bear witness to remain until the flames burned down, an hours-long wait that was meant to show how deeply each respected the departed. The slaves sat on the ground, a proper distance from the family, and quietly observed.

Long after the sun had set and the stars had taken their place overhead, the flames had finally been reduced to crackling embers. The family retired to the manor and the slaves stood to shovel earth over the remains of the pyre, the final element of the ritual. Menri drove his shovel into the earth when the last of the job was done and marched back to his quarters. Ben stayed behind.

"Blind man," called a voice hoarse from smoke and still somewhat shaken with grief. It was Marret, marching down from the steps of the manor.

"Yes, Master Marret?"

"This land," the young man continued when he'd reached his worker. "It is mine now."

"It is. I speak for all of the slaves when I express my sorrow for your loss. I've worked for a number of men, but none were the equal of your father. I—"

"Enough. I'm not interested in sympathy, old man. Father spoke to you about a number of things. Whenever he needed some skill or another, you seemed to have it."

"As I said, I've worked for a number of men. They have had many requirements, and I've done what I could to fill their needs."

"I want you to gather some of the other slaves. Starting tomorrow, I want the stable expanded into a full carriage house. If I am to remain here, it is time that I live the life a man of my means is meant to live."

"Master, the rakka is in season. Pulling any workers will leave berries to rot on the vine, seeds to soak too long. We've already lost a day to the mourning. You—"

"Quiet!" Marret snapped. "Listen, blind man, I loved my father, but I have no intention of following in his footsteps. He fertilized this land with his blood, sweat, and tears. It was his way. It is not mine. I won't bleed for a harvest. I won't sweat for a few bushels of grain, and his death has brought me the last tears I ever hope to shed. I'm not looking for advice on how you think I ought to proceed, and I certainly don't need you telling me how *he* would have. I've got my own way.

You just listen to what I say and make it happen. Understand?"

"Yes, master," Ben said steadily.

"Good. Now get them together. I'll tell you what I want and where I want it, and you get it done. Dismissed," Marret said, turning crisply and marching back to the manor.

Ben stood quietly listening to Marret leave and, after a moment alone, listening to his apprentice pad up to him.

"Marret doesn't sound like half the man his father was," the malthrope said, eyes focused on the door of the manor and sensitive ears twitching.

"Indeed," Ben said with a nod, "If he's smart, he'll quickly learn not to abandon what has made this farm work. If he's stubborn . . . there are dark days ahead."

#

The first days under Marret made it clear to all that Jarrad and his boy had very different ideas of how a farm should be run. Jarrad had fed his slaves well, paid his workers well, and rewarded hard work. He'd poured money back into the land, and bought the best equipment and materials that he could afford.

Marret's priorities were elsewhere. He indulged himself in every way. First was the carriage house, then a carriage to fill it. His father's carriage was sturdy and simple: stout wheels and thick boards assembled into a durable body. The finish was a basic, honest stain. It was easy to repair, easy to maintain.

Marret purchased a slender, sleek work of art. Three different paints, eight different woods, and a dozen different craftsmen were needed to keep the pretty but frail carriage in proper repair. One look at his "suitably impressive" carriage beside the one his father had chosen convinced him to sell the old one rather than sully the sight of the new.

Each new choice he made reflected the same shortsighted and extraneous sentiment. He spent a fortune on delicacies, luxuries, and status. On any given day, half of the workers were toiling at a new addition to the home or tending to fragile but beautiful plants he'd selected to surround the manor. In his mind, he was finally living the life he felt a man of his position ought to live. Paying for these things? That was simple.

He was educated. He understood the give and take of an endeavor such as this. His father had believed the only way to keep the coffers full was to provide the highest quality rakka. There were other ways. He could charge more for the rakka, or find ways to produce it more cheaply. When that did not make ends meet he lowered the salaries for his employees, sold half of the lentils meant to feed the workers, and skimped on everything that he didn't deal with personally. It meant he couldn't justify the cost of offering better treatment for harder work, so motivation came from the other end. Poor performers were to face the strap. In the short term, the budget was balanced. In the long term . . .

The first link in the chain to break was the staff. Slave handlers with too much work for too little silver simply left. Not a problem, though. There were those who would work for less, though they all tended to share a similar quirk. Work for hire is done to meet needs. Normally those needs are simple: money for food and shelter. Others have more . . . unfortunate cravings. They thrive on the feeling of raw power that comes from a bit of well-aimed violence. For them, being asked to administer vicious beatings to those who could not fight back was a dream come true. The handful of silver coins was just a bonus. That suited Marret just fine. Yes, it led to a bit more discipline than was strictly called for, but a dash more motivation would surely help the bottom line. And the fact that a healthy dose of the overzealous punishment found its way to one particular slave most frequently wasn't going to keep the new owner awake at night.

Marret had no interest in having the malthrope anywhere near the manor, so the beast was invariably left working double on the rakka field to try to keep the harvest from being wasted.

He was just finishing the last row of the day's third sweep, a heavy load of overripe berries over one shoulder and a light load of ripe ones over the other. If Straab had believed it had been full-grown five years prior, when the beast's tail had been taken, he would have shuddered at the sight of the creature now. Now, having been on the farm for ten years, he was easily Ben's height. In fact, to the tips of his pointed ears, he stood taller than anyone but the most imposing of the new slave handlers. His barely adequate diet (even supplemented by whatever farmyard pests he could catch) had left him with a lean physique, but what little muscle he had was work-hardened. Wiry biceps like spun steel hefted the bags with ease, and stamina that was the envy of even the elves kept him on his feet until the job was through no matter how much work they heaped on him.

"Mally!" barked one of the more enthusiastic additions to Marret's staff.

"Yes—" the beast tried to reply.

A stiff leather strap whistled through the air and slapped the creature's face. Metal studs on the surface, additions made by the handler himself, began to raise welts almost immediately. The man's name was Bartner, and he was one of the few handlers who was still able to literally look down on the malthrope. He was thick in every meaning of the word: massive arms and legs, barrel chest, and pot belly. The largest of the handler uniforms barely fit him, straining at its seams around his middle. His forehead was glazed with sweat, and his breath was heavy with rotgut. The lack of diligence in harvesting ripe berries had allowed Gurruk's little hobby to flourish, as he had more fermenting fruit than he knew what to do with.

"I thought I'd made it clear that you were to call me 'sir,' mally. And to only speak when spoken to," he sneered.

"I—" Instantly the strap was raised again. The beast flinched and closed his eyes to regain composure. "Sir. Sorry, sir."

"Better. What have you got there?" Bartner asked, nudging one of the bags hard enough to spill a mound of berries to the ground.

"Sir. Rakka, sir."

"Looks a bit light. You been slacking?"

"Sir, it is the third—"

Another lash of studded leather ended his sentence. "I don't want excuses. I want that bag full the next time I see it, or you won't walk away from the next hit you take."

Shaking with anger, the creature crouched and gathered the spilled berries, then hurried on his way. His haste was partially so that Bartner wouldn't do anything else to him, and partially so that he wouldn't do anything to Bartner. The relentless abuse was pushing the beast close to the breaking point, and the worst of it was that the assaults were coming from both sides. Most of his bruises came from the handlers. The rest came from the same place they always had. Even now, Menri was standing at the end of the row, leaning on a shovel and wearing a satisfied smile.

The years had finally caught up with the elder slave. The previous year had seen him earn the second stripe he'd fought so long to avoid, and the effect of the demotion had been profound. In mere weeks, the fierce dedication to his task withered. He was still a hard worker—in truth, likely still the hardest worker on the plantation besides the

105

malthrope—but his heart was no longer in it. He was a tired, bitter shell of his former self. Even his smoldering hate of the malthrope had waned a bit, seeming almost to linger simply out of habit.

But, alas, old habits *do* die hard.

"The man said *move,* beast!" Menri said, aiming a boot at the creature.

With a flash of angry eyes and a smooth and practiced sidestep, the beast avoided the blow and continued on his way. Menri watched for a time, then turned back to find himself face to face with Bartner.

"What are *you* smiling at, slave?" the handler rumbled.

"It is nice to see the monster getting the treatment he deserves," Menri said.

"Well, I'm so happy I could bring some sunshine into your day. Now, I know that we've got a blind slave on this plantation, but I didn't realize we had a deaf one, too."

"Why would you think—"

Once again a blow with the strap cut a sentence short. The strike came so suddenly that it managed to knock Menri to the ground.

"You. Will. Call. Me. *Sir!*" Bartner ordered, punctuating each word with a blow to the fallen slave. "Now get up and get back to work!"

Menri hauled himself to his feet and put the shovel to work reshaping an irrigation ditch, muttering apologies and agreements all the while. Bartner laughed a throaty, mean-spirited little laugh and walked away. With an angry grimace, Menri watched him go, then glanced up to see the malthrope watching. The creature met his gaze for a few moments: long enough to make it clear that he'd seen what had happened—long enough to make it clear it was something he had seen many times, from many people. With the message delivered, he went on his way. There was someone else who needed him.

Ben was across the fields, where the latest extravagance was being installed at Marret's manor. The land surrounding the house had blossomed into rainbow of different flowers and plants, and now Marret had decided that he needed a pleasant surface beneath his feet as he strolled through the splendor. Thus, a polished stone walkway, complete with a carved oak trellis and a dozen other features imported from a dozen different lands that had nothing in common save their high cost.

In keeping with his reputation, Ben seemed to know everything that needed to be known about how best to install these curiosities, and lately his days had been spent directing, instructing, demonstrating, and adjusting as a result. Nothing had been done to lessen his other responsibilities, which meant that there was now twice the work to be done and half the time to do it. When the sun was setting, his apprentice always managed to sneak away from his own responsibilities long enough to help the exhausted old man back to his shack and begin work on the night's repairs.

With one arm over the malthrope, and the other leaning heavily on his walking stick, Ben reached his shack and crumbled into his seat.

"I've got food here. You should eat something."

He heard a bowl placed on the edge of the work table, but when the blind man picked it up, he paused.

"This bowl is full."

"Yes," his apprentice replied.

"Unless our new master has changed his ways, a triple-stripe slave gets only half a bowl at mealtimes. This is a double helping."

"You need it."

"Regardless of whether I need it or not, I'm not entitled to it. If I got a full bowl, someone else got an empty one. Where did you get this food? Did you steal it?" he asked, mustering up a stern tone despite his exhaustion.

"No, Ben. The other share is mine."

"You work harder than me, boy. You should be eating the extra share."

"I don't need it."

"Oh? Don't malthropes need food anymore?"

"The east field had a mole problem. It doesn't anymore."

"Ah," Ben remarked with a nod. He dug his spoon in and hungrily went to work on the bowl's contents. "You know," he said between bites, "I don't know if I should envy you or pity you for that stomach of yours."

"Just be glad it helps me to put a little extra in your bowl now and then," the beast said, leaning against the door frame. The frame found its way to one of the more recent welts left by his handlers, prompting a grunt of discomfort.

"Is that yelp Bartner's handiwork?"

"It is nothing."

"Mmm," Ben said with a nod. "Close the door. And come here."

107

The door was shut, and the malthrope approached until Ben felt he was near enough to reach out and place a hand on his shoulder.

"Listen to me," the old man said, his voice low and serious. "I've seen this before. New owners making decisions like these. Running plantations like this. If it doesn't get better soon, and it doesn't look like it will, it is going to get a lot worse. I think . . . I think it might be time for you to move on."

"What do you mean?"

"Don't pretend you don't understand. Go. Get away from this place. Locked in a place like this with a man like Bartner and others like him? If you give them enough time, they will match any danger that might be waiting for you outside these walls. At least in the outside, you'll have someplace to run."

"What about Straab?"

"That was years ago. No one has seen him around the plantation since that day. Jarrad wasn't eager to deal with him after that. And even if he is still out there, Jarrad is gone. You owed *him* for sparing you. Marret doesn't deserve a second thought. Just go."

The beast breathed a slow breath in and out. It was a strange thing, listening to a heartfelt plea from a man in a blindfold. It is in human nature—and malthrope nature, too—to look a man in the eye to know the strength of his conviction and the earnestness of his statement. A trained ear, though, can find the same window to the soul in a man's voice. The advice, the request, was genuine.

He looked his caretaker over. The old man had aged more in the last month than he had in all of the time that the beast had known him. He was thin, hands speckled with scars and scrapes. There was a waver to his motions, as though at any moment he was in danger of falling unconscious from exhaustion.

"I'm staying, Ben."

"Then you're a fool. There's nothing here for you anymore."

"There's you. Who's going to take care of you when I'm gone?"

"You think I need your help? I got by just fine before you were my problem."

"That was before Marret, and with ten fewer years weighing you down."

"I'll be fine without my red shadow watching over me."

"And you'll be better with it. Now eat. I'll get started on the day's repairs."

Ben set his jaw. It took a fair amount of practice to know when a blind man was glaring at you, but the beast had mastered that little nuance as well. Finally the old man shook his head and dug back into his meal. "I don't know where you learned to be so stubborn."

"The same place I learned everything else."

Chapter 12

It took only a year since Marret had taken control of his father's plantation for the costs of his poor choices to begin to come down upon him. The rakka harvest was barely a third of what it had been the previous year. Under his father, a man perpetually concerned for the future of his land, the shortfall would have been painful but survivable. For Marret, it was a disaster. Any rainy day savings had been spent within months of his father's death, and he'd borrowed against the next three years of harvests since then. If the next year didn't make up for the last one, there would be no fewer than four debtors looking for payment. Some of them would be quite willing to take blood if gold was not available.

The situation called for radical action. Returning to the old ways might have worked, but it would have taken resources he didn't have. It also would have been admitting defeat, and Marret had more pride than sense. There were other ways. Three days of soaking in oak ash water became one. The overripe berries formerly destined for Gurruk's still were now destined for the customers. Roasting would no longer be the nuanced, trained process it had been. Now it was about speed: hotter fires to blacken the seeds quicker, and more roasters to do more at once. The result was rakka by the sack, but the miraculous effects that fetched such a high price would be all but absent. That was something that could be dealt with tomorrow, though. Today, there was nothing to do but return his full workforce to the fields and fill as many bags with rakka as he could.

"This is a travesty," Ben grumbled. He and his apprentice had been assigned to shucking duty, removing the seeds from overripe rakka and dropping them into the oak ash. "These berries are very nearly rotten. A soldier hoping to sustain himself on these would be better eating a handful of sand. These belong in the compost."

"Where they *belong*," countered Gurruk as he squeezed seeds from berries alongside Ben, "is in my still! Last year I turned out some of the finest batches I've ever made."

"Bah. This is a farm, not a brewery."

"Distillery!" Gurruk growled.

"Regardless," Ben said with an irritable wave of his juice-stained hand. "And do you smell that? They aren't roasting seeds in there, they are making coal."

The malthrope raised his head, brow furrowed, and sniffed the air again. "That isn't seed that's burning. That's wood."

"Well, of course it is. What do you think they are firing the roasters with?" Gurruk replied. "Stupid animal."

"The wrong kind of wood. That isn't firewood!" the beast replied urgently.

A moment later voices began to ring out across the farm.

"Fire! Fire! The roasting shack is burning!"

All stood and ran across the courtyard to the shack. Double the roasters and double the heat had been fairly begging the old, dried-out structure to catch fire. It was burning like tinder, and as with any raging fire, there was a ring of panicked onlookers filling the air with a chorus of frightened yells. Buckets were being gathered and a brigade was being formed, but if the first few splashes of water were any indication, the shack and anyone inside would be cinders before the flames could be quelled.

"Is anyone in there? Is anyone inside!?" Ben screamed over the din.

"It was me and Menri," coughed a singed slave, a newcomer for the current season. "I was throwing bundles into the fire. One bounced out. I . . . I don't think he got out!"

"There's a man in there! Someone! Someone has got to get in there and do something!" Ben cried.

The gathered masses just watched in fear, even the handlers doing little more than staring with wide eyes at the flames. Long, pointed ears flicked as the malthrope listened, his keen hearing picking out the gruff voice of his first and most dedicated tormentor as he called for help. His fists clenched, his lip twitched, and a vicious battle raged in the creature's mind. With a glance at his mentor and a throaty growl, his decision was made.

Three bounding strides from his long legs took the beast past the leading edge of the crowd, where the heat of the flames was already nearly blistering. He focused on the shack. One of the roasters had given way and rolled in front of the only exit, spilling its load and blocking the door. The second roaster had been erected in front of one window, and a mound of seeds waiting to be processed heaped in front of the other. The wet seeds seemed to be the only thing that hadn't

111

taken to flame yet, leaving one corner of the shack free of flames while the rest was already beginning to buckle.

Using skills honed by a life of avoiding his fellow slaves, the creature leaped to the roof, where strength stoked by urgency allowed him to tear away a flame-weakened roof slat. Wispy orange flames rushed out in a flash of fiery light, blackening a swath of his fur and stinging his eyes and lungs with smoke. When they cleared for a moment, he caught a glimpse of Menri. The smoke and heat had all but overcome him, as he huddled among the seeds and clawed uselessly at them, desperately trying to reach the window. The beast's wiry, underfed frame slipped effortlessly through the broken slat and down onto the sizzling seeds.

The flames surged again, forcing him to shield his eyes for a moment before desperately scanning the cramped furnace he'd thrust himself into. Menri was too large to fit through the hole in the roof, and even if it could be made larger, the hefty brute was too heavy to make it out and the malthrope lacked the strength to carry him. There had to be another way. He squinted through tearing eyes and was just able to make out the original roaster, still standing on supports badly weakened by the flames.

"Come! Come on! This way!" the beast cried, wedging himself under the arm of his frenzied tormentor and heaving him toward the heavy, seed-filled drum.

The unprocessed seeds had soaked the beast's legs from the thigh down, providing them a tiny measure of protection. He had to hope it was enough. With a roar, he thrust a kick that sizzled against the metal. It was enough to upset the supports and send the roasting drum toppling over, where it smashed easily through the weakened wall. The rush of motion stirred the flames, causing a wave of fire to wash over the beast and the human. A shock of pain shot through the malthrope and he gasped, filling his lungs with black smoke and scalding air. Shrugging off the pain and summoning every ounce of strength he could muster, he heaved the coughing slave forward and staggered through the smoke and flames toward the new exit. The pair rolled out a heartbeat before the shack finally collapsed.

Buckets of water switched from dousing the ruined shack to the half-dead workers. Patches of burning fur and clothing were extinguished, and a few of the braver slaves managed to drag Menri clear. Drawing in ragged breaths and coughing violently, the malthrope crawled out of the worst of the heat and rolled to his back. Neither of them had fared well in the blaze. Menri had a swath of burns across one arm and leg that would leave nasty scars. Half of the fur on the beast's face had been blackened, his nose and left ear was raw and blistered, and his left eye was shut tight. Each was hacking and wheezing, trying to get good air into broiled lungs. A cluster of the other slaves gathered around Menri.

Suddenly, all eyes turned to the edge of the field, as Marret approached amid a battalion of handlers. There was fury in his eyes and his voice.

"No! No, no, no, no, *no!*" the plantation owner cried. "The roasters! There . . . were there any slaves inside?"

"Two. They got out," replied Bartner, a witness to the near-tragedy and little else. There was a casual tone to his voice, and even a weak grin on his lips.

"How much rakka?" Marret fumed.

"Perhaps four bushels. A bit more, maybe."

The owner's hands shook as he paced in tight circles, anxiety burning at him with a sting nearly the match of the fire. "Four bushels. No lives lost, no one to replace . . . Fine, *fine*. I want that shack rebuilt! New roasters. Get the blind man on it. I need roasters turning again *tomorrow!* Half-rations for the rest of the season for the slaves responsible, and half rations to everyone until we're back to turning out rakka seed. I will not have this plantation crumble because of some blasted incompetent slaves!"

With that, Marret stormed away, his men in tow. Those around Menri managed to get him to his feet, but once they did, he pushed them away. He turned to the creature beside him.

"You . . . why?" Menri wheezed.

His savior tried to answer, but the creature could only manage more painful coughing. Finally, he reached up, a clawed finger pointing to the brand on Menri's healthy arm, then to the matching one on his own. Menri nodded once and bent low, the other slaves keeping him from falling. With his burned arm, he grasped the beast and helped him to sit up.

"Listen to me . . . I don't like you. I'll never like you. But what there was between us . . . is over. You may be a monster, but you're one of *Jarrad's* slaves." Menri looked to Bartner, who had taken it upon himself to scatter the crowd of onlookers and "encourage" them to begin work on the new roasting shack. "Right now, we've got better things to worry about than each other."

Ben finally made his way to the injured pair. His voice was steady but urgent. "I'm here. How bad is it? Describe the wounds."

"I've got blisters. The beast has them, too. On his ear and nose. He caught a lungful, too."

"All right. Get your wounds cleaned and dressed. Lots of clean water. Do you need my help for that?"

"I can manage."

"Good, go. And you, you little devil. How bad is it? Open your mouth. Breath for me."

The creature, with care and concentration, was able to pull a shaky breath in and let it out without coughing.

"Again . . . I don't hear anything terrible. Your face. Your ear and nose were burnt. What of your eyes?"

With a quiver and a twitch, the malthrope fought his left eye open.

"It . . ." he struggled to say. "It seems you are still the only blind man on this farm."

Ben smiled weakly and shook his head, snapping quickly back into the proper tone when the moment had passed. "Get him up. Clean water for him, too."

The other slaves paused.

"Do it!" came Menri's booming voice from behind them. "He is one of us. You don't leave one of your fellow workers on the ground."

Even with the strong words of a man they trusted, a man they looked up to, there were few slaves willing to set aside their bone-deep distrust. It was Gurruk and Blondie who finally shouldered their way through the assembled crowd and pulled the burned malthrope to his feet while Goldie fetched water. Burns were treated to the best of Ben's ability with the resources at hand.

Behind them, the fire finished what it started, consuming the remains of the roasting shack and taking any remaining trace of respect or loyalty the slaves might have had to their owner along with it.

#

Marret's sweeping changes and complete abandonment of quality managed to keep the plantation afloat for another season, but it cost him dearly. Buyers who had come to trust the peerless attention to detail that made Jarrad's rakka so sought after had paid the usual premium. When they received their share of the harvest, what they received was rakka in name only. Burnt to a crisp, half-rotten, or nearly green . . . if the seeds had a fraction of the effectiveness of a proper batch, it would have been a miracle. The reaction from the buyers, buyers who had trusted Jarrad for years, was universal. Angry words were exchanged, vicious threats were delivered, and future purchases were canceled. Word spread through Tressor: buy rakka from Marret at your own risk.

A hard-earned and valued reputation that had taken Jarrad years to build had been squandered in the space of two harvests by his son.

Planting season was just a few weeks away, but the land had yet to be prepared. Rakka was too costly in both time and resources to grow without the secure knowledge that a buyer would be waiting for it when it was time to harvest. Marret's newly-earned reputation had left him with no one willing to commit to even a single sack. Another farmer would simply switch to a different crop and weather a few lean years. Marret's debts—and, more importantly, the men to whom he owed them—made that a death sentence. Rakka was the only crop that carried a high enough price to keep his head out of the noose.

Messengers were hired, missives were prepared, and prayers were said. One by one the replies returned, each making it clearer and clearer that Marret had sold his last rakka berry. Then came one final response.

Marret had sent thirty messages. This reply was the thirty-first. It was written on highest quality velum, and delivered one night by a messenger none had seen come or go. The wording was simple and direct:

I am interested in a business arrangement. I will arrive at midnight to discuss it. Meet me at the northern entrance to your plantation and find us a private place to discuss it. No witnesses.

It was ominous, vague, and reeked of danger, but it was the last chance Marret might have to avoid paying his debts with his life. He handed out instructions to his men, and when the time came, he was waiting at the gate on the north side of his land.

There was a chill to the air, one made worse by the uncertainty in the pit of Marret's stomach. He was wearing a finely-woven robe, a single garment that was worth more than his late father's entire wardrobe. Like so much that he'd paid mounds of silver for, it was pretty, but it didn't do the job. The breeze cut through it, leaving the young man to shiver as he waited.

Beside him stood Ben, staff in one hand, a lantern in the other, and a bag slung over one shoulder.

"It must be near midnight by now," Marret muttered, blowing in his hands.

"Quite near, master." Ben nodded. "If you do not mind the observation, this seems an unusual way to begin a simple crop purchase."

"I do mind, blind man. My father liked a bit of back and forth with his workers. I prefer a man who knows his place," Marret snapped.

"As do I, farmer," came a voice from the darkness.

Marret turned to the darkness to see a gray-cloaked figure emerging. There was a strong moon, and the lantern was freshly filled with oil and quite bright. The darkness simply wasn't dense enough to have concealed an approach, but nonetheless, here his visitor was, steps away without so much as a glimpse prior. Worse, she wasn't alone, joined on each side by two figures dressed in coarser, heavier versions of her own gray cloak. The hoods were cavernous, and the light of the lantern didn't seem to penetrate deep enough to reveal even the gleam of an eye.

His visitor stepped closer. She was attractive, in a cold and pale way. Her features were sharp and flawless, skin nearly white and lips and hair nearly black. Rather than the light, billowy clothing worn by most of those who called Tressor home, beneath her cloak she was bundled in a thick coat and heavy leggings. For an instant, Marret thought he'd noticed a few flakes of snow melting on the shoulder of the cloak. There was a look of weary impatience on her face.

"I didn't think my instructions left any room for confusion," the woman said. "No witnesses."

There was a twist to her words, and it was not entirely due to the undertone of irritation. Marret, unable to place it, set the puzzle aside for a moment.

"Madam, as you can see, this man is blind. I give you my assurance that he is in no way a witness."

"Yes, well, I trust you've set aside a suitably private setting for our discussion."

"Yes, yes, we will be discussing it in my study—"

"No, the stable."

"But—"

"You don't have very many options, farmer. Do what I say or I walk away, and you cannot afford for me to walk away. I mean that in a *very* financial way. Let us go."

She marched briskly past Marret, acting for the world as though the plantation belonged to her, and made her way toward the stables without being directed. Marret hurried to keep up.

"This is very irregular, madam," he objected.

"And you wouldn't have been standing at that gate if you hadn't exhausted all of the 'regular' options. Now, be a good little farmer and keep quiet until we are behind closed doors," she instructed sharply.

Marret swallowed his anger and followed. A few minutes of walking led them to the dark and unpleasantly fragrant confines of the stable. Ben shut the door, drawing the attention of the four horses that would be witnessing a business deal that was looking less wise by the moment. Each animal was in its own stall, and as the two silent companions of his visitor moved to the far corners of the room, the creatures became visibly uneasy.

"Now. We are in your chosen location, and I have followed your rules. May we *please* get down to business, Madam . . . I'm sorry, what is your name?"

She crossed her arms and adopted weary expression. "Madam Teht. And, yes, I'd say we should begin. I have a few questions for you, if I may?"

"I . . . I suppose."

"My partners and I are of the belief that there is something very special here on this land."

"You and your partners are quite insightful. This soil has been consistently responsible for some of the finest rakka ever to—"

"No. A man. Or perhaps a woman. Someone here, who has been here for some time. It took some time to pinpoint it, but now we are quite certain."

"I don't understand . . . you are here for a slave?"

"Well, I am certainly not here for *you*. Now, tell me, do you have anyone here who is . . . unique? Someone remarkable?"

Marret was uncertain where precisely the conversation was going, and for that matter, *why* it was going there. Until he could be sure that there was no chance of this meeting ending in a large payment, though, he forced himself to remain in a business state of mind.

"We pride ourselves on having the finest and best-trained workers in all of Tressor."

"Yes, but does one stand out more than the rest? Despite our best efforts, we simply haven't been able to get a good look. Something is blinding us. I'm looking for someone different. Someone truly notable. A swordsman, perhaps? An artistic prodigy? An elemental? A malthrope?"

Marret shuddered.

"There," she said with a smile, "You've got a malthrope. Such was my suspicion."

"I assure you, it is quite legal. He is a worker, and a fine one."

"I'm sure he is. Tell me, does the beast have a mark anywhere? A curve and point? There since birth?"

"I really wouldn't know. Blind man?"

"As I understand it, he as a mark like that over his heart."

"Excellent. I want him. Name your price," said Teht.

"I'm afraid a simple slave sale—"

"You don't understand," she said, snapping her fingers. A bag the size of Marret's head was tossed to the ground at her feet. Presumably it was thrown by one of her men, though neither seemed to have moved. The bag spilled open, dumping out a fortune in featureless gold coins. "Name your price."

Marret's throat suddenly went dry. He opened his mouth, but before the words could come, his servant interjected.

"Master, don't," Ben advised.

"Quiet!" Marret barked, "This young woman and I are discussing the future of this plantation!"

"Master, her voice. Do not tell me you cannot hear that," Ben insisted. "Madam Teht has a Northern accent."

The plantation owner shuddered, turning over the peculiarity of her speech in his head. It had been quite some time since he'd heard such an accent, and hers was weak, but it was undeniable.

"Where, may I ask, do you hail from, Madam Teht?"

She snapped her fingers again, and a second bag of gold struck the ground beside the first. "Is that really relevant?"

Marret's mouth fell open and his eyes widened. Every fiber of his being urged him to politely assure his honored guest that her place of origin did not matter to him in the slightest, and that the malthrope would most certainly be hers within the hour. This, alas, was not so.

"I'm . . ." he said hoarsely, "I'm afraid that it is . . . it is quite relevant. You see, the malthrope doesn't have a tail. My late father cut it off and sold it. The beast was to be destroyed, but it was and is a fine worker, so an arrangement was made to allow it to remain on the plantation, alive, provided that it never leave. If it were to disappear, then my father—and now I—would be responsible for anything it might do."

"I assure you that it will not be allowed to do anything untoward while under my ownership."

"I don't doubt that, but the slave would need to be sold to you through official means. The officials involved would simply assume it escaped otherwise, and even with a proper sale they may not be satisfied. If you are Northern . . . well, our people are at war. An official business agreement would be treason. Either case would leave me in a position with little use for your payment, regardless of the size."

"I see," she said with a sneer. "Well . . . we wouldn't want that, would we . . ."

"Absolutely not. As long as this plantation is my responsibility, that malthrope stays on it."

Teht narrowed her eyes and heaved an irritated sigh. "They always send me on these blasted errands to the South, and they never go smoothly," she muttered to herself with a shake of her head. "Fine. You grow rakka here, yes?"

"Ah, yes! The finest in Tressor," Marret replied, relieved to find the conversation finally returning to the subject he'd been prepared to discuss. "If you'll look here, last season's crop was quite bountiful."

Ben fished the bundle of parchment from within the bag and held it out. Marret snatched it and selected a page, handing it to Teht.

"Now, we have quite a bit of next season's crop available. It . . . it is still somewhat troubling if you are Northern, but . . . well, unlike the slave you were after, we should be able to . . . misplace the record of this transaction. You may reserve—"

"All of it."

"Well, yes, if you wish, you can certainly purchase it all."

"I intend to, farmer. All of it. In fact . . . thrice this amount."

"Err. What you see there is what I will be able to grow. If you would like to reserve the full crop for the next three years, I would be willing to sell it. Properly prepared rakka will keep for well over three years."

"If you want this gold, I want three times what you grew last year, and I want it this year. One bushel less and we do not have a deal. Simple enough for you?"

"I . . . rakka takes a considerable amount of work. To get top quality rakka, there will be some that must be discarded or—"

"I'm not interested in quality. Quantity is what I'm after. You provide this much, and I will buy every last berry, every last seed. And if you manage it the next year, and the year after that, each year, I'll be back."

Marret's eyes locked on the two heavy sacks of gold. Combined, they were enough to take the debtors from his throat and return him to the life he'd grown accustomed to. He swallowed hard. "That is acceptable."

"Master, you—"

"If you utter one more syllable, I swear to you, blind man, I will find a way to make your pathetic life even more miserable," Marret snapped.

"Pleasing to see that you know when to put a man in his place. Keep the gold—though if you fail to deliver, I'll be taking it back. Now, if you'll excuse me, I've got *another* errand to run farther south. Another meeting with the blasted gatekeeper." Teht muttered. "My talents are wasting away working on trivial things like this."

She pushed her way past Marret and continued out the door, her attendants in tow. When the plantation owner attempted to follow, intent on oozing a bit more charm in hopes of making an impression as a social elite, the heavy door to the stable was slammed in his face. He let the false smile fall away.

"What," Marret fumed, turning to his slave with a scowl, "do you think you were *doing* contradicting me? There are *two* bags of *gold*, each as big as that empty head of yours, that could have been lost had you continued your prattle."

"You cannot hope to fill the order, master. Even if we do not lose a single bushel, and even if we deliver every last rakka seed regardless of quality, we couldn't hope to fill *half* of what she's asking," Ben raved.

"Then we shall plant rakka on all of our fields," Marret said.

"You cannot! Rakka ruins the soil if left to grow in it year in and year out. Within three seasons, you won't be able to grow a weed!"

"Within three seasons we will be able to buy half of Tressor if she keeps paying us so foolishly. This soil is the best in all of the kingdom. It has always done what we've required of it. It will not fail us now."

"It has done what you've required of it because it has been cared for properly. It was the last semblance of your father's way that you hadn't abandoned."

"That is all, blind man. Go. Back to your shack. And tomorrow, don't bother coming forward at meal times. You'll find your bowl empty. Tonight you should thank all that is holy that you are so frail. If I wasn't afraid they would snap you in half with their first blow, I would have my handlers teach you a lesson you would never *ever* forget," Marret barked. "Have I made myself clear?"

"Crystal."

"Then go!" Marret growled.

Outside, a crack of thunder pealed across the plantation, near enough and powerful enough to rattle the stable and spook the horses nearly into a frenzy. Without so much as a flinch from the sound, Ben lowered the lantern, pushed open the door, and departed.

Marret took up the lantern and marched after him expecting to see the beginnings of a rain storm, and thus another chance to ingratiate himself to his new benefactor in the form of a loaned carriage. Outside, he found not a cloud in the starry sky, not a drop of rain . . . and no sign of the strange woman or her body guards. Pausing only briefly to consider it, the greedy land owner rushed back inside the stable to see to his gold.

Ben simply marched steadily and slowly.

"The man doesn't understand the harm he does . . . doesn't understand the mistakes he makes. All it takes is the glitter of gold and the fool is as blind as me . . ."

#

Against tradition, advisement, and good judgment, Marret had chosen to completely fill his plantation with rakka. With the temperamental plants occupying the fields meant for lentils, there was some question of where the food for the slaves would come from next season, but this was, predictably, of little concern to Marret. Of greater concern was the fact that there simply weren't enough slaves to properly plant and tend to the additional bushes. Reluctantly, a portion of the gold was spent to purchase enough slaves to shoulder the additional load, and enough handlers to keep them in line and on task. Normally, training them would have taken at least a season, but with the lax requirements set forth by their benefactor, weeks of training were collapsed into two instructions: keep the soil moist, and pick any berry that isn't green anymore.

Once the baskets were filled, a cursory attempt at soaking and roasting the seeds was made, but it soon became clear that there would be no hope of keeping up with the harvest. The already-slashed preparation was reduced to a quick dip in a vat of water and a hasty sear. At the end of a season, all of the compromises and cut corners had produced just enough rakka to fill Teht's order.

At midnight on the last day of the harvest, she arrived as quietly and mysteriously as she had before, instructed a veritable army of cloaked servants haul away the crop, and left the payment in advance for the next year.

Of course, the new slaves had cost a handsome sum, the new handlers needed to be paid, and with no food grown, food enough for the workers needed to be bought. In the end, the gold from the first payment wasn't enough to cover the costs *and* his many debts, but it was little concern. This year's payment more than made up for the difference. All that needed to be done was to match the prior year's harvest and his debts would be clean with more than enough gold left over make him as wealthy as he'd always behaved that he was.

Alas, the soil that had so faithfully served his father for all of these years seemed to have no such loyalty to him. The northern fields, those which had been forced to endure two years of rakka without rest, were reluctant to suffer a third. Few bushes sprouted, and fewer still survived long enough to produce any fruit. Ben used every trick he knew to pry another useful season from the land, and to squeeze extra from the fields that had not yet been taxed to their limit. The end of the season brought a harvest that was still well short of Teht's requirements. With most of the gold spent upon his debts, and thus without the ability to give it back as the mysterious woman would require, Marret was forced to pay dearly for rakka from other plantations to make up for the shortfall.

It was then that Marret finally managed to accept that he could not provide another harvest like this one, and refused to do business with Teht any longer, but the damage was done. There was not a single field on his overworked stretch of land that could yield a decent crop any longer. Before long, new debts began to replace the ones that had so recently been paid. When the time came to pay his yearly tribute to the lord, he could not afford it and was forced to give up the best of his fields and the best of his slaves.

More time passed, and things only grew worse from that day.

#

Five years since the deal with Teht had sealed the doom of Jarrad's once-great plantation, Marret's two sisters had taken their families and moved on, but some combination of pride, stubbornness, and stupidity kept Marret and his brood in the sprawling manor. The young man was convinced that he could somehow scrape enough of a survival from his father's land to one day build it back again—and he was unwilling to give up his home. All that remained of what had, for a time, been nine fields, were the same three that Jarrad had worked when Ben and the malthrope had been purchased fifteen years ago. Combined, there was perhaps enough worthwhile soil among the unsold land to bring in what would have been a shamefully small yield from a single field in the old days.

Worse than the state of the land was the state of the workers. All of the single-stripe slaves had been taken by the lord, and most of the double-stripe slaves as well. Many more had simply escaped. The hellish conditions and starvation rations convinced them that the life of a fugitive—or even the death of one—would be preferable to enduring another day on the land. Only the dozen with bodies or minds too broken to contemplate escape and too weak to be worth selling remained now.

Among them were Menri, Goldie, Gurruk, Ben, and the malthrope. Menri and Goldie were husks of their former selves, the former thanks to the ravages of a hard life finally catching up with him, and the latter thanks to a series of poorly-treated injuries all but crippling him. Gurruk, who had been ornery when drunk and more so when sober, had gotten in more than enough fights to earn three stripes and too low a price to be sold. Ben was nearly bent double with age and had no value elsewhere, and the malthrope refused to leave his mentor's side and could not be sold regardless. The others were mostly the remnants of stopgap purchases made to keep the farm afloat in recent years.

To keep them hard at work and to discourage further escape attempts, there were no fewer than eight handlers, nearly one for every slave. Their leader and most eager member was, naturally, Bartner.

"Up! Up and out!" barked the slave-driver as he marched along the row of rundown shacks that housed the remaining workers. "I want all

123

of you on your feet and ready for the day's orders *now!"*

Slowly, the haggard slaves stumbled from their homes and formed a line. Bartner stalked up and down, teeth fairly grinding as he looked them over, almost eager to find a misstep or misbehavior. When it became clear that they were too weary and beaten to misbehave, his mind churned until he found something suitable to growl about.

"Blind man!" he bellowed. "Get out here!"

The malthrope turned to the door of the shack, his motions slow to avoid drawing a lash from Bartner. It opened, and Ben shakily made his way out. The years had been harder on Ben than anyone else. Now ancient by any measure, the last five years had ruined him. His wrinkled skin hung loose in a malnourished way. What little hair he still had was reduced to a thin, downy, white tangle. He tried to stand tall, but he was bent and stooped with time; if not for his walking stick, the old man likely wouldn't be able to stand.

Bartner scowled and pounded over to the frail old man.

"Listen, blind man. In all of the years I've been here, I've seen you talk, I've seen you teach. I've seen you sit down and tinker. I've never once seen you work. All of these men and the mally get out there and get dirty and sweaty and do the job. Considering how bad this patch of dirt is doing, I think it is time you got out there and put your back into it." His words were delivered with the flicker of a grin at the corners of his mouth, like a boy who had just discovered a brand new toy.

"The spirit is willing," Ben stated. "But—"

"But nothing! If you can lean on a stick, you can lean on a shovel. Get out there and do your job."

"You can't do that! Ben can barely stand!"

All eyes turned. It was the malthrope who had spoken. Though the trying conditions had helped to ease the hostility toward him amongst the slaves, if only by making the slave handlers even more despised than he, he still tended to stay quiet when in groups. When his voice was heard, it was a few quiet words, always the answer to a question. This outburst represented the most that any but Ben had heard him speak all at once in years.

When he realized who had objected, the fury poured off of Bartner. He thundered up to the creature, foregoing the strap for a punishing backhand.

"Don't you *ever* speak to me unless I *order* you to speak to me," he roared, hammering home his words with a second and third strike.

"You. Filthy. *Malthrope!*"

A final devastating blow upon the groggy and stunned creature was enough to drive him into unconsciousness. When the light slowly returned to his vision and the fog began to lift, the creature found himself secured in a leather harness and attached by way of it to a plow. His rattled mind tried to put the pieces together. The tool—a stout, wedge-shaped blade with a pair of handles to guide it and a sturdy rope to pull it—hadn't been used to till the fields since the work animals had been sold two years prior. At the handles was the graying, worn-out man that Menri had become under Marret's leadership.

With muzzy clumsiness the creature worked at the straps, trying to free himself.

"Don't," warned Menri. "Bartner said with Ben as an extra hand on the field, we finally have an animal free to pull the plow."

In the past, the slave would have reveled in the current situation, but the fight had long ago left him. He knew all too well that if the monstrous head slave-driver thought he could get away with it, the scoundrel would have a slave strapped to the plow every day, just to watch them struggle. Somehow, there was no fun in watching suffering when the next day it could easily be your burden to bear.

"Ho there!" came Bartner's voice from the edge of the field. "If our new ox is through with its rest, get a move on!"

The malthrope shuddered and turned to Menri.

"For what it's worth," the man said quietly, "even *you* don't deserve *this*. Now get moving, before he beats both of us."

After a deep breath and a resigned sigh, the malthrope strained at the straps until the blade began to cut through the parched and ruined soil. The work was back-breaking. In minutes, his muscles were screaming and his lungs were burning. It took every ounce of his strength to keep the plow moving, and if a stubborn clump of dirt or cluster of stone managed to bring it to a stop, he had to fight madly to get it moving again. Making matters worse was the agonizing throbbing in his head, a lingering reminder of the throttling Bartner had given him. His vision had yet to clear completely, and the baking sun and suffocating heat wrung the strength from his limbs, but he pressed on. There simply wasn't another option. Stopping even long enough to catch his breath drew Bartner or one of his underlings to administer a lash or two, and threats of worse if he didn't finish the row.

The sun crept through the sky. When it finally reached the horizon, somehow the malthrope was still breathing. Long ago he'd lost the strength to haul his burden with his legs alone. Now he'd resorted to digging his toes and fingers into the dirt and heaving at the straps to inch the blade forward. Most of the other workers had finished their tasks and trudged to their shacks already, leaving at least one handler free at any given moment to provide motivation. The only respite came during the occasional grudgingly-allowed water break.

It was during just such a break, Menri drinking from a dipper and the beast plunging his head into a bucket, that a commotion was heard.

"What's going on over there?" Menri asked, wiping sweat from his brow.

"It looks like they're giving the proper encouragement to the only worker doing a worse job than you two," muttered their current handler, one of Marret's most recently hired. "The blind man."

The words roused Ben's apprentice from the near-trance he'd fallen into. His head shot up and he fought his red-rimmed eyes into focus, scanning the fields until he spotted the meager form of his mentor. The old man was on his knees, clearly without the strength to stand. Bartner was over him, studded strap in hand and vicious grin on his face. The slave-driver muttered something the malthrope couldn't make out over the pulse pounding in his ears. Ben wheezed an unheard reply. Whatever it was, it was enough to prompt Bartner to deliver a lash to the old man's back, knocking him to the dirt.

"No!" the malthrope urged.

"If you're through with your water, you can get back to work," said the slave handler overseeing the beast. "Move."

The words were delivered with a threatening brandish of his own tool of punishment, a cat o'nine tails, but the beast did not heed them. Another blow was delivered to the fallen old man, and the beast shook as though it had struck him instead.

"You've got to stop it! You'll kill him!"

"You should worry about yourself, monster. Now back to work!" the handler ordered with a lash of his weapon. When the blow failed to silence the desperate pleas for mercy, more followed.

Blow after blow rained down on malthrope and blind man alike. Each strike made the creature more desperate, drawing the attention of other handlers, each adding his own lashes and barked orders. They did no good. Each strike was shrugged off as their target screamed for Bartner to stop, tears streaming and voice wavering. He struggled at the straps that held him to the plow, inching it toward his ailing mentor and trying with all of his might to pull free.

#

Half a field away, Ben slumped after another blow.

"Please . . . please . . . you don't understand what you are doing . . ." the blind man struggled to say.

"I am giving you what you deserve for not working," growled Bartner with another lash.

"You can't do this . . . not now . . . not in front of the malthrope . . ."

"Don't worry, old man. The beast will get what he deserves soon enough. Now, are you going to work?"

Another blow knocked the wind from Ben's lungs.

"I . . . can't . . ." he croaked.

The strap tore at him again.

Fingers digging into the soil, Ben pulled together what little strength he had left. "Do not show him . . . this side of humanity. You don't understand . . . how important he is. You don't understand . . . what he'll do if . . . he is a . . ."

The words were cut short by a savage blow.

"He is a monster. And there is only one way to deal with monsters."

Ben coughed weakly, blood speckling his lips. "Yes . . . only one way . . . to deal with monsters . . ."

#

The beast watched with pained eyes as finally there came a blow upon the old man that did not prompt a shudder of pain. There was no motion at all. Ben was still. As the realization of what happened reached its icy fingers into his brain, the malthrope dropped to his knees and hung his head low. The world seemed to dim. Agony, fear, anger . . . each dropped away. All expression drained from his face as a cold, dark emptiness wrapped itself around his soul. It snuffed out the anguish of his mind, then snuffed out the mind as well. In its place rose something else . . . something primal. A smoldering ember inside of him, one that had been stoked by each moment of sorrow and each act of cruelty, flared and sparked.

Ben was not the only thing that had been broken by that final blow. It had snapped the tattered threads of restraint within the beast, torn away the layers of humanity built with such care.

Slowly, the creature raised his head, seeming to notice for the first time that the handlers had never stopped lashing him. Rocking with their blows, he climbed to his feet and turned slowly to the nearest of his tormentors. His gaze was cold and empty, eyes gleaming with an ancient purpose—something in that look was enough to cause the handlers to slow their strikes, then to stop entirely. The wisest among them chose to back away.

"You! You there! Why have you stopped! What's going on?" Bartner cried as he stalked toward the circle of suddenly apprehensive handlers, leaving the motionless old man behind.

The ring of handlers opened to allow their leader in. He stomped up to the creature, his furious gaze locking onto the eyes of a beast that seemed unnervingly calm. In his rage, Bartner had blinded himself to something that man as a species had forgotten on all but the most fundamental level.

When a man envisions a vicious creature, a creature that means to kill him, he imagines a snarling demon of a thing: teeth bared, claws pawing at the ground, ears turned back. In truth, such a beast does not mean to kill you. Flashed teeth and bellowing roars are meant to frighten, to threaten. A creature acting in such a way may fight you, it may even kill you, but what it is most dedicated to is fending you off, proving its strength, and saving itself. It is a cowering reaction to a larger foe, or an intimidating display to a would-be opponent. When a beast truly intends to kill you, it behaves very differently. It watches, intensity in its gaze. Its motions are slow, subdued. It trains it senses, waits until the right moment. In short, it behaves precisely as this beast was. Whether Bartner realized it or not, his relationship with the creature had changed. No longer slave and slave-driver, now they were predator and prey.

"Do you *want* me to do to you what I did to him?" Bartner raged, brandishing his strap.

The beast did not flinch and did not look away.

"Oh . . . so you aren't afraid of the strap anymore?" the handler growled darkly. "Fine. We shall try something new. You, with the nine tails. Give it here."

Bartner's obedient underling tossed him the instrument of torture. It was a bit larger than arm's length, constructed of braided black leather that had taken on a brown tinge with age and use. At one end was a loop through which Bartner placed his hand to keep the tool in place. The opposite side was a tangle of nine loose and dangling strands, each knotted along their length. A few experimental swings whistled through the air. The beast watched, eyes following the motion.

"This has been a long time coming," he said with a grin.

The malthrope turned to face him, expression blank and eyes steady. Bartner raised the weapon high and brought it down. At the same instant his victim raised his arm. Each strand wrapped tightly around the presented limb. When Bartner tried to withdraw, the beast shifted his weight, drawing his arm swiftly back and heaving with his work-hardened legs. With his fist still secured in the loop, Bartner could not drop the tool and was pulled off balance, stumbling toward the beast. Another weight shift and the malthrope was darting toward the overbalanced handler. His jaws snapped open . . .

In less than the time it took the others to react, it was over, a long overdue justice done. Bartner collapsed with a few final twitches. The malthrope spat something to the ground and turned his cold gaze to the next handler. What followed was chaos. Cries of anger rang out and every available slave-driver dove upon the malthrope. Somehow, the beast managed to shred the straps holding him to the plow, and slashing claws and gnashing teeth found their mark again and again. Slave-drivers scattered, but the beast pursued. Muscles worked to near collapse were roused to life again as ancient instincts of the hunt clicked into place.

#

No one truly knows all of what happened that day. It is said that at one point the surviving slave-drivers managed to manhandle the beast into his shack and brace the door, only to learn too late that the tool shack makes a poor choice of prison. A slash of a blade made short work of the door and the unfortunate man bracing it, and out streaked the malthrope, scythe in hand. There were screams that could be heard for miles. There were calls to arms as the personal servants and personal guards of the plantation owner rushed to the fields. There was blood.

For the beast, there was naught but the flames of hate blotting out the thinking part of his mind. For the people of the plantation, there was naught but a nightmare. That day they saw everything they feared a malthrope might be come to life before their eyes.

When the burning fury finally dimmed, the first thing to cut through to the malthrope's mind was a piercing squeal of fear. He shook himself and looked around. He was indoors. Elegant furniture, expensive rugs, and fine tapestries were around him, broken to splinters and torn to shreds. He was inside Marret's manor, and whatever he had done, it had destroyed the once-opulent sitting room. Again the squeal rang out.

He looked to its source, a young boy not more than five. The boy was huddled in the corner screaming his head off, his eyes locked in terror on the creature before him.

With his wits returned to him, the malthrope looked himself over. One of his black-furred hands was drenched, thick drops of crimson pattering steadily to the polished wood of the floor. The other held a scythe, its blade streaked with a muddy red. There was an acrid, metallic taste clinging to his tongue, and from the end of a whisker rolled a solitary drop of blood. He let the scythe clatter to the floor, looking down at his stained fingers and glistening claws. Realization and understanding crept into his thoughts, bringing with it a cold dread that seized the back of his mind and fluttered madly in his chest.

Not knowing what else to do, the creature ran. Through the house he sprinted, past scenes of unspeakable devastation. Through the fields he ran, finding them empty and lifeless in the light of the setting sun. Through the wide open gates, across the road beyond, long into the night he ran. Away from his home. Away from his prison. Away from what he had done.

Chapter 13

The terror of his acts was enough to keep the beast moving for far longer than his tortured muscles should have permitted, but exhaustion can only be pushed aside for so long. As the moon slid below the horizon, he managed a few final steps on shaky legs, stumbling into the tall grass beside a stream.

Sleep took him before he even managed to lie down, leaving him a crumpled heap among the weeds at the mercy of his dreams. They were horrible. The white-hot rage had robbed him of any real memory of what he'd done, but his mind was only too eager to fill the gaps with imagined horrors and half-recalled atrocities. The images came in flashes, vivid and searing. They flickered through his mind in tight cycles, always ending the same way: the squeal of terror and the look of utter horror in the eyes of that little boy.

An eternity of such torture seemed to pass, but finally his eyes opened and his mind tried to make sense of things. It was bright, brighter that it should have been. It had been years since he'd awoken with the sky over his head. His muscles were sore, which was nothing new, but it was worse than normal. He hadn't been so sore since he'd raced Menri to complete his row. On top of it was a horrid, pulsing pain across the whole of his back, where he could feel the breeze fluttering at holes in his tunic. Stiffly, he sat up, swatting away a cloud of gnats.

The back of his mind nagged him with the little tasks he was accustomed to doing each morning. Check outside the door for tools left for repair. Fill the water pail and bring it in for Ben . . . Ben.

He held his throbbing head in his hands as the truth settled in. Ben was gone. Everything was gone. The place he'd called home, his purpose, his mentor, all gone forever. He carefully stood, stopping just when his eyes were clear of the tall grass. There was nothing. No huts, no walls. Nothing between him and the horizon but open fields, dirt roads, and scattered cottages.

At the sight of the sprawling, unfettered landscape, the malthrope froze. Strange as it might seem, he had never truly longed for freedom. His youngest days, the only ones spent beyond the reaches of the

131

plantation's fences, were little more than vague memories. In his youth, all that had mattered to him was finding new ways to make Ben proud. In the years that followed, his every waking moment was spent working the land, performing odd jobs, and otherwise proving his worth to himself, to Ben, and to the others. The plantation had been his world, and the walls were where his world ended. To find himself beyond them gave him a dizzying, plummeting feeling, like he was dangling from the edge of a cliff.

Overwhelmed, he ducked down again, his mind abandoning the terrifying prospect of freedom in favor of smaller, more immediate problems. The long run and the events that came before it had taken far more out of the beast than sleep alone could restore. His mouth felt as though it had been filled with sand, tongue stuck to the roof of his mouth, eyes red and dry. He crawled to the edge of the stream and dunked his head, once to shock a bit of focus into his mind, and again to slake a bone-deep thirst.

Once his thirst was tended to, he hoisted his head out of the water and allowed his eyes to linger on the sight below. His hands, resting on the pebbles on the stream bed, were trailing billowing clouds of red, the dried remains of the crimes of the prior day mixing with the clean water. Madly he scrubbed at his fingers, his arms, his face, and back again, not stopping until long after the last trace of red drifted away. He likely would have continued until his hands were rubbed raw, but a motion in the water shook his mind free and reminded him of the other pressing need he had been neglecting. It had been too long since his meager breakfast the day before, and there had been too much work done since. His stomach was empty, not to the point of hunger but far beyond it.

Flitting in a long and cautious arc around the disturbance of his fingers in the water was a silvery form. The sight of it, the first fish he'd ever seen outside of a stew pot, brought a growl to his stomach and a gleam to his eye. Answering to instincts that had once again taken matters into their own hands, he dove for the morsel.

A clumsy grab sent the scaly meal darting away, and thus sent the starving malthrope splashing after it. After too much time, he finally managed to swat the wriggling form out of the water and onto the shore, where he pounced upon it. Two satisfying crunches sent the catch, bones and all, to an eagerly waiting stomach. Without so much as a pause to catch his breath, he launched himself back toward the deepest part of the stream. There, two more fish were caught with no more skill but much more enthusiasm. They were larger, and combined represented the largest meal he'd eaten in months. Now almost painfully full, he waded back to the safety of the tall grass, his mind able to turn to other things.

He sat back, panting, and tried to work out what had happened and what was going to happen now. Perhaps it was shameful, but his thoughts did not settle upon the lives he had taken. Not at first. His memories of what he had done were too fractured. They were like the nightmares he'd just awoken from: bright flashes and vivid instants, with wide gaps between. He simply didn't know all of what he'd done, and perhaps he never would. Instead, his mind turned to Ben. The old man had been the one constant in his life for so many years. He had always been there, always knew what to do.

For the second time in his life, he felt a hole form, an empty spot in his soul. First his mother, now Ben. When he thought of the blind man on the ground, Bartner over him with strap in hand, he felt the flames of anger again, but as quickly as they came, they were snuffed away by words from his past that had not spoken loudly enough to be heard yesterday, but now rang clear and true.

"If you let that part take over . . . you'll be what they always expected you to be," he murmured quietly.

There was no denying it. What he had done was easily the match of anything they'd told tales about around the fire. He'd done terrible things. Things that could never be justified. Things only a monster could do. And what burned him now wasn't that he had done them—for now, his crimes were too large for his mind to swallow. What truly shriveled his soul was knowing the shame, the disappointment Ben would have felt. It seemed so small in comparison, a sprinkle of rain in the wake of the torrent of atrocity, but it was all he could think about. The old man was the only one who had ever seen any potential in the creature—not as a worker or a trophy or a ransom, but as an individual. Ben had had hope for what the beast could become. And now all of that was wiped away, wasted. In the space of a few minutes, he had lost his mentor and everything the old man had dared to believe.

His eyes stared unseeing toward the sky, the weight of his deeds pressing down on him. He could have lain there forever, tears of sorrow and regret trickling down his cheeks, but in time his keen ears twitched. There were voices, angry ones, in the distance. The words carried on the wind filtered through to his tortured mind. They were after him. It sounded like three people, two on horses and one leading a hound. Almost mechanically, he climbed to his feet and peered out from the grass. Sure enough, a team of men were in the distance, and there was little doubt that the hound had caught his trail.

If he'd thought about his actions, he might have allowed the men to find him and administer the justice he knew he deserved, but there was already far too much fighting for attention in his mind. Staying out of sight was the first and most thoroughly learned lesson he'd learned in his time on the plantation. Sore muscles and weary senses simply took their own initiative. He pulled himself into the stream and guided himself in the direction of the flow, moving quickly but quietly, no destination in mind other than *away.*

For nearly three days, he continued in that way, threading south, then west, always with search parties close on his tail. Word must have spread of what he'd done, because no sooner had he lost one batch of would-be captors than another drew near. There was no time to find food, and sleep came in stolen moments. Each change in direction was dictated by a short, careful scan of his surroundings with nose, ears, and eyes, selecting whatever path led to the fewest people.

He awakened one day, after passing out from hunger and exhaustion, to the sounds of heavy footsteps along the rocky ground. His panicked flight had taken him to the foothills of a series of low mountains. In his daze the night before, he'd managed to find himself a jagged cluster of boulders to sleep behind. The steps that he heard came to a stop on the other side of the stones. There, the men responsible settled down and began digging through their packs. As they did, they spoke.

"You sure they came this way?" asked the first voice, a man with the slow irritation of one who had followed another for a few miles longer than he'd wanted.

"Yes, Latak. I am sure *it* came this way," said the other voice. "How many times do I have to tell you that we're only after one of the things."

"But that whole plantation got wiped out. You telling me that *one* mally could do that, Dihsaad?"

"I'm telling you that I took the job to hunt down one escaped slave, in this case a mally. I don't care how big the bounty is and how many of the things I find, I'm only bringing back one. Besides, you saw the prints. There was only one of them."

"They could have been traveling one after the other."

"In perfect lockstep? Latak, how could you be at this game for nearly twenty years and learn *nothing?* And here I thought the worst part about having you as a partner was how much you slow me down . . ."

The two continued to bicker. From his hiding spot, the malthrope tried to keep silent as he looked over the landscape, hoping to find a path that could take him safely away from the trackers. All around was little more than rolling hills and stubby grass. He was resigned to the prospect of having to outrun the hunters when his empty stomach and sensitive nose joined forces to remind him that if he didn't find something to eat soon, he wouldn't be running for much longer. Sniffing the air, he detected the tantalizing smell of smoked and salted meats. The men were well supplied, a veritable banquet waiting in their packs. There was something about the men themselves, too. Something that stirred an old fear. Despite this, hunger began to outweigh logic, and before he knew it, he was slinking closer to the edge of the boulders to see where the bag was and whether or not he might be able to grab it. Aside from a few tantalizing moments when they were both looking away from their supplies, there seemed to be little chance of him liberating so much as a mouthful from them.

To his great surprise, his trackers managed to get through a heavy meal without noticing him, and were now discussing bedding down for the night.

"I don't think we'll make much more progress tonight," Dihsaad said. "We'll start fresh tomorrow."

"If we're sleeping here, I have something I need to take care of," Latak announced.

"Fine, but do it on the other side of those rocks there. It is bad enough I'm going to have to smell it all night, I don't want to have to see it."

Latak stood and began to pace toward the malthrope's hiding place. The smart thing to do would be to run now, hard and fast. With a meal in their stomachs and sleep on their minds, they wouldn't follow him for very long. But hungry as he was, he wouldn't be running very long either. Finally he made his decision. He burst from his hiding place and grasped the larger of the two packs. Dihsaad was startled, but only for an instant, managing to grasp the creature's wrist.

"Latak! Latak, you idiot, get over here!" Dihsaad cried, scrambling for his blade with his free hand. "It is here! We've got it! We've got—"

In his desperation, the malthrope acted swiftly, swiping his own free hand through the air and raking his claws viciously across the man's face. The tracker cried out, releasing the beast and clutching his bloody injury. It was a cry of savage agony, the scream of a man fearful that the wound might be his last. The beast seized the pack and sprinted for freedom, leaving the pair to deal with the aftermath of his attack. It wasn't until he reached a stream, much higher in the mountains, that the malthrope finally stopped. There he caught his breath and strained his eyes and ears, but there was no sign that the pair had followed. He tried not to think about *why* they might not have followed, and engaged in the increasingly familiar act of washing blood from his hands.

The provisions were enough to keep his body, trained by years of starvation rations, functional long enough to reach one of the inevitable results of choosing the path of least population. Had he continued south, he would have found himself in one of Tressor's massive deserts. As it was, his jinks and dodges had taken him far enough west to reach the heart of the mountains, where the cold wind and rocky soil made things too inhospitable for any towns to take root.

One morning, after a long night of being scoured by flakes of ice too sparse and cruel to be called snow, he awoke to find he was finally free of pursuit. Even after staying still for the whole night, there was no one to be seen, heard, or smelled. For the first time in more than a decade, he was beyond the reach of both masters and hunters. He was free.

#

Earning his freedom, it turned out, was only the first challenge. The next step was surviving it, and that was proving just as difficult. The mountains were deserted for a reason. Stubborn weeds, frozen lichen, and the odd hardy tree were the only things that grew at all. Aside from birds, which were far too wary to let him near and little more than a mouthful even if caught, the only creatures seemed to be skittish little rodents. Unlike their cousins in the plains, these seemed to know that the malthrope was after them even before he did, disappearing down holes in soil too frozen to dig out if he so much as glanced in their direction. On rare occasion he would see, far in the distance, a mountain goat or other such bit of prey, but they were even wilier. Cornering rats in a grain shed had been poor training for hunting for his dinner in the real world, it seemed. Even so, he chose to move farther and farther into the mountains in search of food, rather than risk heading back toward the plains and encountering a hunting party in his weakened state. If he was going to risk encountering humans again, it would be only after he'd had time to recover, or until he'd found a place with ample cover for him to hide in.

The occasional berry bush or fleshy tuft of leaves was sampled out of desperation, though as often as not he learned the hard way not to eat from such a plant a second time. The only thing in ready supply was water, coming from crisp and clear springs and streams that were frustratingly free of fish.

Weeks of scrounging for food eventually took him through a low valley to the other side of the mountains. Some distance down the slope, he could see the tops of frost-covered trees. He rushed as quickly as his failing limbs could carry him toward the forest. One of the only things he could remember clearly from his youngest days was that where there had been trees there had been food. Therefore there *must* be something to eat there, and there would be shelter from both the elements and prying eyes.

He wasn't a dozen paces past the outskirts of the forest when his nose triumphantly assured him that there was indeed game to be found. Unfortunately, there still remained the challenge of actually finding it. In the mountains, the problem had been that food was so rare, he never seemed to catch a scent. In the woods, there was the opposite problem. Every scrap of forest floor was crisscrossed with the scents left by creatures he'd never smelled before. Tantalizing aromas were all around him again, but following the trail to something to eat seemed impossible. Two days in the forest had provided him with a squirrel, some manner of plump little bird that hadn't been swift enough to escape him, and a few handfuls of berries that he'd found to be not too dangerous to eat. If he didn't get any real food in his stomach soon, it wouldn't matter that he'd escaped the hunting parties.

As night fell on that second day, a bit of tracking and a lot of luck led him to a hole in the ground that could only be a rabbit's warren. He'd had to deal with a few of them when clearing new fields on the plantation, and from the smell of this one, it was home to at least a few of the delicious little morsels. Sniffing about, he found each entrance to the burrow and blocked them one by one with stones. When only one remained, he crouched low, locked his eyes on it, and waited.

Hours passed, the malthrope doing his best to keep still, never allowing his eyes to leave the burrow. The wind off of the mountain was constant, whipping at him and droning in his ears with a low wail. His throat grew dry, his eyes reddened, and his eyelids drooped, but he refused to let his attention waver. Now and then, the rustle of stones near one of the other exits could be heard as the rabbits tried and failed to escape. Soon, surely, they would need to leave. When they did, he would be ready. And so time rolled on until no light remained but the faint glow of starlight. Still there was nothing . . . nothing but a strange scraping sound, then the near-silent rustle of fur and patter of feet.

In desperation, he sprang toward the sound just in time to see half a dozen balls of tawny fur erupt from a freshly dug exit, scattering in all directions. A mad swipe of his clawed fingers managed to snatch the two slowest creatures, leaving the rest to bound away into the night. After another quick slash to each made certain they would not be getting away, he held up his prize. It was not going to be the feast he'd been hoping for, but the two rabbits would make a fine meal just as soon as he could find a bit of water. The long wait and constant wind had left him horribly parched, and a mouthful of rabbit wouldn't do him much good if his throat was too dry to swallow it. He trudged westward until he reached a small spring he'd spotted earlier. Lowering his catch to the ground, he knelt and gratefully cupped water into his hands, lapping it up until the worst of the thirst was gone. Then, with a sigh of relief and a hungry rumble of his stomach, he turned to where he'd left his dinner.

It was not there.

Eyes wide, ears alert, and teeth bared, he scrambled to his feet and scanned his surroundings. The rustling of the trees in the wind made it difficult to single out any sounds that were out of the ordinary, and the weak light of the moonless sky did little good, even for his sharp vision. It didn't matter. He'd only taken his eyes off of his catch for a moment. They had been quite dead, so they could not have run. That meant that they had been taken, and whatever had taken them couldn't be far.

Suddenly, farther down the sloping forest floor, there was a pained breath and the crunch of a careless step. He had found his culprit. With the sort of speed only ravenous hunger and vicious anger could foster, he dove toward the noise. Whatever it was, it must have known it had been heard, because it bolted, abandoning stealth for speed and retreating amid heavy, thumping steps.

Frost-nipped trees whistled by him, icy ground crunching beneath his feet. The head start the thief had managed to earn quickly vanished, and as it drew nearer he could just make out a vague form in the darkness. It was running on two legs. A human? No. It didn't move like a human. The strides were longer and faster, the movements more sure, even on ground unsteady enough to make his own feet slip and skid. There was a peculiarity to its run, too. A limp or lameness seemed to rob just a touch of speed each time the left leg came down. Whatever it was, it was heaped with layers of ratty cloth, such that it was a wonder it didn't tangle its own feet in the hem of the billowing hooded robe that served as the outermost layer.

He was closer now, close enough to hear the terrified breaths even over his own. Now was the time. He took one final stride and leaped at the thief, but the scoundrel chose that moment to step hard on its right foot and dart aside. The pounce missed, but just barely, and the thief gained ground. The pursuit continued until his breath burned in his chest and his much-abused legs cried for relief, but there had been too many hungry nights for him let a meal like that get away from him.

His target began to slow, each faltering step on a now clearly ailing leg prompting the tiniest hint of a voice, a barely suppressed cry of pain. Heartened, he redoubled his efforts. Ahead of him, the thief leaped, pivoting in air to come down hard on the good leg and dart aside again, but this time the malthrope was ready, heaving himself in the same direction and wrapping his arms around the legs.

The pair tumbled to the ground, rolling and scrabbling at one another. The former slave was unlucky enough to strike a tree, the wind rushing from his lungs and his prey slipping from his grip. Clenching his teeth, he rolled forward and fought a breath into his lungs, crawling on all fours toward the still recovering robber. He reached out and grabbed the favored leg.

Instantly, the air was split by a cry. It was an agonized, enraged, *female* voice. He caught the edge of the robe and hauled himself on top of the thief, struggling to wrestle it flat as the voice spouted a torrent of vicious-sounding words in a language he'd never heard. With great effort he managed to put a knee on the small of his foe's back, catching an arm and wrenching it up behind its back nearly to its shoulder blades.

"Give them back!" he barked, reaching for the thief's other hand, which still clutched the purloined meal.

"Let me go!" came the angry reply, the first words he'd understood.

"I *said*," he growled, using his free hand to grab the hood and pull it back, intent on looking his enemy in the eye, "give them . . ."

His words dropped away, and for a moment there was nothing but stunned silence. The hood pulled back to reveal a tangle of dark red hair and pointed, black-tipped ears. The head whipped aside to reveal a foxy face, a sandy gray eye wild with anger and fear straining to match his gaze. For the first time since he'd lost his mother, he was staring at another malthrope. His breath caught in his throat and he froze, his mind utterly seized by the shock and confusion. For a handful of seconds, each did nothing but stare at the other, quietly waiting to see what the other would do next. It was the creature beneath him who broke the silence first.

"Whatever it is that you want to do," she hissed, "I promise you I will give you scars to remember it."

The words shook a bit of sense into his head. He eased the pressure on her arm. "You . . . you're a malthrope . . ."

"Of course I am a malthrope, idiot. So are you! Get off me!"

His mind crept forward a few more steps, eyes darting to the purloined prey still locked in her grip. "You stole my rabbits."

"They were not your rabbits. An idiot who puts his rabbits on the ground and turns his head loses his rabbits. *Get off me!*"

"Give them back!"

"Fine," she spat. With what little motion she could manage she heaved the two morsels aside. "You have them back, now get *off.*"

He loosened his grip a bit more, but his eyes shifted to the hand that had released the meal. Tossing them aside had revealed a few more inches of her arm. Her wrist was thin and frail, and even through the layers of fabric he could feel that the one he held was the same. He looked to her head, noticing for the first time that her face, a veneer of indignant pride layered over fear and desperation, was gaunt.

"You're starving . . ."

"And you are crushing me!"

He shifted his weight, intending only to take his knee from her back, but she seized the opportunity to get her good leg beneath her and throw him from her back. She tried to scramble to her feet, but the instant she put any weight on the injured leg she shook with pain and stumbled. By the time she was on her feet, so was he. She dove for the rabbits, but he managed to get in front of her. Shrieking in frustration and pain, she sprang backward, pivoting in air to land with her back to him. After three strides, the shadows swallowed her and she was gone.

"Wait!" he cried. "Come back! I need to talk to you!" There was no reply. He snatched the rabbits and held them up. "Listen to what I have to say and I'll share the food!"

The wail of the wind was the only sound for a time. Then came the irregular crunch of steps, the female approaching. She stopped just near enough for the gleam of her eyes to be seen.

"Say what you want to say."

#

"You did not say you would be starting a fire. You should not start fires," said the female from just beyond the edge of a circle of light cast by a meager campfire.

"It is freezing, and this is the first time in days I've found enough wood to have a decent fire."

"Then talk fast. I do not want to be here when men see the fire and come looking for who it was that lit the fire."

There was a peculiarity to the way she spoke. She never seemed to open her mouth fully, and each word would cling to the next. The vowel sounds were long and muddy, and the consonants were sharp, shifting from one to the other with an audible flip of her tongue. It was as though each sentence had been drizzled in molasses, the words escaping her lips as a rich, dense flow with barely a gap between them. She also seldom looked him in the eye, instead nervously glancing out into the darkness whenever the wind twitched a branch or tuft of shrubbery a bit too noisily for her taste.

"What are you doing here in the forest?" he asked.

"I am living in the forest," she said with a sneer, adding a handful of muttered words in what must have been her native language. The comments were like all of the quirks in her speech combined, each sentence a cluster of harsh, jagged words that fit together into an oddly beautiful mosaic of sound.

"Are there many other malthropes here?"

"There are not many other malthropes anyplace. Certainly there are not any more here."

"What happened to your leg?"

"I hurt it. How many questions before you give to me the food?"

141

"We'll see. How did you hurt it?"

"Why does it matter to you?" she said, her patience already thin.

"Because I don't know much about this place and I don't want what happened to you to happen to me."

She huffed a breath and rolled her eyes. "It did not happen here. I was in the Great Forest. I was chasing a deer and I stepped into one of the . . . what is it? The snapping traps, for the large hungry things that eat the fish? The traps that go like this."

She spread her fingers and moved her hands sharply apart and together, her fingers interlocking like a creature's teeth.

"I don't know, I've never been to the Great Forest."

"They have them in places that are not the Great Forest. Men put them all places when they want to catch the . . . fish-eaters. It does not matter. I stepped in a snapping trap, with the dull bars, not the sharp teeth, and—" She clapped her hands together. "Like that. I got it open, but my leg, it is not right now. It has hurt since then."

"Is that why you are so hungry and thin?"

"I am so hungry because you took back from me the rabbits. But, yes. I have not been able to hunt very well. And it is worse since I came to this place. Not very much good to eat here."

"Then why did you come here?"

"Because there is not very much good to eat here. Nothing much to grow, nothing much to hunt. That means that men do not come here. With my leg like this, I cannot run from men when they come, so I must go to a place where they do not come. Are these enough questions?"

"Were you a good hunter before you hurt your leg?"

She looked at him flatly. "I am a malthrope." The sentence was delivered as though it was all the answer he should need.

He took a deep breath and thought for a moment. "I have an offer. A trade."

She narrowed her eyes. "What sort of trade?"

"If you help me learn to hunt, I will share my food with you and help you recover."

"You are a malthrope. You know how to hunt. This is foolish what you say."

"I thought I knew how to hunt, but I've only ever had to do it in open fields or in closed buildings. Places where they couldn't hide, or couldn't run. Out here, every creature seems to know I'm coming before I even notice them."

"Hunt inside buildings? No, no. This is not true. This cannot be true."

"You almost outran me with a bad leg. You run through a crowded forest like I would run along a path. I need to know how to do these things. I need you to teach me."

"I can do these things because I am a malthrope."

"Then I need you to teach me to be a malthrope."

She huffed again, shaking her head. "That is . . . you need . . . this is not enough. You get everything and I get nothing in this trade. I do not need your help so badly."

"You do need me. More than you realize. That leg has been getting worse, hasn't it?"

"Worse? Of course it is worse! You chased me through the forest. You tugged on my leg and you climbed all over me."

"Before that."

"Some days yes, some days no. How do you know this?"

"I know injuries like that. Your leg isn't broken, not all the way, but it will be soon if you don't dress it properly and give it some rest."

"Rest my leg. I cannot do this, I need to eat."

"I can feed you, if you teach me how to get the food."

"You *mean* this? You mean these foolish things that you say?"

"I do."

"And what if I say no?"

"Then I take my rabbits, you take your bad leg, and we both take our chances."

In the darkness at the edge of the firelight, he could just make out the gleam of her teeth as her lips peeled back in a frustrated sneer. She murmured for a bit in her native language, pronouncing certain words more vigorously than others.

"You say that you can help to heal my leg?"

"I've watched it done a few times."

"How long will it be taking?"

"If you heal quickly, and you stay off of it, perhaps a month."

She muttered more sharply, her emphasis on certain words making it clear without translation what role they played in voicing her anger. "And you need me to teach you to be what you *are?*"

"I need you to teach me whatever I need to know to survive."

She shook her head and tried to stand, but the instant she put

143

weight on the injured leg, she winced and eased back down. With a sigh of defeat, she put her hand to her head. "I will do this."

"Thank you," he said, tossing the larger of the two rabbits to her. "You will not regret this. Eat first, and then I'll look at your leg."

She was already loudly working her way through the meal as though it was her first in days. He wasted no time in digging into his own as well, delighting in the all-too-rare luxury of a meal that would last for more than two bites.

#

Not a word was exchanged between them until the last speck of meat was consumed. With hunger as ravenous as theirs, it did not take the two malthropes long to extract every morsel, down to the marrow in the bones. The female finished first, licking her chops as she tossed the last bone aside after she was certain it was stripped bare. Satisfied, she casually clawed at the icy earth until she'd dug a shallow hole, then gathered the bones and dropped them inside. He watched as she did so, imitating her behavior until his own bones had been buried, the earth brushed smooth over them.

Having a meal in one's stomach, even a meager one, has a way of pacifying one's temper and easing tension. The raw hostility wasn't entirely gone from the female's body language, but it was softened considerably. She edged a bit closer to the fire, stretching her favored leg out with a few hisses of pain.

"You say you can help me with my leg. What is it you can do?" she asked.

"Let me look at it," he said, standing and pacing around the fire.

She eyed him with suspicion, tensing her muscles as he approached in case she had to flee suddenly. He knelt beside the limb and tugged at the multiple layers of leggings.

"Eh!" she interjected, slapping his hands away. "Do not touch my clothes. If you need to see something you cannot, you will ask *me,* and I will decide if you see it."

She eased the hem of the layers of robes and trousers up a calculated amount, revealing terrible swelling beginning just above her ankle. He reached for it, but again she slapped his hand away.

"What did I say to you? There is no touching!"

"I need to feel the bone."

"This you will not do. It is hurting bad enough without your touching."

"Fine. But if we don't do something, it is definitely going to break. And soon. Your leg doesn't even look straight."

"And this is what you can do? Tell me it will break? This does not help me!"

"We need to make a splint. I'll find some straight branches. You stay here. Try not to move it."

He moved swiftly into the forest to gather two of the strongest, straightest lengths of wood he could find. It was a good feeling, a familiar feeling, to be doing something for someone else. In the back of his mind, he had been fearing the day he would find food and shelter enough to make life less than a struggle. The endless task of scrounging up enough food to eat, of finding a place away from the wind to sleep, and of keeping a vigilant eye open for bounty hunters had kept his mind from other things. It kept him from thinking about what he had done, and who he had lost. The forest might well have given him food and shelter too quickly to keep the darkness from settling in his thoughts. Now, though, he had a task, and he threw himself into it gratefully. Stout but smooth branches were selected, along with a few oddly-shaped crooks and forks that had useful curves.

When he was satisfied, he returned to find his would-be teacher sitting just beside the pack of supplies he'd stolen. A hasty attempt had been made to hide the fact that she had clearly been rummaging through it.

"What were you doing?" he asked, the gathered wood held awkwardly under his arm.

She opened her mouth, the telltale hesitation of a forthcoming lie dangling in the air for a moment. When no suitable reply formed itself, she instead pointed to the branches. "Why is it that you need bits of wood?"

"I told you, I need to make a splint. Do you know what a splint is?"

"No, I do not know what this is!" she snapped. "Why would I know what this is?"

"Your leg is hurt. It is weak. A splint is a way to keep it straight and strong."

He knelt beside the pack to retrieve his rope. While he was at it, he carefully tallied the other contents. The meager remnants of the supplies he'd stolen were clearly stirred up by a haphazard search, but it would seem that nothing had been taken. Besides the rope, there was an empty leather water flask, a poorly-kept knife that he had been meaning to sharpen, and the remains of a pair of boots that he'd gnawed much of the leather from when food was especially scarce. He looked to the female. She looked back with a subtle look of defiance, as though daring him to accuse her of something.

"Straighten your leg. Hold it like it would be if you were standing," he instructed, measuring two of the longest, flattest pieces branches against the afflicted limb.

"What are you going to do?"

"I am going to tie these pieces of wood tight against your leg, to keep it straight, and—"

"*You will not do this thing!*" she cried, shoving him away. "I am having difficulty to walk on it, and you want to tie wood to it?"

"I need to do it to help you."

"How do I know this? Maybe you do it to hurt me, to keep me slow."

"Trust me, I know how to help your leg."

"Trust you? You do not have a tail. A malthrope with no tail most times is a dead malthrope. It is not a malthrope who makes good choices. You cannot keep your tail, but you want me to trust you with my leg? No. Do something else," she said firmly, arms crossed.

He sighed and furrowed his brow in thought. "I suppose I can make a crutch."

"A crutch . . ." she said vaguely, her eyes dancing slightly in the act of recollection. They brightened when she found the word. "For under my arm, yes? For helping me to walk?"

"Yes."

"Do this instead."

"It won't help very much."

"*Do this instead,*" she repeated with a hard look.

Not in the mood to argue, he selected one of the longer bits of wood and instructed her to lay back, marking where the thin, carefully selected branch reached her underarm. A line scratched with his claw in the appropriate place, he found a rock to prop the branch against.

"I don't understand why you haven't done this for yourself," he said, lining up the mark with the rock. "It is simple to do."

"No. Hunting? Tracking? These things are simple to do."

"Not if you never had a chance to practice them."

"Then this is my answer as well."

The Rise of the Red Shadow

"That is fair, I suppose." He stood and thrust his heel at the raised end of the branch. Two more such blows were enough to roughly break the green wood near the line. He dug out the dull knife and began scratching at the damaged fibers. "You speak very strangely. Do you not speak much?"

"I do not speak *Tressor* language much. Tressor is not my home. Not for long. A year. Two, maybe. I speak Crich."

"I don't know that language. Where did you come from?"

"I come from Vulcrest. No. When I was born it was Vulcrest. It is not Vulcrest now. Now it is part of . . . it is with . . . what is it, the name for when many places become one place? For war?"

"Empire? You come from the Nameless Empire?" he said, stopping in the middle of a complex bit of lashing to stare distrustfully at her.

"Empire? It is not the word I was thinking, but it is close enough. This is a problem?"

"We are at war with the Nameless Empire!"

"*We* are not at war with anyone. The men are at war. Always they make war. It is nothing for a malthrope to worry about."

He stared at her for a bit longer. It had never once occurred to him that something that was a worry for the other slaves might not have been a worry for him.

She continued. "Men draw lines on the ground, kill you for crossing them. Malthropes, we do not do this."

He went back to work. "Why did you come here?"

"The war is why. Part of why. Things are bad for us, for malthropes, in the north places, the Empire. Men hunt us. When there was war, I thought, 'South there are men who are enemies of these men. Maybe they do not hunt the malthropes.' Stupid thoughts. They hunt us here. Everywhere."

"Well, then why did you stay?"

"If it is the same here as there, why go back? Only it is not the same here as there. Here it is warmer. In the Great Forest, there is food, much more food, and much easier to find than in the Empire. So I stay. What about you? Why do you know nothing?"

"I know plenty of things."

"Nothing you *need* to know."

"Where I come from, I needed to know things like this," he said, shaking the now-completed crutch. It was a simple thing, just one of the lighter of the branches he'd retrieved with a curved piece of wood

147

lashed across the top to give the arm a place to rest. He'd done his best to carve away any jagged edges. "And it would seem that *you* need it, too. Here, give me your hand."

She looked distrustfully at the offered hand, but grasped it after a moment and allowed herself to be hauled up, relying entirely on her one healthy leg. He tucked the crutch under her arm. In a series of short, ginger attempts, she put her weight on it. When she released his hand, she eyed her own leg critically, as though consulting it for an opinion.

"It helps. Some," she allowed. She tipped her head to the side, reassessing him. "What is your name?"

The corners of his mouth drooped. He opened his mouth to answer, but hesitated.

"It is not hard," she said with a shake of her head. She placed a hand on her chest. "I am Sorrel. You are . . . ?"

"I . . . I don't think I really have a name."

"Did no one talk to you ever?"

"I've been spoken to."

"Then what is it that they called you?"

"Well . . . some of them called me Mally."

As soon as the word left his mouth, she nearly knocked him to the ground with a slap across the face.

"What was that for!?"

"This is not a name! This is a word you will not say!" she cried.

"Why?"

"It is a word *they* use. It is a word they use for *us.*" Her voice was shaking with emotion. "It is not a good word. It is a word men use when they tell other men about bad things that a malthrope does. It is a *bad* word."

"I'm sorry. I didn't know," he said quietly, his mind turning over all the slaves and handlers who had called him by that name.

"I am only here for two years and I know this. Every malthrope in Tressor knows this. How do you not know this?"

"I've never met another malthrope."

"That is foolish. You have a mother, a father."

"My mother died when I was very young. And I don't remember anything about my father. I was raised by a . . . I was raised by humans."

Sorrel looked at him and for a moment the hardness in her features faltered. There was a flash of pity in her eyes. "This . . . this explains much." She shook herself, willing her protective layer of defiant independence back into place. "It is late. The fire has burned too long. I will go now. Tomorrow, I will find you. We will begin this."

"You have a safe place to sleep?"

"I do. You do not. Do not follow me or the deal is no more. Understand, er . . ." she began, gesturing vaguely for a few moments while she fished for the word. Finally, she abandoned the search. "*Teyn*?"

"What does Teyn mean?"

"It is like . . . a dead thing that does not leave. Or something that is there, but is not."

"A spirit?"

"It is close enough."

"Why would you call me Teyn?"

"I said before. You have no tail. Dead malthropes have no tails. If you walk around without one, you are a teyn. Now go find someplace to sleep, Teyn. Tomorrow I will find you. We will begin."

She took a few unsteady steps with her new crutch, easing into the pain of her leg and the awkwardness of her aid. As she left the fading light of the fire, her steps quickened and she was gone. With little recourse, the creature she'd dubbed Teyn scooped the loose, sandy soil over the flames until they were extinguished and found a dense stand of trees he hoped would take the edge from the wind and keep him from prying eyes.

He huddled against the driving breeze, alone with his thoughts again. It was astounding. He'd only been with Sorrel for an hour or so, but already her absence burned at him. A part of it, a large part, was the simple comfort in not being alone. A few weeks on the run hadn't been enough to wipe away years of never being without the smell and sound of familiar creatures. Even when the other slaves had all hated him, there was something about knowing that they were there, that they were always there, that gave his mind a foundation. And, of course, there had been Ben . . .

No. Not that thought. He sifted his mind for anything else to think of. Sometimes the emptiness of forgetting someone is preferable to the pain of remembering them.

Pushing the old man out of his thoughts before the tears could start flowing again. Pushing harder when the fear and shame of losing control began to rise up, he focused on perhaps the only thing that had a chance of seizing his mind completely. Sorrel was a malthrope. In all of the years on the plantation, in the back of his mind, he had wondered what it would be like to meet one of his own. He had imagined meeting a creature who wouldn't hate him on sight, a creature who didn't need him to prove himself worthy. Perhaps most important of all, a creature who would finally be able to show him what a malthrope really was. All he knew about his own kind was what the others had spoken of in their stories.

Sorrel hadn't lived her life trying to do the job of a human. She was what she was meant to be. She was what he would have been if not for the plantation. She had the answers to a thousand questions he had never been able to ask. He held tight to these thoughts until, finally, sleep took him.

Chapter 14

"Eh. Teyn. Why do you sleep still?" came a hushed voice, accompanied by a rough nudge with a crutch.

He rolled aside, fighting his eyes open. Through the whole night the steady breeze hadn't once relented, and without a fire or proper clothes, sleep had been anything but deep. The sun had yet to rise, the sky a deep violet to the east and a star-speckled black elsewhere. If not for the sharpness of his eyes, there probably wouldn't have been light enough to see his new tutor. As it was, he was treated to a view her standing in the dim light, most of her weight leaning on the crutch and the healthy leg, and her many layers of clothing keeping the cold at bay. She did not appear to be the least bit weary.

"It isn't even dawn," he grumbled muzzily.

"Of course it is not dawn. Dawn is when animals feed. You need to be *ready* by dawn," she stated, her tone indicating it should have been obvious.

He sluggishly climbed to his feet, leaning heavily on the tree to do so.

"You are still tired. You should not sleep on the side of the trees with the mountain," she said.

"Why?"

"On these mountains—on all mountains I have found, the wind comes down from the top. If you can see the mountaintop, you will have bad sleep. You did not know this? You did not *notice* this?"

He shook his head slowly. She tipped hers to the side and sniffed, a slight frown on her face.

"Hungry days ahead," she said. "Fine. We start at the beginning. You have three ways of finding things to eat. You can see, you can smell, you can hear."

"What about taste and touch?"

"You are finding things to eat. If you can taste and touch, finding is over. So you can see, smell, and hear. Which is most important?"

"Sight, vision."

"No!"

"Hearing?"

151

"No! No, no, no . . ." She shook her head and put her hand to her eyes. "Smell! Always smell! See and you know what is in front of you. Hear and you know what is all around you. Smell and you know what is all around you, where it came from, where it went to, how long it was here, if it was afraid, what it was eating, if it was sick, everything you need to know."

"You can tell *all* of that from smell?"

"Yes! Why do you think you have a nose at the *front* of your head," she asked, tapping his nose with her finger. "It is because smell comes before the rest."

"Does that mean sight is the second most important?"

"No, next you hear."

"But your eyes are in front of your ears."

She stared at him flatly for a moment. "Learn first, Teyn, then think. Smell comes before hear, learn comes before think. Now, use your nose. What does it tell you?"

He sniffed the air, but before he could open his mouth to answer, she was reprimanding him.

"No, no, no!" she corrected, taking an unsteady step closer.

"What?"

"Are you a child? You do not smell like that. Like this. Watch," she said. She drew in a long breath, pulling the air in slowly. "Long-slow. This tells you much. All that is around you. All there is to smell. Long-slow first, always. After long-slow, short-fast." She sniffed the air three times. "Short-fast is little pieces. The pieces are different. You move your head, short-fast. You move your head again, short-fast. Maybe this smell is stronger here, maybe it is weaker there. You know that the thing that makes the smell is moving, or maybe not. Maybe the air is moving. You wait, and you test again. Understand? Long-slow to find something to follow. Short-fast to follow it. Now you."

Somewhat doubtful that it was truly possible to *smell* incorrectly, the one she called Teyn nonetheless did as he was instructed. He breathed in long and slow, letting the scents of the thin forest fill his nose. There was the crisp, clean scent of frost, the potent smell of pine needles, the warm scent of Sorrel, and dozens of scents he couldn't identify. One of them, though, stood out above the rest.

"I smell the rabbits from yesterday."

"Of course you do. Now short-fast. Where are they?"

He sampled the air as she had, three quick sniffs with the slightest of an adjustment of his head, then a few more with his head turned aside. The subtle differences from one tiny taste to the next began to form themselves in his mind. There was more to tracking than having a sensitive nose. Simply being able to detect those things that other creatures could not was only a tool, and, like all tools, it was only valuable to those who knew how to use it. Every breath was like listening to a noisy crowd mingling on the floor of a vast meeting hall. Hearing every voice was simple. Tracking was the art of following a single conversation while a thousand others echoed and droned around it. He tried to focus on the tantalizing thread of a scent, twisting his head and testing the air again and again in search of it. There was undeniably a pattern, but it was elusive, suddenly weaker where it should be stronger, or twisting back on itself rather than leading anywhere. He slowly followed it as best he could for a minute or two before Sorrel, awkwardly thumping along behind with her crutch, growled in frustration.

"Enough. Get down," she said, hobbling up to him and bopping the top of his head.

"What?"

"Down. Nose on the ground. You should have found the trail by now, but you have not. This you should have learned as a child, so get down where your nose would be as a child." She slapped the top of his head again. "Down."

"You don't need to do that," he growled.

"I am hungry, and soon the sun will rise and the food will be ready for us. So you need to be a better hunter very fast. Now get down, Teyn."

He ducked out of the way of a final slap to the head and crouched low, putting his hands to the icy earth and lowering his head. Eyes shut, he sampled the air again. The scent of the rabbits was stronger, easier to follow. Keeping his nose close to the soil, he crept forward. With each step, the trail grew stronger. The crawl turned to a crouching walk. A life of slinking through the shadows, fearful of being heard, had taught him to keep his steps silent without sacrificing speed.

After five minutes of weaving through trees and following the scent, he approached a clearing with a low, dense cluster of thorn bushes. The sun was a bit higher in the sky now, casting enough rosy glow for his keen eyes to pick out the dimples of footprints leading to and from the bushes. Evidently the rabbits he'd chased from the warren had made this their new home. He turned back to see if Sorrel had been able to keep up with him, but if she was behind him, she was far behind, nowhere in sight. Looking back to the bushes, though, earned him a glimpse of a tattered heap of layered cloth, crutch sticking awkwardly to the side and a red-furred muzzle grinning from underneath a hood.

His mind not quite willing to allow the possibility that Sorrel could have beaten him to the prize despite being nearly crippled, he glanced behind him once more. When he turned to her again, she pulled back the hood enough for him to see her eyes. She pointed to them, then to the bushes, and finally raised her crutch like a club. He nodded once and tensed his legs. She nodded again, then swiped the crutch at the bushes, rattling free a crust of ice and causing and explosion of startled rabbits to burst from the other side.

There were five of them, and having the benefit of preparation hadn't done much to tip the odds in his favor beyond the first pounce. The leap had netted him the unlucky creature first to leave the cover. The others scattered. He scrambled back to his feet, locked his eyes on one of them, and rushed after it. Chasing a rabbit turned out to be nearly as difficult as chasing Sorrel had been. The little thing moved in leaps that never seemed to head quite in the direction he was expecting. Nonetheless, he kept after it, digging his feet into the earth and cutting aside to stay on its trail whenever it changed direction. Eventually, his breath heaving and his chest burning from the cold air once again, he managed to dive upon it. For the second day in a row, there would be a meal for himself and his tutor.

He was just catching his breath when Sorrel caught up with him.

"How many?" She asked.

He held up his hard-earned catch.

"Two? Bah!" she grumbled, coming closer and snatching the larger of them to inspect. "This is why I do not like rabbits. Very much running, not very much eating. But still," she said, slapping him on the back, "one lesson, two rabbits. Maybe not so many hungry days ahead after all. Come, we eat now. And you can start one of your fires if you want. I know a good place."

#

The place Sorrel spoke of turned out to be a narrow notch cut out of the mountainside. What had likely once been a much larger stream was now a trickle of icy water tracing a crooked path along a hollowed out alley of smooth stone. A large alcove in the stone wall was wide enough to comfortably fit the two malthropes, with room enough for a fire between them. Best of all, for the first time since he'd entered the mountains, he wasn't being blasted by the merciless wind.

As they had the night before, each ate eagerly and quietly, but for once the hunger was not desperate, and thus the food could be savored a bit more. As "Teyn" chewed at his meal, he looked over his new teacher. A malthrope's eyes were sharp day or night, but in darkness they told little of subtle things like color. Now that the sun had truly risen, the light was enough for him to take in the sight in full. She looked to be older than him, but still young, perhaps a handful of years further into her adulthood than he. He was a bit taller, the tips of her pointed ears coming to eye-level for him. Her clothes were at least four layers of the billowy robes and trousers that the farmers wore, supplemented by a collection of scarfs and shawls, and topped with a thick, gray, hooded cloak which had not been present the day before. Her fur was different from his, a dark mahogany instead of his own fiery orange, but the same cream at her throat and black at the tips of her ears. Her eyes were gray with hints of yellow and amber, and her hair was a long and tangled mass that gathered into a pool in her hood. Three small gold hoop earrings adorned one ear, and a pair of mismatched rings were on her right hand. Her eyes flicked in his direction a few times as he studied her.

"Why do you look at me so much, Teyn?" she asked.

"I've never seen another malthrope before."

"Well, do not look so much."

"I apologize. Tell me, how did you end up ahead of me when I was tracking down the rabbits?"

She smirked. "In the beginning, you figure out how to follow the trail. Later, you figure out where it *leads*. It is faster."   ·

"When will you teach me that?"

"I will not. It is not something someone teaches. It is something you learn by doing."

"I see." He ate a bit more and looked around at the simple but effective shelter. "Is this where you went yesterday? Is this your home?"

She scoffed. "No, Teyn. I did not take you to the place where I sleep. My home is a nicer place than this, but for you, this place is good. Better than sleeping in the windy trees."

"Yes. Thank you for finding it."

He looked thoughtfully in her direction. She weathered his gaze for a few moments before setting her food aside and glaring at him. "You are looking at me too much again, Teyn."

"I'm sorry, but I have so many questions."

"If they are about the hunting, we will talk later, before dusk."

"No, they are about us. Malthropes."

She sighed. "Well, ask, if it will stop your staring."

"Well . . . what *are* we?"

"We are *malthropes*."

"Yes, but what is a malthrope? Humans say we are half fox, half man."

"*Men.* Men know nothing about such things. We are not half man. We are not half fox. We are malthropes. Look . . . here." She plucked a water-smoothed stone from beside the stream. "This rock, it is round, yes? And it is more yellow than the other stones, yes? A lemon is round, and it is yellow. Is this stone half lemon because of that? No. And we are not half man either. A yellow stone is a yellow stone. A malthrope is a malthrope. Men say these things so that he can say that anything good in us comes from men. 'It walks like a man. It thinks like a man.' As if it is only men who can do these things. There are parts of us that are like men, and there are parts that are like an animal, but we are what we are, not half of anything."

"Where do we come from?"

"I come from Vulcrest. I have said this."

"No, our race. What is our history?"

"Where do men come from? Where do elves come from? Dwarves? Dragons? Fairies? Where do these things come from? I do not know. But probably the answer is the same for them as it is for us."

"You speak Crich, I speak Tresson, but these are the same languages that the humans speak. Is there a malthrope language?"

"If there is, I do not know it. I do not think so. I think languages are things for places, not for types of creatures."

"Why did we—"

"This was not the deal," she interrupted. "The deal was for me to teach you to survive, not to teach you these other things. Eat your food and stay quiet. Save strength, yes?"

He nodded slowly and returned to his meal, eating it in nibbles in an attempt to make a somewhat inadequate meal last a bit longer. As he did, he noticed that Sorrel was now staring at him, though not as overtly as he'd been staring at her. Her head was pointed vaguely at the fire just as his was, but in his peripheral vision he could see her eyes dart in his direction every few moments, lingering a bit longer each time. He drew in a breath to ask why she was looking at him, but he decided to keep his silence. It may only have been a short time that he'd known her, but he'd already learned that she had no interest in idle conversation. Instead, he let his thoughts churn in his head.

It was strange. There was no question why Sorrel didn't like him to stare. All of his life he'd felt uncomfortable when others looked his way. It must have been something all malthropes shared . . . except she was certainly staring at him now, whether she knew that he'd noticed or not, and he didn't mind. It didn't stir the same anxiety. He didn't feel the urge to slink into the nearest shadow or tuck himself into a forgotten corner until they left him be. But why? Perhaps it was because she was a malthrope? Perhaps malthropes didn't have the same effect on each other? But then why *did* she tell him not to stare?

As his mind wandered in tight little circles, he failed to notice his eyes were betraying him, drifting toward her until they each were sharing the same askance view of one another. They remained that way for a time, each lost in thought, each observing the other, until their wandering eyes met. The burning flutter of an entirely new sort of anxiety shot through him and he hastily turned his gaze back to the shifting flames. Rather than doing the same, Sorrel shook her head. Though out of the corner of his eye he couldn't be sure, he thought he saw a grin briefly curl her lips.

Chapter 15

In the days that followed, the lessons flowed. Teyn was no stranger to following directions and learning new skills, but this time it was different. When he had been learning to work the land, treat injuries, and repair equipment, he'd been slow to learn. Each new task had been a challenge, a struggle.

Not so now. Hunting, tracking—all of the skills of the forest felt natural, familiar. It wasn't as though Sorrel was teaching him, it was as though she was helping him to remember something that he'd known all along. Even more importantly, this time he was not working to please someone, though every hard-earned word of praise from Sorrel was savored. This time he was reaping his own rewards. A good day's hunt meant a full stomach for both himself and his teacher, and a poor day's hunt meant a hungry night for each of them. One would be hard-pressed to find a more effective motivation.

Regardless of how quickly he learned, or how driven he was to succeed, there was a reason the mountainside had been abandoned by human hunters. The sparse trees and rocky soil were a terrible hunting ground. In his first two weeks under her tutelage, he seldom caught anything larger or more nourishing than the rabbits of the first few days, but even when there was no meat to be found, there were important lessons to learn. A nose trained to follow the trail of a frightened bit of prey was equally useful in sniffing out mushrooms, berries, nuts, and seeds. Finding them was only part of the challenge. The more important lesson was knowing which to eat and which to avoid.

"What about this one?" Teyn asked, crouching down beside a cluster of speckled mushrooms at the base of a pine.

"Ah, no. No, no! Do not touch. Those are bad. They will make you very sick," she said, touching his shoulder to back him away.

"How do you know?"

"Different ways. Look. You see here? There are ants all around. On the tree, on the rocks. Everywhere. But not on the mushroom. If they do not want it, you do not want it. Also, something is probably good to eat of you find bits of it in . . . what is the word? In Crich we say *gohveen.* What animals leave behind."

"Droppings?"

She smirked. "Yes, like that, but my word is stronger, and more fun to use. It is—oh!" Her ears perked up. She began making wafting motions with her hands, waving air toward her nose. "Do you smell that? Smell, smell!"

He drew in a breath, sifting through the tapestry of scents for the thread that she might be indicating. "Is it . . . a sort of sharp smell? And sweet?"

"Yes. Now show me where," she said, ushering him with a tap on the back.

In the days since reluctantly accepting the task of teaching Teyn, Sorrel had warmed to the role. Perhaps it was his eagerness to be taught, or perhaps it was the inherent satisfaction in seeing lessons bear fruit, but her initial almost resentful attitude toward instruction was now practically enthusiasm. She seldom missed an opportunity to turn an errant breeze or a distant rustle into a test of what he'd learned thus far.

After a few floundering moments of trying to follow the faint scent, Teyn picked a direction. Though he'd not yet mastered such nuances, it was clear that the source of the aroma was a fair distance away. As he walked, sniffing periodically, he looked to his tutor. She was limping along, her crutch touching down only every second or third step.

"You really ought to avoid putting so much weight on your leg," he said.

"My leg is feeling better than it was. I do not need the crutch so much."

"It is feeling better because you've been keeping your weight off of it. If you—"

"Ah-ah-ah!" she shushed. "I am teaching, you are learning. Remember this."

"The deal was for me to help you with your leg. If you don't let me do it—"

"Fine, fine," she grumbled, making a show of pounding the crutch to the earth for a few steps.

He nodded and put his nose to the wind once more. They marched up the slope of the mountain, past some thinning trees, and then down again across a rocky stretch before reaching a thicket of thorn bushes.

"There, yes. You see? You see where your nose leads you?" Sorrel said. "Even when you cannot catch food, it leads you to things that you can eat." She thumped up to the bushes. "These berries are good to eat. I would not like to eat them always, but while my leg is hurting, they have kept me from starving. Crouch down. I will show you how you should pick them."

Teyn did as he was told, but before she could give any instruction, he was already hard at work, his hand darting among the thorny branches and gathering berries with practiced ease. The plant wasn't rakka, but the berries grew in much the same way. It made the task a familiar one, so much so that going through the motions that had filled so many hours of his youth began to bring back unwanted memories, which he paused to shake away. Even so, within moments he had filled his palm with perfectly ripe berries. He stood and held them out to her. She eyed the mound of fruit, the corner of her mouth turned up in a smirk, then raised an eyebrow.

"*This* you can do?" she said doubtfully. "You cannot hunt, or track, or do any of the things that you need to be doing, but *this* you can do?"

"It was one of the things they taught me."

She huffed. "Leave it to men to teach all of the wrong things. Bah! No matter. When you eat these, you eat slow. One at a time. You will be sad if you do not," she said, taking a berry from his hand and popping it in her mouth.

He sampled one. It was powerfully tart, almost painfully so, with the slightest hint of sweetness behind it. The flavor filled his mouth, bringing a tear to his eye and twisting his face with the intensity. The sight of his reaction prompted a boisterous laugh from Sorrel.

"You see? Imagine if you eat two. Now, berries, roots, nuts, things like these? You eat them one day. Maybe two. More than that without some meat and you will be feeling not well."

"Why?"

Sorrel glared at him. "Why always are you asking *why?* I am not teaching you *why.* I am teaching you *what,* and also *how. Why* does not keep your belly full. Now, give me these," she said, steadying his hand with hers and brushing the berries into one of her many pockets. "Fetch some more for yourself, and we eat."

He did as requested, stripping another bush of what he supposed were its ripe berries and returning to find her sitting in the awkward position her bad leg required of her. Her back was against a tree, a mossy rock beneath her knee to prop up the ailing limb. She was enduring the punishing intensity of the berries, eyes squinted and head tilted.

"The berries," she said with a shudder, "are a punishment for not hunting better, I think."

"I'll have to do better tomorrow, then."

"Yes, you will."

He took a seat beside her and reluctantly subjected himself to the same trial-by-dinner. After three or four of the fruits, his tongue finally surrendered, refusing to report any more of the sour assault and making the rest of the meal a good deal more tolerable as a result. The days with Sorrel had managed to hammer her dislike of being watched while she ate firmly into his head, and thus he kept his eyes on his meal. Lately, though, she'd been flagrantly defying her own rule, staring directly at Teyn during meals. Her constant gaze prompted the same vague, tingling heat he always seemed to feel when he was seen, but from her it was different somehow. He'd come to expect it at times like these. It was almost comforting to know that there was finally someone from whom he didn't have to hide.

"What are the names of these fruits?" he asked.

"I do not know what is the name for them in Tressor language. In Crich they are called *jhevik*."

A gust of wind chose that moment to scour the thicket, rustling Teyn's fur and cutting through the thin, torn fabric of the tunic he still wore from his time in the fields. While he was moving, either walking along or digging through the rocky soil, the bite of the cold didn't sink so deep. Once he was still, even for a few moments, it seemed to settle in quickly. It wasn't a dangerous cold, but it was constant, driving down on him and wearing at him. If not for his years working in the sweltering heat of the fields, he likely wouldn't have minded the cold at all, but a lifetime adjusting to the heat made adjusting to the cold a slow and uncomfortable process. He shivered lightly at another breeze. It was a motion that did not go unnoticed by his mentor.

"You are cold," she stated, popping one of the last berries from her hand into her mouth.

"I'm getting used to it."

"Mmm. You do not *look* like you are getting used to it. You rely too much on those fires of yours. You are spoiled by the fires. Fur should be enough for you."

"What about you? How many layers are *you* wearing?"

161

"It does not matter. I do not wear the layers for the warm. I wear them because it is easier to carry them that way. And because I am not so foolish as to leave them where someone can take them. You should find yourself some layers, if you cannot stand the cold."

"I'm fine," he said firmly, attempting to will the trembling from his fingers. Another burst of wind sent a visible chill through him.

She huffed a breath, tossed the final berry in her mouth, and began to work at the tie of the thick cloak she wore atop her countless layers. "Here. Come here."

"I don't want your cloak."

"That is good, because I am not giving to you my cloak," she said as a few final tugs released the stubborn knot. A shrug sent the weathered old cloak to the ground behind her. One by one, she tugged and inspected the heap of layers about her shoulders until she found what she'd been looking for. Teyn had assumed it was a scarf, but as she untied the knot and unraveled the tan strips of fabric from around her neck, it was revealed to be an ancient jacket.

"Here," Sorrel said, pulling the garment from her back and tossing it to him. "The arms are too long, and as a scarf it is too heavy. Maybe it is better for you until you can find proper clothing for yourself."

Teyn caught the bundle of fabric and held it out. It was a sturdy garment, nearly as thick as her cloak and very solidly made. The fabric was coarse and woven tightly. At the very least, it should keep the wind out, and his own fur should do the rest. Like the cloak, he'd never seen its like along the fields of the plantation, even in the cooler months. It must have come from her home, from the north.

"Where did you get all of these clothes?" he asked.

"I find them," Sorrel replied. "Sometimes in markets. Sometimes hanging in the wind. Sometimes on the ground beside a man who is sleeping."

"So you steal them."

"No, no." She pulled the cloak up and worked at tying it again. "It is like the rabbits. You put it down, you look away, it is not yours anymore. You deserve to lose it." A third attempt at securing the cloak failed. Glancing up in frustration, she gathered together the ends of the cloak's ties and gestured toward him. "You know how to do things like this."

"That is stealing. You are a thief," he said sternly. He tucked the garment under one arm, knelt beside her, and took the ties, deftly tying a slip knot.

"No, not a thief. A thief steals things for money. Men can be thieves. A malthrope cannot. A malthrope cannot sell things to men, and men will not sell things to a malthrope. So if a malthrope takes from men, it is not stealing—it is getting things in the only way that a malthrope can get things." Not once did she sound ashamed, or even defensive. She explained it simply, as though it was just another lesson. "And a malthrope is not foolish enough to leave things where they can be found . . . most of the time. Why is this a problem for you?"

"I have always heard that malthropes were thieves. I had hoped it wasn't true."

"You hear this from men. Men find ways to hate malthropes."

"Elves and dwarves, too."

"Bah." She flourished her hand. "It is the same. Short and hairy, tall and pointed ears, they are all men on the inside. When you put on that jacket, you should put the thin one over it. The thin one is loose, it will fit better over than under."

He nodded and pulled off his slave tunic for the first time in far too long. A searing sting of pain and guilt speared his mind as he saw the dark brown stain left by a splash of blood. It was along the front of the garment, far from the whip-torn holes and the stains of his own blood. This was blood he had spilled with his own claws. The stinging in his mind turned to a blaze of anxiety when Sorrel spoke.

"What is this?"

"I . . . this . . . I . . . ." He stumbled, his eyes locked on the stain.

"Not the blood. What do I care if you are messy when you are eating?" she dismissed, thankfully misinterpreting the origin of the stain. "This, on your chest."

He looked down. She was indicating the mark over his heart, a black patch of fur among the cream that formed curve with a point between its two peaks. He had long ago forgotten it was there.

"Oh. I don't know. It has been there as long as I can remember. I thought maybe all malthropes had it. You don't?"

"If I did, you would not be seeing it, so do not ask," Sorrel said with narrowed eyes. "Come here."

He stepped closer and leaned low, near enough for her fingers to brush the mark.

"I have never seen a thing like this. Very strange." She tipped her head to the side, and slowly her ears sagged. She dragged her fingers

163

lightly across the remnants of scars old and new. They showed has narrow strips of hairless flesh, some pink and fresh, some white and healed. She glanced up. Leaning near enough for her to inspect the mark had brought his face very close to hers, so much so that with her head raised their noses almost touched. Something about the moment made her smirk. Finally, she shrugged, pushing him lightly away. "Bah. You are strange. This is not new, yes? Get dressed. I have had all the berries I care to eat today. We should go back to near to your little nook."

Teyn slipped his arms through the sleeves of the jacket. They were a bit long even for him, but only slightly, and cuffing the ends solved that. Moments after putting it on, he felt warm without a fire for the first time since he'd entered the mountains. The sash and buttons that would have secured it closed were long ago lost, but even so it was a vast improvement. He picked up the tunic from the ground and made ready to pull it on, but he stopped, his attention once again drawn to the stains. Closing his eyes, he dropped his hand and let the unwanted reminder of that terrible day on the plantation fall to the ground.

"You will not wear it?"

"Never again," he said.

"Then I will take it. It will find use somewhere," she decided, leaning aside to snatch it from the ground. Rolled tightly, it disappeared into one of her many pockets.

"Now, we go, I—"

She was interrupted by a gust of wind. Something carried on the breeze was different, a foreign scent that caught even Teyn's attention. He was new to interpreting such things, but it had a musky, pungent smell, something heavily furred and either enormous or numerous. Whatever it was, it was enough to push all else from Sorrel's mind. Her eyes were pressed shut, her nose pointed in the direction of the wind, drawing a long, slow breath. Another gust from the same direction seemed to visibly shake her. When her eyes opened again, they gleamed with hunger and purpose.

"Come! Come, come, come," she urged, her words almost silent.

He leaned low to help her to her feet, but she swatted his hand away rolled to her hands and knees.

"Down, get down now, this way," she whispered intensely, crawling as best she could toward the leeward side of the berry thicket.

He crouched low and followed her. "What is happening?"

164

She reached up and clamped his muzzle shut with her hand, pulling him down lower and whispering in his ear. "You will be quiet. A thing is coming. To catch it, we must hide."

With that, Sorrel released him and continued, ducking lower and moving with greater care with each passing moment. Teyn did likewise. When his teacher seemed happy with their new position, a small patch of ground where the bushes were sparse enough for her to nestle among them, she nearly flattened herself to the ground. Now she was lower even than the knee-high berry bushes, completely hidden from all but her student beside her.

"What is it? What is coming?" Teyn asked, his voice as low as hers had been.

"Never mind. They will be here soon, you need to be ready. When they come, stay low. Head low. Ears flat. Look at them through the leaves of the bushes to see. They are very strong and very fast, but if you can take one, it is food for days. You have to surprise it, get onto its back, and then go for its throat. Pick one small, do not pick one with the . . . eh . . . with the . . ." She pointed frantically at the top of her head. "Head . . . sharp things."

"But what *is* it?" he asked, propping himself on his elbows and craning his head.

In reply, she glanced through the bushes and became suddenly rigid, eyes glassy and intent. She reached up and planted her hand on his head, forcing him to the ground. Without raising his head, he peered through the waxy green leaves of the bushes and was just able to spot motion weaving among the trees in the distance. The minutes crawled by, Sorrel utterly rigid and motionless, Teyn doing his best to imitate. The forms drew nearer. Now he was certain that there were many. The scent was washing over him in waves, sparking ancient instincts. He felt his muscles tensing, ready to spring forward, even though he didn't know why.

Now they were at the fringe of the clearing, cautiously edging toward the berry bushes farthest from the hiding place of the malthropes. Finally, Teyn got his first good look. On the plantation, Jarrad had frequently brought one or two creatures such as these back from his rare hunting trips. He'd called them thorn elk, and a single look at one of the large males made it clear the name was an apt one. Overall, they resembled a larger, shaggier deer. Their pelts were gray, with patches of pure black and pure white near the belly. The females might have been chest high if he was standing beside them, but the one adult male of the herd was noticeably larger.

Projecting back from its broad head were cruel, barbed antlers. Each forked once or twice, spreading out to the side, and each was covered with short, stout spurs. It stood with its head high, eyes wide and watchful. As the others of the herd approached the bushes, nibbling at the berries and leaves, it watched, its breath leaving in billowing clouds in the chill air. There was an alertness to the group, the sense that they knew danger was near.

Teyn was awash with instincts that had never found use before that day. He found himself scrutinizing the way they moved, trying to pick out some sign that one was a better target than another. His limited vision slipped first to the possible prey, then to their defender. His heart was beating faster, his hair standing on end. Deep inside, he knew that this, the hunt, was the reason he was born. For the first time, he felt the beginnings of what it must be like to truly be a malthrope.

One of the young bulls of the herd wandered a bit farther from the group. The beast was a shade smaller than one of the females. Antlers that would one day soon be formidable weapons were for now little more than bristling nubs. And there was something else—a hesitant step here, a stumble there.

Sorrel's eyes darted first to Teyn, then to the creature. Somehow her glimpse alone seemed to radiate the insistent, primal knowledge that this was the creature, this was the moment. There wouldn't be a better chance. Teyn drew his legs silently up beneath him until he was coiled like a spring, one hand planted on the ground to steady himself, and every sense on fire. He bounced his leaf-obscured vision first to the prey, then to the defender. The instant its vigilant gaze swept way from the bushes, Teyn made his move.

His legs and back straightened and he burst from his hiding place. The world around him seemed to slow. His leap took him in an arcing path, higher than the lowest branches of the pines around the bushes. The whole of the clearing was an explosion of motion. Each member of the herd broke into a bounding, fearful run, disappearing into the trees. The young elk panicked and bolted, its eyes wide and sweeping, but Teyn had chosen well. It lacked the steadiness to move quickly and the experience to choose its motions properly. He came down upon it, his clawed fingers raking across its haunches, but desperation and fear gave his prey just enough strength to wrench itself away.

166

The terrified creature bounded toward the trees, Teyn not two steps behind it, when the air rumbled with a vengeful bellow. The male was thundering toward him, trampling a path through the bushes and nearly flattening the still-concealed Sorrel. Teyn's mind pulled itself from its task, switching suddenly from pursuit to escape. The charging bull was faster than him by far, closing the gap between them in mere heartbeats. Thinking back to Sorrel's attempts to evade him when they'd first met, Teyn took one last step and landed hard on his heel, springing to the side just in time to avoid a razor-sharp antler scything through the air behind him. The move only bought him a few steps, the hissing breath of the stampeding elk already hot against his neck.

Ahead were two pine trees growing near enough for their branches to weave together. He shifted his sprint toward them and, pouring all of the strength he could muster into the motion, heaved himself through the gap between. The elk's hooves plowed up a stretch of frosty earth as it skidded to a stop. Teyn did not slow, rolling once and landing on his feet at a full run toward the base of a stout, ancient tree. He reached it and scrambled high among the branches as the monster behind him recovered. Below him, the elk pounded up to the foot of the tree and peered up at him, fury in its eyes. It reared onto its hind legs and came down with all of its strength, butting the trunk the tree, but Teyn held firm. Once, and again, the bull whipped its head, striking the tree hard enough splinter the bark. Finally, it seemed satisfied, plodding back into the woods.

Teyn remained high in the tree until long after his heart had stopped pounding and his breathing had slowed. He was still there, clinging to the branches and trying to calm his nerves when he heard a voice echoing through the woods.

"Teyn!" Sorrel called out, thumping along with her crutch.

There was something unusual in her voice, a tone he hadn't heard before. When she called again, he realized that it was concern.

"Teyn, you are near, I smell it. Answer when I call you!" she called again, this time the more familiar tones of anger tempering her voice.

"Here," he replied, finally digging his claws into the icy bark and climbing from his perch.

"Ah! A tree. Smart. This was a good thing to do. Come here!" she yelled, hurrying as best she could to the source of his voice.

She reached the foot of the tree a few moments after he reached the ground.

"Let me see you. Turn around," she ordered, scanning him up and down.

He did as he was told, and once she was satisfied, she placed her hands on his shoulders and turned him to face her. "Good. It is good, you are not hurt. You thought fast, and you acted fast, and you ran fast, and you were not hurt. You are learning to be a proper malthrope!" As she spoke, she swept the pine needles and flakes of bark from his sleeves, punctuating the comment with a slap to his chest. "Come. You drew blood. The path will be easy to find."

"You . . . you want me to try again? After what happened?"

"Pff. Nothing happened, Teyn. You are well, your prey is not. That is how hunting goes."

"But the male! The bull will come after me again. Those antlers could have cut me in half!"

"Antlers! Yes, that is the word!" she proclaimed. "Do not worry. You have gotten away once. You will get away again. Once or twice more and you'll have the one you were after. Quickly now. You did not strike so deep. The thing will not be slowed much. It will take time to follow."

"I can't do it."

"Bah. You can. Come. We cannot allow the forest to serve up a meal like that and then let it walk away. We would spit in the face of fortune. You will finish the hunt."

"I *can't do it.*"

His voice quavered with his final words. At the sound, Sorrel looked him over once more, seeming to finally notice that though his body was none the worse, he was badly shaken by the experience. His hands were shaking, and his eyes were flitting here and there, ears twitching and turning at every sound. He had, perhaps foolishly, allowed himself to believe he was safe here. After reluctantly allowing the constant fear for his life to drop away, to have it thrust upon him again was devastating. It brought back powerful memories of his flight from the plantation, and of the final days there.

"Listen, Teyn," Sorrel said, clasping his shaking hands in hers. "You are afraid. It is right to be. You could have been killed. But you were not. This is a victory. You did as you should. It is a good thing to be afraid of that thing. It is bigger and stronger. Around a thing like that, you need to be alert and fast. Fear gives you these things. But you are not so big, and you are not so strong. There will be many things bigger and stronger, so you cannot let the fear stop you, or you will never start. You take the things fear gives you and refuse to give the things it tries to take away.

"There are many ways to beat something. You can be bigger or stronger. You are not. You can be faster. You are not. You can be smarter. You are not, yet. But there is one thing always that you can do to beat something, no matter what it is and no matter what you are not. You can keep trying. Try and fail, try and fail. Maybe many times, but if you continue to try while the others do not, then you will win. So never stop trying. Life will be hard for us, Teyn. We are malthropes, that is the way of things. But so long as we never stop trying, we will find our way. If you learn nothing else from me, learn that."

Teyn listened to her words. Again, there was a tone behind them that he hadn't heard in her voice in the short time he'd know her: sincerity. Other things she'd taught were things that she knew, things that she'd learned. This was something she believed, a piece of herself that kept her going in the face of the endless trials of her life. He took strength from her words—but, more than that, he took comfort in her touch. She held firm to his hands while she spoke, and looked him directly in the eye. Something about it, about physical contact that was not the back of a hand or the heel of a boot, made the words more real, more meaningful. He'd had her to keep him company for days, but this was the first time that he truly felt that he wasn't alone. His trembling slowed, and Sorrel smiled as she saw in his eyes that the fear was drifting away.

"Good. Good. Now come. I will show you where to follow the path. Soon, we feast."

#

It took more than a day and a half and three more close calls, but Teyn finally managed to catch his prize. The young elk was enough to fill their bellies for three full days.

From the moment of that first true success, things changed. It was as though seeing the prey, tracking it, stalking it, had awakened a part of him that he'd been forced to keep tucked away. The lessons began to take root even more quickly now. He was eagerly seeking out each new scent and gaining as much insight and wisdom as Sorrel could provide.

Just as his skills grew, however, game grew more and more scarce. The meager offerings that the barren mountainside could provide nearly vanished as the knowledge of a dangerous predator spread among the prey. The pair found themselves traveling farther each day to find a meal, and coming back with less to show for it each time. Worse, all of the travel was very hard on Sorrel, who, despite his continued insistence, refused to give her injured leg any real rest. As a result, it had barely improved at all.

A few weeks had now passed, and Teyn was hot on the trail of a strong scent. Sorrel limped behind, a near-constant grin of pride and amusement on her face as she watched her protégé put her teachings to use. He'd always trusted her advice before, and it had yet to be proven wrong, but this time his confidence was wavering.

"It . . . it doesn't smell fresh at all," he said with concern.

"Do not worry about that. There is nothing wrong with claiming another creature's kill."

"But it smells rotten. It smells like there are *many* rotten things nearby."

"Only rotten things?" she quizzed him.

"No . . ." he replied, sniffing again. "Some fresh meat, too."

"Yes, good. This is good. Something has brought back many meals here. Not everything cleans all the meat from the bones, and so you smell what they leave. There must be good hunting not far from that smell, or else how would the things get there?"

"There is another smell, too. There is something . . . strange about it."

"Yes. Yes. It is like a thing with feathers, but also a thing with fur. I do not know the smell, but it is an old smell, and there is no path of it leaving or coming. Maybe it is one of the rotten things now, yes?"

Teyn pressed on uncertainly. The journey so far was already the farthest she'd traveled from the familiar section of forest that had become their home, and the source of the scent was quite a bit farther.

Gradually, they began to find signs of what they had been smelling. Here and there were the partial remains of a very large piece of game. Some of the old and moldy remains appeared to have once been full-grown thorn elk. One broken skull still bore a mighty set of antlers. Other piles of bones were too broken or too old to offer any hint of what beast had produced them. They pressed on, hoping to find something with a bit of fresh meat left—or, better yet, something that the hunter that had left these trophies of past meals had not quite been able to kill. A beast half the size of some that they'd come across, weakened by a prior run-in, would feed the pair of malthropes for weeks.

Despite the enormous potential reward waiting at the end of the trail of remains, Teyn found himself growing more uneasy with each step away from his home.

"How do we know that whatever did this to these animals won't do the same to us?" he asked his mentor.

"It would do this to us gladly. But your nose has been getting sharper, your ears and eyes are pointed in the right directions, and I am smelling and listening and watching also. We will know if anything is creeping up to eat us."

He nodded and turned back to the task of rooting out something worthwhile from the veritable graveyard, but her assurance did little to ease his nerves. The mountains in this part of the woods had been growing steadily steeper, eventually leading to a rocky cliff face. The treacherous wall of stone was looming over them as they threaded their way out of a particularly thin patch of trees.

Just ahead was a small waterfall trickling over the edge of the cliff. It began as a strand of water, but the wind pulled it apart into feathery sheets as it fell, leaving it little more than a freezing mist by the time it settled to the surface of the shallow lake below. The cold blue of the sky reflecting in the rippling surface, combined with the majesty of the falls and the tall, proud pines, would have made for a striking and beautiful view, if either of the malthropes had been in the proper mind to enjoy it.

As it was, the burning uneasiness that had lingered in the back of Teyn's mind had spread to Sorrel as well. Her vigilant gaze was now darting in a hunted and anxious fashion. There was a stillness to this place, a lifelessness. It was almost the same sort of fearful hush that their own section of the woods had taken on once Teyn's hunting skills had improved, but to a vastly greater degree. With nothing else to do but keep to his task, he tracked down the source of the latest unknown scent. It had led them just beyond the fringe of the sparse woods, to a narrow stretch of barren ground. Ahead was a clump of chalky substance, a bit smaller than Teyn's head, that the young malthrope could not identify.

"What is it?" he asked, crouched low as he investigated.

When no answer came, he looked to Sorrel. She was distracted, her face serious and her eyes scouring the landscape for anything that might be a solid cause for concern. He turned back to the substance. A nudge with his toe caused it to crumble apart, revealing the odd tuft of hair or twist of gristle and unleashing a fresh whiff of pungent odor.

"Gohveen . . ." came Sorrel's voice in an awed hush.

"That's what I thought it was. It smells like . . ." he began, turning to see her eyes turned not to the fragrant discovery, but to the sky. She seemed frozen, eyes quivering and lips parted in disbelief. Teyn turned to match her gaze, and quickly spotted what had seized her attention.

While the pair of them had been keeping their eyes trained on the ground in search of food and threats, they had failed to notice danger drifting on the wind above them. It was just a dark point against the bright sky, but something about the way it moved through the air kindled an ancient and well-earned dread within Teyn. He squinted, trying to take in the details of the form. There were wings—the massive, broad wings of a bird of prey—but this was no eagle. To earn such a sprawling silhouette, an eagle would have been near enough for him to hear the rustle of its feathers, and this beast was still high in the sky. A thin cloud drifted in front of the sun, darkening the sky enough for him to make out a hooked beak, piercing eyes, and slate-gray feathers. It had stout talons pulled sleekly to its breast. Behind them, pawing at the air as though eager to strike, was a pair of powerful cat-like legs and a sweeping tail.

Teyn had heard the men of the plantation tell stories of such things. They called it a griffin. As they watched, the creature pitched downward, dropping into a dive that was enough to shake Sorrel from her stupor.

"Run!" she shrieked, stumbling backward for a few steps before turning to coax her ailing leg to as near to a sprint as she could muster. Teyn matched her speed. "No! The other way!" she cried between the yelps of pain that accompanied each stride. "We split! It cannot catch us both!"

"But what about you? You're hurt! If it goes after you it will catch you!"

"It is a flier! It will catch whatever it decides to chase. Go!"

"I won't leave you to face it alone. There's got to be a way."

A stride landed hard on the bad leg, sending a jolt of pain that was momentarily intense enough to eclipse the fear and panic.

She tumbled to the ground, her muscles rigid with agony for a few long moments before the wave of pain subsided. Her teary eyes opened to find Teyn had already gathered the crutch and thrown her arm around his neck to haul her to her feet. When they were unsteadily upright again, both of them snapped their eyes to the sky. The beast had wheeled around and was rushing toward them from directly ahead, descending from above the cliff. On her best day, Sorrel would barely have had a chance of making it to the shelter of the rocky crevice. With her leg in such terrible shape, there was no hope of getting that far. Even the nearest of the trees might as well be half a world away.

She heaved a few shaky breaths and pushed herself away from Teyn. "Fine," she said, tears in her eyes and voice. "Head for the cliff, you understand? Head to the cliff and find a place too small for the flier to go. Run fast as you can."

She spoke with her eyes trained on the sky, the desperation and urgency in her tone rising with each beat of the creature's wings.

"Right, let's go," he stated, duty and purpose gleaming in his eye.

"No," she instructed. "You go alone. It will chase you, not me."

"Why?"

She looked to the sky a final time to see the beast just moments away, then turned to Teyn. As if attempting to gather her nerves for something, she drew in a deep breath. With a blur of motion, a cry of fury, and a flash of her claws, she raked a long, shallow slash across Teyn's chest where the open shirt left it bare. He staggered backward, disbelief and shock making the pain seem distant and inconsequential. The wounds were superficial, but already they were beading with blood.

"That is why! Now go. *Run!*"

She sprang toward the trees, favoring her bad leg to the point of hopping. He looked up to the swooping form, and in its cold predatory gaze he saw the same calculations he'd been learning to embrace. It flitted its eyes first to the injured motion of Sorrel, then to the bright red streaks of blood on Teyn's chest. When he saw the creature curl its talons toward him, he knew that it had made its decision. There was only time enough for a pair of bounding steps before the creature was near enough to strike, but he made them count, rushing low to the ground and tucking his shoulder into a roll when he felt the rush of wind from its wings. Claws longer than his fingers cut through the air, missing his head but catching his ear, slicing a notch out of the outer edge.

He rolled to his feet and dashed for the cliffs. Behind him the ground shuddered under the beast's landing. An eagle was an ungainly creature on land. Pity, then, that he was not facing an eagle. As sleekly as its avian aspect had allowed it to navigate the skies, its feline aspect allowed it to match that grace on the ground. It pivoted, dug its hind claws into the earth, and once again Teyn was being pursued by a much larger, much faster creature. Unlike before, there were no trees to serve as cover or obstacles. As the griffin steadily gained, all he could do was pour as much as he could into his sprint and pray that he reached the cliff in time.

The ground grew rockier and more uneven with each step toward the cliffs, but he'd learned to be surefooted in his time with Sorrel. He also knew better than to waste an ounce of his precious strength and coordination to attempt to see how close the monster had come. He relied on the rest of his senses instead. The sound was the most telling, a distinctive sequence of scrapes and slaps as the bony bottoms of the avian feet and fleshy pads of the feline feet alternately struck the earth. At a puff of wind, he reflexively ducked his head, narrowly avoiding a snap of the beast's razor beak. Twice there was a stutter in its step, and twice Teyn shifted directions in time to dodge a swipe of a talon.

Each missed attack gained him a step, and finally he reached the stone wall.

Vast boulders that had been sloughed away from the rest of the mountain by decades of wind and weather littered the base of the cliff. Eroded-away stone alcoves and ice-carved rifts dotted its face. There were dozens of places to hide—hundreds, even—but at a glance, there was no telling which would be large enough to hide him yet small enough to keep him from harm. It hardly mattered, though; his racing mind and pounding heart were both ready to give out, and even a moment's pause would cost him his life. Luck would simply have to be with him. He picked the nearest slice in the mountain that seemed to have a chance to conceal him.

A frantic turn and shuffle slid him into the pocket of darkness within the cliff wall. It was narrow, and the stone on either side was jagged and sharp, but if the alternative was being torn to bits and gulped down by the beast a step behind him the choice was an easy one. He scoured himself across the stone, scraping his already clawed chest and wedging himself as deep as he could manage. His head was turned to the opening without room enough to move it and he could scarcely breathe as the monster reached the wall.

Talons raked and clawed at the stone, scoring lines into it mere inches from his flesh. The griffin unleashed a furious screech as it chipped and scraped at the stone wall with its pickax of a beak, crumbling bits of stone but, mercifully, making little progress. Finally, it angled its head it to cast one last scornful glare at the morsel just out of reach before stalking backward a few steps to sit, rage in its eyes. Teyn's mind turned back to the rabbits, and the day he'd trapped them with a single exit and waited for them to try to leave. He dearly hoped that this beast did not share his patience.

For a few moments, they simply stared at each other, the monster swishing its tail with quick, angry motions. It stood and charged the wall again, making a halfhearted attempt to fish him out before slowly turning its sharp eyes back to the rocky stretch leading to the forest. It scanned steadily, then stopped, body instantly and eerily still. Slow, tentative steps followed, head locked toward something blocked from Teyn's view by its unfurling wings.

It didn't matter; he didn't need to see it. He knew what the beast saw.

"Here!" Teyn croaked, not able to get air enough in his lungs to speak properly, "Here! Keep your eyes on me!"

He raised his arm, reaching out until his fingers were nearly at the opening of the crevice, and slapped the stone. It was no use. The beast had its new target, and would pursue it as doggedly as it had pursued him. Teyn tried to fight breath into his lungs to call out a warning to Sorrel. He'd yet to catch his breath from the run, and narrow shelter allowed only tiny sips of air. The beast kept moving, stalking low to the stone. He twisted and turned his mind, trying to find some way, any way to keep it from targeting her until she'd had more time to find safety. There was one obvious choice. He had to give up his shelter and make himself the more appetizing prey once again.

So close to the monster, it might well be the last choice he made, but he did not hesitate.

A quick shove with his feet heaved him from the crack, sending him tumbling out into the open. This time the sound and motion was enough to draw the attention of the beast. Once again, the stillness seized it, as though it knew that safety was just a step behind Teyn and to betray its intention a moment too soon would send the prey scurrying back. Every instinct, every whisper of intelligence, every corner of Teyn's mind demanded he do just that, but he willed those voices into silence. A moment spent staring down the monster was a step toward safety for Sorrel, and she needed very step she could get. He simply had to hope that she was moving as quickly as she could. The monster took a slow step toward Teyn, but he held his ground, senses attuned to every minor movement, every twitch of muscle in the massive predator. The tension grew more intense, each beast knowing the next move was the last of the game, and each waiting for the perfect moment to make the fateful choice.

A sound pierced the air, one that nearly tore Teyn's heart from his chest. It was Sorrel, her voice twisted in agony. The monster's head snapped toward the sound, and before the shrill echoes had died away, it was already bounding toward her. Teyn's legs moved of their own accord, breaking into a sprint that made his earlier flight seem leisurely by comparison. He trailed behind the beast, pushing himself harder than he ever had. This time it was not his own life on his mind, but hers. His pace quickened further, eyes locked on a crumbled form in a shallow gully among the sparse trees of the forest's fringe. Desperation and fear had driven Sorrel to rely upon her much abused leg and it had finally failed her. Even at this distance Teyn's keen eyes could make out a horridly crooked bend in her now useless limb. Unwilling to give up, she was working her way backward crab-wise, one arm and one leg dragging her along while she brandished her crutch. Even in the face of certain death, defiance gleamed from her eyes.

Teyn pushed himself harder. The fear was gone now. Every step was sure, determined. Even the exhilaration of the hunt had dropped away. His mind, body, and soul were one, dedicated to this single task. Save her. He had only known her for a short time, but Sorrel must survive. Too many others had been lost—by his hand or another. He would not allow her to be taken away.

He was beside the griffin now, running half a dozen strides for each of the beast's, and gaining only a few precious inches. Ahead, Sorrel beat the lashed end of her crutch against the ground, breaking it away and leaving a cruel, jagged spike. A toss in the air and a shift of her hand left it in a javelin grip.

When the beast was ten long strides away, Sorrel sent her weapon flying with a heave of her arm. The charging monster swung wide, curving to dodge the weapon and approaching from the side. Sorrel was unarmed now, but her eyes were wide and her teeth were bared. Her attack did not meet its mark, but it had forced the creature to waste enough steps to give Teyn the time he needed. Approaching from the other side, he hurled himself through the air to collide full-force with the creature, wrapping himself around its neck. The impact forced the air from his lungs and was barely enough to stagger the beast, but he did not allow his momentum to slow.

A rage came over him suddenly and completely, as though it had been a soldier waiting at the ready, eager to be deployed. He plunged his claws deep and clamped down with his jaws. Madly, he tore away clumps of feathers in search of something vital.

The griffin reared, pain finally cutting through instinct. Sorrel scrambled away, managing to pull herself clear just as the monster's claws came down hard, throwing Teyn to the ground before it. He rolled aside, avoiding a lightning-quick strike of the creature's beak. Eyes dancing across his surroundings, he spotted the broken crutch where it had landed a few paces away. He sprang to his feet, ducked below a sweeping claw, and snatched up the weapon. Makeshift spear held tight in his grip, he turned to face the monster once more, stalking sideways to place himself between it and Sorrel. The griffin took a cautious step back. Teyn growled a vicious challenge.

For a moment there was another standoff, like the one at the cliff except that the roles of predator and prey were no longer so certain. When the massive beast let its eyes flick toward Sorrel, Teyn made his move, leaping high and putting all off his weight behind a single strike of the spear. The weapon met its mark and sunk deep into the griffin's shoulder, eliciting an ear-splitting cry from the beast. Instinctively, it leaped, pumping its wings and taking to the sky.

Perhaps it was dedication or perhaps it was blood lust, but Teyn refused to release his grip on the weapon. He was dragged into the air, dangling from the spear. The creature rolled, a motion that whipped him about and shook his grip, but he managed to dig his claws into the pelt and hold tight. It soared higher, and a brief glance over his shoulder treated Teyn to a view of the retreating ground. The sight was enough to cut its way through the fervor that had been clutching his mind. He looked to the griffin's head looming over his own. Even without seeing its eyes, it was clear that hunger had been overruled by fear in its mind. It was fleeing. He'd won. Now all he had to do was survive.

Each thrust of its wings shook the beast, threatening to break Teyn's grip and send him plummeting to the ground. He needed something to hold onto that was more substantial than feathers. The only option was the spear. Scrabbling with his feet and lunging forward, he managed to get his fingers around it. Instantly, the monster cried out, tipping forward into a dive. Soon it was heading directly toward the ground, and for a heart-stopping moment his fingers slipped and he was falling beside it. The wind whistled in his ears and the rocky field rushed closer, but he kept his eyes on the beast. It pivoted and worked its wings harder, pulling itself out of the dive and drifting near enough for Teyn to latch onto its back.

Again he reached forward for the spear in order to have some sort of anchor, and again the beast screeched and shifted in the air, pulling sharply upward. Somehow, Teyn gathered his wits tightly enough to realize that it was tipping in the direction he pulled the spear, trying to get away from the pain each fresh tug brought.

A firm shove forward sent the beast into a dive again, confirming his observation and giving him the tiniest chance at survival. With tugs and nudges of the weapon, he guided the monster as best he could toward the surface of the lake below. It was working, but each attempt to steer replaced a bit more of the creature's fear with fury. He was a good deal higher than he would have liked when it finally twisted itself into a tight roll that successfully tore him from its back, the spear clutched desperately in his grip and sliding free. A flailing fall brought him to the surface of the lake, where he slashed down with punishing force. The water softened his fall only slightly.

The shock of water that was on the cusp of freezing was joined a moment later by the thump of his back against the lake floor. He coughed out a precious breath of air and convulsed as water rushed in to replace it. Drawing together the remnants of his mind that had survived the ordeal thus far, he realized that one aspect of the plan he'd failed to consider was the fact that he didn't know how to swim. It didn't matter. He would not survive a clash with a massive monster and a fall from the sky only to be killed by a pool of water. He planted a foot on the lake bed and pushed himself toward the rippling waves above.

Not a moment too soon, he broke the surface, and after a fit of coughing and spitting, he was able get a lungful of fresh air. What followed was a somewhat undignified sequence of splashes and sputtering gasps as he worked his way to the shore. Finally, his thrashing brought him near enough to feel the silt and stone of the water's edge.

He flopped ashore and allowed himself a few moments to gratefully take advantage of the fresh air and solid ground. Slowly, his mind began to process what had happened, and his body listed its complaints. Every inch of him ached. His heart was rattling in his chest, the cold breeze was chilling his wet fur, and he could feel a dozen different welts and bruises forming.

It wasn't until his breathing began to slow and his heart no longer threatened to beat its way out of his chest that he dared attempt to stand. It took three tries, but he finally managed to remain upright. He surveyed his surroundings, now grappling with the task of determining what exactly he was supposed to do now. His body politely suggested that he lie down for a few hours, but there would be time for that later. He turned his eyes to the sky, searching until he spotted the now-distant form of the griffin. To be on the safe side, he decided to fetch the spear, just in case it decided to return. At some point during the fall, he'd released it, but it was fortunately bobbing at the water's edge. Once it was in his hand, he shook away as much of the water as he could from his long hair and bristling fur. Finally, he limped toward the trees, coughing up a few lingering drops of water as he went.

The short distance to the low hill that hid Sorrel seemed like miles, and even so, his breathing had barely returned to normal by the time reached it. He plodded up the slop until he could see his fellow malthrope ahead. Sorrel was curled in a ball, her hands cupped over her eyes. She was shaking with violent, heaving sobs. Her voice was twisted with pain and sorrow.

"Sorrel?" he croaked, when he had breath enough to do so.

The sound seemed to slice through the agony. She wiped the tears from her eyes and snapped her head toward the sound. Teyn must have been a pitiful sight, drenched and shivering lightly in the breeze, the bloodied and broken remnant of the crutch still tight in his grip.

"You really are a teyn . . ." She uttered.

Without a word, he stumbled down the short hill and dropped to his knees beside her. His motions were clumsy and subdued until the moment his eyes turned to her ailing leg. Then a sharpness came to his gaze.

"We—" he began to say, stifling a cough. "We need to take care of this."

"There is no use, Teyn. It is broken. What could you do?" She

Joseph R. Lallo

groaned. The pain was terrible, and the suggestion that something could be done about it almost made it worse, as though it had a mind of its own and would not be denied.

"I need to bind it. It needs to be straightened and it needs a splint."

"Still you wish to do this? It is not too late for that?"

"If we do it quickly, your leg should recover."

She knitted her brow, a look of pained contemplation on her face.

"It will hurt very much, yes?"

"At first there will be a lot of pain. It will pass."

As she gave the situation a few more moments of consideration, a wave of pain visibly made her decision for her. "It cannot hurt more than this. Do it. Do what you need to do. *Quickly.*"

He nodded and went to work. The broken-away head of the crutch was lying on the ground beside Sorrel. He snatched it up and sliced the lashing with a claw to salvage a short length of rope. Over the course of the battle and fall, the length of crutch that had served as a weapon had earned a fresh break. Placing it below his knee and giving either side a sharp pull snapped it into two roughly equal lengths.

"I need something to pad it, an old bit of cloth, or—"

"Fine. Take! Take what you need, just move fast!" she barked.

One hand propped her in a sitting position while the other danced across her outfit, plunging into her endless array of pockets and pulling out items of all descriptions. There were trinkets, coins, and swatches of cloth and leather so worn there was no telling what they might have been when they were new. Finally, she revealed the slave tunic she'd tucked away when Teyn had abandoned it. He grabbed it and wrapped it as gently as he could around the fractured shin. It was not gently enough for her tastes, prompting her to dig her claws into the cold ground and unleash a string of colorful words in her native language.

"Careful, Teyn!" she snapped, clutching his upper arm.

"We aren't through the worst of it," he warned. He plucked the armrest of the crutch from the ground, wrapped it in one of the swatches of leather, and held it out. "Take this. Bite down on it."

"What good will this do?"

"If you bite this now, you won't bite your own tongue later."

She shuddered with pain again, eyes resting uncertainly on the leather-wrapped wood.

"Trust me," he said, shaking it. "It will help."

After another hard look she opened her mouth and clamped down

180

on the leather. Teyn slipped the lengths of wood into a layer of the wrapped tunic to hold them in place, then looped what little rope he had around the dressed leg and prepared a knot. He turned to her. Sorrel's eyes were locked on the leg, apprehension and agony playing tug of war with her expression. He gathered the ends of the knot. If he'd arranged the rope correctly, a good hard tug of the rope would draw the injured leg firmly against the makeshift supports, aligning the ends of the bone and holding them in place. On the plantation, he had only seen it done a few times, but faces of the men who had needed it done, and the cries made by even the hardiest of them, were burned into his mind.

No matter. It needed to be done.

He placed his foot against one of the supports, bracing it. The stray ends of the knot were wrapped in his fist. With his other hand, he pulled her hand from his arm and clutched it tight. She held tight and wrestled her eyes open, meeting his gaze.

"Ready?"

She drew in a breath, held it tight, and offered up a stiff nod, eyes staring into his. He pulled the rope taut. A screaming sob of pain erupted from her, forcing its way past the tightly-clamped bit of wood and echoing through the trees. She squeezed his hand painfully tight and held it until the initial shock of pain dwindled to a slow, intense throb.

"That's it. It's done," Teyn said.

Her watering eyes turned to the leg. Once crooked and useless, it had indeed been drawn back into the proper alignment.

"I need to finish tying the knot."

At first she tipped her head in confusion, but then she realized she still had his hand tightly clutched in hers. She released it and, once he'd worked enough feeling into his fingers again, he finished the job.

"There. That wasn't so bad, was it?" he asked, grinning weakly.

"Let me break your leg and we will see how *you* like it," she muttered with a scowl.

The two of them were exhausted and beaten, but alive and whole. For the first time since the beast had appeared overhead, the rush and intensity of the ordeal was gone, and it was steadily taking with it the strength and clarity of purpose that had carried them this far. Replacing it was a bone-deep weariness. All of the fatigue and punishment they'd been able to push aside was racing back. The only thing either of them wanted to do was collapse and let a long night of sleep restore some of their strength and wits. Unfortunately, it was twilight, they were far from home, and, as their run-in with the beast had taught them, they weren't safe in the thin forest. They needed to move, to find shelter. And with her leg so badly hurt, there was only one way it would happen.

Without words, Sorrel gathered the things from her pockets and tucked them away. When she was through, Teyn hooked one of his arms around her back and the other beneath her knees. For once, her withered and undernourished form was a blessing. Lifting her was like lifting a scarecrow, which was fortunate, because he scarcely had the strength to lift much more. As carefully as he could, moving slowly so as to avoid jostling the newly-splinted leg, he climbed to his feet and set off toward home.

#

The crash that comes after pushing the mind and body beyond their limit can only be held at bay for so long. After an hour of heading back through the woods, Teyn couldn't go any farther without the fear of faltering and dropping his precious cargo. When he reached a reasonably sheltered notch in the mountain, he carefully lowered Sorrel to the ground and leaned heavily on the stone wall. His breath was ragged and wheezing, still giving way to a weak cough from time to time and slow to return to normal.

"I'll . . . I'll try to find some wood for a fire. I just need . . . I need to catch my breath."

Sorrel winced as she extended her leg and attempted to find a comfortable position. "Forget the fire, Teyn. You try to find wood now and you will fall, and maybe one of those cat-bird things will find you. Or maybe a fish-eater. And then where would we be? You dead, and me soon after. No, Teyn. Rest. Fire later."

Teyn attempted to object, but he was already settling to the ground, his body having decided to take his friend's advice even though his mind felt differently. He sat and leaned against the wall, leaving a respectable amount of distance between himself and the female. After she finished adjusting her leg, she turned to him, eyes flitting over him and taking in the sight of her savior. She seemed to consider him as one might consider a riddle. Finally she squinted, abandoning the puzzle with a single word.

"Why?" she demanded. Like many of her questions, she didn't so much seem curious as impatient, as though he was late in answering a question that should have been answered ages ago.

"Why what?"

"Why what happened back there? Why carry me so far? Why dress my leg so well?"

"It needed to be done," he said simply.

"That is all? You did not do it for any other reason? You did not want . . . something from me in exchange?"

"No. You needed help, I gave it. You would have done the same for me."

"No, I would not," she countered, a chuckle of disbelief behind her voice. "Coming back? Fighting the cat-bird thing? I would not do this for my own brother. It is a hard enough life without fighting battles that are not your battles. You must put yourself first if you want to stay alive."

"That is not what I was taught. You do what you can to help your people when they can't help themselves. If we all did that, then we would all be better off."

"Maybe, yes. But we do not all do that. And if others do not, then why should you?"

He shrugged. "It has to start somewhere."

"Men taught you that?"

"One of them did . . ."

"He was teaching you to be weak, then. To do what they tell you. He was like the rest."

Teyn shot her a dagger-sharp look. "Say what you wish about the rest of the human race, but do not speak ill of that man."

She murmured something, a noncommittal sound that was neither an acknowledgment nor a retort, and certainly wasn't regret or apology. He sat in silence while she resumed her gaze of consideration. Deep inside, he found himself wishing there was a fire crackling, and not just for the badly needed warmth. A fire gave him something to stare at, and it filled the air with a quiet but constant sound. Without it, the mournful wail of the wind did little to cut through a silence that felt thick and oppressive. His eyes felt restless without a suitable focus. The wind gusted enough to curl into their shelter and offer an icy burst that motivated Teyn to tug the front of his shirt a bit tighter. The long walk in the breeze had been enough to take most of the dampness from it, but in doing so, it had chilled him to the bone. Out of the corner of his eye, he saw her tip her head again, something in his body language catching her attention.

"Give me your hand," she said, reaching out.

He took the hand nearest to her from the edge of his shirt and offered it. She clutched it lightly.

"Still cold. That fall in the water chilled you good, eh? You are lucky it was not in the north. This cold is nothing. There, a dunk in the water without a way to get dry quick is a very bad thing. Even with fur you might not survive it."

All he offered was a slow nod. She held his hand a bit longer, the corners of her mouth drooping and her brow furrowed. Teyn closed his eyes, trying to force the cold from his mind so that he could give his aching body a few hours of real sleep. Beside him, Sorrel adjusted herself for a moment, no doubt seeking a position that would offer a bit less pain. Her shuffling left her leaning lightly against his side, her shoulder to his. She shifted, and then came a gentle warmth drifting over him. His eyes opened to find that she'd pulled the heavy cloak from her back and thrown it over the both of them like a blanket. If it had been a proper-sized cloak, it wouldn't have been nearly large enough, but the comically oversized thing was more than enough to cover them both, so long as they stayed close.

"Thank you. You didn't need to do that," he said.

"No. But I am thinking . . . the lessons this one man teaches you. Maybe not all of them are bad." She yawned wide and leaned her head against his shoulder. "Sleep now, Teyn. You have much carrying to do tomorrow."

#

It had taken the pair of malthropes more than twice as long to return from the ill-fated trip as it had to reach the griffin's cliff. Fortune had smiled upon them along the way, offering up a few plump game birds that were too slow to evade Teyn once he'd set down his teacher. It wasn't the meal they'd been seeking when they set off on their journey, but it was enough to give them the strength to return. Now they were making their way through the familiar trees of the place they called home. It was strange—there wasn't anything particularly distinctive about this part of the mountain, nothing to set it apart from the miles and miles of rocky wilderness that surrounded it, but, somehow, being here brought a profound relief. Pacing the land that greeted him every morning filled him with a sort of comfort, a security that he'd not truly felt since the workshop that he'd shared with Ben.

He shifted his path toward the hidden crag of the mountain that now served the same role as the shop of old, but Sorrel stopped him.

"No, go that way," she directed.

She was cradled in his arms, one arm around his neck and the other pointing the way. After that first night of sleep, she'd been foolish enough to second-guess Teyn's advice. The throbbing had subsided for the most part, and the splint seemed strong, so she'd tried climbing to her feet while Teyn slept. The result was a cry that startled him from sleep and enough pain to assure her that, for better or worse, Teyn would be her legs for a few weeks.

"Up there, then down the slope a bit. There is a patch of flat stones and a gap between two tall parts," she said.

"Where are we going?"

"Where are we going . . ." she muttered. "We are going home, Teyn. Where do you think?"

"Your home? But you told me never to follow you there."

"You are not following me there, you are taking me there. It is different. How else am I supposed to get home? Now go, quickly. It has been a long time. I want to be sure my things are where I left them."

He followed her instructions, and soon found his way to a deep overhang nestled in a nook near the mouth of a small valley not far from his own lair. A thin shard of stone that had dropped free of the mountain ages ago served as a wall, closing off the overhang and turning it into a room of sorts. Carefully slipping through the narrow opening beside the stone, Teyn found the place that Sorrel had called home.

The late afternoon sun was filtering through cracks around the edge of the natural door, where something in the stone of the wall made it sparkle and cast points of rainbow light all around. Here and there, a patch of the wall had been rubbed or scraped to reveal more of the gleaming stone, forming simple patterns of the stuff. Most of these designs were centered on the wall farthest from the entrance, where a neat mound of dry boughs had been piled and draped with a rough cloth to form a cozy little bed. A trickling sound drew his attention to the corner of the den, where a natural spring had forced its way between the layers of stone and formed a small pool.

Perhaps it was simply that it was shielded from the wind, or perhaps it was due to two warm bodies occupying a space only just large enough to accommodate them, but the little alcove seemed warmer than it should be without a fire. Scattered around were little indications that this was a home: smooth pebbles of various colors polished to a sheen and piled neatly on a natural shelf, a few delicate bones and feathers strung together on a piece of poorly knotted thread and dangling from a crook in the roof, tiny touches that Sorrel had left behind to make the space her own.

"Home," she said simply.

"It is very nice," Teyn said as he stooped to set her down.

"Bah. It is a hole in the mountain," she said with a dismissive wave. She set down her good foot and hopped along, holding his hand for balance. Once she'd reached the bed, she spun around and walked herself down the wall with her hands. "But you could search for a year and not find a better hole in the mountain than this one. Turn around."

"Why?"

"Because you are in my home and I told you to turn around," she said flatly.

He did as he was told. Behind him there was the grind of stone on stone, then the tinkle of metal. When the stone sound came and went a second time, she spoke up. "You can turn around again."

He faced Sorrel to find her applying fresh earrings. The three hoops in one ear were gone, and in their place was a dangling collection of tiny gems at the end of delicate gold chains. There were also two new rings lying on the ground beside her. When she was finished with the earrings, she slipped the other bits of jewelry on each of her fingers one by one until she found a finger that fit.

"It was time for a change, yes?" she said with a smile, admiring her new accessories.

"How much jewelry do you own?"

"Hah. Not enough. Always this is the answer."

"And all of it is stolen?"

"No, no, I said before, Teyn. Not stolen. Found in places that men weren't watching close enough."

He sighed. "It is one thing to take something you need, but this?"

"No, it is the same. I see the earring and I say, 'This I need.' And even if it is different, it does not *make* a difference. So I am a thief. And so they say we all are. They say we all are killers as well, and that is not true. I am not a killer, and you are not—"

186

She stopped as she saw a look come over his face. Killer . . .

The word brought with it a flash of the fear and shame he'd felt on the terrible day, and a flicker of the anger that had driven him to the deeds. His breathing quickened, his heart pounded, and his mind burned. It was the same feeling he felt when the other slaves would stare at him, but a thousand times worse. He felt exposed, as though she could read the truth on his face. Perhaps she could. Already her hand had moved subtly aside until it was hovering over a large, flat stone beside the bed. He turned away.

"You . . . are not a killer, are you?" she asked, voice unsure now.

He tried to find the words. If he could deny it, if he could convince her it was not so, maybe things would not change.

"Look at me," she demanded.

Without thinking, he turned, locking eyes. Just like that, all was lost. In his eyes, she saw what he'd been hoping to hide. In her eyes, he saw the hardness—and behind it the fear—that he'd been hoping he would never see again.

"What did you do, Teyn?" she asked in a hushed tone.

"I'm sorry. I'll go."

"You will answer!" she snapped. The stone was in her hand now, raised and ready to be put to use. "Tell me! Who? How many?"

"I . . . I don't know! I was a slave. It was at the plantation. They beat the man who raised me. They *killed* him! Then . . . then I don't know. All I remember is how much I hated them, how much I wanted them to pay for what they'd done to me, to him, to us *all*. There were dozens of men and women on that plantation, Sorrel. It was empty when it was all over. Just me, the owner's youngest, and . . . broken, ruined bodies."

His eyes were lowered, unwilling to look her in the face and see the fear again. A soft clack echoed off the walls of the alcove as she placed the stone on the ground.

"You are not a killer, Teyn."

"I am."

"No, you are not. Look at me, Teyn."

Reluctantly he raised his eyes to hers. There was no fear in them. If anything, there was pity.

"I'm telling you, I—"

"You killed. You lost control and you struck out at those who wronged you. They would have killed you, so you killed them. It is

187

what you did, not what you are."

"It doesn't matter why I did it."

"To me it does. How long have I been helping you? Weeks. That much time and you do not think I would know it if I was spending my time with a killer? You insult me, Teyn. You are a malthrope who has killed a man. Maybe many. You know how to kill and you can do it if you need to. In this world, with the things we have already faced together, that is a useful thing to have around."

"You don't want me to go? You aren't afraid of what I might do?"

"My leg is ruined. It has been since I first met you. If you wanted to do something, why wait? I see the things you can do. I watched you fight the cat-bird thing, and I saw a fighter in you then. But also I watched you after the antler beast chased you. Shaking. Scared. Not a fighter. Then I think, maybe if the thing came for me instead, you would not be scared, you would be a fighter again. I think it is something that only comes when you need it. I think you protect things. So you may be dangerous to men, but to me you mean no harm. I will keep a close eye on you, I would be a fool not to, but this I was already doing. And even if none of this was so, we had a deal. We *have* a deal. Until my leg is better, I do not have a choice but to keep you near."

Teyn stood at the entrance to the den, his mind awash with clashing emotion. The pain and fear of having his secret revealed was mixed with the disbelief and relief of her acceptance. He was without words. Perhaps sensing this, Sorrel didn't allow the silence to linger.

"I have been too long away from this place, my home. I have things that I must do. It has also been far too long since my stomach was full. Do you think you can find a meal without me? My nose tells me something tasty is near. Did you smell it?"

"I . . . I think so," he replied, wrestling back enough of his wits to form an answer. "The rabbit warren. I think new rabbits have claimed it."

"Yes, I think the same. Very good. Go, catch them and bring me some. But ask before you come in. This is my home, not yours."

With a grateful nod, he turned and began to follow the scent. Just as he had done so many times before, he coped with the turmoil in his head and heart the only way he knew how: he buried himself wholly in the task. Moving on instinct and practiced tactics, he let the thinking part of him slip away. By the time he was returning from the hunt, with four plump rabbits to show for his efforts, the edge of his emotion had been blunted somewhat. He was not himself, but the rapier sting that had tormented his mind was replaced by a dull ache.

Sorrel, meanwhile, was behaving as though nothing had happened at all. She ate her first hearty meal in days with her usual relish, and when she was through, she began to muse aloud.

"The place where you sleep. It is near, is it not? You can hear me here from there if I yell?" she asked.

He nodded.

"And if I call, if I need help. How fast until you reach this place?"

"A minute or two."

She pondered for a moment. "I think," she said, gesturing with a bone as she spoke, and gnawing at it between sentences, "this is not fast enough. Maybe a fish-eater comes, yes? With a *bad* leg, maybe I could get away. With a broken leg, no. So I call, and a minute or two passes and you find me." She drew the bone across her throat like a knife, punctuating the motion with a slicing sound. "Dead. No. You need to be closer. There is another place, farther that way. It is a hole like this. No water there, and no rock to keep out the wind, but it is as nice as yours I think. You could sleep there instead. It would be shorter for you to come here, and that is good, because you will need to come here very much." She looked to her leg and her ears drooped a bit. "*Very* much. How long until my leg is better?"

Teyn didn't answer, his eyes staring sightlessly at an indistinct point on the wall of the den, mind swimming in thought.

"Eh!" she exclaimed, snapping her fingers, "Listen to me when I talk to you!"

"I'm sorry. I was—"

"You were thinking. You do this too much. Sometimes it is best to let the mind rest. Now, how long until my leg is better?"

"A month until you can try walking again. Another month before you won't need a splint or a crutch."

"Gohveen," she muttered. "This is very long."

"That's if things go well."

"Then you will make sure things go well. If I cannot walk then you will come here and I will teach you things to help you hunt without me. And when you finish and bring the food here, you will stay and I will teach you more. If I have to trust you to bring all of the food for us both and do it alone, then I will make sure you are as good as you can be."

189

"I'll do my best."

"Good. And after you do your best and we eat our fill, you will stay here for a while. If I cannot move around much, I will need something here to keep me from losing my mind looking at these walls all of the time."

"You're sure you want me to—"

"Yes, Teyn. Stop asking. Until my leg is right and you learn what you need to learn, it will take the two of us working together to stay alive. That is the way it is. Maybe you were a killer yesterday, and maybe you will be a killer tomorrow. I don't care. What I care about is today, and today you are my legs and I am your mind. Now open your ears, because there is much to learn."

Chapter 16

The weeks that followed were trying for both of the malthropes. Though Teyn had learned a tremendous amount from Sorrel about the arts of hunting and tracking, it wasn't until he set off on his own that he realized how much he still relied upon her gentle guidance to find the first hints of a trail that would lead him to his prey. Worse, while their hunting trips had been taking them farther and farther from their dens in order to find food enough to survive, with Sorrel all but helpless Teyn found himself unwilling to leave her alone long enough to make the trek to the patches of forest that had been most fruitful. Some days he found nothing at all, returning instead with a meager collection of nuts, roots, and berries. Sorrel, perhaps understanding the reasons behind his struggles, accepted whatever he had to offer, listened to the troubles that had denied him the day's prize, and advised on how to overcome them.

However, she was not always patient. Often her words would come with the jab of sarcasm or the irritated hiss of frustration; they always made it clear that she knew he could do better, and she knew precisely how. She was an endless fountain of information, sketching out on the sandy earth of the cave floor the tracks he might find, or explaining what parts of the mountainside were the best bet to find plants and animals he was after. Her tips were simple and small, often obvious in retrospect, but each was a new piece to the puzzle, and slowly his skill grew.

More curious though was what came after the lessons of the day: they spoke. Not about the hunt, or about her injury, or any other topic that Teyn would have thought she cared about. In fact, seldom was the subject the same from day to day, or even minute to minute. They never seemed to talk about anything of consequence at all. They just talked, for hours on end, long into the night. And though the conversations couldn't have been more different from his lessons, he learned just as much from those words as he did from her advice.

He learned that Sorrel had a twin sister, and both of her older brothers were twins as well.

"Of course they were twins," she remarked, "For malthropes, twins

191

Joseph R. Lallo

are not so strange. Not always are there twins, but not so strange."

"So I may have had a brother? Or a sister?"

She tipped her head at him. "You may have had a brother or sister, yes. But not a twin, I don't think. You are too big. All the twins I know are not so big as you."

"If you had a family, why did you leave them?"

"Why do I do anything I do not want to do? Because of men. They hunt us, and a family of malthropes is easier to find than one. So we go. We go our own ways. We try to be safe. If one lives, then the family lives. Sometimes that is the only way."

Other times she would talk about places she'd been in her life. Though she was only a bit older than Teyn, she had spent time all over the Nameless Empire, near places she called Kenvard and Ulvard, in a place called Ravenwood, and mountains called Rachis. He marveled at the stories she told, and pressed her for more.

"The mountains are strange in some places," she said. "Stones of many colors, colors you don't see anywhere else. Here, like this."

She shuffled aside and plucked a shiny pebble from beside her bed. It was a deep blue, perfectly even in its coloring, and almost glassy in its smoothness.

"I found it in a river halfway up a mountain. I do not remember the name of it. There are mountains where I find red, like this, and green and blue. All colors are someplace, I think. My favorite is purple, but, of course, purple I do not find. I saw one, up north a bit, near where the fighting is. That was the day I stepped in the trap and started this whole mess." She grimaced. "It is what you get. You go in a deep river, where there are lots of fish, and of course they put a trap for a fish-eater nearby."

"What *is* a fish-eater?" Teyn finally asked. "You talk so much about them, but I don't know what it is."

"It is a thing, a big animal. In Crich it is *medeev*. I do not know it in Tressor language. It eats fish."

"If it eats fish, why do you worry if one will show up?"

"It eats anything it can catch! It eats fish because it can catch fish without much trouble. If it can catch *me* without much trouble, then it will be a malthrope-eater."

"Well what does it look like?"

"It is big. It is . . . like a dog. Only larger."

"A wolf?"

192

"No. Much larger, and rounder and thicker. As big as the cat-bird thing sometimes. Also, a wolf comes many at a time. This is just one always. And a wolf walks on four legs. The fish-eater walks on maybe four, maybe two."

Teyn turned the imagery over in his mind, trying to match it to the stories he'd heard told over the nightly fires in the old days of the plantation. "A bear?"

"Yes! Yes, this is the word. A bear. And my leg, it was hurt by a bear trap," she proclaimed. "Bear. It is an easy word, too. So long I could not think of it. You are not so foolish sometimes, Teyn."

Sometimes the conversations would last longer than either of them realized. Occasionally, dawn would break before they were through, and Teyn would help Sorrel outside to watch the sunrise.

Weeks passed in the same way, and, gradually, the final pieces of the puzzle began to take shape. The trails, however faint, revealed themselves. A few sniffs of the wind told the tale of a dozen creatures crisscrossing a glade. He knew where they were going, where they had come from, and which were best to seek out. Some were still a challenge, leading him on a chase or putting up a fight. Many would escape him, but more and more he prevailed, bringing home his prize and raving about how clear it was to him now. At those times, Sorrel simply offered a knowing smile, as though all of this time she'd been waiting for these very words.

Teyn was not the only one who learned things in those days. On a day when he proudly brought back a young elk and there had been more than either of them could eat, he showed her how a bit of the right kind of wet wood and a long, slow fire could smoke the meat and it would last for ages. He showed her what he'd learned of tanning skins and preparing furs. A needle fashioned of bone combined with some twisted sinew was even enough to cobble together a warmer pair of trousers and a sturdier coat.

From time to time, he checked her leg, crafting a better splint or checking that the healing was going well. It had taken constant scolding and reminders, but Sorrel hadn't put any real weight on her leg since the day it had finally broken. Of course, that didn't stop her from fidgeting, sliding, hopping, shuffling, and otherwise putting the rest of her restless body to work when she needed to get around.

#

At the end of a month and a half, Teyn's skills had grown to the

193

point that he was able to provide a hearty meal two days out of every three, and on the lean days, preserved food kept the hunger at bay. It had been just such a day, a poor hunt and a salty meal of smoked meat behind them, when Teyn was inspecting the progress of her leg.

"I think maybe you did not use the right wood for this one, Teyn," she said, tongue scraping against her teeth. "Maybe next time you use one of the needle trees. Maybe that will taste better."

"No. They told me never to use pine," he said, kneeling beside her leg. He pressed his fingers to her shin. "How does that feel?"

"It feels like you are pressing on my leg," she said with a shrug.

"And now?"

"It feels like you are pressing harder," she said, impatience working into her voice.

He grabbed at her. "Give me your arm," he said, stepping quickly to her side and pulling her arm across his shoulders.

"What is this about, Teyn?"

"Two weeks ago you screamed when I pressed on that spot. Come on, try to stand."

"You are sure?" The impatience was gone now, replaced with guarded excitement.

"Come on!"

He shouldered as much of her weight as he could manage, lifting her slowly and steadily from the ground until she was teetering on her good leg, the injured one bent at the knee with its toes lightly resting on the ground. He slipped out from beneath her arm and grasped it firmly to keep her steady from behind. She put weight on it for the first time since her panicked flight from the griffin. Her eyes squinted a bit, and her teeth bared, but she waved off any attempt to support her again. Bit by bit, she leaned on the favored leg. Finally Teyn stepped back. She was standing, unsteady but without help.

"How does it feel?" he asked, ready to catch her if she seemed ready to fall. She did not answer. Her head was lowered, and she was wavering slightly. Teyn stepped around to the front and found her staring at her leg, tears in her eyes.

"Does it hurt? What's wrong? Here, take my arm," he said urgently, stepping forward to steady her.

First, she raised her hand, palm forward, silently instructing him to keep his distance. After a slow, shaky breath, she raised her eyes to him.

"It barely hurts at all, Teyn. *It barely hurts at all!*" She stumbled forward, tears flowing freely now, and threw her arms around him.

Teyn staggered back a step to steady himself before slowly returning the embrace. It was the first time in his life he'd ever received such a gesture of affection.

"It is healing, Teyn," she wept, her chin on his shoulder. "I can feel it. It is actually getting better."

"Of course it is. We took care of it. Why wouldn't it get better?" he asked, not sure what to make of her reaction.

Sorrel loosened her embrace enough to look him in the eyes. "Because never do things get better for us. Always they get worse. We are chased and we are hated and we are hungry and we are cold and we are tired. Each day another thing. It gets to be that you are afraid always. You are afraid to trust your own. You steal things from your own. The day I stepped in the trap, the day I felt the pain, I knew it always would be there, because never has anything that has gone wrong ever gone right again. Not until you," she added, her tone a reverent hush. "Thank you."

"It was the least I could do."

"How long now?" she asked, wiping her eyes and sniffing. "How long until I can walk without you there to catch me?"

"It . . . it should be a week or two. Try a bit more each day and the strength will come back. And then . . . that will be that . . ." With his final words, his voice dropped, and his spirit with it.

"Why do you not sound happy to say this, Teyn?"

"Because that will be the end of this. The deal will be done. Once your leg is strong enough, you'll have no more use for me, and by now I've learned everything I need to know."

She looked him in the eye, saw the earnestness there, and erupted into a bout of boisterous, howling laughter, fresh tears running down her cheeks.

"Teyn . . ." Sorrel managed to say when the fit had run its course, "Teyn, Teyn, Teyn. This you do not need to be sad about. You are a handy one to have around. I think I can find a use for you still. And if you think after all of this time together you will just leave," she added with a devilish grin, "you have very much more to learn."

She hugged him tight once more. He returned the favor.

"Let us go! Let us leave this place!" Sorrel declared when they finally separated.

The statement came suddenly, prompted by nothing in particular and yet spoken with the utmost of conviction, as though it was a decision arrived at after long debate and careful reasoning. Teyn furrowed his brow and tried to comprehend why she would say such a thing.

"Why do we have to leave? What's wrong with this place?" he asked, certain he was missing something.

"Bah, what is *right* about this place? It is too windy, and too rocky, and too gray. There is little food and no place to stay but holes in the mountain, and I am sick of it. It is time to go." As she spoke, she was gathering what few possessions she had, snatching up stones and bits of cloth, even going so far as to pull aside a well-concealed stone and fetch a satchel of jewelry that, until that moment, she'd never allowed Teyn to see.

"But it is safe here. It takes some work, but we can find enough food to survive."

"Teyn," she said, with a sad shake of her head, "I do not *want* to survive. I want to *live.* It is very much a different thing, and you do not know it because you've only done the first, never the second. One taste of life and survival will never be enough for you again."

"But where will we go?"

"Wherever we want! Those stories I tell of the Great Forest. Always you are eager to hear them. Don't you ever want to see the place? Don't you want stories of your own?"

"But . . ." he objected, though now he was not sure he knew why.

Her words fizzed and sparked with energy, and steadily those sparks began to flare in his mind. So much of his life had been lived in the rigid confines of the farm. Large though it was, the boundaries were never out of sight. He never tried to leave, because he knew that beyond those walls was a world with no place for him, and if he were to go there, he would have to face terrible consequences. It was now dawning that, in a way, he'd never truly escaped that place. When he ran, he was moving only because if he didn't, those consequences would catch up with him. His life had been nothing but a desperate search for a safe corner to hide away, and though he'd left the plantation behind, he'd taken the walls with him.

As she so often did, Sorrel saw the flicker of life in his eyes long before he found the words to express it.

"Come on," she said, holding out her hand. "We'll see how far this leg can take me in a day, yes? And the next day, we'll try to beat it. When we find a place that looks like home, then that will be our home until we decide to find another. It isn't an easy life, but it is a life, and that is better than the other choice. You say soon I will be able to run again. When I do, I want to feel grass beneath my feet."

A part of him resisted, the part that was still the frightened little whelp cowering behind the legs of the one man who wouldn't strike him. For once, though, the fear was countered by another voice, a louder voice that cried out for all that it had heard but not seen. More than that, for once he had a friend, someone who stood by him not because they shared a plight, but because she wanted to. And he knew that where she went, he would follow.

He took her hands and, together, they walked into the sunlight.

#

What followed was a glorious time in their lives. Sorrel's leg recovered completely, and shortly afterward, they reached the Great Forest of Tressor. Never had Teyn seen a place so filled with life. The ground was an emerald carpet of lush vegetation. Trees of every type towered over them. Most days the sun beat down upon the woods. Others times the driving rains that had fed the fields of his youth hammered down, but it didn't matter. Fine, broad leaves provided shade and shelter such that even on the worst of days there was someplace cool and dry to stay.

Hunting had never been easier. Herds of deer lived and thrived there. There were plump birds that Teyn had only ever seen while they were being prepared for the master's table. The air was heavy with scent of prey, and for once there was more than enough to eat. Steadily, Sorrel's withered and malnourished form regained the muscle and curves it had lost, and similarly Teyn ate well enough to replace his wiry frame with one that was healthy and strong.

But all of this bounty came at a price. Whereas the barren waste of the mountain was theirs alone, humans and their like frequented the forest in search of all of the same things that had drawn the malthropes there. Evading the eyes of humans was a skill that Teyn had learned quite well over the years, and Sorrel had raised it to an art form—so much so that when the rare need arose that could not be fulfilled by the forest alone, the two would venture out to the surrounding villages and cities. There, Sorrel would inevitably "find" what they were after, often with a few shiny baubles to show for her trouble as well. Teyn

197

learned these lessons with the same hunger for knowledge he'd shown when learning to hunt and track. Soon, the city was just another hunting ground, no more dangerous than the woods if they took care and didn't linger.

Those hours that were not spent hunting or exploring were spent learning all that the other had to teach. Teyn picked up what he could of Crich, and after that the beginnings of a language she called Varden, which he soon learned she spoke nearly as poorly as Tresson. She eventually gained a firmer grasp of that language as well, though it was largely the consequence of their long conversations than any hunger for knowledge. Her interests tended toward whatever talents and skills he'd gathered during his time on the plantation. His miraculous treatment of her leg had sparked a fascination in any other talents he might have "stolen" from the humans. Most things he tried to teach her were not enough to hold her interest, but fashioning tools, weapons, and clothing soon became a passion of hers.

The weeks and months marched quickly by until in the blink of an eye two years since had passed, by far the best of Teyn's life. He and Sorrel seldom left each other for more than a few hours. Many warm days and wonderful nights were spent together. For all of his life, even when he was with Ben and the other slaves, he had never been anything but alone. Now he had someone. Not just someone to keep him company, but someone to call his own. His heart belonged to her, and hers belonged to him.

Through all of that time, though, despite having Sorrel by his side, more freedom, and a better life than he'd ever had before, Teyn could not shake the feeling that there was something missing. He didn't feel unhappy. Far from it. Until these precious years of freedom, he'd hardly known the meaning of the word happiness. What he felt, he could not describe. Something at the edge of his mind felt wrong, as though there was something important that had been left undone. He did his best to put the feeling out of his mind, to enjoy this rare and treasured string of good fortune, but whenever he had a moment of solitude, it was there waiting for him. It was no surprise that Sorrel sensed his troubles. Her concern surfaced from time to time, but she had the unique and admirable ability to set such things aside to live in the moment. Teyn could do little more than try his best to follow her example.

Most of their time had been spent in one corner of the Great Forest or another. On this day, the two malthropes were winding their way along the bank of one of the handful of rivers that flowed through the forest. While Sorrel was well-versed in the names of every little hamlet and glade on the northern side of the steadily smoldering war, she'd made it a habit of classifying Tresson landmarks by their meaning to her. Thus she spoke of "our mountain," "the place where we usually find the fat birds," and in this case . . .

"The river where the trap was," she said with a sneer. "Watch the ground. We are close to where it happened."

"I know. We were here last spring."

"And if you did not step in a trap, then you can thank me for this."

She tugged at the neck of her shirt and brushed an errant strand of hair from her eyes. In the mountains, she and Teyn had weighed themselves down with layers of clothing to ward off the cold. As they made their way down to the fields, Sorrel had shed one layer after another, bundling each up and carrying it along rather than wearing it. Since they'd reached the forest, she had whittled her wardrobe down to a faded green tunic with frayed gold embroidery and pair of worn brown leggings, each of a thin fabric made thinner by age and use. Teyn wore a vest and trousers he'd made himself from crudely tanned deer hide. Each carried a pack of the same material, bulging and dangling with their belongings.

"Why are we coming back this way?" he asked. "Hunting parties come through this patch of woods all the time."

"Here, yes, but that way for a while was a place I liked very much, remember? That place where the men never seemed to go? There wasn't very much to hunt, but there were places near to it that had plenty. The rain was never very bad there. It is a place that we could stay for a long time without having to move."

"You've never been interested in staying in any one place for a very long time."

"Yes, well. Sometimes there are reasons to. Sometimes it is nice to know that you can be safe somewhere, in case—What are you looking for?" Sorrel asked impatiently.

Since they'd reached the river, Teyn had been glancing at the surface every few moments, and for the last hour he had hardly taken his eyes off of it.

"It was something you said once, while your leg was recovering."

She put her hands on her hips. "If I said something back then that

199

would make you ignore me and look in a river, I think I would remember it. It must have been quite a thing to distract you so much. What if I had something important to tell you?" she asked, adding under her breath, "Something you would not need to be told if you had grown up with other malthropes . . ."

"There!" Teyn said, suddenly dropping his pack and bounding it into the water.

"What are you doing now?" she called out, confounded. "There aren't any fish worth going after. Certainly not if you splash around like that."

He ignored her, slowing his pace as he waded waist-deep, his eyes trained on the rippling surface. Finally, he plunged completely below the water, emerging a moment later with a handful of gravel and sloshing back toward the bank. He blinked water out of his eyes and shook it from his long hair, unwilling to take either hand from the double scoop of stones to wipe them.

"What did you find?" Sorrel asked, now interested.

She peered down at the assortment of water-smoothed stones as he laid them out on a patch of moss and shifted through them. Shifting one or two aside, he uncovered something that made Sorrel squeal with excitement. There, among the glossy river rocks, about the size of her palm and roughly the shape of a flattened egg, was a deep purple stone. Her eyes gleamed as she held it to the light.

"The color, it is perfect. How did you know where to look for one like this?"

"You said you'd thought you'd seen one in the river near where you were hurt. I thought there might be more."

"Sharp eyes," she cupping his dripping wet cheek with her hand, "Sharp eyes, sharp mind. That's my Teyn. These other stones I carry, but this one I will wear. I think something around my neck, yes?"

She held the stone to her chest, where it might hang if it were set in an amulet. Her mouth opened to speak, but a shift of the wind snapped her attention to the east. Teyn had turned at the same moment. Neither of them spoke. There was nothing to say. The scent of humans was on the air. What came next had been reduced to a reflex. Find cover until it was clear why they had come and what they were after—and, if they were seeking malthropes, run. It didn't matter how large or how well-armed the hunting party was, there was no catching a malthrope in the woods without surprising it or surrounding it, and neither Teyn nor

Sorrel were careless enough to allow that to happen.

It was the work of moments for each to find a place among the bushes, disappearing into the shadows and flora to watch and wait. A few short minutes passed and there came the quick steps of a pursuit. Next there was the crunch of gravel, the splash of water, and finally the thunder of hooves. A man burst into sight; at the first glimpse of him, dark thoughts from long ago gripped Teyn's mind. It was a slave, dressed in the same distinctive tunic he'd worn for most of his life, and bearing a two-stripe brand. Below the stripes was a brand he'd never seen before—a plantation owner from nearby, no doubt. His feet were bare and battered from a long run over rough ground. There was a madness in his eyes, a terrified need to escape that Teyn knew all too well.

A faint whistle of twirling rope came next. From the trees behind the fugitive flew a trio of heavy leather pouches joined by lengths of rope. It spun through the air and caught his legs, wrapping them tight and sending the slave tumbling to the ground. He tugged at the restraints, but not a moment later a horse and rider crunched up to the fallen runner. The horseman was an older man, well into his forties, and he wore cheap leather armor, little more than heavy clothes made of layered hide. What showed of his skin told the tale of a hard life. His hands were covered in calluses and were blackened with dirt.

Despite the rest of his distinctive appearance, there was one feature that captured one's attention above all. There were four parallel scars beginning at the back of his scalp and continuing across his right ear and down the side of his face, ending at his jaw. The wounds were thick and deep enough to show as hairless furrows across his head and left his ear a serrated and perforated mangle of flesh. His expression sagged unnaturally on that side, as though the slash had severed something that had never been properly restored.

"All right. All right," said the horseman. "It was a good run, but you're caught. Enough struggling, or I'll have to make sure you don't do any more running. That's something I'd rather not do. It'll cost me money, since a slave with no feet won't fetch much of a bounty."

There was something about the horseman that chilled Teyn. The sound of his voice, the look of his face, and more than anything his scent brought back half-remembered flashes of the day he had been found and taken by the slavers, and again when he'd escaped the plantation. This man . . . he had been there. He was responsible. A rage rumbled in Teyn's chest, but the icy fingers of fear locked it deep inside of him. The same fear that he had felt as a child. It was a helpless certainty that if he moved, if he was seen, then he would be locked away once more. So he watched, frozen in terror.

The slave hadn't heeded the warning. He fought with the restraint for a few moments, then abandoned it and tried to drag himself away. The slaver simply marched toward him, dispassionately drawing his blade with the same weary irritation of a shepherd about to deliver a motivating thump. With every motion, the anger burned hotter inside Teyn, boiling away more of the fear, and with it the reason and caution. His fingers dug into the soil, his lips curled back, and deep in his chest came a deep, grating growl.

The sound prompted an uneasy shuffle from the horse and drew a sudden cautious glance from the slaver. The realization that he had been heard briefly snapped sense into the malthrope and he managed to silence himself and creep a bit deeper among the bushes. The slaver took a half-step toward the thicket that concealed Teyn, but then thought better of it, turning back to his bounty and delivering a sharp blow with the base of the knife, dazing the struggling man. The slaver then drew a looped length of rope from his belt and pulled it tight around the wrists of his prisoner.

"You aren't worth tangling with a wild animal," he grumbled, hauling the slave from the ground. "Ugh. It is times like this I wish that idiot Latak didn't get himself killed. No brains, but he could tote dead weight well enough."

The captive slave was unceremoniously dumped across the back of the horse, and once a few straps had been secured, the slaver rode back from whence he came. For a moment Teyn simply watched, eyes focus intensely in the path through the woods that had brought the darkest part of his life rushing back to him. Then came a sharp tug at his collar, yanking him to his feet.

"What was that?" Sorrel hissed, slapping him in the back of the head. "Growling? Are you a child that cannot control himself?"

"I need to follow them."

"That is foolish. They were humans. You do not follow humans unless you want to get killed."

"I *need* to follow them," he repeated, finality resonating in his tone and iron resolve in his eyes.

He didn't know what he would have said if she asked him why.

There was no answer. He simply knew that this was something that had to be done. It was as though a piece of his mind had been patiently waiting for the slaver's arrival. Now that the time had come, that part of him would not be denied. Fortunately, he wasn't asked to explain it.

"Fine then. Let us go," Sorrel grumbled angrily.

"You don't have to come with me."

"I do if I want you back alive. I have seen that look before. That is the look of someone who stopped thinking here—" She tapped his head. "—and started thinking here." She tapped his chest. "It is the look you get before you do something stupid. Eyes like that see only what they are after, not the things that lie between. So I have to come, or you will walk off a cliff trying to get something on the other side. Let us go. We will do what you need to do. Just do not ask me to like it. And when you are through, when you do this thing, we will come back here, we will find the safe place, and we will talk about why this cannot happen again."

He nodded, drew in the scent, and followed the trail.

Compared to a herd of deer or a frightened rabbit, tracking a human on a horse was simplicity itself. Man was a beast unused to being hunted, except by other men. Thus, if he could not be seen, he believed he could not be followed. And so he would continue forward, his path straight and obvious. This man was no different. Even with a horse to speed his travels, the slaver may as well have been leading the way.

The journey took days, bringing them beyond the edge of the forest and well into the plains surrounding them. As they moved into the parts of the land that humans called home, Sorrel became increasingly uneasy. Small towns bustling with life and activity dotted the roadside, and soon it seemed that before one ended, the next began. The slaver traveled only during the day, forcing the malthropes to do the same, and before long there simply wasn't enough cover to conceal them. Any other time, Teyn would have eagerly turned back, retreating to the safety of the woods while Sorrel chided him for his nervousness. Not this time. Now the roles were reversed. The normally fearless Sorrel wanted to turn back, while Teyn wanted only to press on, to reach the end of the path. And so they spent days darting desperately through alleys and moving along the bases of walls.

The longer they traveled, the more obsessed Teyn became. Too often Sorrel had to catch him by the arm and haul him back, lest he be seen.

Finally, just as a driving rain began to fall, the slaver peeled off from the main road and approached a secluded valley. It was precisely the sort of place favored by those engaged in the more unsavory professions: easy to reach, hidden from view, easy to defend, and easy to escape. The entrance to the valley faced the plains and would certainly be under constant watch. There was an exit on the far side which might be easier to infiltrate, but without spending hours scouring the landscape, it was difficult to know how to access it. None of that mattered to Teyn, though. He didn't want to enter—he just wanted to see it with his own eyes, to hear it, to smell it. With his sharp senses, he could do all of that from afar, so long as the rain didn't get much worse.

He and Sorrel climbed the steep slope to the top of the valley, then crept low to the muddy stone until they reached a sharp drop-off that led down into the wide, low valley floor. Sorrel remained far from the edge, huddled in a leather cloak she'd drawn from her pack and keeping her eyes and ears open for danger. Teyn, wearing a matching cloak, slithered along the rain-slicked ground until his gaze fell upon the slave camp below.

His breathing quickened. It was all the same. The hastily-erected tents, the wheeled cages . . . all of the things that had haunted his dreams for so long, he'd forgotten they were real. He shuddered, the chill of the cold rain combining with raw, burning emotion. He focused, trying to hear past the patter of rain. Voices came in half-heard whispers: the name Dihsaad, a price, the name of a mine to the east.

He took a deep breath, sampling the air. Even in the rain he could smell the sweat, fear, and filth below. He could almost taste the swill they'd fed him, and feel the lash of the strap. Beside him, Sorrel had made her way to the edge and was staring with quiet disgust.

"No wonder they treat us the way they do. Look how they treat each other," she murmured. "Come. You've followed the man. You've seen what you came to see. Let us go. It is not safe here."

Teyn didn't answer. He was still staring at the slave camp below, but he was no longer seeing it. Deep inside his mind, all of the pieces were coming together: the distant uneasiness that plagued his mind, the certainty that he had a job to do that he'd been neglecting. He understood now. He knew what he had to do, what he should have been doing all along. He quietly stood tall and bold against the gray sky.

"Do not!" Sorrel gasped.

The words fell on deaf ears. With a step forward, he dropped off of the cliff's edge, catching his heels on the loose rocks and skidding down the slope like an archangel descending on a village of sin. This was not the madness of his dark day on the farm. This was something else. Something that had been missing from his life since that day. This was purpose. Voices rang out as he reached the ground, his hood billowing in the wind and his red fur drenched. Swords were drawn and bows readied, but none of the slavers had faced a foe able to move so quickly. He was little more than a blur to them as he dashed through the heart of the camp, charging for the man they called Dihsaad.

The space between he and Teyn, combined with the cries of warning from his fellow men, had given the slaver time enough to have his sword ready. He met the charging form of the malthrope with a slash. Teyn rolled beneath it and drove his shoulder hard into the man's stomach. The momentum was enough to lift the man from the ground, forcing the breath from his lungs with a guttural wheeze. A moment later man and malthrope tumbled to the ground. Teyn had no weapons but his claws and teeth. Scrambling atop the fallen man, he put them both to use. Unfortunately, the thick layers of leather armor were more than a match for them. He'd only just managed to open a hole in the defenses when a boot met his shoulder, knocking him sprawling to the ground.

Instantly, the whole of the camp seemed to be on top of him. Slavers too near to each other to put their blades to use chose instead to batter him with their fists. Others were more reckless, jabbing at him with swords, knives, and pikes. Teyn struggled, distantly aware of the attacks, but his only concern was that they would keep him from his task. If death would prevent him from doing what he had to do, then he must not die, not yet.

A lifetime of dodging attacks allowed him to shift away from or knock aside the deadliest of blows even while pinned to the ground. Finally a twist and roll managed to throw free enough of the men for him to slip out from beneath and spring back to his feet. He heard a blade swing, and he felt a tug at his cloak, but Dihsaad was still on the ground, and his sword was free from his hand and out of reach. Teyn swatted the hands of a man between him and his prey, managing to jar the blade from his fingers. With a deft snatch, Teyn plucked it from the air and continued his bounding sprint toward Dihsaad. Another dodge and three more strides brought him to target. The older man had rolled to his knees and was crawling for his weapon, but Teyn kicked him to his back again.

"Look at me!" he roared at the dizzied slaver. *"Look at me!"*

Dihsaad locked eyes with those gleaming from beneath the rough-hewn hood. When Teyn saw the look of fear and hate of a man staring into the eyes of a monster, he drew the blade in a quick swipe across the man's cheek, opening a gash.

"This is what you made of me," Teyn hissed, blade rising for a final blow.

He paused, eyes smoldering with hate. Never in his life had he wanted so badly to see a weapon meet its mark, to plunge the stolen blade hilt-deep into Dihsaad's chest. But deep inside him, a voice he'd been able to silence until now reminded him that he had felt this way once before. He'd felt this need in the moments before he lost control. Though he was driven by purpose now, the blood lust was straining against his will, screaming for him to take his revenge a hundred times over. Yes, he could take the life of the man who had taken his freedom, but what of the others? How much blood was he willing to have on his hands?

"Never again," he murmured, driving the blade into the ground beside Dihsaad's head with a single swift stroke and snatching up Dihsaad's sword instead.

There was a more important task to be done. He stood and bolted, dashing toward the nearest of the slave pens. The cages were cheaply built, little more than trimmed lengths of wood lashed to one another. Three quick slices managed to cut a crossbeam loose, and the cage began to buckle. It was more than the slaves inside needed to break free. A dozen men flooded out, and in the chaos Teyn managed to hack away at another cage, and another. When the last of them had been breached, he dashed for the mouth of the valley. The remaining slavers had their hands too full with the escapees to give chase.

The rain came down more heavily as Teyn fled the valley. With the intensity of the moment past, the consequences revealed themselves to him one by one. One eye was almost swollen shut already. Bruises and welts were forming everywhere his attackers had landed blows. There was a searing pain in the small of his back. He felt the warm trickle of blood from his nose. Worse, it was still day, and the rolling plains held no fewer than three roads, all heavy with traffic. He and Sorrel had made it this far only with extreme care, and even then only because no one suspected that there were malthropes about. Any one of those men could have seen him for what he was, and Dihsaad certainly had. They would be after him. They would raise the alarm. Soon the only place they could be certain that they would be safe would be deep in the Great Woods, in familiar territory with endless cover, but they were days away.

Panic burned his mind—and, mixed with the darkly familiar horror and shame conjured up by the sight of the blood he'd drawn, he hadn't wits enough to do anything but run. Ahead, he saw a carriage trundle out from behind a grassy hill. He skidded to a stop, eyes wild and breath heaving. He couldn't go back; the slavers would surely catch him. He couldn't go forward, or the people in the carriage would see. Before he could venture another thought, though, there was a rough tug at his arm.

He turned to see Sorrel dragging him desperately away from the road. The pair of malthropes scrambled a short distance through the roadside field until they reached a narrow brook, then followed it to where it met a side road. A simple wooden bridge spanned the water, and Sorrel and Teyn crawled into the dark, damp shadows beneath it.

Several tense minutes passed as the two sat, listened, and waited. Twice they heard the heavy wheels of a cart rattle the boards over their heads, and once the pounding hooves of a horse did the same. Then there was no sound but the drumming of rain against the planks.

When she was sure that the danger had passed, at least for the moment, Sorrel turned her attention to Teyn. He was a miserable sight. His fur was matted down with rain. Blood still dripped from his nose, and it had gathered at the swollen and split corner of his mouth. One hand was pressed to his side, blood leaking through his fingers from a blow that had sliced its way through his cloak and vest and carved a shallow gash along his side and lower back. The other hand held the grip of the stolen sword so tightly that it was shaking.

"Is it bad? Do you need anything? Anything that I can fix?" Sorrel asked, radiating concern and anxiety.

"I'm fine. It . . . it is nothing. Nothing serious," Teyn answered, pulling his hand from his back to find that the bleeding had nearly stopped.

"You are sure of this?"

"Yes."

"What is wrong with you!?" she barked, delivering a fresh smack to the head now that she knew he wasn't at death's door. "I warn you about stepping off a cliff, and you do that exact thing! Do you have any mind left at all?"

She dug through her pack and pulled out a rag. After dunking it in the brook, she began to dab at the many patches of blood that Teyn's assault on the camp had earned him. All the while, she muttered with increasing intensity in her native tongue. Despite the fact he'd learned quite a bit of her language, Sorrel had never stopped reverting to it when she wished to say something she didn't think he would want to hear. When the rag was saturated, she rinsed it and resumed her ministrations. It took nearly a dozen rinses before she seemed satisfied. She then passed the rag to him to hold to his back injury. Thus cleaned, he looked a good deal healthier. More than once, he'd returned from an ill-fated hunt in worse shape.

"Well? You have nothing to say? You just sit there?"

"It has to end," he stated, eyes turned low.

"Yes, it has to end. What you did today, it will make life hard for us. You cannot do that again!"

"No, I mean what we saw today. That camp. The things they do there. The reasons they do it. All of it. It has to end."

"This is madness what you are saying. This not our concern."

"It *is* my concern."

"There were no malthropes down there. Let the others fight their own battles. It has nothing to do with you. You need to think about yourself. About *us*. Worry about your own people."

"They *are* my people, Sorrel," he growled, throwing open his cloak and revealing the brand on his arm. "It has everything to do with me. You've never lived that life, you don't understand. Even *I* didn't understand until I learned what life was like out here. Imagine waking every morning, seeing a fence, and knowing that your world will never extend beyond it. Imagine spending the rest of your life in a place that you can walk from end to end in a few minutes. And imagine knowing that before the sun has set, you will have worked yourself to the bone in exchange for a meager meal and a night's respite before doing it all over again, day after day, until your body is ruined and they have no more use for you. Imagine that at any moment a strap or a whip could lash into you for being clumsy, or disobedient, or simply because the slave handler didn't like the way you looked at him. And all the while knowing that it can never be any other way, that there is no hope of anything better.

"Everything am I that I wish I was not, I owe to that place. All of my nightmares, every dark blot on my memory, every stain on my soul, every drop of blood on my hands was born in that place. If I am a monster, and I know that I am, then it is because that is what they made of me. And every day, those cages find new people to fill them. Every day, more people are thrown into that life. I can't allow it. I must stop it. Any way that I can."

"And what of the life of a malthrope? Running from humans always. Being hated by all for no reason. Is this life any better?"

"It is a terrible life, but at least it is a life! At least you can hope to find a place where you can be happy. Inside those walls, you aren't a living thing. You are a tool, a piece of equipment. Your grave is as good as dug the moment they press the brand to your arm."

"They are men. They deserve what they get."

"What you say about them is no different than what they say about us! We are the *same,* Sorrel. Neither of us may realize it, but humans and malthropes are just creatures, living in a world, doing what we believe we must, and hoping to see another day."

"If you do things like you did today, there will be little hope for *you* to see another day. What do you think? That if you can do this thing, what happened to you will be undone? Do you think that if you get killed doing this thing, then you will be redeemed for the things that you have done? You are what you are, Teyn. You cannot change the past."

"This isn't about the past. This is about the future. It is about what I can do to change things for the others. I can't just hide in the shadows and live for the sake of living, Sorrel. Life needs a purpose or there is no point in living it. This is mine. It is the reason I am here. And now that I realize it, there is *nothing* more important to me."

Sorrel's eyes narrowed and she pulled back, a hard expression on her face. "Nothing?"

Teyn's eyes widened as he realized his words. "I didn't mean that—"

"Stop, Teyn."

"We can do this together! We can—"

"*I said stop!*" she cried, for the moment forgetting that they were hiding. "I am asking you to forget this. This is a dangerous thing."

"You and I have done dangerous things before."

"That time is gone."

"Why?"

"Because it is, that is why. Listen. You need to choose, and you need to choose right now. Do you want to do this, or do you want to be with me?"

"Why do I have to choose? Why won't you tell me why you aren't willing to take this risk?"

"Because if something is important to you, you don't need to know the reason to make the choice. You don't need time, you don't need to think. Like that—" She clapped. "The choice is made. You did it when you saw that man and followed him to this place. Now I ask you to do it again. Choose this thing, whatever it is, or promise me that you will come with me and you will put this out of your mind forever."

"But—"

"No but, Teyn! If you do not make this promise then one day— maybe tomorrow, maybe in years—you will go, you will do this thing, and you will not come back. I will not give my tomorrow, I will not give my years, and I will not give my heart to a malthrope who would let that happen. Now promise me, Teyn."

He looked into her eyes. The resolve he saw in them dispelled any hope that her mind might be changed. He tried to will himself to say the words, to promise her that he could set this epiphany aside and return to the paradise that he had with her . . . but he couldn't. His mouth hung open, but he could not bring himself to say the words when he knew they weren't true, to make a promise he knew he couldn't keep.

"I understand."

"We can—"

"There is no we in this, Teyn." Her voice was shaking now. "If you want to spend your life doing this thing, that is fine. But do not expect me to do it with you, and do *not* expect me to watch while it kills you."

"But . . . but, Sorrel, I love—"

"Do not," she said, putting her fingers to his chin and pressing his mouth shut. "Do not say those words. Not anymore. Maybe you believe them. Maybe I do as well. Maybe even they are true, but it will be easier for us both if you do not say them now." She gathered her pack and cast a careful eye to the surroundings to see that the way was clear. When she was certain, she stood, tears running freely but her face steady as stone. "I hope you find peace one day, Teyn. And I hope you never learn the real price of your purpose. Do not try to follow me. Goodbye."

"Sorrel, don't go," he pleaded as she turned away. Her footsteps sped to a run. "Sorrel! *Sorrel!*"

Teyn gasped with pain as he fought to his feet and rushed out from under the bridge. All he saw was the back of her cloak as she disappeared over a rise and down into the field below. He tried to climb the bank of the brook, but his battered leg betrayed him and he stumbled. By the time he reached the crest of the same hill, she was gone.

He stood there for a long time, in the open and heedless of the pouring rain. He could follow. He could run after her for days, following her scent and tracking her footprints, but he knew it would be no use. Over the last two years, in those rare times that she'd decided she wanted to be alone, he'd never once been able to find her. If she wanted to disappear, she would disappear, and nothing he'd learned would lead him to her.

Even if he could, there was truth to her words. What he had resolved to do could very well mean his end. It was wrong to bring such a fate upon her as well. It was his purpose, not hers. The pain of his body fell away as the pain of his heart surged. It felt as though the foundation of his world had been torn away and he was tumbling downward into an uncertain darkness. Worse than the feeling of loss was how common such a feeling had been. His mother, Ben, and now Sorrel. Everyone he'd ever cared about . . . they were all gone.

But Sorrel was the first who had *chosen* to leave him, and that was what stung worst of all. She hadn't been taken . . . she had slipped through his fingers.

At the edge of his vision, he saw movement far along the road and managed to coax himself back under the bridge lest he be seen. He crumbled to the ground, tears brimming in his eyes, and looked aside. Among the river stones beside him was the rag she'd held just moments before she left. He picked it up and held it tight in his fist. To the other side lay the sword, blood staining the handle. He grasped that as well. For a time, he remained there. Hidden from the world. Alone with his thoughts.

As time passed and the day slid into night, the darkness crept into his mind as well. He thought back to those who had been taken, and those who had left. He thought back to the many times he'd endured this pain . . . and he resolved never to allow it to happen again. This was the last time he would be abandoned, left with a hole in his heart. If that meant hardening his soul, closing it to others, then so be it. The purpose was all that mattered.

After a final, reverent squeeze, he tucked the rag safely into his tunic and hauled himself to his feet. He slipped the blade into his belt and turned toward the nearest city. From this day forward, there was a job to be done.

Chapter 17

Now that he was alone again, there was no reason for Teyn to return to the Great Forest. It was safe there, but he was through being safe, and there was little he could do there to make any difference. Instead, he found his way to an old shack in a rough and overgrown patch of unworkable land at the edge of a cluster of farms. From the looks of them, neither the shack nor the path leading to it had been used for years. It still wasn't the best choice of shelter—humans had a way of reclaiming places like this without a moment's notice—but until he had healed some of his more troublesome injuries, it would have to do.

Keeping himself fed was tricky with so many towns and so few hunting grounds in the area, but he'd learned quite a bit from Sorrel when it came to "finding" things he needed among the humans. Local farmers lost a chicken or pig from time to time, and bakeries in nearby towns began to lose loaves of bread. He was careful not to prey upon any one place too often, and ate only what he needed to survive. His attack on the slave camp had no doubt put the fear of malthropes into the area, and he could not afford to have the locals suspect that there was one hiding nearby.

While he nursed his wounds, he tried to develop the skills he would need to achieve his goals. It was humans and those like them who seemed to control the plantations and the slave trade, so if he wished to end the slave trade, he would need to be among them. He would need to learn from them. Each time he ventured into the towns to scrape together a meal, he lingered longer, opening his ears and learning the dark corners and unwatched areas that would hide him from prying eyes.

Taverns and inns were valuable sources of information. People gathered there and spoke freely about anything and everything that had happened in their world. He trained his ears to follow conversations, listening closer to voices that sounded hushed or anxious. Those who spoke loudly seemed as often as not to be boasting or lying, telling stories to impress their friends and entice the affections of others. The truth always seemed to come in whispers.

While information was easy enough to come by, hiding places

were much trickier. Back alleys seemed, at first, to be the best choice, but the fact of the matter was that only the largest of the towns in the area had them, and too often they were already occupied by townsfolk engaged in dealings of their own that were best kept from prying eyes. Once his injuries had improved enough to permit it, he found that rooftops were a much better choice. People very seldom thought to glance upward when seeking out the source of an unexpected sound, and the poorly tanned hide of his cloak was a close match for the color of the thatch that made up most roofs in the region. If he moved with care and chose carefully, he could spend the whole of the night along the roofs of a village without turning a single head.

The most stubborn of his wounds, the slash to his side, had finally been reduced to a dull soreness by the time he was comfortable abandoning his adopted home. He'd taken to moving from place to place, scouting out a safe shelter to spend the day and sneaking into the cities at night. Though he'd believed he was choosing the cities to target at random, he realized in time that, without being aware of it, he was following a scent. Through some instinct or perhaps simple fate, he'd found the weak and lingering scent of the man he'd injured, the man called Dihsaad. Since then, he had been working his way along the path forged by the scent. Each day it grew a bit stronger. Here, he found the inn where Dihsaad must have spent the night not long ago. There, he found a market at which he must have lingered.

Teyn couldn't explain why, but something compelled him to find the slaver again. Perhaps he felt if he knew how the slavers moved, where they went, he would be better equipped to combat them. Or perhaps it was because it had been Dihsaad who had drawn him out of the safety of the Great Forest and revealed to him his purpose, and thus in finding him again the next step might reveal itself. Or perhaps it was just the darkest part of him urging him forward, eager for a second chance to take the life that had been spared.

After a few weeks Teyn found himself at the northern edge of the smaller of Tressor's two deserts, the Makaat Oduun. There was a chill to the air now. This far south, the mild nippiness to the breeze at sundown was as near as Tressor came to feeling the bite of winter. As the plains gave way to dusty scrublands; the thatched roofs had steadily shifted to mounded and sculpted curves of red clay. At first, he'd been concerned that he would not be able to blend himself with the bright red masonry, but after a few strong gusts of wind, anyone outside was coated with a layer of the same red dust, stirred up from the parched ground. It was reason enough for the people of the area to move quickly, keeping their heads down and eagerly rushing indoors to get out of the dust and wind. It was thus even simpler to escape notice here, and he was able to spend a good deal more time listening and less time watching and worrying. It meant that he could devote more time to tracking Dihsaad, until it was not his scent but his voice that Teyn was following.

Currently, the malthrope was nestled in the crook of an oddly-shaped roof. Below him, the patrons of a tavern they called The Last Makaat Oasis were washing the dust from their throats with a strong-smelling drink that Teyn could not identify. The scent reminded him of Gurruk's concoction from his plantation days, but not quite to the same nostril-burning intensity. The customers called it "bahk," and drank it by the pitcher. Apparently Dihsaad was a regular here, and he was having more of the potent beverage than he usually did. Teyn knew this because the tavern keeper had started up a conversation that had already become so familiar, the malthrope was beginning to wonder if each such man had received the same training.

"That's your fourth tankard," came the standard line, "something troubling you?"

Dihsaad made a sound of disgust. "Where do I start?"

"Something go wrong?"

"Everything."

"How so?"

Dihsaad grumbled. "A few weeks back. I was attacked. That's where I got this nice little slice on the cheek. The scoundrel released a fortune's worth of slaves."

"It was *you* that got attacked? Word's been getting around about something like that. I've been hearing some strange tales about what happened."

"Doesn't surprise me. I've heard a dozen different stories from my own men. Half of them insist it was some sort of demon. Ten feet tall. Strength of three men. Moved faster than you could blink. Complete rubbish. They think it came down from the sky, and went straight for me. They say it was like a ghost, swords and clubs passing through it without any effect."

"Not the way you remember it?"

"The thing took a few lumps. One of us drew blood. It was no demon. I looked it dead in the eyes. Trust me. It was a creature of this world."

"If you looked it in the eye, you must know what it was."

Teyn held his breath.

"It was . . ." Dihsaad began, pausing as if he didn't like what his mind was telling him to say next. "I was meant to *think* it was a mally."

"How's that? Meant to think it was a mally?" the bartender said with confusion.

"It had a muzzle, like one of those blasted beasts . . . but it was too big. Yes, too big to be a *real* mally. And the muzzle was red, but it was dripping. Could have been paint dripping off it, or maybe blood . . . anyway, it caught me by surprise. Got me down. It carved my cheek up, and it said to me, 'Never again.' Then it stuck the knife in the ground and left me there."

"If it looked like a mally, it was a mally."

"Couldn't have been a mally," Dihsaad insisted.

"Why not?"

"I faced down plenty of mallies in my day. I used to hunt the cursed things. A mally never could have got me down like that. You ever hear of a mally that could beat a man in a fair fight? And not just against me, but against a whole slave camp? Not likely. And even if it did make it through the camp and straight to me, have you *ever* heard of a mally who would pass up a chance to kill a man?"

"You can never be too sure with those things. Sometimes they get wrapped up in dark magic and the like. Remember that story they tell about that farm back east."

"Which one is that?"

"Oh, you must have heard it. This is years ago. Rakka plantation."

"Doesn't sound familiar."

"Let's see . . . been a while since I heard it . . . it was a place that made those seeds the soldiers carry. Used to do a good job of it, but then something happened, new owners or some such. Place went bad awful quick. People say he made some deals he shouldn't have, trying to scrape things back together. Guess one of them came due. One day, everything is just as it had been for years, the next—" There was a snap. "Dead. The owner. The owner's family. The slave-drivers. Everyone. 'Cept for a little boy, screaming about a monster doing the deed. Everyone figured the kid was seeing things, but then the slaves

216

started to pop up. Seems whatever it was that did the killing, it had left the slaves alone. As each one got caught, they all told their own stories about what happened. Some of them said it was a mally that the owner kept."

"The owner kept a mally? What, as a pet? Feh. That'll be the reason his farm died out. Those things will bring a curse upon your land. Who ever heard of a mally as a slave . . ." Dihsaad's voice trailed off. A moment later he began to mutter, so quietly, Teyn had to strain to hear it. "Mally slave . . . rakka farm . . ."

"What's that now?" the tender asked.

"Nothing. Nothing. No. You listen to me, I know a mally couldn't have done what happened to me, and I know that it couldn't have done what you said happened on that farm. Mallies are cowards. No such thing as a fair fight for one of them. They only stab you in the back, or in your sleep. I hear they'll turn tail and run if you stare 'em in the eye. And I stared this thing down. But you say this thing let those slaves go? And it let mine go. We could just be dealing with the same scoundrel. He said 'Never again' . . . I'll bet you, I'll just *bet* you that it is another slaver. Or someone working for him. I've got quite a reputation. Made my share of enemies. I'll bet someone with deep pockets, someone looking to be the only slave trader around, sent him in to shut me down. Disguised himself as a mally to do it, to keep people guessing."

"I suppose that's one explanation."

"Well, they're going to get their wish. I've had it. Watching those idiots at the camp rounding up those slaves he let out was reason enough to call it quits. It took them *weeks* to fetch them all. If someone out there has the money to hire a blade to play dress-up and warn me never to track another slave, then so be it. I'm through! Now, you going to stand there all day spinning yarns, or are you going to pour me another?"

The conversation continued, but Teyn had heard enough. He'd heard too much. Eyes shut and fists tightened, he let the voices recede into the general din and struggled with what they'd taught him. The slaves he'd freed had been caught, and those who had shared his suffering under Marret had been caught again as well. Nothing he'd done had mattered. Blood had been spilled, lives had been taken, and for nothing. It wouldn't be enough to simply release the slaves.

If he wanted to free them, to truly free them, he would have to find another way.

217

He'd also learned that a man would rather deny his own eyes than admit that he might have been beaten—or, worse, he might have been shown *mercy* by a malthrope. It was a valuable lesson, but it couldn't take the sting from the other things he'd learned.

When he was certain there was no one to see, he leapt down from the roof and made his way into the moonlit dunes to find a meal and collect his thoughts.

#

Weeks more passed, and he traced a crooked path along the roads and fields of Tressor. If his mind had not been turned so dutifully to his task, he might have marveled at the sheer variety of the human race. They had found a way to live in any setting. Deep in the desert there were tribes of nomads, their homes little more than coarse cloth lashed to light wooden poles. There were homes of clay, of stone, of wood— anything that could be found and coaxed into the right shape. Where there was good soil, there were farmers. Where there was precious stone or ore, there were mines.

Eventually, he found his way to the west coast, where he stared toward the sunset across the waves of a sea that seemed to have no end and watched fishing boats harvest the waters. It was almost difficult to believe that so many different paths could be taken by the same race of creatures. Dark-skinned, light-skinned, every shape, every size. And among them mixed the other races, the races most like them. Malthropes with their beastly features were shunned, but for those creatures who were merely taller or shorter, with pointed ears or scraggly beards, a place was made for them.

He breathed in a whiff of the salty air, smelling the hundreds of humans, elves and . . . dwarves. He sniffed again, now certain. There was a familiar scent, one he'd known all of his life. For once, curiosity got the better of him and he set off in the direction the scent led him.

The port town was different than most that he'd encountered in his travels. Most Tresson villages were small, or else they began and ended slowly with houses spreading thinner and thinner as one moved away from their centers. This was a sprawling, bustling place. The streets were paved with cut stone and the houses were pressed close to one another. Though he could not read the sign he passed upon entering, the people seemed to call it Sarrin. It was a crowded, active place even late into the night, and some of the buildings were three or four stories tall, making traveling by roof both a trickier and less reliable proposition. Still, he did his best, slipping into alleys and over fences when he had to, and across roofs when he could, always moving closer to the source of the familiar scent.

Eventually, the trail led him to the shore. Stretching far into the water was a narrow pier, and sitting at the very end of it was a single-room shack.

Teyn scanned his surroundings from the shadowy mouth of the last alley before the shore. A handful of people were still lingering on the docks. There were not many, but more than enough to spot him if he made a wrong move. The pier was wide enough for perhaps two people to walk side by side, and years of sea air had warped and curled the planks. Any one of them would likely sing like a nightingale if he stepped on it. Even if he managed to move silently, he would still be a lone form, obvious and clear. It was the only way to the shack, though, and he refused to come so close without finding out if what he smelled was real. His mind offered up only one possibility, and he reluctantly prepared to put it into action. He tied his hide cloak tight around his neck, pulling the hood as far forward as he could manage. Hunching down, he shouldered his pack and lowered his head. All that remained was to wait. When the moon was hidden behind a cloud, he knew it was time. He took a deep breath and walked out from the alley.

Instantly, he felt the burning sensation of discovery and exposure, as though a thousand eyes were turned to him. The night was dark, but not so dark that a keen eye wouldn't pick out the end of a foxy snout peeking out from the hood. He had to stride steadily and confidently, as though he belonged on that pier, and pray that those who noticed him wouldn't give a second look. The dozen or so paces across the road that ran along the shore were the longest he'd taken in his life. He'd done his best to pick his moment—but, as luck would have it, a tipsy couple had chosen the same moment to stumble out of pub a short distance away. He turned his head away from them, keeping his pace steady and doing his best to appear as though he had someplace very important to be.

"Ho there!" came the slurred call of the man, his woman giggling and hanging from his neck as though she would fall if she let go.

Teyn froze, fear cutting through him. There was no doubt that the words were directed at him. Swallowing hard, he grunted a vague response without looking.

"My darling Greta has a taste for something sweet. You wouldn't know a place with something that would suit her craving at this late hour, would you?" he asked, amid more giggles.

The malthrope sampled the air again. Amid the potent mix of seaside aromas was the scent of burnt sugar, the sort of smell that he would catch drifting from the windows of Jarrad's house on the evenings of holidays and feasts. A glance aside revealed the lantern-lit doorway of a tavern a short distance away. Still without turning, he raised his hand and pointed, silently thanking his foresight in acquiring gloves.

"There."

"Ah! Many thanks to you, good sir, and good night on this . . . good . . . night," came the reply in the best imitation of gentlemanly eloquence the inebriated young man could manage.

The pair wavered away. Teyn breathed a sigh of relief and stepped out onto the pier. Sure enough, it was as shaky as he'd feared, swaying slightly with the motion of the water. Each step had to be taken with care to avoid a chirping squeak that would draw the attention of anyone near. After too long, his laborious and meticulous journey reached the door of the shack. The scent was strong and clear, and a dim light was flickering through the cracks of the weathered and rotten shack. Teyn stood at the door, not certain what he'd hoped to accomplish by coming this far. There had only been two people he'd ever known who would have welcomed him. One was dead, and the other had left him. This could only end poorly . . . but it had to be done.

He rapped on the door. From inside, there was a stirring. Thumps and rattles rang out for a few moments, and finally the door opened. Before him stood the dwarf named Gurruk. One of the stout fellow's hands held the door's handle, more to steady the dwarf than to steady the door. The other hand was wrapped around a clay jug, a match for three more that lay discarded on the floor of the shack. He gazed up, red-rimmed eyes measuring up the figure before him and lingering for a moment on the fox face that stared uncertainly down at him. The expression on his face, one of weary irritation, didn't so much as flicker. Finally, he took a long, sloppy swig from his bottle, wiped his mouth, and spoke.

"Well, come in then," he stated, as though the visit was an unwanted but not unexpected inconvenience.

Teyn quietly stepped inside, closing the door behind him. The shack was almost bare and horribly cramped. There was scarcely room for the two of them to stand, and the only furniture was a net hammock strung from two of the walls and a plank shelf nailed beside one end of it. The floor had a few meals' worth of bones and what for another person might have been several weeks' worth of liquor bottles. For Gurruk, it was probably just a few days. The dwarf heaved himself up onto the hammock, using the sling as a seat.

"Gurruk," Teyn said.

"Mally," he replied. He took another swig. "I suppose you're here to kill me then."

"No . . . no, of course not."

He shrugged. "You killed everybody else. Never did know if it was out of mercy or carelessness that you spared the slaves. Should have known it wasn't carelessness. You always struck me as the thorough type. Why are you here, then?"

"I found this town and I picked up your scent. I needed to see if you were really here."

"Why?"

"Because I had heard that the other slaves had all been caught."

He nodded again. "Most were. Goldie and I stuck together. Menri, too, for a while."

"Are you on the run? A fugitive?"

"No, I'm a dock worker. I'm not much of a runner if I can avoid it."

"But how? How have you managed to avoid getting caught? Surely one look at the brand on your arm . . ."

"What brand is that?" he said, pulling up the ratty sleeve of his shirt to show the slightest of scars where once had been the brands of value and ownership.

"But how?" Teyn asked.

"A decent healer can get rid of a few scars. It isn't legal to take off a slave's brand, but it isn't hard to convince a reasonable businessman to forget that."

"How did you do that?"

"Same way I got the bounty hunters to look the other way. Gold. It greases the wheels, greases the palms, and makes the sun rise and set. Why do you think my brethren spend so much time in the cold, dark ground looking for it?"

Teyn's eyes opened wide. Of course. It was so simple. Gold. It was the one thing that every gathering of humans seemed to share. Whether they were fishing, cutting down trees, hunting, farming, mining, or

221

anything else, gold was always part of it. It was the way slaves changed hands. If a slave could be bought to work, then surely the same price could buy his freedom.

"How did you get your gold?"

"I didn't. Goldie did. Turns out the skinny devil wasn't a complete liar when he said he was from an important family. I wouldn't call him a favored son, and I wouldn't say they were exactly noble, but when he needed money, he got it. He spends his days on the east coast now, running ships between Delti and . . . that town on South Crescent . . . Qualia. Smuggles people and goods. Like I said, not a noble family. Menri's further north. Heh. I heard he got himself started with a farm of his own near Bellarah."

Teyn considered the words for a time while Gurruk drained the bottle. When he was convinced he'd gotten the last drop from it, he dropped it to the ground with the rest, causing a clink and rattle that jangled the nerves of the malthrope. He'd been taking care to be silent for so long, the thought that someone could be so careless and not worry about it was jarring.

"It is lucky you chose tonight to pay a visit. You might not believe it, but I don't do a lot of drinking these days. Spend a lot of time on the ships. Fell in the water a few times. Strong drink doesn't do much for the sea legs. Today's the day I get paid and get my days off, so today's the day I do my drinking. If I wasn't in such high spirits, you probably wouldn't have got past the door. I can't say I was keen to see your face again. I'd rather not see anybody's face from those days, but yours least of all. I see it enough in my nightmares." He shuddered and fished around to see if any of the discarded bottles had anything left in them. "The things you did . . ."

"I know."

"But still . . . the things *they* did. When Goldie and me got out, when we were hiding and waiting for the money so we could clean ourselves up . . . we talked about it. All of it. And for maybe the first time, we agreed about something. He said he saw it start. He saw them kill the old blind man and set you off. And he said that if those boys had their way, if they'd been given the chance, they'd have done as much to all of us. It wasn't like under Jarrad. *Bartner*—he'd have killed us and he'd have smiled doing it. You saved our lives that day. Even the ones who got caught again. There isn't a farm or mine or quarry in all of Tressor that wouldn't be an improvement over that place. Even the war with the Nameless Empire would be better. At least on the front, death's coming from a man who believes he's killing for a good reason.

"You did a dark thing, Mally, but you did a dark thing that needed doing. And I owe you a debt for that. I know Goldie would say the same. Menri, too." He wavered slightly and emitted a worrying sound from deep in his gut. "But I'm in no condition to pay any debts tonight. And I won't be tomorrow either. You get what you came for?"

Teyn nodded slowly.

"Good. I see you once more, you ask for something, you get it. After that?" He paused, as if in thought. "Just don't let me see you after that, understand?"

Again the malthrope nodded.

"Good. I'm done for the night. Close the door behind you."

With that, the scraggly little fellow more or less collapsed back into the hammock. Before Teyn had made it out the door, a snore loud enough to rattle the planks of the pier was rumbling out.

#

Knowing how he could achieve his goal did little to bring it any closer to completion. Teyn had never in his life had the need or desire for gold or silver. He had no idea how to gather it, and likewise hadn't a clue how much he would need. Worse, as Sorrel had so frequently observed, there was no legitimate way for him to earn a living in human society, and despite his recent travels he had yet to find any settlements of his own kind. Knowing how to craft the odd bit of clothing or perform simple repairs may have been more than enough for a human to earn a living, but no customer would buy from a monster, and no employer would hire one.

If he could not earn money the proper way, then his only recourse seemed to be to employ Sorrel's method. Alas, while he was quite adept at getting from here to there without being seen, locked doors were another matter. Worse, he simply didn't have her knack for finding valuables. Food was easy—he could just use his nose—but jewelry and coins could be hidden anywhere.

A few nights of observation taught him where the townsfolk tended to stow the things they didn't want stolen, but a week of attempting to pluck them from the pockets of passersby or pry open strongboxes led to near-discovery twice a night, at least once resulting in a long chase by an angry merchant with a very fast horse. In the end, the fruits of his labors were a copper necklace he wouldn't be able to sell and a handful of coins. In time he might develop some sort of aptitude for thievery, but without a mentor, he was left at the whims of trial and error, and the mistakes were costly. Until he could find a better way, all he could do was keep at it and hope that he learned quickly.

It didn't take long for him to learn that larger cities were better targets than smaller ones—but, just as in the forest, more prey meant more predators. He was hardly the only would-be thief prowling the dark corners, and most of the others were far more skilled. That was fine. If he needed to learn, let him learn from them. His ears were sharp, his eyes were keen, and he was patient. The rest would come in time.

Some lessons were of no use to him. Many hours were spent crouched on a roof, listening to sly men and women approach strangers and lull them into a state of trust or pity. Sometimes they would be friendly, helpful to those visiting from other towns. Other times they would be pathetic, fallen upon hard times. When two or more worked together, complex vignettes unfolded. Perhaps one thief would play the role of a fellow out-of-towner, behaving in a way the scoundrels hoped the victim would imitate. Other times, one thief would make a blatant and intimidating attempt to rob someone, allowing his partner to come to the rescue. Vast, well-orchestrated schemes played out, always to gain the trust or earn the gratitude of their chosen prey, only to abuse it and disappear into the night. These games were stunningly effective, and genuinely fascinating. Seeing how quickly the thieves determined just the sort of person that their target would trust, and just how simple it was to prey upon that trust, was humbling. He even began to understand the signs and habits that the thieves watched for, and how to identify them himself. Without a face someone could trust though, none of those tactics would do him any good.

More useful were the little tricks and skills employed by the criminals who worked alone. By watching them, he learned how they spotted a likely target. He observed clever acts of misdirection: a tossed pebble drawing the attention of a target to open them for a grab, or choosing a less-likely hiding spot to strike when the target investigated the more likely one. When the target was a house or shop, he saw robbers slip hooks and string over the top of a window or door to snag and lift a brace. He saw locked gates lifted from hinges, loose bars twisted free of their mountings, and unguarded upper windows used to bypass well-blocked lower ones.

After a bit of observation in any given town, he knew who the thieves were, where they hid, and how they worked. Still, he couldn't seem to master their own methods for himself. Here and there, he had successes, but too many failures and it was no longer safe for him to stay in the town, forcing the process to begin anew elsewhere. Lingering in the back of his mind was the concern of just how he would put the money to use when he'd earned it, but he knew if he didn't focus on the first step, he would never reach the next. So he soldiered on.

Finally, he struck upon a solution. He could only do half of what the other thieves did, and he could only do it half as well as they, but he could shadow them flawlessly. Inevitably, they would make their way to an out-of-the-way den or wilderness cubbyhole to stow their earnings. Most of them were painstakingly hidden, but almost without fail they were a target far enough from prying eyes for Teyn to attempt to pilfer them. There was something about stealing from thieves that was soothing to his battered conscience, and thus it quickly became his favored method.

Chapter 18

One particularly chilly night, Teyn was perched in the trees a night's journey away from a rather notable town. He'd never bothered to learn the name of the place because it was far too grand and too crowded for him to consider remaining there, but the sheer spectacle was impressive, even to his untrained eye. It was sprawling, every bit as densely built as the coastal city of Sarrin, but far from the coast and much larger. The bulk of the city was hidden behind a wall. It was not the meager wooden fence that might surround a farm, or the rough stone wall that might surround a wealthy lord's land. This wall was a work of art, many stories tall, its surface smoothed with some sort of tan plaster or mortar such that it appeared to be carved from one massive stone. There was even the faded blue evidence of fine patterns painted along its top edge, where curved and sculpted battlements now and again revealed archers patrolling its catwalk.

Three large gates stood nearly twice the height of the rest of the wall, heavy wood and metal gates hoisted high within their towering arches. At the center of the city within was a single building easily the match in size for some of the villages he'd visited. It was a castle, two small towers standing on either side of one massive one, each square in shape and reaching high into the air. The tops of the tower walls tapered together in a smooth curve, meeting in a pointed spire that bore a waving flag.

Teyn was watching a trio of thieves divide up their night's haul, after having followed them as they worked their way away from the cities walls. It was instantly clear upon first spotting them that these three were trouble. Some of the pickpockets and scofflaws he'd watched were careful not to alert their victims, let alone hurt them. Not so for the ones chuckling and counting out shares below him. Two of them were men, the sort of burly masses of hair and muscle that tended to be found hauling heavy loads from one end of a town to another for a living.

The other one was a woman dressed in clothes revealing enough to provide all of the distraction the group ever needed. Night after night, the woman would lure an unsuspecting man out into the wilderness,

226

where her two accomplices would beat him to within an inch of his life and take all that he had, threatening to finish the job if he ever told how he got his injuries. It was a detestable thing to watch, and Teyn knew that these were tactics he would never put to use. The looks in their eyes as they descended upon the hapless victim, the unmasked glee and shameless reveling, brought back visions of Bartner and his ilk. It boiled his blood. The sooner he could take their ill-gotten gains and be done with them, the better.

After striking four victims along the roadside, the group gathered at a thicket of trees and shrubs far enough from the road to keep their fire from being spotted. Their cackling and bragging to one another about the night's haul was boisterous enough that they didn't notice the crunch of dry grass just beyond the fire's light, nor did their eyes turn to the five forms approaching on horseback. Teyn skillfully retreated to a higher branch, unsure of what would come next and unwilling to be caught in the crossfire, should there be any. The figures drew closer, spreading until they surrounded the still oblivious brigands. One horseman stopped at the trunk of the tree below him. His equipment was much like that of Dihsaad: light armor and a full complement of nets, ropes, and snares. He slowly readied a rope net, weighted at the edges and large enough to capture all three of the outlaws if well thrown.

Perhaps sensing that something was wrong, the banter among the thieves tapered off. One by one, they turned their eyes away from the fire, scanning the darkness. Before time enough had passed for their eyes to adjust, chaos erupted. A net was heaved, instantly entangling the woman and the larger of the men. The remaining thief bolted, but two horsemen cut off his path, each twirling a rope with a weighted end. He tried to turn and run in the opposite direction, but one of the horsemen released the rope in a long low arc, entangling his leg and sending him to the ground. Two horsemen dismounted, and restrained the first two criminals; two more restrained the third. In the space of a minute, the unlawful trio had been gone from smiling and preening about how clever their scheme was to spitting profanities and threats while they were dragged behind their captors.

Fascinated, Teyn dropped down from the tree when it was safe to do so, gathered what coins and valuables had been spilled during the scuffle, and followed. The men looked and acted like slave-trackers, but these three had certainly not been slaves. The five horsemen made their way toward the town, one stopping to scoop the woman from the ground and throw her across the back of his horse, while the men were dragged a good deal longer when it was clear the fight had not gone out of them yet.

When they reached the outskirts of the city, they followed a curving road around its walls until they reached one of the well-fortified gates. They passed through and approached a small courtyard with a lower wall made of the same stone, as though it was just a looping outcrop of the main wall. In his first sweep of the town, Teyn had spent little time there. The streets around it had no thieves of any sort, and the men within the walls were well-armed and vigilant. It had simply been wisest to stay away.

"Well, if it isn't my favorite rat catchers," piped a portly and particularly sunbaked fellow. He had a carefully cropped beard that tapered along its length, making the second of his two chins seem even larger. A round hat of stiff red cloth was held on his head by a thin tan strip that wrapped tight around its base. He wore mail made with large, thick rings, and layered on top of it was a red tunic with a tan swath that began at his shoulders and narrowed a bit as it drew tight over his belly. At his belt was a simple wooden cudgel on one side and sword with a curved blade on the other. It was one of the uniforms that always seemed to be worn by the best-armed of the townspeople, and Teyn had supposed that it belonged to the "watch" that pickpockets and the like always seemed worried about. "What have we got today?"

"The roadside bandits," answered the lead horseman. "Alive and mostly unharmed."

This final claim prompted a fresh smattering of harsh language from the captives, but seeing the watchman put his hand to the grip of the cudgel was enough to silence them. The watchman then paced to a sign board beside the gate of the short wall and looked over one of the postings, a coarse bit of paper scrawled with the complex and flowing script of Tressor. He glanced from the page to the captives a few times, then nodded.

"Near enough to the description to satisfy me," the watchman said. He gave a sharp whistle and spoke, raising his voice enough to be heard through the walls of the watch house. "Three to go in, and . . ." He checked the posting again. "One hundred and fifty entus."

A trio of younger, thinner watchmen in less impressive uniforms scurried out and dragged the captured thieves inside. A moment later a jingling sack was brought out and presented. At the sight of it, Teyn's eyes widened. Even if it was filled with copper, it represented nearly as much as he'd been able to gather since he'd begun collecting money—but it was silver. The pieces fell together in his mind. Bounty hunters hunted anyone who was free but should not be—not just slaves, but criminals as well, and they were rewarded handsomely to do it. This! This was how he would earn his gold. He already knew the face and scent of every criminal in each of a dozen towns, and if there was one thing he could do better than any human, it was track down a target.

"A bit late for you, isn't it?" asked one of the horsemen.

"Our night man is sick," the watchman explained with a scowl.

"Anything new you can tell us about other folks you're after?"

"You know the way it goes, boys. New bounties get announced at sunrise. No one gets advance knowledge. The patriarch thanks you for your service," the watchman replied wearily. "Now off with you!"

Teyn heeded the request along with the horseman. Sunrise would come before long, and there were preparations to make . . .

When sunrise came, Teyn managed to find an unseen place among the buildings beside the watch house and trained his ears and eyes on the door. Before long, a small crowd began to form. All told, there were less than a dozen of them, including the five from the previous night. Each new member of the gathering nodded in recognition of the others, clearly familiar with one another from countless mornings such as this. All but two of them were men, and every last one of them exuded the same aura of intimidation. Though not fully armed or armored, each had at least one weapon conspicuously at his or her belt. They eyed each other and their surroundings with measured looks, checking for danger or disrespect, and traded stories of their recent exploits.

These were not heroes. There was no sense of honor or duty to them. They were predators, like Teyn, hunters who had chosen a very special sort of prey.

After a few more minutes of waiting, the portly watchman who had dealt with the bounty the night before stepped out into the courtyard of the watch house and rattled a heavy and weathered copper bell that hung from a stand by the door.

"Step forward, step forward!" he bellowed with a sing-song cadence. "By decree of the noble patriarch of the city of Gallishasa,

229

the following men and women have violated the laws of this land and are to be brought to this watch house alive to receive their punishment."

The whole of the speech was delivered with the sort of mechanical, flavorless tone of a man who had uttered the words so many times that they had lost their meaning.

"For the crime of theft, Bultim of Denith. Brown eyes, black hair, dark skin, average height and build. He has got a scar over his left eye. Last seen near Denith. Bounty of twenty-five entus. Next, for the crime of murder . . ."

And so the list went on, one by one listing off the scoundrels who littered the streets and describing what little was known about them. Crimes like murder fetched high prices, and crimes like treason higher still. After the list of those to be brought in alive was a list of those who could be brought in alive or dead, and, finally, those to be killed in sight.

". . . and, of course, blue-suits and mallies."

The final words—"blue-suits and mallies"—were delivered in the obligatory manner of a thing that should go without saying. They'd almost been blurred into a single word. Teyn had to dig deep into unpleasant memories of his youth to recall precisely what was meant by blue-suits. Finally, it dawned on him. That's what Marret had called soldiers of the Nameless Empire.

In a way, it was almost comforting to know that there was another sort of person—a *human*—out there who shared the same level of open disdain that malthropes did.

Once the group had broken up, Teyn made his way unseen out of the city walls. The descriptions the man had given were not very helpful. They could have applied to half of the humans he'd seen that morning, but a few of the details were familiar. Combined with the accused crimes and the last location, he was reasonably certain he knew where at least three of the bounties could be found. All he had to do was get close enough to catch a familiar scent and there would be no escaping him. Finding them would be simple. As for the rest? He would soon find out.

A short sprint took him to a cluster of tall weeds beside a dried-up stream. Among them was a leather bundle he'd been storing there. Traveling among the humans was dangerous enough without being weighed down by extra equipment, so he always found a place to stash his things before venturing someplace risky. Inside the bundle was the meager but growing collection of coins and trinkets he'd accumulated, the tools he kept, the rest of his clothes, and the pair of objects he'd managed to prepare in the hours before sunrise. The first was a simple cloth sack with a string to cinch tight around the opening.

The other was the visor of an old helmet he had found. It was the sort he'd seen worn by soldiers heading north to battle, an odd cone of metal that stuck out like a beak from a faceplate with slits to allow him to see and breathe. A bit of hammering had reshaped it such that he could *just* wedge his muzzle into it. The result was uncomfortable and locked his mouth shut such that any speech would be through clenched teeth, but combined with the deep hood of his cloak it might just be enough to convince a human that he was one of them for a single glance. That would be enough. He had no intentions of lingering long enough for a second look.

A length of rope and a knife completed the equipment for the hunt. The rest was returned to its hiding place, and he was off.

The trip to the town that hid his prey was a long one. At his best, he could match the speed a man on horseback preferred to travel, but it was enormously taxing, and life in and around the cities had not been doing him good. There was never much in the way of hunting, and the farms and such he preferred to prey upon were all too far away. He'd been living on the meager scraps he could steal from the shops or scrounge from the trash, and it showed. Like so many other times in his life, though, he closed his mind to the hunger and pain, forcing it aside and focusing on the task. If he could not move faster, he would simply stay at it longer.

All through the night he traveled, and long into the day. He slept sparingly, and only when travel carried too high a risk of being seen.

In time, he found himself in the "town" of Rell. It was a simple little cluster of buildings—a tavern, a place of worship, and a market. In the capital, it would have been little more than a forgotten street corner, but here in the country, it provided the bare minimum that the locals needed. A similar crossroads could be found at the center of dozens of such communities across the landscape, each proudly bearing a sign post informing passersby of where they were and where the next such place could be found.

Long before reaching the town center, Teyn had picked up the scent of his quarry. Perhaps the man was not aware that he had been marked for capture, or perhaps he didn't care, because he had taken no precautions to hide himself. He was sitting out in the open, reclined in one of the wood and canvas chairs set up outside the tavern, not seeming to have a care in the world. Teyn found a safe place to lie low among the roadside weeds and kept an eye on him. The sun was still high in the sky, and the man was too exposed for Teyn to strike, so the malthrope was left with time to consider how it was possible that this man could be behaving as he was. The price on his head had been measured in gold, whereas the other bounties were all in silver entus. As far as Teyn could tell, none of the other hunters had come for this man, despite the fact that for a mounted bounty hunter he wasn't more than a few days from the capital, Gallishasa.

The concern fluttered across his mind that he may have tracked the wrong man. One by one, he pulled to mind the descriptions. A gold ring with an opal. A tattoo of thorn vine wrapped around his right wrist. The little finger of his left hand missing the last knuckle. This was certainly the man, someone who the watchman had called "Duule of Sarrin." Finally, Teyn shook the concerns away. It had become clear that trying to figure out the workings of the human mind was far beyond him.

The hours crept on. Now and again, a man or woman would ride down the road, speak to Duule briefly, drop some coins into his hand, and leave with instructions given in terms too vague to be anything but code. There was certainly something strange about him. For one thing, he seemed a bit old to be capable of the magnitude of crimes necessary to earn so high a price. Black hair was giving way to gray at the side and baldness on top. His skin had the leathery texture of a man who had spent his life in the sun, but his posture and attitude suggested it had been years since he'd worked an honest day's labor. He simply dozed in the sun, waking to deliver orders and accept payments, until evening came. Then he made his way to the stable adjoining the tavern and mounted a rather expensive-looking horse. Teyn followed.

Duule took a leisurely ride down one of the dusty roads that ran beside the fields of a sprawling farm. In this part of Tressor, there was seldom a frost, even this deep into winter, and thus crops of all sorts could be grown year-round. This particular field was overgrown with wheat that should have been harvested ages ago. It now stood tall and dry, bending stiffly with the breeze. After a few minutes of riding, he went over a gentle rolling hill, such that the city center was no longer visible. He then took a subtle glance around, and when he was satisfied that he'd not been followed, he guided his horse into the fields, rustling the wheat as he went. It was a remarkable method to avoid being followed, Teyn had to admit. Anyone trying to sneak after him would make a great deal of noise trying to move among the dry grain, and a quick search for swaying stalks would betray precisely where the unwelcome guests were hiding.

Of course, Teyn had learned to follow deer and rabbits, and the most cautious human was nothing compared to a nervous woodland creature. He slipped among the stalks, moving when the wind blew, disguising his motion as little more than the results of an errant gust. As he made his way deeper, the scents of at least three men and horses concealed among the tall stalks gave him still more reason to move with care.

His bounty emerged, after a meandering trip through the grain, into a patch of field that had been kept clear. Not long afterward, the rustle of wheat announced the arrival of six men and two women, each bearing heavy bags. Teyn sniffed the air and realized he knew half of them from his time spent observing nearby towns. In fact, as they stepped into the fading light of the sun, no fewer than three of them matched descriptions that the watchman had given. He took note, reminding himself to return and follow their trails once his current target had been delivered to the watch.

"Nice and prompt today. Good. Good," remarked Duule, with the tone of a noble addressing his subjects. "And the earnings seem to be improving. No trouble with the law, then?"

"Never for very long," replied one of the lesser thieves, a greasy young man with a smile that made Teyn's skin crawl.

"That's right," proclaimed Duule. "And as long as you continue to pay me, there never *will* be trouble. My boys will make sure of that. Now, unless any of you have got something that needs to be said, give me my money and move along. It has been a long day, and I'm certainly not leaving while any of you are here to follow me."

With the grudging obedience of a group that would gladly put a knife in his back if they thought they could get away with it, each of the subordinate thieves dropped their bags of coins and disappeared into the wheat. Their superior watched them slink away and kept a watchful eye and a vigilant ear until he was sure they were truly gone. Satisfied, he hopped down from his horse and pulled open each of the bags, surveying the contents with a smug smile. His mind was fully on the heaps of copper and silver, gathering the smaller sacks and combining them into larger ones, keeping a running tally, and portioning out which coins would be spent on business and which on pleasure. It was a precious drop in his defenses. Teyn tensed. The three men he'd smelled among the stalks as he approached were still near, and he now realized that they could only be bodyguards; if he struck, they would be upon him in no time, but this was the best opportunity he would have to make his move.

The distraction of his earnings was just enough for Duule to miss a shadow separate itself from the swaying wheat and creep behind him.

One moment his eyes were feasting themselves on the gleaming piles of tribute and his mouth was wide with a self-satisfied grin. The next, a knotted piece of cloth was shoved into his mouth and the world went black. In two lightning motions, Teyn had gagged him and thrown a sack over his head, drawing it tight around his neck. With a muffled cry, Duule lurched forward, clawing at the hood, but the malthrope caught his wrists, wrenched them back, and bound them with a few deft twists of rope. A few more twists and his ankles were similarly tied, leaving the man completely restrained and grunting furiously through his gag.

Teyn allowed himself a moment to savor the victory before turning his ears to the field around him, scouring the sounds with trained precision until he was certain that none of the others were heading back. There was nothing but the sound of the wind and eight sets of hoofbeats becoming progressively more distant. It had worked. It had worked *perfectly*. Not even the guards had heard. The only thing that seemed aware of him was Duule's horse, which had taken a few uneasy steps away when Teyn appeared. However, now that what he'd expected to be the hard part was through, there remained the task of getting him back. The man was half again his weight, and carrying his struggling form for several days and nights wasn't likely to end well.

At the edge of the clearing, the man's horse had calmed a bit and was nibbling at one of the dry stalks. Teyn flicked an ear, eyes narrowed in thought. The horse would ease the journey, but he had never ridden one before, and staying hidden while riding one would be impossible.

With no obvious solution, he set the problem aside for a moment and rummaged through the pile of fist-sized bags left by his bounty's underlings. His time on the plantation hadn't given him much of a formal education. He didn't know how to read or write, so the slips of parchment within each bag did him little good, but he'd learned a bit about counting and tallying, and the sacks of assorted coins were perhaps a match for the reward for this scoundrel's capture.

The wind carried warnings, the sounds of fresh and purposeful rustling as well as the heavy scent of men and horses. Time was running out; the guards were moving closer. He abandoned the thought of gathering the coins, snagging only the bag that his prey had sorted most of the silver into before heaving the bound and gagged form from the ground and dumping it across the back of the horse. The painful realization flitted across his mind that far too many of the lessons he'd learned in recent years had been panicked guesswork to avoid being killed. Riding a horse would be the latest.

Vaulting onto the beast's back was simple enough, foregoing the stirrups entirely. The flash of motion as he leapt and the sharp impact of his feet on the saddle, for better or worse, shocked the horse into motion. Teyn hopped down to a seat on the saddle and reached back to keep his prisoner from sliding free. Dry wheat whipped by them, snapping and crunching as the frightened horse charged on. The sound must have been enough to bring the men nearby to full alert, because calls rang out and steeds quickened to a run.

Teyn turned and gathered up a few of the jingling straps that the horse's former owner had no doubt intended to use to secure the sacks of payment and used them instead to hastily lash the restrained man in place. By the time he was finished, the horse had begun to slow and the others were nearly upon him.

Teyn thought quickly, trying to recall the proper way to coax a horse into a gallop. On the plantation, they had never needed to do so, and though he'd seen it done countless times, he'd never once thought to take note of how it. Memories of a hundred different times he'd seen riders set off flashed through his mind and he tried everything he could recall. He snapped the reins, jabbed with his heels, jostled in his seat, and called out a dozen muffled commands through his iron mask. The pounding hooves of his pursuers drew nearer; in desperation, he pulled the mask free to dangle at his neck and called out again.

"Ha! Forward! On! Heeyaa! Move! *Move!*" he urged.

Time was up. Growling in frustration, he leaned back and jabbed his claws into the horse's flank. The beast reared, whinnied, and burst into a gallop that threw Teyn from the saddle. He tumbled to the ground amid the tall wheat, and an instant later three riders nearly trampled him as they rushed after the now-riderless horse. Shaking away the daze of the fall, he sprinted after them. The wheat was tall enough to hide horse and rider alike, and thus was well over Teyn's head, but that suited him fine. Bounding periodically into the air to get his bearings, he dashed unseen toward the riders. He saw them in fleeting glances among the swaying stalks, three hulking men on stout horses and weighed down with weapons. They were clearly muscle, hired to chase away and intimidate. Neither task called for speed, so they were woefully ill-equipped for the task at hand. Even on foot, Teyn was able to close the gap between them, and before long he was running along in the wheat beside the rear-most rider. Baring his teeth and pulling back his hood to make the most of his beastly features, he released vicious growl and lunged toward the horse. Instinctive terror took over and the beast tried to reverse direction, sending the unprepared rider to the ground in much the same way that Teyn had been thrown. Without missing a stride, Teyn launched himself toward the next horse.

By the time the runaway horse had emerged from the field and was galloping madly along the road, all three of the thugs were chasing uselessly after their own steeds. Teyn slipped the mask back in place as he ran, and managed to catch up to the escaped horse a short distance down the road. The panicked run had all but dislodged his prisoner, who was now dangling upside down, a single strap securing his legs to the equipment harness. The malthrope managed to snag the reins and coax the horse to a halt so that he could properly secure his prize. He worked quickly, hands darting over the straps and shoving at the struggling form. The gagged mumbles were becoming more distinct. The ride must have dislodged the knotted cloth enough for him to force it bit by bit from his mouth.

"Ugh. Augh!" he struggled to say, finally spitting the gag free. Instantly he began spraying profanities and threats, now muffled only by the thin cloth of the sack over his head. "You are dead! You understand me? Dead! Do you have any idea who I am? How powerful I am? Either you let me go right now, or I promise you, you'll never be able to see the light of day again! I'll have all of my men after you! You'll be hunted everywhere you go! I'll send men after your friends, your family, everyone you hold dear! If you had any idea who you were dealing with, you would thank your lucky stars I'm even giving you a chance!"

"And if you knew who you were dealing with, you would choose your threats more wisely."

He pulled a final bit of rope from his equipment, pulled it tight over the sack-covered mouth to quiet his bounty once more, and finally mounted the horse to guide it forward into the fading light of the setting sun.

#

A few days later, Teyn rode his stolen horse into the capital once more. The journey hadn't improved his horsemanship much, but he knew enough to keep the horse calm and to keep it moving. That was enough. Along the way he'd shown his prisoner a measure more kindness than he himself had been granted during his trip to the slave camp so many years ago. Food and water were given once a day, provided he was able to find a place far enough from prying eyes and curious ears. The vicious words that poured out whenever he loosened the gag made him more certain each time he heard them that every ounce of compassion he showed was more than the scoundrel deserved. The man spoke of men he'd had killed for so much less, of deeds that had been done in his name that were nearly the match for his own dark day on the plantation. With each savage story, his voice resonated with a sort of terrible pride. Teyn was relieved that he kept the sack covering the man's eyes. A window into that soul was something he wouldn't dare gaze into.

As the journey had rolled on he felt a spark of pride, long buried, begin to flare. What he was doing was right. Men like this did not deserve their freedom, and bringing them to justice would earn money enough to free a handful of those who were more deserving of the gift of liberty. For the first time in too long, he finally felt that he was moving in the right direction, and with every moment, he was more certain that this was why he woke every morning. This was his purpose.

The hour was midnight, or very nearly, when the streets outside the watch house finally began to empty. He watched the coming and going of people, and when he deemed it to be the safest moment, Teyn steeled himself and guided the horse into the small courtyard of the watch house. Three hard knocks on the door prompted footsteps. There was the sliding of heavy braces, the irritable grumbling of a groggy watchman, and finally the door creaked open. A bleary-eyed underling stared out into the darkness of the courtyard, flickering lantern in hand. Teyn stepped away from the glow, shoving the bound and gagged criminal forward to lie at the young man's feet.

"Who is it?" the watchman asked, stifling a yawn.

"Duule."

The sound of the word hit the man like a splash of cold water. In a frenzy, he snatched away the gag and hood. The long journey had taken most of the fire from the criminal, but he still mustered the strength to mutter a few choice words.

"Commander! Commander!" The watchman grabbed the bound man by the collar and dragged him inside, while a considerably more irritable voice complained of being awakened. The two officials then engaged in a hushed conversation they likely thought Teyn could not hear.

"You are certain it is him?"

"It is! Look at the tattoo, and the bad finger!"

"We've . . . we've got to get him locked up. Get some men in here. Wake them up. I want him in and out by morning." It was the commander who said this. His voice had the unmistakable tone of someone who had taken his current shift and position specifically so that he would not have to deal with things as serious as the current task. "And get the bounty. I don't know who brought him in, but he's going to need that money so that he can disappear before someone *makes* him disappear. Gads . . . let me get a look at him."

The commander came thundering up to the doorway, grabbing a lantern and quickly shutting the door behind him to keep the new prisoner from being seen by passersby. Teyn stepped back again, trying to stay clear of the light and turning his head to keep his eyes in shadow. He didn't know how much of his eyes could be seen through the mask, but it wouldn't take much to convince a human he was not one of them.

"You, sir, bought yourself a bucket of trouble," said the commander.

He was older than both the official who had answered the door and the portly day commander, though he wore a uniform matching that of his daytime counterpart. His face was not quite so immaculately kept, with a scruffy beard on his chin and a tangle of gray hair escaping his hat. He raised the lantern high, holding it forward, but Teyn turned entirely away.

"Please, no light," he muttered, his teeth clenched and his voice muffled by the ill-fitting mask.

"Mmm, yes. I suppose I'd be shy about showing my face after bringing in that man." He lowered the lantern and snuffed out the flame, reducing the courtyard to near blackness. "You'll have a hard time from now, boy."

"Why?"

"Why? Why? You . . . you don't really know who that man is, do you? Gads, boy. How can I put it to words? Thieves and thugs, they don't have a lord, but if they did, it would be the man you just captured. Half of the hired blades in Tressor work for him, and half of the thieves we haven't been able to catch pay him for protection. He has an army, it is as simple as that. No one would nab him, even if he was out in the open, because they knew there would be a crowd of murderers tripping over each other to earn a little extra for slitting the throat of the poor fool who took him. Why do you think the price was so high?"

"It doesn't matter."

"So you say, but you just wait. It is all we are going to be able to do to hold onto him until we can get him into a proper prison. Sad to say, he's probably got some watchmen working for him, too."

Behind him, the door opened and the younger of the men of the night shift handed out the small pouch of gold, hands shaking and eyes locked on the prisoner within. "Ten gold rhysus."

"If you are wise, boy," said the commander as he passed the pouch to Teyn, "you will take this gold and disappear. Find someplace dark to hide and hope he doesn't have any men hiding there with you."

Teyn took the pouch and turned silently away, leading the horse as he went. It was remarkable how deeply the humans feared a life that had long ago become normal for him. He'd given up imagining what it would be like to walk through a city without having to worry about the threat of discovery. Perhaps there was a time and place where such a dream was a reality, but it was not here and it was not now. Better to focus on what could be done than to dwell upon such things.

Though the horse would be helpful, keeping it and remaining hidden among the people of Gallishasa could not be done, and he had no means to sell it. Briefly he considered butchering it, but doing it properly would take more time and space than he had to spare. Besides, he felt a sort of gratitude to the beast for carrying him to his first real

239

victory. Thus, he set it free. If the time came that he needed another horse, they were simple enough to find.

He made his way back to the well-hidden bundle of belongings. The leather roll was still there among the tall grass, untouched in his absence. He pulled it open and poured out the coins, piling them with the others and sorting them into stacks.

All told, his fortune now numbered two hundred and six copper coins, what the people called porus, forty-eight silver entus, and now ten gold coins, evidently called rhysus. It was enough for a slave—it had to be. He didn't know how many copper coins there were to a silver, or how many silver to a gold, but surely he had enough now to buy the freedom of at least one man or woman. All that remained was the final obstacle. A towering wall between himself and his goal. He needed to make the purchase. He needed to come face to face with the sort of men who had bought and sold him, and he would need to convince them to take his money.

This wasn't going to be like the bounty, hastily exchanged in the dead of night. There would be haggling, bargaining, and all of the little games people play when money is involved. It wasn't something a mask could help him through. He needed help now. He needed a favor.

#

Though much of the justice of the region was meted out in the capital, the people of Tressor had better places to send those who were to be locked away. The ruling classes had no interest in sharing their city with the filth of society. Those found guilty were thrown in sturdy carriages and carted to places tucked far from the proper, law-abiding people of the kingdom. Duule, as one of the most notorious members of the underworld, did not receive so much as a mock trial. He was quickly ordered to a place called Makaat Prison, a sunbaked labyrinth of stone and steel tucked as near to the center of the Makaat desert as possible. A trusted and faithful messenger, a member of the day watch, was put in charge of his transportation, and Duule was sent rattling along the roads to where he would spend the rest of his days.

The journey was less than a day old when, for no clear reason, the messenger guided his horses off of the main road and to a little-used path through the rolling hills and scattered groves of the countryside.

"This isn't the usual way," remarked one of the three guards assigned to the carriage.

"This way's faster," the messenger assured. There was a

nervousness to his voice that the guard attributed to an understandable fear of the wrath of the man behind the bars of their carriage.

The carriage was a simple cage with wheels, similar in most ways to the slave transport carriages, though higher quality. It was open to the air, displaying the condemned criminal to all who passed. The shame was considered part of the punishment, and also served as a warning to any would-be criminals of the consequences of their crimes. Duule had been strangely silent since he was loaded inside. The torrent of profanities and threats that had been hurled at anyone in a watch uniform had tapered off shortly after their journey began, and now he was simply sitting in the center of his cage, arms crossed and eyes fixed on the guards seated at the head of the vehicle.

After following the road until it had taken them well away from the nearest towns—and any witnesses—a half-dozen men on horseback came into view ahead. One was leading a horse with no rider. Instinct honed by years of transporting criminals began to nag the guards.

"Don't slow down when you get to those men. I don't like the looks of them," advised the senior guard. The messenger, now visibly anxious, did not respond, simply guiding the carriage forward with his eyes turned to the road.

One by one, the horsemen ahead began to separate. Now they were near enough for the guards to see that they were far more heavily-armed than any mere traveler should be.

"It's an ambush. Move! Faster!" the guard demanded.

Instead, the messenger halted the horses. The bandits pulled the guards from the carriage and put their weapons to work. Before any could comprehend what had occurred, their lives had been brutally taken. The messenger watched miserably, untouched and unthreatened. Once all of the guards were dead, he climbed down from his seat and opened the cage. Duule stepped down.

"You weren't supposed to kill them," the messenger said, fear and awe in his voice.

Duule delivered a vicious backhand, knocking the messenger to the ground. "And *you* weren't supposed to allow me to be locked away. What am I paying you for!?"

Even in the grand capital city Gallishasa, the salary of a watchman was a meager one for a man with a large family to support. By dropping a rhysu or two into the proper hands once a month, Duule had secured himself a small contingent of men within the watch. Each

Joseph R. Lallo

of them knew that they could not continue to enjoy the life to which they had become accustomed without ensuring that their benefactor's generosity could continue. The scheming criminal was skillful in his selections, always making certain to gain the aid of those watchmen entrusted with the task of delivering men and information. Today, his investment in this man had paid off nicely.

The bribed messenger curled into a ball on the ground, fearful of receiving more blows. "It wasn't my fault. It was a bounty hunter who turned you in, and you haven't got any men on the night watch yet!"

"Who was it then? Which bounty hunter had the audacity to claim the price on Duule of Sarrin?"

"I don't know! They say he wore a mask. Those who dealt with him swear they've never seen him at the morning bounty announcements."

"Well, if he's wearing a mask, how would they *know* that?" Duule taunted, raising his hand for another slap and grinning as the man flinched. "Listen carefully. Go back to Gallishasa. If this masked bounty hunter shows up again, I want to know. Find out anything you can. And I suggest you impress upon your fellow watchmen that a masked bounty hunter is not the sort of man they should be dealing with."

"What do I tell them about you?"

"Tell them you were ambushed and I got away, obviously. Though you'll need a few scars to show off. Wouldn't want them to get suspicious." He turned to the heftiest of his bandits. "Make it convincing, but don't kill him. It costs a fortune in bribes to get a decent man in the capital."

The grin returned to his face as he turned away and climbed onto the back of the spare horse. Behind him, his men delivered a beating that would certainly be enough to convince even the most skeptical of watchmen that he was at the center of an ambush. The grunts and cries of pain faded into the back of his mind as he began to think aloud.

"It must be someone from the north, or maybe someone from the Crescents. Surely there's no one in Tressor who hasn't heard about the dangers of crossing me," he mused. "I want a description of this new hunter, and once I have it, I want to know where he lives, I want to know who he loves, I want to know where he spends his money . . . and I want them all in *ashes!*"

#

The Rise of the Red Shadow

In the seaside town of Sarrin, a jovial and hard-working dwarf had just loaded the last bit of cargo and untied the last line of the week. The sun was just at the horizon, and with a smile and a wave, he set off toward the city to buy a few bottles of ale to pass the long night. His favorite tavern was a squat little building tucked among a cluster of the tallest in the city. It had been built long after them, and was set deep in what was either a narrow courtyard or a wide alley. Curiously, it had its door facing away from the street. One would think that such an arrangement wouldn't attract very many men and women—and it didn't, but men and women were not the desired clientele. This was a dwarf tavern, one of the only ones that could be found beyond the foothills of the mountains. The tall buildings kept the place in shadow, dim and cool, just the way a person raised in the mountains and mines preferred it.

Sarrin was a large port, and thus saw its share of every race as ships came and went. Enterprising members of each race saw the potential profit in giving their people a little taste of home, and thus places like The Wayward Vein opened their doors. In the case of the dwarf named Gurruk, it was half of the reason he'd settled in this town.

He was jingling a fresh payment of coins in his pocket and looking forward to a cool bottle of ale or three when he heard a sound from a side alley.

"Gurruk."

The dwarf stopped. He knew the voice, chiefly because he'd made special note of it as a voice he hoped never to hear again.

"Back so soon?" he grumbled under his breath. "Do you want to kill me now?"

"No."

"Never hurts to ask," he said with a shrug.

Gurruk turned to the dark little notch between two of the towering buildings that surrounded his trusty watering hole and saw the gleam of animal eyes.

"You said that the next time I saw you, I would get what I asked for."

"Is it my soul that you want? Because I don't think you'll find much use for it. Not exactly the purest one around."

"I'm not interested in your life or your soul, Gurruk," Teyn growled. "I want you to make a purchase."

"What sort of purchase?"

Joseph R. Lallo

"Slaves," Teyn said, tossing the sack of coins and trinkets to Gurruk's feet. It landed with a weighty thump. "I want you to take this money and use it to buy as many slaves as you can and pay to wipe away their scars. I want them to be freed. And when it is through, give what money remains to them to start their lives."

Gurruk knelt and pulled open the sack, rummaging through the contents. He glanced back to the darkness. "Why?"

"Because it needs to be done. Because it should be done. And because no one else will do it."

Gurruk considered what had been said. "True words. True words. Sorry to say it, but it takes a lot of money to set a slave free. At least, the way *I* know how. This is probably only enough for one."

"So be it."

"What good will it do to just free this one slave? Once he's out, what'll you do for the next one?"

"That is my concern, not yours."

Gurruk hefted the bag, deep in thought. "I promised you I would do what you asked. I promised when I was *drunk*, but drunk promises mean more. When you're drunk, silly things like reason and good sense don't get in the way of the truth. For the life of me, I can't imagine how a mally like you, a mally who would do what you did to those slave-drivers, would do this, too. I don't know if you're a saint with a mean streak or monster trying to atone. That's not for me to figure. All I know is that after I do this for you, you don't darken my door again. No voices out of the shadows. No knocks on the door in the middle of the night. You keep your bloody claws and your lost causes far, far from me."

"If you do as I ask, you have my word that you will never see me again. But know this: if you take those coins and do not keep your promise . . . you will not see me *then* either."

There was a whisper of motion and a cascade of dust from high in the alleyway, and then silence. Gurruk felt that the creature was gone, but that the same time he felt that it was staring at him from every shadow and every corner. He glanced down to the sack of coins. Best to get it done. The sooner that thing was off his back, the better.

244

Chapter 19

Gurruk was as good as his word. The coins were only enough to buy the freedom and wipe the slate of a single triple-stripe slave, but it was proof that it could be done. For a time, Teyn watched the liberated slave, an elderly man with the dark complexion and faded tattoos of those tribes hailing from the very deepest southern parts of the vast Tresson kingdom. After what must have been a lifetime of labor and captivity, freedom did not come easily to him. Though the dwarf had indeed provided the man with what little remained of the hard-earned coins, it wasn't nearly enough to buy a home in a city, and he was far too old to be carving out a life of his own. And so the old man simply drifted, eyes distant and unsure. The shackles had been taken from his wrists, but they lingered in his mind.

Finally, clarity came to him. It was a clear, crisp morning, and the former slave roused to see the rising sun over an endless, sprawling desert field. After that moment, it was as though a weight had been lifted from him. Perhaps he knew this field. Perhaps the sight of so much land without a fence or wall to stop him finally reminded him of what freedom was. Perhaps he had finally found a place that looked like home.

Whatever the reason, from that day forward the man moved with purpose. When Teyn finally left him, the man had found a tribe of his own people, and they had welcomed him with the warmth and joy of a dear friend returning after a long hard journey.

Watching the life return to the old man's eyes had been rewarding, but it also had taught him that there was more to this than simply paying to have them freed. There needed to be something for them to move on to, some life to return to. How could he provide that? The answer wasn't clear, but there was little doubt that when it came to him, it would bring with it the need for much more than the small fortune it has cost to free this man. There was much work to be done.

In the weeks and months to follow, Teyn threw himself into his task like never before. He needed money, and quickly. Once or twice, he tried to steal again, but it quickly became clear that for better or worse he was far more skilled at hunting men. Day and night, he kept his nose to the breeze and his eyes to the streets. He matched scents to faces, and faces to descriptions. He found bounty offices in half a dozen towns and sought to catch what scoundrels he could from each of their lengthy lists of wanted men and women. Sometimes he succeeded, wordlessly accepting his payment and disappearing into the night. Other times he failed, either when another bounty hunter chose the same moment to strike, or when the target noticed him and put up a fight. Word was spreading about the masked hunter who dragged away his prey in the shadows. The brigands and burglars were growing more wary. More and more often, Teyn ended a long journey bruised, bleeding, and empty-handed.

With each failure and each success, though, came wisdom as well. If others were reaching his targets first, then he must be faster. If the targets were ready for him, then he must be bolder. He must strike when they thought they were safe. So he found the narrow gaps in their defenses, and slipped through them even in the light of day. His boldness came at the cost of greater exposure. It was difficult to breathe while wearing his mask, let alone follow a scent, so too often he relied only upon his hood to hide his face until the time came to strike, and more than once he had been seen. Though witnesses caught only a glimpse each time, rumors and stories were quick to spread.

There was a malthrope lurking among men.

There would be consequences—that much he knew—but there was nothing left for him to fear. He had no home to be taken away. He had no family to threaten. He had squandered his only friendship to pursue this purpose. The purpose was all there was now. Anything to get the target. Anything to earn the bounty. If it cost him his life, so be it. It was a small price to pay.

#

In the cramped office of General Bagu, deep in the heart of the capital of the Northern Alliance, the icy and impatient Teht was sitting in one of the chairs before his desk. She had been there for nearly an hour, which was well beyond the limits of her razor thin patience. Her fingers drummed on the arm of her chair, and her lips were pulled back in a sneer.

"Where is that blasted—" she began to mutter, but a creak of the door startled her into silence. It was one thing to curse her superior under her breath. It was another to be overheard doing it.

The door creaked on its hinges and in walked a man Teht didn't recognize. He had an unremarkable face mostly hidden behind a heavy beard and the brow of an ornate hat. The headpiece was tall and trimmed with expensive fur. It was formed of stiff cloth and seemed round from the front and pointed from the side. The rest of his outfit was similarly ornamental and foolish-looking, all gold embroidery and needless detail. Tradition seemed to dictate that such elaborate garb be worn by all official representatives of a government when discussing important matters.

"I don't know who you are, but this is a private chamber for . . ." Teht began. Her voice caught in her throat when she noticed that the stranger was holding a thin but similarly ornate halberd with a gem set in its blade. "Oh . . . my apologies."

A sly smile crossed the lips of the newcomer as he shut the door behind him. "None necessary, Teht. It has been some time since our paths have crossed. It is only natural you would not be aware of my latest 'role.'"

"Yes, General Epidime," she said with a nod. "That is quite true."

"I see Bagu is late. Again," he observed.

"He is," Teht fumed in response.

"Well, then," he said, leaning against the wall near the door and absentmindedly tapping his halberd. "What has he got you working on?"

"More to do with that prophesy he's so enamored with," she grumbled. "He's got me back to chasing a malthrope around the south. *Again.* Slippery thing. Every time I think it is dead or caught, it pops up again."

"Mmm. Yes, they tend to be wily devils," he remarked. "But, then, they would have to be, to still be alive these days."

"I honestly don't understand why he's assigned this task to *me.* Surely *you* would be perfectly suited to it."

"I assure you, nothing would make me happier than taking a jaunt down to Tressor and spend some time tracking a malthrope. Fascinating creatures. But you know our noble leader. Once he makes a decision, he clings to it tenaciously. Besides, Kenvard has been giving us trouble of late. Strong-willed people, those Kenvardians. After twenty years of war, they are having doubts about the future of the Alliance. They are considering pursuing a separate peace. It has taken some careful manipulation to quiet them down and get them to fall back in line, and there's much more to be done. Even if I succeed, that whole land has got a rebellious streak. We'll have to deal with this sort of thing once or twice a generation, I suspect. People like that need a good deep scar to brood over before they will fall in line for good." He tapped the halberd a few more times, then raised an eyebrow. "Is this the same malthrope that you were 'quite positive' could not have survived a few years ago?"

"Most likely," she muttered. "It is madness to suggest such a thing. Two years ago, he ran amok. Murdered nearly everyone on that damned plantation Bagu had me ruin. A creature who is already hunted performing an act like that? It should have been dead in days. Yet in the fleeting moments that I can detect him, the blasted creature gallivanting down there today has the same shape, the same aspect to his soul. There was an outburst not long ago that felt precisely the same as the one that ruined the plantation. I think we are following the wrong creature. I am quite positive that the sort of creature who would commit such an atrocity is the precise opposite of the noble warrior we've been charged with locating."

"In light of recent developments, I should think you would be cautious of anything about which you are quite positive." He grinned. "I love a good riddle, and this does seem to be a stimulating conundrum. What precisely is keeping you from your prize?"

She grumbled something under her breath and crossed her arms. "The blasted creature has got an undeniably powerful soul, but he never uses it. It is nearly impossible to find him with magic. The only time I am able to gain a glimpse of him is when he lets his emotions take hold, and he rarely allows it. As I said, it happened again not long ago, so I know that he is alive. No matter how many times they send me to that blasted place, though, I cannot *find* him. The spells simply do not exist to track him properly."

Epidime shook his head. "Teht, my dear. I can appreciate that the mystic arts are your particular area of expertise, and thus it is attractive to solve every problem with your skill in that regard, but you must learn to use the other resources at your disposal."

"*What* resources? They only ever let me bring some of Demont's worthless cloaks. If they granted me a strike force of reasonable size, I'm sure we could have him in no time."

He sighed. "I shall forgo the usual speech about why force must not be used in this situation. If the first dozen explanations haven't taken root in your mind, once more won't do any good. Instead, consider this: the greatest bit of good fortune we've had since our arrival here was the simple fact that one of the creatures we would one day need to eliminate was a malthrope. A race already hated on the entire continent? We couldn't have *wished* for better luck. I've put a good deal of work into whipping that hatred into a blind fury on both sides of the battlefront. Have there been any stories circulating about malthropes lately?"

"There are *always* stories of malthropes doing every manner of crime. I'm beginning to think those people see malthropes in their sleep."

"Anything notably different of late?"

"You expect me to listen to the endless prattle of those simpletons?"

"Fools may be fools, but they *always* outnumber the wise men, so it is best to know what they are saying."

"There was . . . well, lately there have been more criminals complaining about malthropes than anyone else."

"Yes . . . yes, yes, yes. You see? There is your answer," Epidime said.

"What possible answer could you find in that?"

"We are seeking a creature destined to be a hero. A hero does not decide one day to fight for what is right. It is a part of them from the day they are born, present deep inside and perpetually bubbling to the surface. Given the slightest excuse, a hero will take up a cause. This is our target stepping into his role. After all, who has more reason to complain of a hero's actions than a villain?"

She looked at him doubtfully. "Even if that is so, what good does it do me?"

"Things such as this have a way of rippling upward, both on the side of law and against it. In time, the malthrope will run afoul of whatever figure stands tallest among the thieves. Failing that, then he will need to deal with those who administer justice. I would be very much surprised if he was not already being sought by some very influential figures on both sides of the law. And the chances are very good that these men are skilled at finding their targets through conventional means, rather than mystical."

Teht considered the words. "So if I am able to find those seeking him, they may be able to point me in the proper direction . . ."

"Or, better yet, they may be able to do your job for you, which I've always found to be far preferable. If you were to provide them with a few specialized gifts to aid their cause, this malthrope will be yours in no time."

Teht nodded, a grin on her face. "I tell you, Epidime, the threads you choose to tug at always seem to cause things to unravel. This is why Bagu should have sent you rather than me."

"Perhaps, but you should relish this opportunity to learn and grow. Why do we live, if not to learn? And in the spirit of education, let me suggest that you put this new knowledge to work. Obedience is praised, but success is rewarded. I would begin your task now, rather than await Bagu. And focus your attention on contacting the bandits rather than the law. They tend to be a bit more receptive to the aid of strangers with questionable motives."

"Yes—yes! Anything to be through with this once and for all," Teht proclaimed, throwing open the door and marching off to put his advice to work.

Shortly afterward, Bagu finally arrived. A seething anger was rumbling just beneath his rigid expression. It was an emotion that seemed to warp the very air around him.

"Epidime," he fumed. "Where is Teht?"

"She was here, preparing to give you excuses, but after a word of advice, I believe she had an epiphany."

Bagu clenched his fists and pounded the table. "Useless!"

"To you, perhaps. She's easily manipulated, at least. That tends to be quite handy for my purposes," he suggested. "Am I to infer from your attitude that things are not going well with the king?"

"The king is my concern, not yours. Give me your report on Kenvard and go," Bagu growled.

"Ah, well. You will be happy to know that I've got good news. Kenvard has renewed their dedication to the Northern Alliance once more, after an assassination plot was uncovered during this most recent gathering. Seems a Tresson sympathizer somehow infiltrated the great hall . . ."

"Assassination plot? Epidime, I made it clear I wanted the whole of the ruling council killed, and you assured me you could accomplish that without taking direct action."

"I did assure you of that, Bagu, but I hadn't anticipated a dedicated and rather remarkable young elf who recently became a commander. Her name is Trigorah Teloran, and I believe that you will be *quite* interested in meeting her . . ."

Chapter 20

In time, Teyn's mound of money grew, but it wasn't enough. It was never enough. No bounty ever came close to matching the price of Duule. The coins handed over in exchange for the scoundrel had been the last gold he'd seen. Since then, anything more than a handful of entus was a rare occurrence. It would be months before he could match the amount he'd needed to free the previous slave. Knowing this, however, changed nothing. All he could do was keep at it.

Midnight once again drew near as he waited in his usual spot, tucked quietly in an alley near the watch house in Tressor's capital. Beside him was the tightly restrained young woman that he'd tracked down over the course of the last few days. She was wanted for various crimes of petty thievery. Nothing that would fetch a high price, but enough to make her worth his while. Streets were slow to empty, and from the smell and the sound, the watch house was unusually full.

Though there was nothing tangible to give him pause, he found himself becoming uneasy. Something was wrong.

When the streets were finally clear, he hoisted his prize to his shoulders and dashed to the courtyard of the watch house. He delivered his customary three sharp knocks to the door, lowered his prisoner to the ground, and took a step back. The door was open almost instantly, as though someone had been standing at the ready. Rather than the elderly night commander or one of his underlings, the man who answered the door was the portly day commander. He looked first to the bound woman, then to Teyn.

"Chandra. Twenty entu bounty," Teyn said quietly, his voice muffled by the mask.

The day commander glanced to a watchman, who scurried off to fetch the payment. He then turned back. "So. You are the man who brought in Duule." He had a wide, genuine smile on his face as he spoke, as though this introduction was long awaited.

Teyn nodded once.

"After all of the success you've had in recent weeks, I just had to meet you face to face. Odd that I never see you during the day when I announce the list." Teyn gave no answer. "Duule escaped shortly after you turned him in. No doubt his men have been after you. Had any trouble?"

"Some."

"I imagine you would." The watchman returned with a small sack of coins and dropped it into the commander's hand. "I've got to say, you've done an awful lot of good for Tressor. How about you take off that mask so that I can look you in the eye and thank you properly?"

"That isn't necessary."

"I appreciate your humility, but there are rumors. Some say you're just one of Duule's men, fetching the ones he doesn't care to protect any more. Others say you're a criminal thinning the herd to make things better for himself. Both claims are laughable, of course, but no sense letting them linger when we can put them to rest by having a look at your face."

Teyn's heart began to hammer in his chest. His sensitive ears twitched beneath his hood as the sound of a half-dozen men readying weapons filtered from within the watch house. The shuffling of feet in a nearby side alley caught his attention. It felt like a noose was tightening around his neck.

"If I show my face, Duule's men might see. I could be in danger."

"I can vouch for my men. Just let us see who we are dealing with and it will be over."

"Just give me my money and let me go."

"You sound nervous, sir," the commander said, his expression hardening. "Now answer me this: what reason would an *innocent* man have to be nervous about showing his face to the watch?"

The commander took a lantern from just within the doorway and pulled it out, holding it high. Teyn recoiled, turning away and retreating further.

"I brought you who you wanted. Just give me my payment!" He growled.

"I've heard enough. Grab him," the commander ordered.

A bell began to ring out and armed men poured from the alleys around the watch house, but Teyn had been tensed for flight since the moment that the wrong man answered the door. They tried to close in around him, but they were expecting a man, not a malthrope. He moved in a blur, charging through a gap and rushing down the short street toward the city gates. At the sound of the bell, though, the rattling of chains had begun. The gate was dropping. He was barely three strides away when the massive gate struck the ground with an earsplitting clash, blocking his way with iron bars less set too close for even his narrow frame to slip through.

Without missing a step he launched himself onto the gate, climbing the crosspieces toward the top. The creak of bowstrings being drawn turned fear to desperation. A wall of sturdy wooden slats covered the top of the gate, preventing him from simply slipping over, but he knew that he could not afford to stop moving. The hiss and thunk of an arrow shooting past his face and driving itself into one of the slats drove the point home. He swung hand-over-hand along the gate, working his way toward the point that it reached the walkway along the top of the wall. There were men stationed there, swords ready.

He managed to heave himself from the gate to the edge of the walkway, but before he could pull himself up, the soldiers there were upon him. He glanced desperately around, his sight limited by his mask. Behind him was a tall building with a flat, open roof. Bracing his feet against the wall, he leapt backward, pivoting in air. The leap was panicked and ill-timed. With a sickening smack and a huff of lost breath, he struck the edge of the roof. An arrow sliced through his cloak and grazed his side before he could climb up, but he shrugged off the pain and rolled to the dusty surface. More arrows followed, but once he was on his feet, there was little hope of hitting him.

Leaping bounds sent him from roof to roof, moving in straight lines, while those below were forced to work their way through the streets. By the third roof, he was too far into the town for the archers to take aim any longer, lest a stray shot strike a resident of the capital. Word spread from person to person, and eyes raised to the roofs, but panic and confusion are the enemy of coordination. The watch fell further and further behind; in time, Teyn was able to drop down to the streets.

Long before word could reach any of the city's other gates, he was outside the walls and disappearing into the countryside, bleeding, exhausted, and empty-handed.

#

In the weeks that followed, the same scene played out in one bounty office after another. Word from the capital reached each one, and at best he was told he could not do business with his face hidden. At worst, there were weapons and concealed men waiting for him. None were so well-equipped or prepared as those in the capital, and thus none did so much as send him away with a bruise, but it didn't matter. Doors were slamming shut. With no one to pay him his bounties, he could not earn any money this way, and no other way had even come close. All he could do was continue to try, until he was sure that no bounty office would have him.

It was thus that he found himself in the northeast of Tressor, in a town called Millcrest. It was a place quite close to the front of the still-raging war with the Nameless Empire. Things were different this far north. For one, most people had at least a touch of the same accent that had flavored Sorrel's speech. The houses were different, too. They were stouter, with sloped roofs and shingles to help withstand the frequent rain and occasional snow. This particular town was also nearly deserted, no doubt thanks to its proximity to the front. Three bad days of battle could easily mean that the war would be at one's doorstep.

Though mostly empty, the town was still quite an interesting one. A mighty river that flowed roughly southeast wrapped around two sides of it, twisting in a wide loop and forming both the northern and eastern edge of the town. At the northwest corner of town, the land was level with the river, and no fewer than three mills dipped now-broken and forgotten wheels into the rushing water. From there, the town stretched eastward, built upon a gradual slope that rose to a bluff a few dozen feet from the water's edge at the northeast corner. At the highest point of the bluff, there was another mill, this one driven by wind. Though only two of the five blades of its fan were whole, a stiff gust caught it from time to time, causing it to turn.

In a ruddy little building tucked among a few empty houses on the south side of town was the smallest, and last, of the bounty offices that Teyn knew. If he was denied here, it was likely the end of his bounty-hunting career. He had spent little time here, but when he did, it was frequently for a swift and easy hunt earning a meager reward. The closeness of the battle meant that war profiteers, traitors, and deserters could often be found nearby, and thus the bounty list was always packed with fresh names and the ground was always crisscrossed with fresh trails. He didn't even need to hear the names and descriptions most of the time. The scent was always the same: blood, sweat, fear, and panic. They could always be found hiding in a dark corner, and they seldom put up much of a struggle.

He tracked down the first that he could find, bound him, and brought him in.

Unlike the capital, there was no need to wait until the streets cleared in Millcrest, and no need to knock on a door. The one responsible for dispensing payments and announcing bounties was an exceedingly fat and unmannerly woman who could be found sitting in the light of an oil lantern from sunset to sunrise, eating nuts and swatting flies. She was dressed in a grimy and formerly white linen dress beneath a scarred leather scale armor coat with short sleeves. She smiled an incomplete grin when she saw the masked figure approaching.

"Well, well. Been a long time since my favorite hunter came a-calling. Who do we have here?" she wheezed. Her voice had a smoky and abused sound to it, though Teyn had never seen her with a pipe. Hefting herself from her seat, she ponderously reached down and pulled the hood from the prisoner's head. After a few moments of staring him down, she referred to a slate board attached to the front of the rickety wooden building. She turned back to the prisoner and pulled the gag from his mouth. "Your name Rittleh?" When an answer was not forthcoming, she gave him a kick to the ribs. "Your name Rittleh?"

"Yes," he groaned.

"Well, well, well. This boy's fresh to the list. Just got the description a few hours ago. Not exactly the highest bounty on the list. Seven entus." She suddenly raised her voice. "*Boys*! Seven silver! Now! And both o' you get out here!"

Teyn stepped a reasonable distance away as there was a stirring and a pair of thickly-built and heavily-armed men lumbered out. One held a small chest.

"Honestly, boy. You need to learn to count," she grumbled, tipping open the chest and counting out seven coins. "Now, go lock up the prisoner and get lost for a bit. Both o' you. The hunter and I need a bit of privacy."

The pair glanced at Teyn, who stood far enough from the light to be little more than a silhouette against the night landscape, and set off for the only other building with any life in it, an inn a short distance down the road. Her chair creaking under her weight, the woman tugged the table beside her a bit closer and dropped the coins in a neat stack. As she spoke, she picked up the stack and let each coin drop to the table, then swept them together and repeated it.

"If you've come this far, I imagine you know that I'm not permitted to conduct official business with masked men in general anymore, and *you* in particular."

Teyn growled. "I brought your bounty . . ."

"Calm yourself. I said *official* business. This close to the fighting, 'official' isn't enough to keep food on the table. Now, you'll have your money for this one. I'll say one of the boys tracked him down. But, in the future, if you want to work for me you'll doing a different sort of job."

"What sort?"

"As a part of the string of nonsense the Tresson authorities make me say, I've had to inform you that you won't get a bounty unless you bring in a prisoner alive and unharmed or if the crime was such to warrant their death. The sort of people you'll be working for aren't so choosy about safety, and mostly they don't care about what the target may have done. Matter of fact, most of them are rather insistent that a good deal of harm be delivered regardless of guilt."

"You want me to hurt people."

"No. I want you to *kill* people. Well, my clients want you to kill people." She swatted a fly on her neck. "I just want what the clients want."

She made the statement without a hint of nervousness or shame, as though it was the only reasonable thing to say.

"I can't do that." The mere suggestion of it quickened his heart and made his hands shake with the memory of last time.

"No? Well, very few can. That's why they pay so much. See, that piece of rubbish you brought me just now? He was worth seven measly entus alive. Just seven pieces of silver. If he'd been on my other list, if someone had wanted him dead? Well, we don't deal in silver for jobs like that. Strictly gold. And not less than five pieces of it. Most jobs, not less than twenty. Sometimes more." She eyed his darkened form intently. "Sometimes a *lot* more."

"I can't. You're asking me to take a life."

"Is that really so hard? What do you think will happen to half of the people you bring me once I turn them over?"

"That is different."

"Not to the prisoner, it isn't."

"I won't do it."

"Fine," she allowed, in a tone that made it seem like her

willingness to let him pass on the offer was an act of the utmost charity on her part. She fished among the broken nut shells littering the ground beside her until she found a small cloth sack that had once contained walnuts and dropped the coins inside. In a smooth toss that he neatly caught, she delivered his payment. "You ever change your mind, come back and see me. I don't figure someone in your position has too many other options, and you certainly aren't in the position to spread the word to the authorities about my little side business. Just remember, you've brought me your last official bounty."

Teyn turned and quickly retreated into the night. His stomach was a knot and his heart was heavy in his chest as he searched for a place to sleep once the sun rose. Her offer had stirred up terrible thoughts, but more pressing on his mind was her assurance that the door was officially shut on bounty-hunting. The money he had earned bringing criminals to justice had enabled him to free his first slave, and the jingling sum in his pocket might give him just enough to free another . . . but there was no telling how long it would be before the next.

With little else he could do, he decided to find the slave he had freed, find some way to convince him to do as Gurruk had done, and give another of his brethren their freedom. Doing so would require that he cross nearly the whole of Tressor and spend a long time tracking, but that was just as well. He would need the time to think up a way to coax a favor from a man who had only ever been given reasons to hate him, and to decide what could be done after.

#

Night and day he journeyed. A part of him, deep inside, marveled at the ease with which he moved about the kingdom. Not so long ago, his only recourse to remain hidden was to stay far from the cities and roads. He had learned much since then. The bone-deep drive to stay hidden had been honed to something deeper than instinct. A single glimpse revealed to him the shadows and unseen corners that could safely conceal him. A moment of observation traced out the movements of a crowd: where they were headed, where they would not be, where he must go. It allowed region after region to whisk by him as the days rolled on, and all the while he was deep in thought.

So lost in his thought was he, it was not until the landscape began to take on strangely familiar shapes that he realized where his path had taken him. A bright moon was lighting the endless fields of a stretch of farms. He skidded to a stop, one memory after another hitting him like a hammer. The trees, the roll of the horizon . . . the house.

He had unwittingly found his way to what had been Jarrad's farm, then Marret's. Now a new name graced the deed, it seemed. The much-abused land had healed somewhat. Not enough to match the legendary output Jarrad had coaxed from it, but enough to nurse a few simple crops from the soil. And if land could be worked, then there must be workers. Teyn's eyes clouded with tears as he saw green shoots sprouting through the ground that had been stained by his crime. At the edge of the field, the same simple quarters still stood, weary and hopeless laborers sleeping within them or pacing restlessly between. The smell, the sound. All of it was the same.

Nothing that had happened, nothing that he had done, had changed anything.

He stood tall, fists tight, and turned to the north. They would change now.

#

"I knew you'd be back," remarked the heavyset bounty officer with a smug grin. "Follow me."

She hoisted herself from her seat and began to waddle toward a deserted patch of the city. Whether it was for Teyn's benefit or her own, she elected to leave the lamp behind, moving with practiced confidence through the darkness. As she walked, she rambled.

"This one's a stone-cold hunter, I said. Knew it from the start. And all the really great hunters I've known, they've all been animals, deep down. They don't just *like* to hunt. They *are* the hunt. And the hunt is about the kill. There are only so many times you can have the rabbit's neck in your jaws without wanting to give it a good shake . . ."

Teyn released a breath that was just barely audible as an irritated hiss. Her words bothered him. Not only because she spoke so casually about despicable acts, but because she spoke of him as an animal. She could simply be using colorful language . . . or she could know what face lay behind the mask. She continued as though she did not hear him.

"You know something? You've returned a few bounties to me, but I don't think you ever told me your name. What do you go by?"

He hesitated. Sorrel had dubbed him Teyn, and in the years that he'd known her, that was how he'd come to think of himself. But Sorrel was not in his life anymore. The thought of this horrid woman, of

259

anyone else calling him by the name burned at him. He'd been called Mally, but he would not and could not be known by that name. His mind flitted far back, landing upon the only other thing he could remember having been called.

"Some call me the Red Shadow."

"Eh. You want to keep your real name a secret? Suits me, Red. Probably best for both of us. Name's Maribelle, but you just call me Boss," She remarked.

They reached a building that looked as disused as the dozen they had passed before it, save for the fact that this one had a sturdy door with a high-quality lock. His employer dug shamelessly down the front of her armor coat, tugging out a gleaming bronze key. With a quick twist, she clicked the door open and slipped inside. He stopped at the doorway.

"What are you waiting for, Red? Inside," she coaxed.

"I will wait here."

"Your type never seems to like having too many walls around you. Fine, wait here." The woman slipped inside for a few moments and returned with a rough slate board. "Since this is your first job for me working off of the black list, we'll start you with something small and simple. The man's name is Crilless. He lives in cottage a short distance north of the battlefront. Easy to find. Due north from here until you hit a river, then east along it until you find a dock with black slats. He's the first cottage west of it. Red door with a horse shoe on it. He carries a leather bundle filled with parchment. It is always on his person. Kill him, take it, and bring it here as proof. Should be done in a few days at most."

"Why does he need to die?"

"Because someone is paying us for it. Listen, Red. This isn't a job where you ask questions. The less any of us know, the better."

"Does he *deserve* to die?"

"Someone is willing to pay good money to see him dead, so I'd wager he's no saint. And what did I just say about questions? Bring me that bundle and you get eight rhysus. That's all you need to know. Now off with you. These things have a way of going stale, and I don't want the price going down because you decided you were curious."

She ambled away, leaving him behind. Knowing that if he hesitated any longer he might change his mind, and knowing that this dark opportunity represented quite possibly the last real chance he had to earn enough to make a difference, he set off for the battlefront.

Little care was needed to stay hidden as he left the city. The soldiers traveled on the main roads, and none but they would dare venture so near to the battle. All of his life, twenty years now, Teyn had heard of the war. When he imagined it, he imagined clashing swords and butting shields. He imagined men on both sides fighting and tearing at each other. His mind had never turned to what those battles might have left behind.

These skirmishes had raged off and on for a generation. The closer he came to the line that the lives had been lost to defend, the more he saw that the land had not been spared. The scars of dozens—if not hundreds—of battles fought on this stretch of the land were everywhere. Houses reduced to charred ruins. The broken remnants of stone walls. Hastily-erected and even-more-hastily abandoned shelters. Broken arrow shafts stuck from the ground like some manner of ghastly crop. He passed through what might once have been a town, but the only evidence was a scattering of foundations and a single stone-paved road. Now it was a place so ruined, so long-deserted that only wildlife called it home. He took the opportunity to stop in this forgotten place long enough to catch and consume a meal before continuing on his journey.

Then, looming in the distance, there was the front. It was a sight to behold. He had heard the people of the nearby Tresson cities refer to this place as Red Band. Here, the border between Tressor and the Nameless Empire ran through a wide stretch of low, flat land between two sloped ridges. It was a war ground that might as well have been designed to foster a stalemate. Each day, the men would descend the slope, spill blood, and retreat when the battle was through. If the line moved too far north or south, the high ground would bring it to a stop.

Beyond the slope was a patchwork city of tents, lean-tos, and other makeshift structures. Horses slept, or shuffled uneasily. Heaps of red armor streaked silver with scrapes and gouges lay outside each temporary residence, awaiting the morning when the soldiers would suit up once more. The air was heavy with the scent of smoke and blood. Most of the soldiers slept, but along the top of the slope, a line of campfires glowed, warming the patrol that kept watch over the killing fields, lest some of the northern scum try to slip by. Far in the distance, a string of similar glows served the same purpose for their opposite number.

Joseph R. Lallo

The task of crossing to the north mercifully stole away what mind he had left to dwell upon what he had seen, and what he was planning to do. Where the ground was steady enough for a squad to attempt to slip through, there were scouts and lookouts. To make the land elsewhere less forgiving and more likely to betray those who would sneak across, the soldiers had littered the field with bundles of cruelly-sharpened sticks sunk into the soft earth. That suited him fine. One did not become a successful hunter—at least, not one of the sort that Sorrel had taught him to be, without learning to step lightly and carefully. Selecting a route heavy with traps but virtually without patrol, he began the long, treacherous trek across the border.

There was an eerie, cold feeling as he moved across land. A part of it, a small part, was how far north he had come. Unlike most of Tressor, which was warm for much of the year, the air became sharply cooler near the border with the north. However, a stiff breeze and an icy bite to the air was nothing compared to the graveyard pall that hung over the place. So many had died here. There were no remains of soldiers, save the stain of blood here and the dislodged bit of armor there, but the atmosphere seemed sickly and poisoned by the horrors it had witnessed. The smell, likely too faint to be noticed by the men and woman who fought here, was almost nauseating to him. A single whiff was all he needed to know that it was a scent that would linger for years, a stench of death that would be a part of this place for generations to come.

He pressed northward, senses alert. The border was behind him now. He was in the land of the enemy. As he traveled, swift and low to the ground, he found himself glancing toward the fires at the top of the ridge ahead, hoping for a glimpse of those who fought on the side of the north. These were people spoken of with nearly the same fear and hate as malthropes. As he drew nearer, though, and he began to see faces and forms near the flames, he found that they were merely humans, identical to those he had left behind him—albeit clad in blue rather than red. Somehow, he'd expected them to look different, to be monstrous or ghastly.

Seeing more of the same left him baffled. How could something as arbitrary as which side of an invisible line a man called home make him worth killing? With a shake of his head, he logged it away as yet another thing about humans he simply could not understand.

When the battleground was well behind him, his mind began to

262

drift back to his target and how to find him. First came the river, if it could even be called that. It was a narrow, shallow stretch of water. More than a stream, but not by much, it must have been one of the tributaries to the river that wrapped around Millcrest. He had to take care as he followed its banks east. A well-traveled road ran alongside it, and flat-bottomed skiffs loaded with goods and passengers were drifting along its surface even as dawn was just beginning to break. Both the goods and the passengers were destined for the war, so special care had to be taken to remain unnoticed. Everyone would be well-armed.

Pier after pier passed with faded gray planks until the rising sun fell upon a row of black adorning a pier near a small cluster of cottages. Three had red doors. One had a horseshoe. He approached it. There was enough light now that he was in real danger of being seen, but the fertile ground of the riverside had resulted in a lush and dense area of high weeds, and whoever called this cottage home had done little to tame them near his walls. He crouched among them and breathed deeply of the air. There was only one human scent, the scent of a man. It formed trails, new and old, leading toward and away from the cottage. The trails all led to the single door of the structure, and they always approached from the riverside road. It smelled as though he was not home now, but he'd left very recently.

He closed his eyes, removing his mask to draw in a better sample, and unraveled the story the scent told. The man spent his nights here. He returned after the sun set, and left before the sun rose. Others passed along the road, but no one ever came to the cottage. So long as he could weather the day unseen, Teyn was certain he would find the man alone after nightfall. All he had to do was wait . . . and hope that when the time came, he still had the resolve to complete his task.

The wait was agonizing. Constant traffic on the road put his nerves on edge, allowing long overdue sleep to come only fitfully and in shallow dozes. The dreams that came whenever he drifted off were dark and twisted, filled with troubling memories. Finally the sky began to darken. Not long after, the crunch of purposeful footsteps approached the cottage. Through the weeds, Teyn could see the man he was to kill.

A heavy jacket, made from rough cloth and stuffed with down, covered a wiry and unwashed form. His hair was long and greasy, his face bearing the wispy beard and mustache of a man not meant to grow facial hair. To look at him, one would almost think that he'd been warned. His eyes were sunken and red, dark bags beneath them. His head darted aside to scrutinize the source of any sound, real or imagined. His left arm was held tightly to his side, clutching at a vague form beneath his coat. His right was at his hip, clutching lightly the hilt of a dagger. This man was no stranger to being a target.

He approached his door and cast a wary glance around him, eyes sweeping over the very patch of overgrowth that hid Teyn. They lingered there for a moment, but Teyn knew better than to abandon his hiding place due to a simple lingering stare. Sure enough, the man turned back to the door, reluctantly taking his hand from his weapon to work the latch. In the moment of distraction as the door slid open, Teyn slipped from the weeds and pulled himself to the roof of the cottage. The motion was smooth and nearly noiseless, but the crackle of a tuft of weeds was enough to raise an alarm in the jittery man's mind. His hand shot to his dagger and pulled it free, and he launched himself into the weeds, stabbing viciously at the spot where Teyn had been moments before. As he struck at the underbrush, he screamed threats in one of the languages Sorrel had attempted to teach.

The man stopped stabbing and stood stone still, eyes wide and wild. When the only sound to greet him was the babble of the distant water and the swish of windblown weeds, he made his way quickly to the door and pushed it open, hurrying inside to latch it again. He threw himself against the door and listened once again, ear against the sturdy wood. The only light within the cottage was the faint glow of embers still weakly alive from the previous night's fire. It wasn't enough for the man to see, but it was enough for Teyn.

The malthrope had slipped inside when the man was stabbing at the weeds, and now he stood behind his target, a knife in his hand. His breathing was slow and controlled, his eyes steady and locked on the man's back. Every part of his body was still, but his mind was a storm. It had been his fear, ever since the dark day at the plantation, that if ever he found himself in a position to take another life, he would not be able to resist. He was certain that he would lose control as he had before, that he would become once again what the men had believed him to be since birth: a monster, a killer. Now he stood behind a man who had been marked for death by other humans, and he couldn't bring himself to put his blade to work.

As the man stepped away from the door and fumbled in the

darkness until he found a taper and a lantern and set about lighting it from the embers, Teyn continued to struggle with himself. This was for the others like him, the others denied their freedom. Taking this one life would provide him with enough money to give back the life of at least one worker. This man had his freedom and look where his choices took him. It was time to give someone else a chance.

Now the man had lit the lantern, filling the cottage with its dim glow. If Teyn was going to do something, he had to do it now. His target began to turn. Teyn grabbed him by the arm and twisted it behind his back, forcing him forward and slamming him into the wall. The force of the collision knocked the lantern from the man's hand, spilling lamp oil onto the floorboards and setting them aflame.

"Listen to me!" Teyn hissed through teeth clenched by the mask. "There is a price on your head. People want you dead for the bundle of parchment you've got clutched beneath your coat. Give it to me!"

After struggling and screaming in pain until it was clear there was no breaking free of his assailant, the man spoke, his voice brimming with insanity. Teyn knew little of the language. He didn't understand half of the words, but those he knew were filled with hate and madness. Words like "kill" and "wealth," words like "war" and "children." Teyn repeated his offer as best he could in the same language, but it was clear that this madman had no intention of accepting. He struggled and shoved, all the while the flames growing higher. Finally, an awkward twist of his body and a furious thrust of his foot managed to shove Teyn back toward the flames. It was enough to force the hunter to release his grip on his prey.

In a flash, the man was upon him, knife drawn and screaming. The two tangled, rolling atop one another. It was clear after just a few moments that this man was no stranger to combat. Crazed though his eyes and voice seemed to be, he moved with precision and purpose. He was barely as strong as Teyn, and far slower, but it took every ounce of advantage that the creature had to keep his opponent's weapon from meeting its mark. The fire spread around them as the fight intensified. The man's raking fingers caught the edge of Teyn's mask, pulling it free. The sudden sight of animal eyes and a beastly face were enough to briefly seize the mind of the man. Teyn took full advantage, kicking him off and springing to his back. One hand grabbed a handful of greasy hair and pulled the man's head back, the other held the knife tight. Teyn's teeth were bared, his mind aflame as he breathed great heaving breaths of the scalding air. He lowered his weapon . . .

#

Outside the cottage, men and women were beginning to gather, calling out for water to extinguish the burning cottage. A bucket brigade was already forming when a form finally burst from inside the fiery cottage. Despite the many witnesses, none caught more than a glimpse of the fleeing form. It was little more than a blurred silhouette rushing from the brilliant flames. Some claimed it held a tight bundle in one hand. Others were certain it held a crude, armored mask to its face. The only thing that was certain was that it was not the man they knew to live in this place. When hours of work and countless buckets had been hauled from the river to the cottage, they revealed the remains of the cottage's mysterious resident. Though the fire had done its work, it was clear to all that he had been dead long before the flames had reached him.

#

Two days later, the woman who had hired him smiled as a leather bundle dropped to the table beside her, crunching spent nutshells.

"Well, well, well," she said, slapping an insect buzzing by her ear, "look who came back." She snatched up the bundle and pulled it open. "Did you look inside?"

The malthrope simply shook his head.

"Good. Glad to see you got that curiosity under control. Me, on the other hand . . ." she commented, pulling open the roll and sifting through the pages. "Need to be sure you brought back what they were after, rather than any old pile of parchment." She read over a few of the sheets. "Yes. Yes this is what they were after. *Boys!* Eight gold!"

Inside the building, he heard the woman's two assistants moving crates and chests.

"It'll take them a bit to get to it. We don't do business in gold much these days. See, two out of three of the people I've got working off the black list don't come back from their first job. Some of them lose their nerve. The rest lose their lives. But I had a feeling about you, Red. Like I said, I looked at you from day one, and I thought to myself: this one, he's a killer, through and through."

His eyes lowered. He did not argue. There was a time, however brief, when he was whole. When he was a person with a name and a life. That time was over. The creature who had earned that name would never have done what he'd done. Teyn was gone. Now he was only the

266

Red Shadow.

After a few minutes of laborious searching and three miscounts, the men finally exited the building and dropped the coins into his gloved hand. Eight rhysus. Eight gold coins for the work of a few days. He gazed at the glittering payment. What he held in his hand was the freedom of one of his own—or more.

"Feels good, eh? Something about the weight of a gold coin. Just feels right. Now that you've gotten your feet wet, I've got a *real* job for you. Something a little more substantial."

"No. I have something I need to do first," he said, clutching the coins tight and turning to the south.

Now that he had the money in his pocket, and the blood on his hands, the weight of his deed was ravaging his mind. He'd been able to make it this far because he knew that what he did, he did to achieve his goals. It was for his purpose. Now that it was within his power to sever a set of chains, to give back a life, he needed to do it. Every moment wasted stained his soul more and robbed this horrid act of any redemption.

"Fifteen rhysus for this one," she called after him.

He paused. "I'll do it when I return. A few weeks."

"Weeks? No, no, no, Red. It won't be here in a few weeks. These things dry up. The opportunity passes, they dismiss the job, and no one gets paid. Fifteen's the top of the list right now, but I've heard from this man before. Fifteen is nothing to him. Once he trusts a hired blade, twenty, thirty, fifty rhysu jobs start to show up. I don't know how good you are with numbers, but what would you rather? A handful of coins today or a pocketful in a week? Or a sack in a month? I don't know what you're off to do, but don't tell me you couldn't do it better if you were a few coins richer."

He looked down to the coins in his hand. What had moments earlier seemed like more than he could have hoped for now seemed pitifully small. If what she said was true, in the space of a month, he might earn enough to free a dozen men. In a year, he might earn enough to buy the very plantation out from under the slaveholders. His conscience and his reason tugged at his thoughts. This wasn't about money, this was about lives. Who was he to be making these decisions? But if he didn't do what needed to be done, who would? There was so much to consider, so much at stake.

Finally, he cleared his mind and did what he always did when something seemed beyond him. He thought back to the one person he'd known who had the mind and heart to make such a decision. He thought back to Ben. What was most important? The purpose. Could more be done to achieve it? Yes. Then so it must be. If it can be better, then it isn't good enough. He quieted the part of his soul that still resisted, and turned back to Maribelle, eyes still low.

"What do I need to do?"

Chapter 21

While the Red Shadow was near the northern border receiving his orders, deeper in the heart of Tressor, Duule was meeting with a group of his underlings. A meeting such as this would normally have taken place in the wheat field, but in light of his capture there, he wisely decided to find a less open and more secure place to conduct his business for the time being. He selected an isolated barn some distance from his home and stocked it with six of the burliest bodyguards he could hire. Joining him were eight messengers, each carrying reports from his endless network of scouts and spies. Thus far, none of them had managed to provide him with what he considered to be a simple bit of information.

"How can you look me in the eye and tell me that *no one* has any idea who this man is?" he growled. "I ordered people to be stationed at every bounty office and watch house. You should have had his head on a platter by now! You!" He stabbed his finger at a young female messenger. "You came from the capital, right? Explain to me why he wasn't piled with half a dozen armed men the moment he showed his worthless hide to turn in a bounty there?"

"Whenever we had an ambush ready for him, he never showed. It was like he knew they were there!" Her arms were raised, shielding her face. "Even after you had your inside men sic the rest of the watch on him, he still got away. It isn't our fault!"

"I don't want to hear your excuses!" He raised his hand to strike her, then grinned at the flinch. Instead, he turned to the next messenger in line, an older man with the scars of a long and unpleasant career. "At least tell me that *you've* gotten some replies."

"Of course," stated the older man. "Most of the bounty offices you sent me to investigate have turned him away, and I managed to speak to a few of the less scrupulous hunters. Most were thrilled to see him gone. They say he was taking an awful lot money off of the table for them, and there were more than a few who were interested in the generous bounty that was anonymously offered to bring him in. Seems none of them are eager to risk having him back on the hunt again."

"Good. I want his head. And I'm not being colorful. The man who pulls that worthless wretch's empty head from his shoulders and hands it to me will have his pockets lined with gold."

"I think that trophy may be a good deal more interesting than you realize," came a sharp, smug voice from the other side of the barn door.

There came the very distinctive and threatening sound of more than a dozen people revealing a weapon simultaneously as all eyes turned to the door.

"Which one of you fools managed to lead someone here?" he growled.

"It wasn't very difficult to find you. You are a highly visible man. Open the door. I'm here to make your task a good deal easier," the voice replied.

"Who are you, and how fast and far do you think you can run? Because if you don't leave me to my business, I'm going to have my men start carving—"

Before he could finish the threat, he was silenced by a sudden and sharp drop in temperature. In moments, the air around the door fell from the warmth of a Tresson night to bitter, biting cold. Frost began to form on heavy wooden planks, and the black metal of the hinges and nails began to emit a piercing whine, rattling in place. Finally, fractures spread across the whitened wood and the whole of the doorway crumbled into a heap of frozen shards.

It revealed Teht on the other side, arms crossed and face humorless.

"Listen. My associates typically prefer that I 'comport' myself with 'tact' and 'subtlety,' but I have had quite enough of the stubborn, backward ways of this primitive, whimpering society. Listen closely, because I haven't got the time or inclination to repeat myself," Teht stated.

"Kill this wench!" Duule roared.

Teht clucked her tongue and raised her hand. Fingers curled into a curious and unnatural gesture, she swept the hand upward. A black aura coalesced around the weapons of each of Duule's men. A downward sweep of her hand sent each weapon solidly to the ground—in some cases, much to the detriment of the hand that had been holding it.

"For reasons that are beyond your capacity to comprehend, I am forbidden from engaging in open hostility toward any of you, but I am well within my rights to defend myself if needs be." She gestured upward again. The weapons launched from the ground and hung menacingly in front of their former wielders. "Do any of you feel the need to press my patience further?"

The others wisely held their ground.

"How were you able to find me?" Duule rumbled.

"I was able to find you because you shout your name and tout your influence from the rooftops. Your shriveled up little soul is a burning beacon of hate and greed. If you haven't guessed, I am a powerful sorceress. That is all that someone like me requires."

There was only an angry silence as a reply.

"Good. Then I'll make this brief," she said. "If I understand correctly, you are after a bounty hunter who turned you in, yes?"

"Yes."

"And you are also aware of the reports that a malthrope has been menacing the area, yes?"

"Yes."

"I suspect they are one and the same."

"That is preposterous! Whoever did this outwitted and outmaneuvered three of my best men. He transported me, on my own horse, from my home to Gallishasa. You would have me believe that a mere beast could have achieved such a thing."

"Much as it pains me, I'm forced to acknowledge the rather remarkable elusiveness of this particular malthrope."

"I won't hear it."

Teht looked around the room. "As I understand it, you've spread word among the watches that masked hunters are not to be trusted, yes? I assume one or more of you have spoken with watchmen who witnessed the hunter in question when he was asked to remove his mask."

"I did," answered the older messenger.

"How did he react?"

"He ran. Sometimes impressively."

"What sort of a man would rather be chased by the whole of the watch than show his face?"

"I can name any number of men who would be killed rather than willingly reveal themselves to the watch."

"Fine, then. The mask. Was it large enough to conceal the face of a malthrope?"

"They say it had an oddly-shaped visor. It may have been big enough."

Joseph R. Lallo

"All of this proves nothing," Duule snapped.

"Perhaps not, but you've been hunting a man and you've come up empty. I know for a fact that Tressor has got is share of malthrope hunters. Hire one."

"If the beast running amok near the capital is indeed who we seek—and I do not for a moment suggest that it is—then it has been the target of every malthrope hunter in the region since the day it was first sighted."

"Yes, but they have not been offered the bounty that you've placed on your delinquent hunter. 'Lining their pockets with gold' might be a bit more motivating. And when you find one willing to take on the job, you can give him these."

Teht reached into a small pouch at her belt and revealed a braided leather strand with round gems woven into the braid at regular intervals. They were each a bit smaller than a grape, and in total there were five. She also revealed a netted bag with a half-dozen more of the same gems loose within it. Each gem in the bag and strand had a dim blue glow about it. She dropped the strange accessories to the ground at Duule's feet.

"What are those?"

"They are a few aids. Affix the strand to whatever weapon you choose. It will provide an enchantment that, in the right hands, should be sufficient to bring the finest warrior to his knees. You need only use your weapon normally. If you strike your target even with a grazing blow, he will experience pain you cannot imagine. It will also disguise the scent of anyone near it. The loose gems have the same enchantment and can be thrown. Now, I'm supposed to tell you not to kill him. It suits our purposes that he be brought to us alive. Frankly, I'm sick to death of coming down here on these blasted errands, so I leave it to you. If I find that the beast has been killed, that is your decision, but it will not break my heart." She turned and stepped over the rubble of the door. After a few strides, she stopped and turned back to them. "And by the way. Those gems will only trigger if used against a malthrope, so don't bother trying to use them for your own foolish pursuits." She stirred the air with her fingers, summoning a swirl of black that steadily grew until it was a column a bit taller than she. "Don't disappoint me."

Teht stepped into the column and, an instant later, the weapons held in the air by her will clattered to the ground. Seconds after that,

272

the column tightened to a filament of brilliant violet light, then vanished with a flash, a clap of thunder, and a rush of force. When the shock of the event passed, Duule's men gathered their weapons poured from within the barn, gathering around crater where once had stood their uninvited guest.

"Useless!" Duule raged, grabbing one of the messengers and throwing him against a wall. "All of you are utterly worthless! Is there no one in this blasted kingdom who can follow a simple order? Kill anyone who would threaten me! Simple!"

He knelt down and fetched the strand of gems.

"What now, sir?" asked the burliest of his bodyguards.

Duule investigated the braid. Without taking his eyes off of it, he answered. "Find me some malthrope hunters. The best you can find. Tell them I want a word with them. And *someone* find me *someplace* where I can do my business *without being interrupted*!"

#

The Red Shadow moved swiftly through the night, a heavy sack held tight with one arm to keep it from jingling. He'd so far taken five jobs from Maribelle, and taken five lives as a result. The first had nearly killed him, and left his mind in tatters. The second never saw him coming, but his heart and soul ached afterward. Each time, he earned more gold than he could have hoped to earn in months otherwise. It was a black, bloody path to his goal, but it was taking him there. He saw each target for only a short time—a few hours at most—but each had clearly been neck-deep in dealings that would inevitably lead to a vicious end. He told himself that if it had not been his blade it would have been another, that their lives were lost long before he'd accepted the job. It didn't do any good. It took all of his will to stamp down his feelings of disgust, to deafen himself to the voices of resistance in his mind.

And what had been the price? Fifty rhysus. Fifty heavy gold coins weighed him down, the fruits of his labors. It was a staggering sum by any measure. He didn't know how many slaves it would free, but he knew it would be a few. Now all that remained was to find a way to make the purchase. The question of how he would arrange to have the money put to its intended use had been heavy on his mind for weeks, and the answer had been slow to form. Even after he'd devised a plan, he had his doubts that it was even worth a try. As had so often been the case though, he had no other options.

It had taken some doing, but over the course of the tracking he'd had to do to find his various targets, he'd found another familiar scent. One of the targets had been a blacksmith in a town called Bellarah. The name of the place had sounded familiar when he'd first been sent that way. It wasn't until he'd caught a scent on the breeze in the countryside surrounding it that he'd realized why. Now he had nearly reached the source of the scent again.

It was a farm, though the word hardly seemed appropriate. In a land dotted with sprawling plantations that grew enough crops to feed and clothe a city, this place was a garden in comparison. A single-room hut stood at one corner, and the rows were planted with simple, hearty crops. This was not a place where a fortune was made. This was a place where a man could grow enough to keep food on this table and clothes on his back. As the sun slipped from the sky, that man could be seen leaning on the handle of a shovel, eyes staring vaguely over his land. It was Menri. He might have been old to be starting anew, but he was not broken. A long life of hard work had hardened him in a way that even the years under Marret couldn't completely ruin. Under his skilled hand, this patch of land had flourished.

Careful to stay out of sight, Shadow approached him. "Menri," he whispered.

Menri's head snapped aside, his shovel raised defensively. At first, his eyes swept the darkness beside his hut without seeing, but after a moment they settled on the figure of the Shadow. He was wearing his mask, and despite the temperate night and the long run, he was bundled in his cloak, the hood firmly in place.

"Who goes there?"

"Someone from your past," the Shadow answered.

"My past is behind me now. I'm done with it."

"A past like ours never truly fades away, does it?"

"Who are you? What are you doing here?"

"I'm here to ask a favor of you. I'm here to ask you to do something that we both know needs to be done."

"You'd ask a favor without showing me your face?"

The Shadow took a steady breath. In a motion deliberate and slow, he slipped the mask from his face and pulled back the hood.

"You . . ." Menri said, fingers squeezing at the shovel handle. "*You* set foot on *my* land?"

"I've spoken to Gurruk. He told me of his escape, and yours. He told me that despite the deeds I had done, he had me to thank for his freedom and his life. He told me you would feel the same."

"Just because I owe a devil for my freedom doesn't mean I'll welcome him the day he returns."

The Red Shadow dropped his heavy sack of gold. "You were able to buy your freedom. There is enough gold there for you to do the same for several more. I want you to do just that. Buy back the lives of some others. Give them what they need to be free."

Menri kept a cautious eye on the figure before him and tugged the sack open. "How did you get this money?"

"Any way I could."

He shoved it with his toe. "I don't want it."

"It isn't for you. It is for the others. Those who are still trapped within the fences, feeling the lash of the strap. What you think of me doesn't matter. Do this one thing and you can go on hating me until we are both in our graves."

The older man eyed the gold for a bit longer. "You want nothing in exchange?"

"All I want is for you to make it clear to them what needed to be done to free them, and make them aware that they may one day be asked to do the same for others."

"Is that your plan? Pay the last freed men to free the next?"

"It is."

"Why? Do you think this will wipe the blood from your hands?"

"It doesn't matter what I think, and it doesn't matter why I choose to do it. All that matters is that it needs to be done, and that you can help make it so."

Menri considered the words. "And how will you know which men owe you their lives? How will you know where to find them when the time comes to do it again?"

"I'll be watching," the Shadow said.

"And what if I don't do it."

"You will. We lived the same nightmare. I don't think you would force that on someone else to spite me, no matter what I am."

"You killed a dozen or more humans in a single day, mally. I'd be in the right if I buried this shovel in your chest."

"It doesn't change anything."

He was quiet for a long time. Finally, as though it caused him physical pain to utter the words, he answered. "I'll do it."

The Shadow didn't linger. Without another word, he slipped on his mask, pulled up his hood, and swept off into the night.

\#

Menri did not delay. The following morning, he set off for a marketplace at a nearby crossroads, and from there learned of the location of a plantation owner on the other side of the territory looking for a buyer for some of the slaves he'd picked up to get through a particularly rough harvest. No one thought twice about a land owner buying a few slaves from another. He made some excuses about why he'd rather keep the sales from the local lord. He must have been a more skillful negotiator than Gurruk. Three more such deals netted him fifteen men and five women, all double and triple- stripe slaves. They were freed, healed of their labels, provided with the remainder of the gold, and sent on their way.

The Shadow watched it all, doing his best to memorize faces, to burn the scents into his mind. He would need them. There was no doubt about it. As he watched men and women who days before had been resigned to a life of servitude walk out into lives of their own choosing, there was no longer any doubt in his mind. What he had done was worth it. Anything would be worth it. So he would need them all, because this was just the beginning.

Chapter 22

Duule grumbled miserably. After Teht had violated his last attempt at a secure meeting place, he'd left nothing to chance. His new headquarters was the basement of a blacksmith's shop. It was sweltering, cramped, and the air was thick with the choking smell of burning wood. It was also a veritable vault: completely underground with sturdy stone walls and a single entrance. The fact that a blacksmith's shop wouldn't look out of place with a few strong men with intimidating weapons didn't hurt either.

"He's here," came the muffled voice of the thug Duule had guarding the door at the top of the stairs.

"Well, send him down, idiot!" Duule snapped.

The door opened and down the stairs thumped an aging but threatening man. He was short and his advancing years had left him soft around the middle, but something in his posture was unmistakably intimidating. Red mud was caked into a sun-blocking layer on his skin. His clothes were ancient and handmade, stitched together from hides and baring his scar-notched arms. An irregularly-trimmed beard and wild thatch of hair was gray with the slightest hint of black. He gnawed a stem of sugar-stalk, absentmindedly scratching at the four deep scars dominating his face. Dust flaked away as he did so. When he reached the only vacant chair, he sat heavily, sending a cascade of reddish earth to the ground beside him.

"You are Dihsaad?" asked Duule, making no attempt to hide his disgust at the man he'd been forced to deal with.

His visitor nodded slowly, spitting a bit of sugary pulp to the ground.

"My men tell me that you are malthrope hunter."

"I have been," he stated.

"Have been? Am I to believe that you are not a hunter anymore?" Duule's expression could have shattered stone, and in his eyes, one could see his mind at work crafting a suitable punishment for those responsible for this waste of time.

"Not a hunter. I track, mostly. Until recently it was slaves. Tracking a malthrope is a bit harder. Killing is a young man's game

277

though."

Duule calmed somewhat. "Fine. That's fine. I've got no shortage of men willing to handle that part of it. I trust your services are available for hire?"

"For the right price, my services are always for hire."

"Good, good. I assume you're aware of the rash of mally attacks up and down eastern Tressor."

He grunted. "Attacks? Thought it was just sightings. Anyway, yes, I'm aware. Strange. Mallies don't all do things at once. It makes me think it's all the same one, except mallies like to keep to familiar ground, mostly. Maybe you see a string of sightings in one direction, but not the other, not so soon after."

"Yes, well," Duule began, a hesitation in his voice suggesting that he was reluctant to say what came next. "I've had some problems with a bounty hunter who wears a mask. He has been unwilling to remove it and . . ." He chuckled. "It has been suggested that the mally and the hunter might be one and the same."

The unscarred side of Dihsaad's lips peeled back in a grin, revealing gleaming white teeth that seemed out of place amid his otherwise grimy features.

Duule sneered. "Laughable I know, but—"

"No. Just means it's a feisty one. A feisty one gave me this," he said, running his fingers across the scars.

"You mean to tell me that a malthrope could be smart enough to find a mask and deal with humans without being detected."

Dihsaad's eyes drifted. "I didn't used to think so, but something happened a little while back." He rubbed a fresher scar on his other cheek. "Malthropes . . . you don't really know them until you know them. If you think they're mindless, soulless, bloodthirsty animals? You're right. If you think they're vile, deceitful, manipulating fiends? You're right about that, too. They are those things and plenty others. I guess it just depends on which one you're taking about."

"How could anything be all of those things?"

"Look in a mirror and you answer me," he said with a shrug.

Duule turned the words over in his mind for a moment before abandoning them as incompatible with is favored way of thinking. "If you can track this creature down, you can name your price, but only on one condition. I need to hear its voice."

"You want it alive?"

"No. I want it dead, and I want it to suffer. But you only get the full price on this thing's head if I hear it with my own ears first. If it and the hunter really are the same, then this thing had the gall to turn me in. I heard it speak, and I want to be sure the beast I kill is the same one that dared cross me. I'll pay any price to make an example of someone who crosses me, but I am not in the habit of paying a fortune for the extermination of a simple pest."

Dihsaad pulled the stalk from his mouth, spat, and nodded. The men stood and slapped the shoulder of the other.

"Start immediately. My men will be in touch."

Dihsaad made his way up the stairs and out of the basement, leaving Duule to brush away the filthy red hand print on his shoulder and quietly curse the man or beast responsible for the humiliations he'd been forced to endure.

#

Once assigned one of Duule's more reliable hired blades, Dihsaad went to work. Tracking something like this one, a target who moved over half the kingdom, was a daunting task. Dihsaad was a meticulous and experienced tracker, though, and Duule had eyes in every corner of Tressor. The tracker gathered rumors, sifted through them, and selected a place to start. It was a stretch of shrubs and tall grass, some distance from a road near a town on toward the east coast.

"You sure we should be here? No one said they saw the thing here," said the muscle that Duule had assigned.

Though the man in question was named Munn, he could just as well have been any of the legion of stout strongmen in Duule's employ. His scalp and face were both poorly shaved, with a filthy rag tied tightly to his head to keep the sun off and a heap of knobby crocodile-hide armor draped across his hulking body. He carried a curiously shaped blade as well. It was the length of a longsword, but with a broad, single-edged blade that made it resemble an oversized cleaver.

"A mally that's smart enough to survive more than a few years doesn't spend much time in a place where people might see it," Dihsaad said. "Around the same time, people claim to have seen one in each of the towns surrounding. This is the best cover near to them all. It spent time here, if anywhere."

While his dimwitted assistant watched with an equally vacant mind and expression, Dihsaad crouched stiffly and began to crawl across the ground, sweeping his eyes and sifting the sandy earth with his fingers.

279

This was the third likely hiding place that they'd searched. The last two hadn't had a scrap of evidence to suggest that a malthrope had even passed through. This one felt different, though. The usual signs were still absent, but there was the sense that they had been removed, covered up. It was difficult to be sure. Here was a patch of dirt a bit too smooth, as though a footprint had been swept away. There was a pile of stones that seemed to have been arranged. He was about to give his knees a much needed rest when his fingers came upon something in the dirt. He dug down a bit more and revealed . . . a bone.

"What's that?" Munn asked.

"A rib. Chewed by teeth a good deal bigger than anything around here ought to have. Broken for the marrow. Buried. Yes . . . this is one of the clever ones."

#

As the Red Shadow continued in his task, clearing Maribelle's "black list" and quickly becoming her most valued asset, Dihsaad continued his search. He knew from experience that a malthrope was not like a fugitive or slave. One did not capture a malthrope by chasing it. Once the beast knew someone was on its tail, it would run faster and farther than one could hope to follow. The secret to capturing one hinged upon getting ahead of the creature. He would find a place that the beast returned to frequently, someplace it felt safe. Gradually the trails revealed themselves, and they all seemed to lead to a single place.

#

Maribelle reclined, eyes half shut and mouth half open. The front of her armor was covered in crumbs from some manner of pastry, and a strong-smelling glass of bahk sat on the table beside her. As quietly as the wind rushing over the roadside weeds, her best blade approached. He stood before her for a moment before finally making his presence known with a deliberate scuff of his feet along the baked stone walkway running in front of her place of business.

"Ah," she said, attempting as she always did to appear as though his appearance hadn't startled her. "Right on time, as usual. Follow me."

She eased herself out of the chair and ambled toward the deserted section of the city. Out of justifiable paranoia, or perhaps out of eccentricity, she never seemed to keep the specifics of a job in the same building twice in a row. It meant that there was always a bit of a stroll before he could be told precisely what she was after. This time, the journey took them up the slope, toward the windmill at the high point of the town.

"You speak much Varden, Red?" she asked. She had a strange habit of engaging in idle chitchat as they walked, as though she were giving him mundane little errands to run, rather than sending him to take a life.

He shook his head.

"Millcrest. Refers to all the mills, see. That's what the blue-suits call these things here. The ones down by the water and this one up here. This town used to be part of Ulvard. For a while, the border went right through the middle. That was before the war, naturally. Couldn't tell you what they used to grind in these things. Before my time." She began to breathe heavily as the slope got the better of her. By the time they had reached the windmill, she was mopping sweat from her brow. "I hate heading up here. Don't know why I even use this old place."

She led the way around to the back of the windmill, where a large courtyard was roughly enclosed by a tall, decrepit fence. At some point in the last few years, a section of the bluff had sloughed off, taking a sizable portion of the fence with it. The water could be heard rushing below. Most of the courtyard was scattered with broken carts and carriages, as well as bits of machinery that were degraded well beyond recognition. The windmill itself was surprisingly intact, a tall, roundish stone structure with a long, low wooden building about the size of a stable attached at the base. He'd never come this close to it, and now something about the place was putting the Shadow on edge. He shifted his mask forward a bit and drew in a slow whiff of the air. There was nothing but the scent of rotten wood and grain.

Maribelle dug out her keys and began to flip through them.

"Well, I've got good news for you, Red," she said. "Just one job on the list, and it's an easy one. Pays quite a bit, too."

He stood silently.

"You interested?"

He nodded.

"You'll be helping get rid of someone who made an enemy of a few folks with deep pockets and not much respect for the sanctity of human life. Same as always, I suppose. Sound good?"

Again, he nodded.

Her expression hardened a bit. "You interested in the specifics?"

Another nod.

She rolled her eyes. "Maybe I haven't paid much attention, but I don't remember you being quite so quiet."

He simply stared in reply.

"You got something against talking, Red? Something happen to your tongue?"

He shook his head.

"Then do me the courtesy of a yes or a no when I ask you a question. Now, do you want to help me get this job done?"

"Yes," he said.

She turned her head vaguely to the side for a moment, then rolled her eyes again. "Yes *what*?"

"Yes, I want to help you get this job done. Please. Just tell me what I need to do."

There was a trio of rattles from somewhere in the mill building, prompting him to snap his head in that direction. Nothing seemed to be swinging loose in the wind. He shifted his attention to Maribelle again just in time for her to open the windmill door.

"Good. Stay put. I expect the payment is as good as earned already," she said, shutting the door again with him outside.

He stood alone in the courtyard, anxiety building steadily, though he could not pinpoint a cause. Another few sniffs turned up nothing worthy of alarm, but each passing moment made him more certain that something was wrong. He adjusted his mask again, now attempting to align his eyes more appropriately with the slits. He scanned the courtyard slowly. Tall grass pushing through the paving stones of the courtyard rustled in the wind. The barely visible shadow of the windmill's blades shifted and slid in the moonlight.

Then there was a motion, a glint of blue that flared and darted toward him. He sprang aside, dodging whatever it was and leaving it to shatter on the stones beside him. In a heartbeat, his hand was on the small dagger at his belt and his eyes were turned in the direction from which the blue stone had come. Then a sensation of raw, blinding pain wrapped itself around his leg.

Breath stuck in his throat as the pain drove further and further into him, cutting beyond mere flesh until he was certain it was tearing into his very soul. He looked to his leg and found that a pulsing tendril of black was curled around it. The darkness wasn't something physical, but rather a shifting and writhing ribbon of dark energy rolling across the surface of his leg. The spell blackened and deteriorated the hide of his trousers, then his flesh and fur until finally his leg failed him and he fell to the ground. The pain was so intense now he couldn't even wrestle enough air into his lungs to scream. When finally he was able to turn his teary eyes back to the world around him, he was surrounded by a series of figures, some of whom he didn't recognize, but several he did.

"Yes, that is certainly the voice of the elusive idiot who thought he could lock me away," said the first figure, Duule. He gestured aside to one of the bulky cohorts who flanked him. "Hand out payments. Glad to see I've finally found a few people who can deliver."

While his man rummaged through a sack over his shoulder and pulled out jingling bags of coins, Duule stepped forward and delivered a punishing boot to the downed malthrope's chest.

"I wouldn't waste any time finishing this one," said Dihsaad, pocketing his payment.

"Oh, I assure you, he's breathing his last breaths. I've just got a few things to do first. You, with the sword. Get that mask off him. I want to see what he is with my own eyes," Duule ordered.

Munn stepped forward, planting a boot on the Shadow's shoulder and roughly pulling the mask free. His beastly face revealed, all in observance recoiled, leaving him twisting on the ground.

"It *is* one of those things," Duule said, turning his head aside.

"I could have told you that. It certainly wasn't any human I was tracking," said Dihsaad. "I'll tell you, that gem strand that hid our scent. I wouldn't mind having that. I could make a job like mine a good deal easier."

"No, tracker. A one-of-a-kind item like that stays with me. I'm not in the business of donating priceless enchantments to the locals. Hand over the gems."

Dihsaad shrugged and tossed the bag of loose gems to Duule. The criminal tugged it open and plucked one from inside, admiring it for a moment.

"Still. These things only work on mallies. Seems a shame to let them go to waste."

He tossed the gem toward his prisoner. With a desperate heave aside, he managed to avoid being struck. The gem shattered with a spark of violet light, and a curl of smoky black energy curled forth like ink spreading in a glass of water. Then, as though it had a mind of its own, the energy struck, wrapping itself around the malthrope's arm and bringing a fresh wave of agony. His hand tightened, fingers curling like a dying spider.

A horrid smile twisted Duule's face.

"Remind me to acquire the services of a few wizards. They make some useful trinkets. Enough amusement. Munn, kill the thing before it finds a way to wriggle out of our grasp again."

His henchmen nodded and grasped the creature by the tunic, hauling it from the ground. He twisted his weapon, leveling it with his victim's neck and bringing it close. The braid of gems was tied to the handle, and under its influence, the cutting edge of the weapon danced and shimmered with black and violet.

"I always wanted to see if I could get a head clean off in once slice," he mused.

The others spread apart to give the executioner room as he recklessly took a few test swings, pulling the blade back and bringing it forward until it just barely touched the beast's neck. Satisfied with his technique, he brought the blade back and heaved it forward. The Shadow took that moment to thrust the heel of his good leg hard onto the foot of his attacker. At the same time, he threw his head back. The swing went wild, coming near enough to graze a few hairs of the beast's chin before the sword wrenched free of his grip, twirling off to clatter into to a bit of ancient equipment. The hulking brute stumbled and reeled, creature still in his grasp but struggling madly. The pair lurched toward the edge of the bluff, Munn fighting to steady himself and the malthrope doing all that he could to keep him off balance.

"Get in there and help him, you idiots!" Duule ordered to his lackeys.

They rushed in, but by the time they reached the tangled pair, they were on the unstable ground where the fence had fallen away. The telltale patter of tumbling soil warned that the precipice was in no condition to support two men, let alone four. They stopped short and watched as Munn finally got control again and wrapped both hands around his foe's neck.

"Little monster! Little demon! I'll squeeze the eyes out of your mangy skull!" he growled.

"Munn, you idiot, get away from the edge!" Duule ordered.

The Red Shadow fought for breath, eyes wild and searching. Behind him was a long fall into raging water. He didn't know how deep it was, or how fast it was moving—and, regardless, he still didn't know how to swim properly. But his vision was already growing dim, and if he didn't make a decision now, he never would. He used his last ounce of strength to lash out with his knee, driving it into Munn's midsection. The mountain of a man pitched forward, breath rushing out in a ragged grunt, and took one final step forward. The crumbling earth at the edge of the courtyard finally reached its limit, breaking away beneath his boot and sending the two of them tumbling over the side.

Both man and beast clashed against the face of the bluff and plunged into the rushing water. Each was weighed down by too much clothing and too many weapons, and thus each was promptly swallowed by the roiling surface.

Duule and those in his employ crowded as close to the edge as they dared, watching the floundering forms sink from sight. The criminal was trembling with anger, and those henchmen who remained were wise enough to hold their tongues and thank their lucky stars that they were not the target of the anger. It wasn't until Maribelle exited her safe house and joined them that the furious silence was broken.

"So. Job done then?" she asked. "Do I get my gold?"

"No," fumed Duule. "Once again I am confounded by the idiocy of my underlings."

"What happened?"

"Somehow, even when the thing was half-crippled, it managed to drag the both of them into the river."

"You're going to go after it, right? I don't want that thing coming after me," Maribelle said, her voice heavy with the very reasonable concern of a woman who has learned that the skilled tracker and efficient killer she had just betrayed might not be dead.

"If a musclebound behemoth with his hands wrapped around the blasted thing's neck couldn't kill it, I'll be damned if I'm going to trust a river to do the job." He turned to Dihsaad and the rest of his men. "Get back on its trail. Find it. If it is dead, bring it to me. If it is alive, *kill it* and bring it to me."

The tracker and the thugs were quick to comply, leaving Maribelle behind.

"Wait! When *do* I get paid?" she cried. "I practically handed that beast to you with a bow on its head. It isn't *my* fault you let it get away."

Duule turned and glared at her. "You. Gold," he said to the

strongman in charge of carting around the payments.

The meaty underling reached into the sack at his side and pulled out a tightly packed coin satchel. Duule took the payment and walked up to Maribelle, holding it out for a moment. He then turned and pitched it off the bluff and into the river.

"What was that for?" she griped.

"I asked you to give me the malthrope and it wound up in the river. Now I've got a lot of searching and frustration ahead of me to get it. Seems your payment should be the same. And as far as I'm concerned, at this point your *real* payment will be if we manage to kill the malthrope before it comes back and kills you. The rest is just generosity."

Maribelle grimaced and looked to the water below as Duule and his men departed. "I'm beginning to think I sided with the wrong murderer."

Chapter 23

The mighty river grew wider and calmer as it approached the crescent sea. At a place where it was widest, a section near enough to the coast for the air to have a salty tinge to it, the Red Shadow's motionless body drifted to the muddy northern bank. Minutes passed before he stirred, and when he did, it was with a violent coughing fit. He rolled aside, pulling himself farther ashore and hacking up river water until his lungs were clear. When his breathing was finally back to normal, he slithered through the mud to the shelter of some tall weeds and tried to pull his thoughts together.

He was chilled to the bone by the icy water. Where his body wasn't numb, it was throbbing. The arm afflicted by his attacker's dark magic hadn't recovered much. Three of his fingers were twisted and useless, and a stabbing pain still curled itself around his forearm like a thorny vine. His leg was similarly lifeless below the knee and wracked with pain. His weapons were gone, his equipment was gone, and the payment from his last job was gone, all claimed by the river. He was worse off now than he'd been upon escaping the plantation. Searching weakly, he discovered that the only thing that had not been claimed by the water was the old rag Sorrel had left behind, which had been folded safely into its own pocket in his shirt.

If he'd allowed himself to dwell upon what had happened, he likely would have been overcome, defeated, but he'd been a free malthrope in the world of man long enough for certain survival instincts to become little more than reflexes. He had to assume that people who had done this to him would still be after him. He would need to get to a place they could not reach him. Where would the people of Tressor never follow? Only one answer came to mind: the Nameless Empire. It was a place where they, like he, would be killed on sight.

He didn't have a firm enough grip on his wits to formulate a better plan, so north he would go.

It took time and effort, but he managed to wrestle enough control over his damaged leg to climb to his feet. Once standing, he moved in a daze, eyes barely focused and breath ragged. Every few minutes he paused to cough up another splash of the river, but he kept going. He

Joseph R. Lallo

hadn't the presence of mind nor the physical strength to avoid soldiers from either army, but through a rare stroke of good fortune, the soldiers defending this stretch of the border must have been called to battle elsewhere, because three full days passed before his mind cleared, and by then he was well north of the front. During that time, his meals were composed of whatever plants he could stomach and whatever else he could scavenge.

Now it was night. The journey so far had taken him north along the east coast of the northern land until the grassy fields turned to the rocky beginnings of a mountain range. All around him were pines, and far to the north he saw snow-capped peaks. He'd just managed to snatch up his first fresh meat since the attack, in the form of a squirrel that had not been wary enough. What little the meal did for his hunger was sufficient to set his mind to the long overdue task of processing what had happened.

He had been a fool, that much he knew. He had been careless, weak. It had cost him everything. Had he been stronger, perhaps he would have been able to fight off the ambush . . . but they had been using magic. There had simply been no way for him to have been prepared.

His eyes turned to the twisted fingers of his hand, still not quite recovered even now. With his other hand he touched a sore spot on his forehead, only to discover a crusted-over gash he'd not noticed before.

A wave of anger swept over him. It didn't make any sense! He had fought off the griffin, he'd savaged Marret's farm . . . why couldn't he fend off a single man with a sword, magic or no? What good was it having a monster lurking inside if when he needed it most it wasn't there?

His face twisted in pain as he tried to flex the fingers of the arm that had felt the touch of whatever dark spell had been at work. Swords and whips, straps and arrows, none of them had been enough to stop him, so they'd turned to magic. It seemed hopeless. Perhaps if he was any other being, or if this had been any other time, he would have considered abandoning his cause. Not now. He'd sacrificed too much. He'd let his only chance for happiness walk away from him. He'd committed irredeemable deeds. He'd felt his soul wither, shut his heart and his emotions deep away. The purpose was all there was. So the answers must be found.

The solution had to be out there. Until now, he'd learned all that he needed by listening and observing. Ben, Sorrel, even the criminals of Tressor had taught him lessons that he'd used to come this far. But now he needed to know how to fight, how to kill. He needed to know how to combat mystic spells and how to escape dedicated trackers. No one would teach a malthrope such things. He could find his way back to the front and watch the soldiers do battle, but surely the tactics one used as part of an army were of little use to one working alone. Perhaps he could seek out battle on his own, find warriors and challenge them . . . no. If he was not flawless from the beginning, he would be hurt and have to recover, or be killed outright before he could learn anything. There had to be a way. There had to . . .

His eyes swept over the scene before him. The clouds were thick and heavy here, blotting out the stars and leaving the moon little more than a dull glow. He'd climbed a fair way up the slope of the foothills, and from that vantage, the dim light revealed much of the land. This place was not like Tressor. There, a view such as this would have included flickering fires and rattling carriages even at this time of night. There would be signs of life and bounty. Not so in this place. He could see only one town: a small, tightly-packed hamlet that hid behind tall, crude walls. He looked farther north, where the forest grew denser, and something about the way the trees met the mountains stirred a memory from long ago. It was something Ben had told him when he was young, a story about a cave that was home to a mighty beast. Ben had said that the greatest warriors in the world would seek it out to battle, and they would fall.

He let the story unfold itself in his mind. Decades of warriors entered the cave to face this thing, and none returned. It had done what he hoped to do. It had battled the best and emerged victorious. It *must* have learned much in those years. Become savvy in the ways of battle, either through instinct or wisdom. Slowly, he came to a decision. He would find this cave, and he would find the beast within. If it was an intelligent creature like himself, he would implore it to teach him its ways. If it had struck down so many warriors, then it was no friend of man. Perhaps then it would be a friend to him. If it was mindless and wild, then he would fight it. If anything could pull to the surface the rage and fury that had carried him through the battles with the griffin and the slave-drivers, it would be this beast. And if the monster killed him? Well, whatever the outcome, his troubles would be over.

By the time the sun was beginning to add color to the clouds, his mind was made up. He would sleep, and when he woke, he would seek the cave.

#

For a time, the Shadow traveled steadily northward. The temperature dropped sharply as he went. Before long, the ground was covered with dense snow. The need to remain unrecognized as a malthrope had long required him to dress heavily enough for the stifling heat of Tressor to be nearly unbearable. Even stripped of his cloak by the river, the handmade hide shirt and trousers were more than enough to make him uncomfortably warm when he was south of the front. The cool air of the north was at first a blessing, though the farther he traveled, the deeper the wind sunk its teeth. By the time he'd reached what he presumed to be the heart of the forest, he was grateful for the layers he still had. Sorrel hadn't been exaggerating when she suggested that the cold of the Tresson mountains was nothing compared to what the north had to offer.

For all of the faults of this northern land, there were benefits as well. The farther north he traveled, the fewer humans and the like could be seen outside of the cities. Once within the forest, there was seldom so much as a whiff of a human on the breeze, and little sign that a human had ever been to a given stretch of woods. Hunting was good in the forest, too. True, he was lucky if he smelled half as many creatures in a day as he did on the Tresson plains, and a fraction of what he smelled in the Great Forest, but there was more than enough to make meals quick and easy to secure. It was a dense forest, plenty of shelter and places to hide. He could make a fine home here . . . but a home was not what he was after. He was seeking the cave of the beast.

For a time, he worried that he would never find the place. It wasn't that he couldn't find a cave. Quite the opposite—the mountainside was littered with them. The problem was that he didn't know which cave was the one he sought. He had no map, and even if he'd had one, he wouldn't have known how to read it. Some of the caves were marked with signs, but he couldn't read *them* either. Even if they had been in his native language, he wouldn't have known what they said, but these were in Crich, or Varden. Despite his troubles, he pressed on.

To this point, everything in his life had been a struggle. He hadn't expected this to be any different. He reasoned that the cave of the beast would surely be marked, if only to warn the unwary of the dangers ahead, and it would need to be large if a creature was to live inside without ever being seen. Caves that met the requirements were rare, and those that seemed to be likely candidates didn't stand to scrutiny for very long. Either the place stunk of humans coming and going—certainly not something one would expect of a monster's lair—or a quick search turned up nothing.

After weeks of searching, he finally found something. The cave itself was rather unassuming. It was somewhat taller than he at its mouth, and a narrow stream flowed from it. Surrounding it, though, was a veritable thicket of signs. They seemed to be written in all manner of languages, as the shapes and symbols were vastly different from one to the next. Others had no words at all, only showing human skulls and other strong and forbidding shapes. More threatening than them all, though, was the smell. It was far too faint for a human to detect, but unmistakable to him: death, rot, fear. Lives had been lost in this place.

He breathed deep and looked into the yawning mouth of the place. He expected to feel anxious, fearful. Instead, he felt only resolve. Somewhere within this cavern was a being that knew more about how to kill and how to survive than any other. If he ever left this place, it would be with some semblance of that same knowledge. Whether he earned it through necessity or through experience, he would learn it well or he would lose his life. It was the way forward or the way out, and regardless of which, it would be well-deserved. There was nothing to fear for him now but leaving this place no better than he entered.

He hesitated only for a moment when he realized that he was without a weapon, but pressed on regardless. He'd had no weapon when he faced the griffin. It was just as well that he had none now.

Beside entrance to the cave, hanging beneath a large and detailed sign inscribed with every conceivable word or image that might dissuade someone from entering, was a cluster of torches and a few bits of flint and steel. The mere fact that neither had been stolen spoke volumes of how feared this cave must truly be. He took two torches, sparking one to life and pocketing a flint. Without another moment of hesitation, he marched into the maw.

He wasn't a dozen steps into the cavern when it became clear that this place was unlike any he had been before. During his time in the Tresson mountains, he'd been in and out of many caves, and in his search for this one, he had explored many more. This was entirely different. The stream running along the ground had made the floor and walls slick with ice and frost. Then there was the sound. For the most part, he was following the running water to its source, and its trickle and flow filled the air constantly. It echoed up and down the tunnel, and into and out of more side tunnels than he could count. The sound multiplied and fractured, becoming a cacophonous din. For a creature such as he, a creature with ears sensitive enough to paint nearly as clear a picture as his eyes, it was confounding and disorienting, like looking into a pair of parallel mirrors and seeing an infinite hallway. Worse, it meant that the beast could approach him from any side and there would be no simple way to detect it.

He moved more slowly, forced his breath to be as steady as possible, and sifted his every sense for anything hidden within the shadows and echoes.

Time passed, though without the sun or stars to go by, it was difficult to know just how *much* time had passed. Gradually, the torch began to dim, but he pressed on, following the trickling water. The farther he traveled, the more the cave changed. It grew warmer. Where once had been a crust of ice was now a glaze of inky water coating every surface. The air became heavy and muggy, with a stale and lifeless quality to it. The passage that contained the stream was quite large, but the tunnels branching from it varied greatly in size. When they seemed large enough to be a potential home for the beast, he would explore them. Some seemed to fan out forever, but most led downward until the way was blocked by water. Indeed, anything that reached downward into the depths of the mountain seemed inevitably to reach a point where only water could be found.

Just as the torch was burning its last, the stream that he had followed reached its source. The tunnel had opened into a vast alcove, large enough that the weak light revealed only the rocky and uneven floor, while the walls and ceiling were lost in the darkness. When he finally reached something else, it was a natural wall, smooth where the water flowed but riddled with jagged fractures and splits elsewhere. The flow that made up the stream was formed by a dozen rivulets leaking through faults in the wall. The trickling sound of water, constantly with him through his journey so far, was louder here. It almost sounded as though it was coming from within the very stone beneath his feet.

He lit the new torch from the old and raised it high. There was little to suggest which way was best, but he noticed that a rotting scent was strongest to his left. Reasoning that where there was death, there was likely to be the beast responsible, he marched off in that direction. It led to a long, wide tunnel with a low roof and a slight downward slope. He feared that it would end blocked by water as so many others did, but instead the slope leveled at a point where murky water was only ankle deep. The roof of the tunnel was only just tall enough to keep his ears from brushing the roof, and the water covering the floor was biting cold, but the scent guiding him forward was certainly stronger here. He pressed on.

Progress was slow, as he was forced to slosh carefully in order to be sure there were no pitfalls or jagged stones hidden by the cloudy water. The floor must have kept a bit of its downward slope after all, as more than an hour of twists and turns brought the water level first to his knees, then to his waist. The clash of frigid water and muggy air was shocking, but the scent still beckoned. It wasn't until the water was chest-high and he hadn't found any trace of what he was after that he decided to turn back.

After a few minutes of backtracking, though, something wasn't right. The water level stayed high, and may even have crept a bit higher. He stopped, eyes wide with chilling realization. The floor hadn't been dropping—the water had been rising! He forced panic aside and quickly assessed his options. The last branching cavern that led upward was well behind him. The water had been below his knees when he passed it. At the rate he was moving, the tunnel would be entirely flooded long before he reached it. His eyes turned back in the direction he'd been heading. He had no way of knowing if it would lead to safety or doom, but he had little choice. If he had to die, let him die moving forward.

Heedless of any dangers the water might hide, his urgency drove him forward. Almost as though it sensed it had been discovered, the rising water seemed to quicken its pace. Before long, it was hissing against the head of the torch and he was forced to sweep against the flow with his free arm to make any progress. Now it was neck-high, his feet only barely able to stay on the floor. Soon after, it was to his chin and the torch was all but extinguished, but there was a whisper of hope. He couldn't see it, but ahead he could hear the hollow echo of an alcove. The water continued its rise until he had to tip his head up to keep his nose above the surface. The torch finally went under, leaving him in total darkness. He released the useless light source and abandoned the ground entirely, pivoting to float on his back and scrabble along the ceiling with his hands and kick with his legs.

Only the top of his snout was above the water now, and he was moving blind. His submerged ears told of little more than his thrashing motions, dulled by icy fluid. That left him with only his sense of direction to lead him onward. He tried to shut desperation out of his mind. It would do no good. Precious sips of air came fewer and further between until finally the water met the roof. His lungs were burning and heaving when finally his clawing fingers reached for the ceiling and instead found only more water. He worked his arms and legs hard, and not a moment too soon he broke the surface.

He threw his mouth wide and took a deep grateful breath. Though they were no longer under the inky water, his eyes were still useless to him in the darkness. Worse, his skill at swimming hadn't improved much. Floundering in the darkness eventually took him to a wall. It was slick with the same coating of slimy liquid as the rest of the cave, but there were deep striations that made it at least climbable. He pulled himself from the icy water. Once free of it, he paused only long enough to cough his lungs clear. If the water was rising, he wanted to be as far from it as he could manage. He located solid grips with slow, deliberate searches using numbed fingers, and eventually found his way to a reasonably level platform to crawl onto. Once there, he collapsed, trembling from the cold and stress. The oppressive warmth of the cave chased the cold away in time, and the rest was forced aside. There were other things to deal with now.

The torch was gone, and with it the only source of light he had. Without it, the darkness was complete. For one with eyes as sharp as his, even the darkest night provided light enough to give him shapes to navigate by. Darkness, true darkness, was something he had never faced. It was unsettling, and might even have been terrifying if there hadn't been far greater concerns to consider: he had no food, and the path to the outside was blocked. Perhaps there was another way out, but he'd been walking with purpose for many hours, and with a light to guide him. Trying to find his way blindly through unfamiliar tunnels would just as likely lead him to the bottom of a chasm as to daylight.

Just as his mind began shifting and swirling with the first moments of panic, something else broke through and seized his attention. The scent that had brought him this far was near. Very near. The moldy, sickening stench of decaying remains was doubtlessly coming from this very ledge. He felt his way along on his hands and knees, always mindful of the edge. Steadily the ripple and splash of water was joined by the skitter of hundreds of tiny legs. Finally, his fingers brushed something rough and metallic.

It was difficult to be certain by touch, but he seemed to have discovered the remains of a knight. There was certainly a shield, and with it many metal plates and leather straps. He maneuvered himself to a crouching position, balanced on the balls of his feet, and felt for the only pieces of equipment he had left, his flint and steel. He dragged it in a short, swift motion and conjured a brief spray of sparks. It wasn't much light, and it only lasted for an instant, but his eyes didn't need much. Using the light of the flash without washing out his vision was difficult, but in it he saw a swarm of tiny black beetles scatter. They had been feasting on what little remained of a fallen warrior. Sturdy armor that must have cost a fortune was orange with rust. It was draped over what was now little more than a skeleton with scraps of flesh clinging to moldy bone. Beside it lay a pack, discarded and open.

It was a gruesome scene, but as he turned it over in his mind, he couldn't help but think that there was something wrong. He scratched out another rain of sparks, then another. Things were missing. The armor was undamaged. No bones seemed to be broken. There was no stain of blood. The sword had not even been drawn. There wasn't any evidence of battle.

He grasped at the ground beside the remains until his fingers closed around the pack. Inside he found a lantern, dry of oil. There was rancid cloth that still smelled of salted and smoked meats, and wineskin that had been utterly drained. One corner of the skin had been chewed—not by insects or rodents, but by large, blunt teeth. It had been teeth like the man's own. This was someone who had come prepared. He had brought plenty of provisions, and he had exhausted them. It was no beast that had killed this warrior . . .

The deeper meaning of the discovery had only just begun to come together in his mind when something demanded his full attention. There was a rumble just below the level of hearing. It began as just a tremble beneath his feet, but steadily it grew until it was rattling his bones. His heart raced and he crouched low, clawing for the grip of the sword and pulling it free, scattering the rest of the remains. He stood tall and planted his feet, eyes pointlessly sweeping the darkness. Gritting his teeth, he strained his ears, but they did him no good. The sound was coming from all around him. A deep breath told only of the stench of the fallen warrior. All the while the sound built, unrelenting. It reached a crescendo, the rumble shifting to a deafening grind and finally to a rush of water. He felt an icy spray of mist against his face and hands. The sound must have been a cave wall giving way, or perhaps some ancient natural dam releasing. It was no beast, but it was no less deadly. Already he could hear the lap and splash of water creeping higher against the wall that he had climbed to reach his current perch. He needed to find higher ground, and quickly.

He made his way as quickly as he could along the platform, heading away from the edge. In just a few moments, he reached another wall, one that wouldn't be nearly so simple a climb. The floor at its base seemed to slope upward toward the left, and the echoing seemed more distant in that direction, so left he went. Eventually it led to a tunnel just barely large enough to crawl through. Tunnel after tunnel passed in the same way; wedging himself through whatever opening seemed to take him upward and away from the sound of water.

Before long, the splash of water was well behind him, but he didn't stop until he couldn't hear it at all. The trek quickly taught him that, with a bit of care, it was possible to navigate by ear. A wide-open room sounded quite different from a narrow tunnel. Likewise, a dead end, even a fair distance away, sent more echoes back to him than the hollow reverberations of a clear path. It wasn't ideal, but a few hard raps with the pommel of the sword on the stone floor could give him a rudimentary image of the cave ahead. At the very least, it was enough to prevent him from falling into any chasms.

An hour or so of tapping and crawling led him to what seemed to be a relatively dry and quiet nook in the mountain. He dragged the flint along the sword a few times, providing him with enough of a glimpse of his surroundings to see that there was no obvious danger lurking unheard around him. Satisfied, his mind was finally given the time to dwell upon his situation.

The remains had not painted a picture of a heroic battle with a legendary foe. That warrior had withered away. He had consumed his supplies, run out of light, and lost his way. By the end, he had been reduced to gnawing on leather to try to ease his hunger. He had starved, and with a pack that size he must have been in the cave for many days before it happened. Surely if the beast were anywhere to be found, it would have encountered him in that amount of time . . .

His stomach rumbled. Though he couldn't be sure, it may have been a day since he'd entered this place. He would need food soon, and he'd found nothing here that might begin to provide nourishment. A creeping coldness gnawed at his mind. After all he had been through, all he had survived, was this how it would end? Would he just waste away in the bowels of a mountain?

The iron-hard shell of determination that had kept the dark feelings and thoughts away until now had finally buckled. Despair and fear were rushing over him. The impenetrable darkness surrounding him seemed to press down, closing in. It was over. He'd made the wrong decision, taken on a task too great for him, and now he would pay for it with his life. His heart hammered and his breathing became swift and shallow. Images raced through his mind as the maddening feeling became more familiar. He'd felt this same hopeless fear once before. His memories settled upon the day he had tried and failed to catch his first thorn elk. He'd found himself up a tree, cowering just as he was now. Shaking, his fingers found their way to the inside of his shirt, to the pocket he'd sewn there, and the simple swatch of cloth within it. He clutched it in his fingers as the scene progressed in his memories. Sorrel found him. She talked him down from the tree, took his hands in hers, and confided in him the one lesson he was never to forget: never stop trying.

It wasn't over. He hadn't been beaten yet. He was still breathing, he still had his wits, and he still had his senses. He would not die as that knight had. There was too much left to do. Raising his nose he took a breath, long and slow. There was the lingering stench of the remains he'd left behind. Mixed with it were the scents of other fallen adventurers, older than the first and scattered. The dank smell of the cave itself seemed to be all that remained . . . no. There was something else. Something deeper. He couldn't identify it, but it was undeniable.

Three quick sniffs selected a direction, two quick taps gave him a mental picture of the way forward. When the cloth was safely stowed again, he was off toward it.

The way was treacherous. Despite being so far above the water, there seemed to be a permanent glaze of moisture on the stone. Even as his skill at navigating by feel and by ear grew, several times he lost his footing, and once he nearly fell down a drop that would surely have killed him. Finally, he abandoned the boots he wore. It was worth losing their protection to gain a firmer grip on the treacherous surface.

When untold hours of travel brought him to a pool of still water, he approached it, hoping that a few swallows of it would hold his hunger at bay. Something was wrong, though. The water had a subtle smell to it that Sorrel had warned him away from in the past. Poison. Two more tainted pools had to be avoided before a pure one could be found. Near the second poisoned pool was the skeleton of another warrior, one who had learned too late of the water's hidden danger.

It was not until what felt like days later that he finally seemed to be nearing the source of the mysterious scent. By then he was weak with hunger, almost lacking the strength to drag himself forward. As the smell grew stronger, he became certain that it was coming from droppings of some kind, and they were fresh. That was welcome news. Fresh dung meant that somewhere near there was fresh food. He forced himself to continue, and steadily the odor grew stronger, until it was almost choking. With it came a new noise. It wasn't the drip of water or the grind of stone. The endless tunnels smoothed and distorted it until it was nothing but a wavering, high-pitched tone.

He was delirious with hunger and on the brink of collapse when he stepped into something pasty that oozed grotesquely between his toes. The sound was more distinct now, but his mind was too dulled by hunger and fatigue to work out the source. It was just a vague chatter at the edge of hearing. He fumbled for the flint and sparked a flash of light.

What happened next seemed to occur in stages. First, there was an explosion of sound. The chattering became a thousand times more intense and was joined by an unholy rustling all around him. Random bursts of wind buffeted him from all sides, and he felt the sting and slice of claws and teeth. His addled mind first was bewildered by the blast of sensations. He then believed that he'd at last found the beast of the cave. Things latched on to him, screeching and clawing. He dropped the flint and tore at one of the wriggling forms, managing to pull it free. Finally he realized that it was a bat. Another time he might have run for cover lest he be shredded by their claws and teeth, but his shriveled stomach reminded him that he was surrounded by thousands of flying morsels.

He swatted his hands and snapped his jaws, making a meal of as many as possible before the flapping and screeching died away. In the end, it was hardly a feast, but it was a source of food, and for now that was enough. He took a few minutes to recover, then many more to find the flint and steel he had dropped during the madness. It was an unpleasant task, but necessary. Now that he had a reliable source of food, and safe water could be found without much effort, survival was possible. That meant that come hell or high water, he would find what he was after, no matter how long it would take.

#

In the absence of light, the passage of time ceased to have any real meaning. For Shadow, life quickly came to be measured in how long it took for him to become hungry or how long it took to become tired. When he was awake, he explored. It wasn't only because he felt the need to escape, or perhaps even find the beast which may not exist. He had to explore, because if he didn't, there was nothing to keep his mind from unraveling. His sanity was like a handful of snakes, wriggling and trying to get free; every time he loosened his grip for even a moment, he could feel more slip away. So he focused on the task, unwitting adopting many of Ben's habits.

In the back of his mind, he was always counting steps. He became familiar with the feel of the walls, the smell of the different caves. With each sleep-wake cycle, it became more mechanical, more innate. Soon he could identify a tunnel by the sound of his footsteps echoing off of its walls. The step count ceased to be a number and became something of a new sense. He simply knew how far he had gone.

The tunnels etched themselves into his mind, and in time he came to notice differences from one visit to the next. As before, many of the caves and tunnels had ended in water. One in particular, despite being a long journey from the bat cave, seemed to have the coolest and cleanest water. He made it a point to return there regularly. It was almost a treat to refresh himself with water that wasn't tepid or stagnant. Slowly, it became clear to him that the water was a few steps farther each day. It was a puzzle, and thus a welcome distraction, so he returned more and more, filling his stomach as much as he could so that he could linger there.

With each inch the water retreated, the stone it revealed felt smoother.

Finally, there came the day that, as he began the trek toward the water, something was new. He couldn't place his finger on it at first. When he did, he realized that it wasn't something his fingers or his ears or his nose could tell him. It was his eyes. They'd been useless for so long, relying on the spark of the flint to do any good, even his dreams had become little more than sounds and sensations. Now he was seeing the dim flicker of light. For an instant, there was fear, as though this glimmer could not be natural, could not be real. When the moment passed, he rushed down the slope as quickly as its glassy surface would allow.

Without his notice, a deep longing had begun to form in the back of his mind. Sunlight, a fresh breeze, the sounds of nature and life. They were such small things, but he had been denied them for so long that a craving had formed. Lurking faintly in the back of his mind, always present, it had grown steadily into a gnawing and desperate hunger. At the sight of what might well be the outside world after all of this time, the desperate need leaped to the forefront and would not be denied. His lungs screamed for a proper breath of air. His stomach raged for something besides bats and insects to eat. His eyes demanded to see color again, to see the world in more than flashes and moments. Everything else—the beast, his purpose, caution, *everything*—was thrust aside as the promise of an open sky called.

As he drew closer to the point of light ahead, his darkness-adjusted eyes ravenously drank in the details. The walls were a marbled gray color, polished smooth as fine marble. He drew in a whiff of air and found hints of things he'd been without for so long he almost didn't recognize them: grass, trees . . . people.

Sanity and control fought their way back into his mind and he drew in another breath. Wherever he was heading, it was thick with life. It was not long before the echoing expanse of the tunnel began to offer up voices. They were quiet, and they spoke a language he had never even heard, but they were undeniable. He forced himself to slow, to let the old instincts trickle back in place of those that had sustained him in the darkness. Now he was near enough to make out that the light he was seeing was certainly sunlight. It was reflected from the curved floor of the tunnel's mouth. He could feel a breeze now, the air drifting into the tunnel from the outside. It carried hints of humans, elves, dwarves, and other things. There were both creatures he'd learned to hide from and creatures he'd never smelled before, and there were dozens of each.

It didn't make sense. It had been ages since he'd entered the cave, but he was certain that this was not what the entrance was like. If this was a new entrance, it was nowhere near the old. He'd walked for days to find the cave. There had been no cities anywhere near. Had he found his way through miles of mountain and ended up in an entirely different part of the kingdom? The caverns had been so twisted, and he'd been lost within them for so long that anything was possible.

He'd entered this place seeking a beast. That danger he had been prepared for. This was something else entirely. There was no telling what he would find beyond the mouth of the tunnel. For a brief instant, he considered retreating back into the cave and finding his way back the way he had come, but the thought was quickly banished by the feverish need to feel the sun on his face once more.

He crept farther, scouring his long-disused sense of sight for all it could tell him. He looked at his hands. They were raw from weeks or more of climbing rough stone and feeling along walls. His clothes were ragged and torn by a thousand snags on sharp rocks. His bare feet had been shredded and scarred. Every inch of him was caked with filth, silty gray muck from the stone walls and reeking droppings from the bat-filled cavern. He was withered and thin. It became clear that it didn't matter what he might find out there. If he stayed inside much longer, there wouldn't be anything left of him.

Shaky legs and tense muscles brought him to the bottom of the tunnel, where he stopped at the very edge of the light. What lay before him now was a smooth bowl of stone, the last remnants of water pooled in the lowest point. The air held none of the chill of the icy land he'd left behind when he entered the cave. If anything, it felt like a brisk spring day. It took all of the strength of will he had left to keep himself from crawling down into the light to bask in the sun, but two unmistakable shadows stretched out across the bottom of the bowl. He held still, eyes on the shadows, but they did not move any more than a minor shift here or there.

It couldn't be a simple coincidence that these two individuals were here. They were guarding the exit to the cave—or, at least, watching it. He listened as they two spoke to one another. It was a male and a female. A sniff of the air confirmed that one, the male, was certainly a man. The other was an elf. Both had a steady, weary tone to their voices as they spoke, as though the task at hand was horribly dull. The man seemed to be speaking Crich, Sorrel's native language. He'd learned to understand a bit of it in his time with her, but even so he could only follow half of the conversation, as the elf spoke another language entirely: a complex, nuanced language that sounded a bit like the one Goldie and Blondie had muttered in from time to time.

"No, no. That is madness. A weapon shaped in that way would be impossible to use," the man said, if Shadow understood correctly. "If one blade curved out, and the other in, you would scarcely be able to move it without slicing your arm."

The human's companion spoke a spirited response.

"Well yes, perhaps as a *thrown* weapon it could work," he replied, "but that is a great deal of craftsmanship to put into a weapon that can only travel as far as one can throw it. Granted, with a bit of levitation it might be useful, but can you think of a single apprentice who would use it?"

The conversation continued in that way for hours while the sun climbed higher into the sky and the shadow slipped farther forward. He followed it down, wading into the water. The dip in the water washed away a layer of the filth that had accumulated in his time in the cave, and it earned him a slightly better view of the place to which the cave had led him. Beyond the mouth of the tunnel, the smooth stone pit spread to fill his view, looking like a clay bowl if it were the size of a small lake. When he edged a bit farther, he found that along the south side, a rope ladder had been rolled out, dangling down to the surface of the shallow water.

By midday the sun had shifted the shadow of the tunnel mouth sufficiently to afford him a view of the lookouts. They still hadn't left, though he had little doubt that whatever they were, they were not guards. Each was dressed simply—the man in what appeared to be a padded cloth approximation of armor, and the elf in a gray tunic. Neither was armed, and neither seemed particularly concerned with the dark tunnel before them. Nevertheless, there they sat, glancing into the darkness from time to time and debating the merits of a nonexistent weapon.

Shadow below waited and watched. Finally, another figure approached, this one a dwarf like Gurruk. He carried with him a tray with two steaming bowls that instantly grabbed the attention of the lookouts. They stood and greeted the newcomer, taking the bowls and enthusiastically involving him in their discussion. It left the three of them with their eyes diverted, a momentary lapse in their vigil. That was all he needed. With smooth, careful motions he slipped from the mouth of the tunnel, wading silently through the water. The ladder was an obvious trap, but his time in the cave had made him an expert at navigating slick terrain. With a bit of effort, he managed to scramble up the north side of the bowl. There was a scattering of rocks and boulders along the face of the mountain at the edge of it. He nestled among them and held still as the lookouts briefly turned back to the tunnel, then the ladder, before continuing their discussion. He had not been seen.

Now he had a full view of the place he had discovered, and he could scarcely believe his eyes. Behind him was a sheer cliff rising up to the very clouds, and on the horizon opposite was an endless sea, but between them was an idyllic setting: a village, bustling and lively. Though the kingdom on the other side of the mountain was frozen solid, here the air was temperate, the grass green and the trees lush with leaves. Small huts, built simply of wood, were scattered on both sides of a central path that led to a large courtyard with a more elaborate meetinghouse of some kind within.

Walking the grounds of the place were creatures of all shapes and sizes. Humans, elves, and dwarves could be seen. Here, a person spoke before a group of others, all seated and observing. There, a pair sparred while another watched. Tiny winged fairies flitted through the air . . . and just a short distance away, what could only be a small gray dragon was sliding from a stone hut. Its head was raised, nose in the air.

A thousand questions flooded his mind, but he didn't have time to ponder how or why any of this might be. Lessons honed by years clicked instantly back into place. The dragon was a hunter, and he would not be its prey. Moving quickly before the beast could turn in his direction, Shadow scanned the village for someplace forgotten or ignored, someplace where he could hide and figure out what came next. Near to the northernmost part of town was an odd gleaming structure. It looked like a massive crystal tooth, jutting from the ground and carved with symbols. More of the same could be seen nearby. From what he could see and smell, it was the one place no one had chosen to linger. If he was to have any chance to avoid being discovered, he would have to make his way there.

He sprinted silently along the cliff face until the boulders no longer offered any cover, then darted among what few trees and shrubs there were. He stuck to the shadows—what few there were at midday—and drew upon a lifetime of instincts to avoid detection. The long stay in the cave had not taken their edge at all. None of the people had looked in his direction, but a brief glimpse behind him revealed that the dragon had its nose to the ground now, and was standing precisely where he had been hiding moments before. If he wanted to be safe, he had to keep moving.

The scaly hunter, little more than the size of a large dog, followed him slowly, sniffing and licking at the ground a few dozen paces behind, but Shadow refused to panic. He moved quickly and carefully toward the deserted section of town near the crystal spire. It was quite near to the cliff, and as the crystal spire approached he saw that it was at the edge of a roughly circular patch of identical crystal, smooth and gleaming like a frozen pond. Something told him it was best not to step onto the crystal surface, so he instead dashed across the narrow ground between the gleaming ground and the face of the cliff. When he made it to the farthest spire he hid behind it, venturing a peek when the sound of claws on earth stopped far behind him. The dragon was standing at the edge of the crystal patch. It seemed unwilling to go any further. After a long look in his general direction, it turned and paced back toward the center of the village.

Two days passed, Shadow slowly adapting to the sights and sounds that he'd been denied for so long. It wasn't clear just how much of his sanity he'd lost within the endless tunnels of the cave until he was forced to cope with reality again. The voices, the sights, they were too much for a mind that had been whittled down to the husk that he'd become inside. This at least was like a normal city in that during the darkest hours it was nearly still. He slipped from his haven behind the field of crystal and stalked the town when most of the villagers were sleeping. Just south of the city's center was a building that hung with the heavy sent of cooked food. He slipped inside and found steaming cauldrons. He almost scalded himself attempting to fill his stomach before he could be seen.

He explored the outskirts of the place, first as far north as he could, then as far south. It became clear that there was no way in or out, save the cave.

It was not only the temperature of the place or the diversity of its population that made it strange. Shadow found that there were people here, particularly in the northern half of the village, who became uneasy and curious in his presence even when he knew he had not betrayed himself with sight, sound, or scent. For some, simply being near seemed enough to set them on the prowl, checking dark corners for him.

Worse was the dragon, though. When it wasn't sleeping, the blasted thing seemed to spend almost every moment on his trail. It was confounding, because rather than the panic one might expect when a fire-breather of any size entered a town, this beast walked freely among the people. Some even seemed to speak to it, offering up a friendly hello or even answering questions that, if asked, had come as little more than a growl. Shadow's only respite from its waking searches came when a small gathering of villagers would assemble before its stone den and it would sit before them, surrounded by ghostly and unnatural lights and flames.

Perhaps inevitably, while Shadow was making his way back to his haven behind the crystal field near dawn of the third day, dragon's vigilance paid off. Its eyes were turned to him as he slipped from one hiding place to another. As soon as it saw him, it raised its head and rattled a low sound in its chest. A dozen nearby heads turned first to the dragon, then toward the place that Shadow was hiding. It had alerted them. He'd been discovered.

The air filled with cries in a dozen languages as people rushed from their huts to answer the call. Those few words he understood made it clear that he was their subject: "stranger"; "to the north"; "from the cave." He abandoned all stealth, running full speed directly for the crystal structure. A plan, such as it was, formed in his mind. He would make his way to the northernmost spire and climb it. From there, he could survey the village from above to hopefully spot a new place to hide, then leap over the mob as it gathered at the bottom of the spire and sprint to his new refuge. Legs adjusted to moving slowly in darkness were already cramping with the sudden intense exertion, but he'd learned to push such things aside. The voices called louder as he reached the edge of the crystal patch. There was no time to slip around the edge, so in one bounding step he crossed the perimeter of the circle of crystal and landed . . . nowhere.

Chapter 24

Shadow slid to a stop. No sooner had he crossed the threshold of the circle of crystal than the world seemed to vanish utterly. He was standing in a void, blackness all around. It felt almost as though he had been thrust back into the cave, but he could see himself clear as day. He looked down to see nothing but more black, nothing even resembling ground, yet his feet stood firm on some sort of smooth surface. The chorus of cries coming from the mob on his trail dropped to nothing. He heard only his own breathing and hammering heart. Before he could begin to grapple with what it was that had happened, a voice seized his attention.

"Well, what have we here? I don't recall being informed of any forthcoming trials," said the voice.

It was a woman, and she seemed to be speaking Tresson . . . though it was difficult to tell. It didn't feel as though he'd heard the words; instead, the understanding of them had simply thrust itself upon him. He turned to see the source of the voice. She was nearly a match for the malthrope's height, and dressed in a flowing black robe. Rising up from the hem of the robe were patterns of white. They looked to be flames, and, impossibly, they seemed to flicker and twist along the surface of the robe as though they were truly burning. Her hair was white and fell to the middle of her back, but her face was anything but old. There was a grace and wisdom to her bearing, and her expression was one of genuine interest.

He turned away from her and burst into a sprint again, but he made it only a few strides before her form appeared again, wafting into existence in front of him. Her expression had hardened a bit.

"Not so quickly now, let me get a look at you," she said.

Grinding his feet into whatever it was that he was running across, he changed directions and doubled his efforts. He didn't know where precisely he was hoping to go, but he knew that whatever this woman was, she was not something he wanted to face without time to prepare for it.

"I said," she began, an edge in her voice now, "*stop!*"

And so he did. It was not through any choice of his own. She simply said the word and his body obeyed, arms and legs locking in place.

"Stand up straight now." Again, the mere suggestion prompted an instant obedience from his body. She paced around him, looking him up and down thoughtfully. "A *malthrope*," she said, an eyebrow raised. The word was spoken not with disgust or fear as he'd so often heard it, but with intrigue. "I wasn't aware we had any of your kind about." She pinched away a bit of the silt clinging to his fur and sprinkled it to the ground. "No, I see. You're fresh from the cave, or relatively so. And there is the residue of a nasty little spell clinging to your arm and leg. Best to be rid of it." She swept her hand and the last trace of a pain that had lingered since the bounty hunter's spell had struck him finally faded away. "Odd that they would send you to see me before even getting cleaned up." She brushed away a bit more of the silt. In doing so, she knocked aside one of the tattered shreds of his shirt and revealed a bit of the mark on his chest.

Leaning close, she flourished her fingers and the grime covering it whisked away. "Well. That *is* interesting, and it warrants an explanation." She looked him in the eyes. "In a moment, you'll find yourself free to move once again. I know that you're thinking of swiping those claws of yours across my throat and running. I mean that literally; I can see the thoughts in your mind. Please be aware that, as your host, I would find that act terribly rude. I ask little of my guests beyond basic civility, and I want to make it clear that any such insult to my hospitality would be inadvisable."

With a jolt he found he could move again. He took two wary steps backward.

It took a few incoherent moments before he could find his voice after so long without using it. "I don't know who you are or what this place is," he pleaded, "but I need to go. There are people out there who will kill me if—"

"I am sorry to interrupt," she said, "but I can assure you that no one here will do anything that may harm you. At least, not without your expressed permission. As for who I am and where you are, follow me. We shall have a nice little chat."

She turned and walked away. As she did, an impossible thing began to happen. Gray stone formed a path beneath her feet, and beside it, vivid green blades of grass sprouted from nothingness. In a wave spreading out from her, a world formed. The grass traced out

Joseph R. Lallo

rolling hills. Mighty trees curled from the ground in moments. The path assembled itself forward and back, crunching up beneath his feet and leading on to a charming cottage of wood and thatch that faded into existence. By the time she reached the door of the cottage, he was standing in the center of a field that stretched as far as the eye could see in all directions. There was no hint of the village, mountains, or sea.

His instincts told him to run, but where? And even if he did, he was at the mercy of this woman. She could stop him with a word. Who knew what else she could do? There was no other choice but to do as she said.

He stepped into the cottage to find it warm and inviting. The door led into a sort of all purpose room. At the center was a long table set with trays of fresh fruit, meats, cheeses, sausages, and bread still steaming from the oven. Fine, cushioned chairs surrounded the table, and windows let light in gloriously to fill the room. Counters and cabinets lined each wall, and the whole of the place had neat but lived-in atmosphere. At the far end of the room was a fireplace, an inviting fire burning within it, and on either side were arched doorways hung with heavy wooden doors.

"There is a basin with hot water through that door if you wish to freshen up," she said, gesturing as she took a seat at the head of the table.

The malthrope merely stood, muscles still tense and head slightly bowed. Again, he felt as powerless and small as when he was a child. Worse than the way that she seemed to bend the very world to her whims was the disarming sense of calm she seemed to radiate. She was positively matronly and refined. It was like a demon singing a nursery rhyme.

"Well?" she asked.

"No. Thank you."

"Very well, then." She motioned with her fingers and the dirt and grime covering his body pulled away, like a layer of dust blown from a disused piece of furniture. One by one, the tears in his clothing began to close as well. "We can't have you mussing my nice clean home. Now, have a seat, you look fit to collapse. And eat something—you're nothing but bones."

He quickly obeyed, settling into a chair. Sitting on anything but the ground was a rare pleasure for him, and sitting on something with a cushion was unprecedented. He looked hungrily to the food and briefly wondered if it was some sort of trick, but his stomach overruled his mind. His eager fingers snatched up a small ham and he tore into it. The woman merely smirked and leaned back in her own chair. It was the work of a minute to reduce the meal to a bone, which he then set about snapping with his teeth.

"Tea?" she asked. "Wine, perhaps?"

He shook his head, finally succeeding with the bone and licking away the marrow. The task done, he set the remnants of the bone on the table.

"Thank you," he said.

"Manners," she observed with interest, eyebrows raised. She poured herself a cup from a teapot and breathed in the aroma. "Now, you had questions?"

He thought for a moment, turning over in his mind the raw power she seemed to have. When he spoke, it was with complete seriousness.

"Are you the beast of the cave?"

She burst into a delightfully musical chuckle, covering her mouth as she did. "Heavens no," she said, laughter still in her voice.

"I came here seeking the beast."

"Mmm, yes. Didn't we all?"

"Then what is this place and who are you?"

"Oh, yes. I *am* sorry. It is so rare that I entertain these days. Introductions. My name is Azriel. I was the first of us to come through that cave seeking the beast. As a result, I'm sorry to say, I was the first to discover that the creature doesn't exist."

"It doesn't exist . . . then it *was* the cave that claimed them, not some beast inside," he surmised, his suspicions confirmed.

"A great deal of them were claimed by the cave, yes. The rest made it here. After any time spent in that cave, and finding the paradise that you've seen here, it should hardly be a surprise that few who came this far felt the need to go back. Thus this village was formed. The finest wizards and warriors of the world, honing our crafts together, undisturbed by the rest of the world. We call it Entwell Num Garastra. An ancient phrase. It means 'The Belly of the Beast.' I'm surprised none of the others explained it to you."

"I . . . didn't speak to any others."

"What of those who greeted you when you exited the cave?"

"I managed to avoid them."

She paused in her tea-drinking for a moment.

"You were able to sneak into this place?"

"Yes."

A wide grin came to her face. "That, my dear, is unprecedented. And bordering on the *absurd*. What is your name?"

"I don't have one."

"None at all?"

"Not anymore. There was one of my own who gave me a name. She called me Teyn. When she left me, as far as I'm concerned, she took the name with her. The only other name I've had that I care to repeat is Red Shadow. It was what I was called when I would follow the man who raised me, and it was the name I selected for myself when I needed one. But it is what I am, not who I am."

Azriel looked aside for a moment and took a thoughtful sip of her tea. "Red Shadow. And Teyn. It seems you may have a name after all."

"I don't understand."

"Did your friend ever tell you what Teyn means?"

"She said it meant spirit."

"Spirit? Yes, it does mean that, but it also means shadow. I think perhaps 'shade' might be the most accurate translation. And the name you've selected for yourself speaks of shadows as well. Furthermore, you slipped out of the cave without being seen, an act well suited to a shadow."

"I only made it a few days before a dragon picked up my scent."

"Ah, yes. Solomon does hold quite tightly to his predatory nature in some ways. Still, a few days is a good deal longer than anyone else. 'Shadow' seems to follow you, if you will excuse the play on words."

He watched as she leaned farther back into her chair. Closing her eyes, she sipped again at the tea, as though it took her undivided attention to enjoy it properly. She was the first human, if she was a human at all, to lower her guard around him for quite some time. Even with the mask, those who saw him were either certain to keep their eyes on him or were anxious for every moment that he was out of view. Even Maribelle, for all of her seeming indifference, smelled strongly of fear when he was near her. This woman, Azriel, was perfectly at ease.

"May I ask another question?" Shadow said.

"Certainly."

"Are you afraid of me?"

"I'm a rather powerful sorceress, dear. It wouldn't be far from the truth to suggest I've got no reason to fear anyone."

"Do you hate me?"

"*Hate?*" she remarked with a tone that suggested the very word itself was laughable. "I've been alive a very long time. I've learned a great deal over the years, but possibly the most important lesson is this: take nothing to heart that you have not seen proven with your own eyes. So many years I wasted believing what I was told. So many things I thought were impossible until I tried them. I've heard the stories about malthropes. I know what people say. You're the first I've met. I don't imagine you deserve my hate until you've earned it. And I'll warn you that it isn't the sort of thing that one should be eager to seek."

"Do the others here feel the same way?"

"How the others feel is immaterial. How they act is what is important, and they will treat you with honor and respect. That is our way," she said. She drew a deep breath of her tea's aroma again. "Bless me, I had another question I wanted to ask and now it escapes me."

"You said you could see my thoughts. Why do you ask questions at all?"

"Most people consider mind-reading to be a horrid violation. I certainly count myself among them. It would be terribly rude of me to pluck the thoughts from your mind without permission unless it was absolutely necessary. Ah, yes, that was it. Tell me, that mark on your chest. There since birth, I suppose?"

"Yes."

"And the quickening? I have you experienced something like that?"

"I don't know what that is."

"Let me ask another way. Has there been a moment in your life, and you needn't tell me what, that was searing in its intensity? A moment that sliced your life in two and left you only with what came before and what came after?"

He shuddered.

She nodded, "That's answer enough." She looked to one of the walls and gestured toward it. A bookcase came into being and from it floated a thick, leather-bound tome. She flipped it open and turned a few pages with deliberate motions, her eyes running over their contents. "A master of every weapon . . . he will have the blood of a fox . . ." she muttered quietly, "Why did you seek the beast? Glory?

Wealth?"

"Every great act of combat I've ever managed was at the risk of my life or that of someone I cared about. I believed if I fought the creature, I would learn how to repeat those deeds. Or perhaps it would be intelligent and it could teach me."

She snapped the book shut, a wide and genuine smile lighting up her face. "You came to learn," she remarked, adding with a triumphant laugh, "and learn you shall."

She set down the book and held her hands out to her sides. Into one, there appeared a quill pen; into the other, a sheet of parchment. She set the parchment on the table and wrote a few lines in a complex and impressive script. As she wrote, she spoke.

"Teyn is a Crich word. Here we use another word, related but much older. It, too, means shadow—in a way. That word is Lain. It is a title, one that is rarely earned. I think, for you, it is something to strive for. Keep that in mind, should such an opportunity present itself." She folded the parchment and casually produced a drizzle of red sealing wax, then a signet ring to leave an impression in it. "Let us go. On your feet."

He did as she instructed, and the moment his weight was off the chair, it wafted away, with the rest of the cottage and the whole of the world around it following. There was only he and his host once more. She was ushering him forward with a hand on his back.

"It will be difficult, I am sure, but you must be calm and open with the people here. Be honest. When you leave this place, there will be people waiting. Give this to one of them," she instructed, pressing the parchment into his hand. "You will be taken to the elder. When you meet him, be as forthcoming as you have been with me. He will see to it that you learn what you wish to learn."

"But," he began, stopping as she turned to face him, "you do not even know why I wish to learn these things."

"But I do, dear, though perhaps you do not." She brushed his shoulders and clasped them tight, looking him in the eye. "You carry a heavy weight, child. Perhaps you do not feel it, but it is resting squarely upon your shoulders. There is a darkness about you, but a great light within you. I see the strength to do what fate asks. It is up to you to find that strength. Now, go. And good luck to you."

Her final words were delivered as her figure drifted apart like smoke in a breeze. The darkness around him did the same; without moving, he found himself once again standing in the shadow of a cliff, the cool smoothness of crystal beneath his bare feet and a semicircle of anxious and excited villagers staring at him expectantly. They kept their distance at the edge of the crystal, unwilling to enter.

Foremost among them was a woman, an elf. She was perhaps thirty years old to look at her, but one of her race could easily have been decades older without showing a hint of the additional years. She was tall and slender, ears pointed and deep brown hair woven into a braid. She looked him over, judging something about his posture before turning and addressing the others. She spoke in short precise instructions in a language he didn't recognize and motioned for the crowd to back away. When she alone stood near the edge of the crystal, she took a step back and beckoned, uttering foreign words in a reassuring tone.

He stepped over the threshold, feeling the pressure of the stares of half the village. The woman spoke again, nodding and indicating the parchment. He held it out to her and she took it, investigating the seal before breaking it and reading the message within. When she was through she nodded once and looked him in the eye.

"Follow me," she said.

#

The crowd parted as the malthrope was led through. Though being the focus of their attention still bored into him, there was something different about the way these people looked at him. On the other rare occasions he'd been paraded before a group of "civilized" creatures like men and elves there had been outright, unmasked disdain. The disgust was not wholly absent here, but where it was present, it was kept beneath the surface, hidden from him in the same way that they may do each other the courtesy of setting their prejudice aside when face to face. Many, though, seemed fascinated. No doubt most had never seen a malthrope in the flesh. Whereas people elsewhere seemed grateful for that fact, here there were those who were clamoring for a better look. It did little to decrease his discomfort.

He had come to this place expecting to clash with a bloodthirsty creature. At this moment, he would have greatly preferred if he had.

"Are you well? Do you need a healer?" the woman asked. She spoke Tresson, and did so with a practiced precision. Only the slightest twist on her words betrayed the fact that it was not her native language.

"No," he stated.

313

"Do you require a meal?"

"No."

"Though you had no way of knowing, I must inform you that what you did, entering the crystal arena without time to prepare, was foolish. Azriel is a phenomenal wizard, but her diplomacy and patience are each something less than desirable," the woman said. "I trust she did not do anything regrettable."

"She didn't."

"She has written that you are from Tressor, is this correct?"

"I am."

"And that you have no name, but that you may be called Shadow. Is this correct as well?"

"I suppose."

"Very well, then."

She stopped and turned to him, prompting him to stop as well. Extending her left hand, she reached toward him, but he backed away. She furrowed her brow.

"This *is* how one initiates the traditional Tresson greeting between friends, is it not?" she asked.

Shadow brought to mind the handful of times he had seen Jarrad or Marret greet their friends on the plantation. Reluctantly, he stepped forward and allowed her to clasp his right shoulder with her left hand while he returned the gesture.

"I am Ryala of Entwell. Welcome," she said. The more she spoke, the more it became clear that there was a crispness and efficiency to everything she did, as though she was checking items off of a carefully prepared list as she went along. She turned back to the path ahead and continued. "I am the personal apprentice to the Elder. As is traditional for all newcomers, you are to be brought to him for review. Do you speak any languages other than Tresson?"

"Some Crich. Less Varden."

"In Entwell, we speak the languages with which we are most comfortable, and we expect our fellow villagers to do us the courtesy of learning to understand. You will find that we all can understand Tresson, and some may speak it to you, but for the others you'll need to listen and learn. The Elder speaks an ancient dialect native to South Crescent. I will translate for you. Can you read or write?"

"No."

"You will be taught to do so."

"What have I done to earn any of this?"

"You have reached this place, Shadow. You faced the trial of the cave and you overcame it. It takes skill, perseverance, and luck to do so even if you know the way. Having passed that test, you are one of us."

"You don't care that I am a malthrope?"

"We have humans, elves, fairies, dwarves, nymphs, dryads, and a dragon. Never before have we had a malthrope, but any creature with the wisdom to teach or the desire to learn has a place here." She raised the parchment. "Azriel believes that you have both, and much more. From what little I have seen thus far, her judgment seems sound."

Their journey took them to the center of the village, where the largest and most grand of its structures could be found. It was tall, its two-tiered roof rising to perhaps three stories and slanted gently along its length. Like many of the cottages, it was round, and windows were spaced at regular intervals along the walls. They revealed a mostly open interior. The wood was left mostly in its natural color, though intricate symbols and ornate script had been etched along the edges of the planks and beams. She led him to the tall double doors, which currently stood open, and motioned for him to stop.

Inside, men and women dressed in tunics of various colors, and one or two dressed in simple armor, seemed to be engaged in half a dozen different discussions. Some were huddled over books and spoke quietly. Others spoke with raised voices and threatening gestures. Presiding over them was an ancient-looking man, bent under the weight of many years but seeming to be the embodiment of wisdom and respect. He wore a long robe of simple cloth. It was embroidered with the same script and sigils that adorned the outside of the building. He was on his feet, looking over the pages in a book offered by a dwarf in a brown tunic.

"I will announce you, and you will come inside. The Elder may choose to test your abilities. If he does, behave in any way that you feel is best. Nothing will be done to threaten your life, and I will inform you if you've done something wrong."

She stepped through the doorway. At her appearance, the Elder dismissed the dwarf and spoke quietly with Ryala. After a short exchange, he nodded and sat in what would have been a throne in another setting. Instead, it was a tall but simple seat at the opposite end of the room, situated atop two shallow steps. He spoke a few words and the various lively discussions were silenced. Ryala turned and motioned for Shadow to enter.

He stepped inside, trying to will away the terrible feeling that this was all too familiar. He was being asked to step forward, to be judged. The last time it had happened, it had cost him his tail. What would it cost him now?

The Elder spoke. When he was through, Ryala translated: "What are your skills? What are the things that you do best?"

"I track and hunt."

The old man nodded and spoke again.

"The Elder observes that these are valuable skills, but ones we have little use for in this place. Food is plentiful without the need to hunt," Ryala said. The Elder smiled and muttered a few more words. Ryala continued. "Unless, of course, you hunt a different sort of prey."

"I hunt what I am told to hunt, what I am paid to hunt."

"The Elder wishes to assure you that there is no need to be evasive. Are you a bounty hunter or an assassin?"

Shadow looked to those around him. None seemed apprehensive. Those who were armed were not reaching for their weapons, and those who were unarmed were not eying the exit. "I have been both."

The answer caused no stir.

"There are many such hunters among us. Are you skilled?"

"Not skilled enough."

The Elder nodded, and held out his hand. Ryala handed him the parchment. He looked it over, then spoke again.

"Azriel speaks of a mark on your chest. Show it."

He opened his recently repaired shirt. At the sight of the mark over his heart, the interest in him intensified, and whispers were scattered about the room.

"Tell us, have you any family?"

"No. My mother is dead. I never met my father. There is no one else that I know of."

"Have you received any mystic training?"

"No."

"You have a powerful soul. You might consider it. Have you been trained in any weapons?"

"No."

There was another stir and a wave of whispers. The Elder closed his eyes for a moment, then began to issue orders not only to Ryala, but to several of the younger occupants of the room. When he was through dispatching orders, Ryala turned to Shadow.

"Follow me," she said, leading him out the door. "An opponent is being selected and you will be asked to defend yourself."

"Why?"

"Because the Elder wishes to see what combat skills you may have. He believes that though you claim to have no training, someone of your species having selected your career would not be alive unless you had attained some level of proficiency in defense."

"What if I refuse?"

"Then we will be unaware of your abilities, and you will have far greater difficulty finding a master willing to take you as an apprentice."

"I don't understand."

"In Entwell, we are all students, and we are all masters. You will share with us what you know, and we will do the same. Whatever you wish to learn shall be taught to you, but only if you can convince a master to take you on as a student. Showing what you can do will go a long way to easing that process."

"What sort of things do you teach?"

"Armed and unarmed combat, stealth, weapon-crafting, elemental magics, white magic, black magic, and many other things besides. Like you, each master entered this place alone or as part of a group, and each believed that they would find a creature that had bested every warrior before them. As such, each is among the most skilled in their craft, and each has been honing those skills against one another since their arrival. You will find no better teachers anywhere in the world."

"And you would teach me even knowing that I have been an assassin?"

"The nature of your role is of little importance. There is no inherent evil to being an assassin, any more than there is evil inherent to any manner of warrior. Indeed, an assassin, working as an individual, can often achieve through a single kill what would otherwise require a pair of armies and thousands of lost lives. What could be more noble? As with so many other things, the virtue or sin comes not only from the act, but from the purpose as well. If you serve a virtuous cause, then you are virtuous. And even if you were a villain and scoundrel before entering the cave, in reaching the village, you have been given a chance to better yourself and in doing so to better us all."

317

There was an odd quality to the words as she spoke them. She did not speak as though she were preaching a philosophy or doctrine. It felt more as though it was a simple explanation, a fact of existence of which she was helpfully educating him. How she said it didn't matter, though. What mattered were the words themselves. Shadow had resigned himself to the path of darkness when he allowed himself to take a life. It had never occurred to him that such an act could be considered righteous or just. To hear such words now, to hear that perhaps in the right cause he might find redemption, caused the tiniest glimmer of hope in his soul. It may be that what he whispered to himself when his shame was at his greatest, that the good of his deeds might outweigh the bad, could have the ring of truth. He let the word sink into his mind, then he tucked them away and turned back to the matter at hand.

The people here were wise. They were powerful. They knew how to do things that he didn't. There may not have been a beast for him to fight, but all of the skills and knowledge that such a creature might have had to offer were present in this place. They seemed to accept him, or at least tolerate him, and they claimed to be willing to teach him. It was too good to be true. He would have to be vigilant for the inevitable moment when their true intentions became clear—but until then, he would absorb all that he could.

He was led into the center of the grassy courtyard surrounding the Elder's building. Many of those within the building, mostly the ones dressed in combat garb, had followed. A flood of similarly-dressed people from the south side of the village had begun to assemble into a wide circle with Shadow and Ryala at the center. Scattered amongst the crowd were more than a few individuals with a less overtly military look. They invariably wore brightly colored garb—white, black, blue, red, yellow, and brown. Fluttering above the crowd and watching with rapt interest was a dragonfly-winged fairy dressed in a swatch of red cloth, and snaking its way through the crowd was the dog-sized gray dragon that had revealed him just a short time ago.

"Step into the center of the courtyard," Ryala instructed. "Your opponent will present himself and the match will then begin. It will continue until the Elder is satisfied. You may request any training weapon you wish, and padded armor will be provided if you wish."

"I require none."

"Very well. Do whatever you feel you must to defend yourself, but do not attempt to take a life."

He nodded, and a moment later a man stepped out of the crowd toward him. The man was lean and tall, though Shadow was taller and leaner. He had dark skin, his hair cropped short and a scar interrupting one eyebrow. In one hand, he held a wooden pole with strips of cloth braided about its center, a quarterstaff. He was layered in padded clothes, but when he saw his foe, he turned to Ryala and spoke. She nodded. He handed the weapon to her, stripping off the padding as well. When he wore only a shirt and trousers, he stepped up and assumed a defensive posture. Shadow did the same.

The moment felt strangely serene. It was raw, simple. He had entered the cave seeking trial by combat, and finally the moment had come. It didn't matter why these people were here. It didn't matter why they seemed to accept him when no one else would. It didn't even matter if this was a trick and they wished to kill him. In this moment, the intention was pure. He wasn't wearing a mask. He wasn't pretending to be something he was not. Instincts of survival and combat—things that he had needed to lock away to live in the world of man—came alive. His pulse quickened in anticipation. His clawed fingers flexed. His senses sharpened. They wanted to fight him, to see what he could do. He wanted to show them.

His foe made the first move, coming in with a thrusting kick. The man looked to be a human, but he moved far faster and far more precisely than Shadow had ever seen. Even so, the attack was not quick enough to meet its target. Shadow sidestepped the attack, but the fighter somehow smoothly continued into a second strike. He narrowly dodged this one, too, and now the man was upon him. Fists, elbows, knees, and feet came at him in a flurry of attacks. Some he dodged, some he slapped away, others he blocked with crossed arms or raised knees. A few slipped through. He tried to make sure that those strikes that landed were those targeted at the least vulnerable areas, but precious few were so aimed.

In a practiced motion, the fighter swept a leg behind Shadow's knee and threw him off balance. He stumbled and fell backward, catching himself on his hands and scrambling awkwardly away. His foe closed in to capitalize on the vulnerable position, but Shadow threw himself to his back, coiled his legs, and planted his heels on the warrior's chest. A swift double kick forced the man back, and while he was still reeling, Shadow sprung to his feet and the fight continued. It was getting faster and more furious with each moment. Though the Entwell resident had precision and strategy on his side, the malthrope's wild and unpredictable combat kept him off balance. Both fighters were taking a fair amount of punishment as a result, but there was no indication that either was ready to admit defeat.

Perhaps it was the fact that he was finally letting his raw aggression take hold after it had been suppressed for so long, but as the battle raged on he found himself slipping further and further away, letting the simplest parts of his mind take control. Grunts of exertion became growls. Dodges aside became darting strikes forward. His teeth were bared, his senses on fire. It wasn't blood lust or anger—it was the raw exhilaration of the act.

Had he not been so focused on the battle, he might have heard the mutters at the edge of the battle. There was a shifting of spectators and the quiet whisper of orders. Instead, he fought harder and reveled in his opponent's ability to meet the challenge in kind. The last ounce of real thought was used to keep his teeth and claws out of the battle, leaving it a contest of fists and feet. He was dancing from foot to foot, watching as his opponent held his ground and tightened his defenses. Each met the gaze of the other, and for a moment the circling and shifting came to a stop, each waiting for the other to make a move. It was then that the moment came.

There was no single cause for his next decision. It was not merely that he heard something, or smelled something, or felt anything else in any measurable way. Some combination of his senses reached his mind as a command and he obeyed. He shifted his weight to one foot, tightened his fist, and turned, swinging his right fist in a wild backhand strike. It connected with the nose of an until-now unseen figure who had been approaching from behind. The blow instantly bloodied the face of the sneak-attacker, and the sight of the blood brought Shadow's mind charging back. Fear clutched his mind and he sprang back a few steps, eyes darting between the stricken man who had been approaching from behind and the opponent who had now dropped his guard and stood with his hands at his sides.

The malthrope tried to watch all of the crowd at the same time, certain that someone among them would draw a weapon or call for a guard.

"I didn't mean to do it! He came from behind! I didn't know that he was there!" he insisted, reflexively trying to diffuse the fury of the mob that had mysteriously failed to form.

The Elder spoke, again translated through Ryala. "Calm yourself, student. The Elder is satisfied."

A pair of white-robed villagers approached the downed combatant while the original fighter offered a stiff nod of respect before weaving back into the crowd.

She continued: "Your combat skills are rough, but promising. The stealth master wished to see if your skills of detection were more refined, so he sent one of his pupils to approach from behind you. It seems in doing so he discovered an aptitude of yours. Go now. Eat. Rest. I am sure you will learn much, and teach much as well."

Shadow's mouth hung open a bit as he tried to understand what had just transpired. The crowd was dissipating without anger or fear. The man he had bloodied was waving off the two villagers in white. They were presumably healers, and the bleeding man had no interest in their service. Strangest of all, he was chuckling.

"Go, go, off with you. A bit of blood now and then is good for a man. Keeps him humble," he said, his words spoken in perfect Tresson.

For the first time, Shadow allowed himself to observe what the young man looked like. He was young, not far into his twenties. His hair was short and reddish-brown, and his face was clean-shaven. His clothes were black and tied close to his body with various thin straps. There was no weapon to be seen anywhere on the outfit, but there were plenty of loops and holsters to hold them if he'd chosen to arm himself. He pulled a rag from a pouch on his belt and wiped his face, then his hands. When most of the blood was gone, he smiled at Shadow.

"A fine blow. You'll have to tell me how you knew where to strike! Thrilled to meet you," he said, extending a hand and widening his grin. "My name is Leo."

Chapter 25

Shadow stared uncertainly at the hand that was offered.

"It's a greeting we have out west," Leo said, reaching down to clasp Shadow's hand in a shake. The malthrope pulled away. Leo's smile turned to a smirk and he shrugged. "Very well, we'll try that again once you've had some time to get settled. Let me show you around."

The young man strode confidently to the south. Shadow looked around. Now that the spectacle of battle was through, members of the crowd had each returned to their prior activities. No one was looking in his direction anymore. He was standing in the middle of a village, revealed yet ignored. Without any better options, Shadow followed the man who had moments before seemed intent on attacking him from behind. The man began to speak again without looking, as though it hadn't occurred to him that Shadow wouldn't have followed immediately.

"You're a Tresson speaker, eh?" he said. "We don't get many native Tressons since the war began. It stands to reason, of course. The only reasonable entrance to the Cave of the Beast is in Ulvard. I don't imagine they would be eager to let a warrior from the opposition cross the border just to test himself against the beast." He turned back to Shadow and noticed the look of vague unease on his face. "Something wrong?"

"No one is staring at me."

He grinned. "You'll need to get used to that. It takes an awful lot to hold the attention of a denizen of Entwell. We have our own interests."

"But I'm a malthrope."

"That you are," Leo said, looking him up and down. "Forgive me if I'm not treating you with the proper fear or revulsion, but, to be perfectly honest, I thought your kind was a myth. Now that I'm meeting one face to face, I expected something with more muscles—and some bigger fangs, perhaps. Still . . ." He blotted a fresh trickle of blood from his nose. "You don't disappoint."

As they walked, the strangely jovial fellow pointed and described the various sights. They were entering the southern half of the village.

The huts and cottages here were just the same as those to the north, but the people were markedly different. Weapons abounded, and not only the wooden training sort. Small courtyards were marked off, and racks of weapons of every type could be seen. There were simple things like axes and swords, but also odd contraptions he couldn't identify. Some were made from chain and wood. Others were curves of metal that seemed too delicate or complex to be of use. There were slender longbows, stout crossbows, slings, bolos . . . an armory of equipment and each with an avid user. There were mock battles happening outside many of the huts: graceful elves clashing with needle-thin swords, hearty dwarves heaving clubs at one another, humans fighting with bare fists.

Strangest of all, everyone seemed utterly at ease with it.

"That is Domar. He's at his best with pole arms, but lately he's been giving daggers a try, of all things. Trilla and Mia are doubtlessly our best knife-throwers, but which of the two is best is a point of debate, particularly between *them*. The food is served in a hut back in that direction. If you'd like to talk about having a weapon made, our smiths are the center of Warrior's Side and the carpenters are closer to the mountain. Basic weapons are done by Kafner and his apprentices. Croyden is our higher-level crafter for edged weapons . . ."

"Where are you taking me?"

"We're heading down to your hut. We've got a few built down at the southern fringe of town that aren't occupied yet."

"You are giving me a place to live?"

"Of course! Unless you are more comfortable spending your nights under the stars." Leo looked to Shadow and grinned again. "You look like a fellow with an awful lot of questions. We are all students here. If you've got a question, ask. We live to find answers. Is there something wrong?"

Shadow stopped and looked around him once more.

"All of this is wrong. This isn't how the world works. This isn't how people behave. Not around someone like me."

Leo laughed. "Look around you. Those two?" He pointed to a pair of humans engaged in an animated debate. "They come from warring tribes. Those elves over there? Their families are ancient rivals. Anywhere else, they would kill each other on sight. Here they wield weapons against each other every day without a drop of blood to show for it. Half of the people here have got a reason to kill the other half, and yet once they reached this place they found their common ground. Don't ask me why it works. Maybe it is the cave. Perhaps having to survive something like that makes you treasure every moment that comes after. Or perhaps it is the fact that every man and woman in this place came seeking to prove that they were the best, and when they reached Entwell they found the very opponents best able to challenge them for such a title.

"I swear, you can come here looking to learn anything in the world, and the one answer you'll never find is how this place could have come to be. The stars simply aligned. All that is certain is that once the wizards and warriors of the world reached this place, they found their peers, and few have ever felt the need to leave."

"What is expected of me?"

"Not much more than you would expect from yourself. You will be asked to learn at least two skills from the Wizard's Side and two from the Warrior's Side. If you attain a mastery level, you will be expected to take on at least one apprentice as well. The rest is up to you."

"The Wizard's Side? I will be expected to learn magic?"

"We won't ask you to learn to cast any spells necessarily, but yes, something of that sort."

"I haven't seen much of magic, but what I have seen makes me certain that I do not trust it. I don't want anything to do with it."

Leo looked about briefly, then leaned close. "To be perfectly honest, neither did I," he whispered. "But they've got some interesting tricks to share."

"What do you study?"

"Ha! Until now, I thought I'd been doing a rather fine job of learning the ways of stealth. Seems you've provided me with a new hurdle to leap before I can make that claim again."

"And what of the mark on my chest?"

"What *of* the mark on your chest?" Leo asked, clearly confused.

Shadow tugged the edge of his shirt aside to reveal the black mark. "I was asked to show it in the Elder's quarters. Those who saw it seemed to react as if they knew that it meant something."

"Birthmarks and meanings . . . I couldn't say." There was a call and Leo looked. Beside a small oak tree between two huts was a young woman waving him over. A wide smile came to his face. "My apologies, my friend, but I'm needed elsewhere. That hut there is yours if you want it. And about the mark . . . it sounds like more of the sort of thing that they would concern themselves with on the Wizard's Side. Better to ask there." He trotted off toward the woman, calling back, "If you need me, just come looking. I dare say that you are one of very few around here who won't have much trouble finding me!"

The strange man ran off and joined the woman, greeting her with a peck on the cheek and a few jovial words. A few other denizens of the village greeted him and the group set off to whatever activity they had planned before Shadow's discovery had interrupted.

The malthrope let his gaze linger for a few moments, watching the friendly young man who had cheerfully accepted a bloody nose without an ounce of ill will. He then swept his eyes around the section of the village. At any other moment, if he'd found himself in the middle of a village, surrounded by people armed to the teeth, he would be running by now. Indeed, it was taking all of the strength of will he had to keep himself from doing so. And yet all he earned here was the occasional sidelong glance. The people here simply didn't care what he was. He turned now to the hut. It was a simple thing, perhaps even a bit smaller than the space he'd had on the plantation, but if what they said was true, it was his. A bed, a roof, and four walls to call his own. He sat on the bed and let his poor mind struggle with the events of the day.

Something deep inside of him rebelled, the part of him that had fought for every scrap he'd ever swallowed and every breath he'd breathed until now. This couldn't be true. How could it? He must have died in that cave. Or he was huddled in the darkness still, delirious from hunger and exhaustion. A place like this, a place where he was just another creature, couldn't exist. But the blows he'd taken in the sparring match were real. He could feel them throbbing. He closed his eyes and gripped the wooden frame, trying to focus on it. It was solid. Real. If he could push the rest aside, let it trickle in slowly, he might be able to accept this place. He breathed the fresh air, heavy with the scent of a hundred nearby people. He listened to the sounds of the place, voices in the distance and the nearby buzz of an insect's wings.

It was just another place, he told himself. There was nothing so strange about it.

"Mr. Malthrope, sir?" asked a small voice.

His eyes opened to a sight that did little to aid his mind in accepting the reality of this place. There was a tiny feminine form fluttering on gossamer wings in front of him. She was drifting to and

325

fro, just barely beyond the tip of his snout. It was the same creature who had been watching his battle, dressed in a doll-sized outfit of thin red cloth. She was slender, and appeared to be quite young. Black hair was cut short and flared along its length around a pert and energetic face. Her wings had a dim glow to them, a deep orange around their edge like a candle that had moments before been snuffed out. Brilliant green eyes stared sheepishly into his. She had an apologetic posture, hands clasped before her and bottom lip chewed between her teeth.

"I'm sorry to interrupt you so soon after being assigned your quarters, but I am an apprentice to the master of flame magic, Master Solomon."

"I have no interest in flame magic, or magic of any kind."

"Perhaps not, sir, but he has got an interest in you. If you are fatigued or unwilling to see him at the moment, please take your time, but he would like to see you as soon as you are available. He asked me to bring you to the Wizard's Side at your earliest convenience. Please consider coming with me? I would really rather bring you to him quickly. I don't get many chances to impress him." She raised her clasped hands into a pleading gesture and bent one knee, her expression turning hopeful. "Please?"

He sighed through his nose, the rush of air jostling her slightly, though she didn't seem to mind.

"Why wouldn't he come himself?" he asked.

"He heard you speaking Tresson, and newcomers like you usually only fully understand one language. He doesn't like speaking Tresson, he considers it too flowery, so he sent me to greet you." Evidently suspecting his flat expression was evidence of an impending refusal, she darted forward, clasped hands held out imploringly. "Please! I will owe you a favor! He likes my partner Duncan much better than he likes me, and this would go a long way toward evening us out, I know it!"

He sighed again, though this time she deftly flitted aside to avoid it. "Very well."

"Thank you!" she said brightly, punctuating the statement with a twirl. She flitted around his head once before darting to the doorway. "This way, please! I promise it won't take long."

He reluctantly stood and followed her. The pair walked along, fairy leading the way. She had a peculiar rhythm to the way she moved, bobbing twice to one side, then darting and bobbing twice to the other.

It was as though there was a song playing and she was joyfully keeping the beat.

"My name is Fiora, by the way. And I meant what I said about the favor. I'm very serious about that sort of thing. I don't have very many friends here on the Warrior's Side, and you'd be a great one to have." As she spoke, she pivoted in air and floated along backward, facing him. Any words that she felt deserved a bit extra inflection received a full-body gesture, darting closer, bobbing upward, pointing with a full arm or kicking her legs. He was beginning to think she felt that someone her size needed to make a grand showing of emotion, lest it be missed entirely. "I know what you're thinking, by the way."

He looked to her sharply. "Azriel suggested that was frowned upon."

"What? Oh, no, no, no. I'm sorry. Not literally. No, no. I'm afraid I never got the knack for that. And it *is* frowned upon. Very much so. I would never do that. No. What I mean is that in a situation like this, it is only natural that you be thinking a certain thought, and I know what that is."

"What?"

"You are wondering how it came to be that a *fairy* became an apprentice to a master of *fire* magic."

"I wasn't thinking that."

"You weren't?" She seemed disappointed.

"I don't know anything about magic."

"Oh. Well, if you did, you'd be thinking that. Very much so." She hung in the air, attempting to suppress the look of expectation on her face. When he refused to supply the question, she helpfully supplied the answer. "Most fairies, if they have an affinity for any one magic, have an affinity to wind, you see. But not Duncan and I. It is true that we both know more than a bit about wind, we both saw the way embers floated through the air and it spoke to us. Yes indeed."

Fiora continued talking without pause, until her voice seemed to fade into the drone of her wings as just another constant noise. The only time a statement stood out is when it rose with the telltale inflection of a question.

"You know something? I don't think I've ever seen a malthrope before," Fiora said.

"And I've never seen a fairy," he replied.

"Well, that's no surprise. We try to make sure that no one sees us."

327

Joseph R. Lallo

"We do the same."

"Why?"

"Because people try to kill us when they see us."

"Oh. Well, it could be worse. For fairies, the problem is that people find us *useful*." She said the final word with a shudder.

"What is so bad about being useful?"

"Different *parts* of fairies are useful for different *things*," she clarified. "And even if they want to use a whole *live* fairy for something, they usually find them *so* useful that they don't let us *go*. My great-great-grandmother used to tell us about malthropes sometimes." Her mind flitted about nearly as much as her body, it seemed. "She said that they are clever. You look clever. You *must* be clever if you made it through the cave all alone."

He glanced at her. "That's all she said? That we were clever?"

"We don't pay attention to what the folks on the ground do much," she said with a shrug and a bounce. "Do other people say different things? Well, I guess they *would*, if they want to kill you. I guess maybe things are different in North Crescent. That's where Gran-Gran-Gran was from. Well, here we are!"

The journey had taken them past the stone bowl that had served as his entrance and stopped at a hut that was quite different from those around it. Most of the huts he'd seen were made from wood alone, or perhaps wood and stone. This one was built entirely from stone. It didn't even have a thatched roof. The size was curious, too. The structure wasn't even tall enough for a man of average height to stand, and it had a smaller footprint than a normal hut as well. The whole of the area smelled strongly of char, and patches of the hut and the ground surrounding it were blackened. A low pedestal was set up, and in a claw atop it was a rough chunk of uncut crystal.

Fiora drifted to the doorway of the hut and produced what at first seemed to be a whistle. After a few lilting notes, however, it became clear that it was her voice, likely forming the words of her native language. From within the hut came a grunt and the jingle of coins. Finally, a form slid from within.

It was a dragon, the same one that had discovered him. This was the closest he'd been to the creature, and the clearest he had seen it. The beast was perhaps the size of a wolf, covered in dark gray scales on its back and lighter gray on its belly. Its head was angular and reptilian, cold gray eyes with feline slits staring down the length of its

328

long snout. Horns jutted back from its head, with smaller spikes sweeping back from its cheeks. The neck was long and serpentine, leading to a stout body with strong legs. Its fore claws had a hand-like quality to them, slicing finger-long claws into the gravel of the ground. Last to emerge from the hut was its lashing tail, nearly as long as the rest of the body and curling with prehensile grace. It thumped down to its haunches, rustled a folded set of wings on its back, and locked the fairy in its gaze. There was a brief exchange of trilling chirps from the fairy and rattling grumbles from the dragon before each turned to face the newcomer.

"Mr. Malthrope, sir. I present to you Master Solomon, our master of fire magic. He promises me he won't waste much of your time. He understands Tresson perfectly well, but he will relay his responses through me, as he is uncomfortable with his mastery of your language."

"Very well," Shadow said.

"Excellent! Please hold still while he takes a proper look."

Solomon stood again, stalking around the malthrope. Instinctively, he turned to keep the creature from moving behind him, but this prompted rumble from the dragon.

"Hold still, sir," Fiora reminded.

He managed to will himself into stillness.

Solomon circled him twice before planting himself on the ground before him and sweeping his eyes up and down, tongue flicking. The penetrating gaze came to rest on his eyes, staring into them for nearly a minute. Slowly, it closed it eyes. It growled what must have been a question.

"He asks if you are certain you have no use for magic."

"Yes."

Solomon's eyes narrowed.

"He says if you change your mind, he will gladly have you as a student."

"Why? What is so special about me? Is it the mark?" He once again revealed it.

"He says the mark may mean everything or it may mean nothing, but what is most important is the spirit."

The dragon rumbled one last comment before slinking back into its hut.

"He says you may go now, and he thanks you for coming. And he thanks *me* for fetching you." Fiora added this last statement with no small amount of pride.

"That's all? He wanted me here to say so little?"

"I'm surprised he said *that* much. He's very terse. Why? Did you have more questions? I'll take you back to Warrior's Side, you can ask along the way. We shouldn't stay here, Master Solomon is probably going to sleep."

She drifted off. He followed.

"Why is there so much interest in the mark? Azriel, the Elder . . ."

"Hmm . . . mark. Mark, mark, mark . . . I suppose they are probably thinking it might have to do with the prophecy. It *is* pretty intricate to be a simple birthmark."

"What prophecy?"

"The big one. Tober's Opus. The one about the war. He finished working on it after he got here, though, so I suppose it might not be so well known outside of Entwell. It fills volumes, and it was never really my area of interest, but let's see what I remember. Mostly it deals with an unnaturally long war. A war that will never come to an end on its own. There are forces that wish to prolong it indefinitely, and naturally there are opposing forces. There are to be five chosen warriors who will unite to end it, and they will each bear the same mark. What were they? Well, one is to be a swordsman, and one a strategist. I believe one is to be a prodigy. Another will be an elemental, I know that. Then there's the weapons-master."

"Master of every weapon. Azriel read that from a book. And something about the blood of a fox."

"*Oh*, she was reading from an *old* interpretation of the prophecy. Newer interpretations record that blood of a fox bit as 'He will be a trickster by nature.' I haven't heard anyone use the 'blood of a fox' wording in ages. Funny, when you say it like that, it is a wonder no one was assuming it would be a malthrope all along."

"What would it mean if I was one of these chosen warriors?"

"You'd go off and save the world, eventually. Around here, though, it mostly means you'd be expected to take part in the Blue Moon Ceremony. Every blue moon, we try to summon the shape-shifter. The prophecy says that she will only show herself if a Chosen is among those joined in the ceremony. There won't be another one of those for a few years, and because of its intensity, they don't usually let warriors participate unless they are exceptionally well-trained or hearty." She

330

assumed proud posture. "The mystic arts are no place for the frail. You'll need—"

There was an odd tone in the air, one that had been approaching since shortly after she'd begun to speak, but it finally rose to the point that she could not ignore it. She turned with a smirk to a point of light that was approaching from the north.

"Oh, here he comes. Excuse me for a moment," she said.

Fiora flitted into the air. With three swift and precise arm motions, each trailing successively brighter strands of flame, she seemed to spark into an equally brilliant point of light. She flared and charged forward, clashing with the approaching fireball. The flames surrounding each form burst into a cloud of embers, leaving Fiora face to face with a similarly-sized and identically-dressed male fairy. He had youthful and oddly cherubic features. His round face was twisted in anger, fingers pointing in accusation and voice piping in a multi-layered symphony of tweets and whistles. Fiora began a conversation with the agitated fairy.

"Yes, Duncan, he's seen Master Solomon already. . . . I convinced him to, that's how. . . . With persuasion and diplomacy. Mystic endurance isn't everything, you know. You need to be well rounded. . . . I am not *that* far behind you in his lessons. . . . I'm *not*! That's it!"

She twirled, flames sparking up around her again. Duncan did the same, and the pair began flitting clashing, sending splashes of flame and bursts of light spraying through the air. All the while, they made sounds somewhere between the buzzing of an angry hornet's nest and two piccolos in a spirited discussion. Shadow backed away to avoid being singed by a curl of flame. The spectacle continued until the whorl of flame that hid Fiora began to dim, her strength presumably flagging. She shifted from her own language to Tresson, interjecting between clashes.

"Enough. . . . Duncan, enough! Hey!" she declared. "Listen!" This last outburst prompted Duncan to pull back and douse his flames. "We are being rude to our newest resident!"

Duncan turned to him, buzzed up and gave a brief and courteous bow. He furrowed his brow and glanced aside, then squeakily managed to say, "Welcome, friend." He looked aside again, twittered something to Fiora, then gave a nod and blazed away.

"He is *such* a child sometimes. I'll get you back to your hut now. I'm very sorry about that."

The lilt to the little creature's motion was considerably more subdued after the battle, and her chattering conversation was reduced to a few cheerful comments here or there as she bobbed along. She reached the hut, gave a bow of her own, and fluttered off to her side of the village once more.

Shadow stepped inside, shut the door tight, and leaned heavily on the bed.

He closed his eyes and did his best to push away the sounds of life and community that filtered through the walls. It was too much, too quickly. He felt as though he'd been thrust into a new body, shoved into the life of one of the people he'd watched from afar when he first began to observe humans in his quest to find a way to free his fellow slaves. A tiny slice of his mind had craved something like this, a place where he could belong, where he could be accepted and live among others. Now presented with such a life, he was overwhelmed, almost terrified. Nothing had prepared him for this.

He very much doubted that *anything* could have prepared him for *this*. Magic all around him, hurled without effort or care. Clashing weapons everywhere, but none of them used in anger. A place where no two creatures seemed to share a common history, and yet all seemed dedicated to the same ends.

"A curious place, eh?"

At the sound of the unexpected voice, he turned and struck, the motion complete before his mind had even fully processed what he had heard. With a meaty slap, his balled-up fist was caught in a tight grip. When Shadow had been given time to exert a measure of control over his actions again, the grip was released and the fist pushed away without retaliation.

The man responsible was a match of Shadow's height. He was a human, perhaps a few years past fifty. His body had the sort of lean, durable muscle that is earned through a lifetime of training. His hair was a uniform mix of gray and black, and thin, but well short of bald. His clothes were dark—not black, but near to it—and had the same general features as those worn by Leo. Straps secured loose patches of clothing tight to his limbs, allowing maximum mobility with minimum rustling or risk of snagging. To one side hung a similarly-secured satchel.

Shadow looked around, but there was no obvious place the man could have been hiding, and he was certain the man hadn't slipped in behind him.

"My apologies for the invasion of privacy, but after seeing your skills earlier, I was curious how deep they ran." He spoke in perfect Tresson. Not only did his words lack the influence of Varden or Crich, it lacked even the regional differences one might hear from various parts of Tressor. Each word was pronounced precisely as it was intended to be. The result was vaguely unnerving. A normal person shouldn't have that sort of detachment or precision.

"How did you do that? Where did you come from?" Shadow demanded.

"In due time, in due time." He reached to his belt and flipped open a pouch, pulling a metal flask that had been tucked snugly inside. He popped the small cork from its mouth. The room filled with the sharp and spicy scent of a strong drink. He took a tiny sip and offered one to his host. When it was refused, he continued. "I've seen the look you were wearing when you walked in. I wore it myself when I first came to this place. When I saw the light at the end of the tunnel after wandering in that cave for too long, I thought I'd finally found it. The slice of the mountain the beast called home. Instead, I found this place. A village. It was devastating.

"I had no use for these people, no use for *people*. The cave was supposed to serve up a beast that I could use to secure my legacy. If I could have, I would have marched right back into that cave and found my way home. At least *there* I could have a chance to find glory. Alas, the cave did not treat me as kindly as it treated you. I was near death, so I allowed the healers to do their work. The sort of withering wear that the cave put on me couldn't be solved with a few simple spells. Even with the best healers they had, my strength wouldn't return for weeks, so I waited and kept my eyes to the cave.

"I wasn't alone among those convalescing, though. There were warriors recovering from sparring matches gone wrong, and in listening to them and watching them, I began to see tactics and techniques that I'd never seen elsewhere. Some seemed simple enough to counter. Others appeared fiendishly difficult to counter, if a counter even existed. The falls had started again by the time I was healed, so I decided until they relented I would invest my time unraveling these secrets. Those lessons led to others. I was asked to share my knowledge, and in teaching I learned even more. By the time the falls dried up and the cave opened again, there was so much I needed to know, I didn't even consider leaving. Now, twenty years have passed and I still don't know half of what I would care to know."

He sipped again.

"Leo is one of my apprentices," he continued. "A promising pupil, but for the last few months I've been having a problem with him. He's got some things to learn in combat and defense, but in stealth the boy is a step ahead of the best of his peers and two steps behind me. He can't best me. He can't even make enough progress to truly improve himself, but at the same time he has nothing left to learn from his fellow students. It is as though he has been climbing a ladder and he's reached a point where a few rungs are missing. Can't reach far enough to go any higher, and there is nothing to help him reach any farther. You? You're different. I would wager you've got a good deal to learn from very nearly anyone here, but your detection skills are more than enough to challenge him. I think you could help each other.

"Now, I know I didn't like being told what to do, and I have no intention of telling *you* what to do, but bear this in mind: you have a blind spot. I found it. That is how I was able to surprise you. If you've got any interest in learning how to overcome your shortcoming, I am the man who can help you."

"It was magic. It must have been," Shadow insisted.

"Does that matter? If it was magic, unless you can trust your enemies to kindly refrain from using such tricks, you've still got a problem. If it wasn't magic, you've got a greater problem still. Either way, if you want to know, I can teach you. Keep that in mind. And if you decide to seek me out," he began, deftly unfastening his satchel and pulling free a bundle of cloth, "you'll need this."

He tossed the cloth to the bed.

"Ask them for Master Weste," he advised, and paced calmly through the door.

"Wait," Shadow said. "What were you saying about the falls? What falls?"

Weste turned to the mountains and smiled. "That tunnel that led you here? There's a reason it is so smooth. Most of the year, it is rushing with icy water, scouring it away, flooding the cave, and keeping what's inside in and what's outside out. Why do you suppose so few people make it through to this place? It is as much luck as skill. The falls are the gate to this place . . ."

Shadow's ears twitched and his heart dropped.

"And that is the sound of the gate slamming shut for at least three months."

The malthrope ran to the door and watched as a silvery sheen began to cascade down the face of the mountain, emerging from between peaks and crevices and gathering together into a ribbon that plunged down into the center of the hollow bowl he'd climbed to enter this place. It began as a trickle, but in moments it thickened until it was a thundering wall of water, filling the bowl and beginning to convert the gravel-covered courtyard surrounding it into a wide, shallow pond. Weste looked to Shadow, a sly smile still on his face.

"Timing like that suggests that either fate has plans for you or the gods have a sense of humor."

With that, he went on his way, leaving Shadow to shut the door behind him, panic seizing his chest. When he'd left the cave, this place was an oasis, a place with food and water and light. Someplace to recover. He didn't feel comfortable, but he knew that the darkness and safety of the cave was always just a few bounding steps away. Now that path was shut, and he'd seen no hint of anything that could afford him safe passage away. He was trapped here, held until the falls relented.

The knowledge of that simple fact made the sprawling village seem tight and close. The towering cliffs were the walls of a new prison, closing in. He glared at the bundle of cloth on the bed. Picking it up, he unfurled the bundle to discover a suit of clothes very much like the one Weste and Leo had worn, some manner of uniform. Memories surfaced. He had been assigned clothes before, in the dark days before his freedom. As was so often the case in times of confusion and uncertainty, his mind reached back to the words of Ben.

"All of these people share a common goal. The same goal. To do what they must, to make things better, to live their lives, and to serve their purpose. You share that goal, and that means that these are your people."

It had been a dark time, his youth on the plantation, but it had taught him much. He was here because he needed to learn, and it was for the same reason that each had come to this place before him. Most important, though, was the fact that this time he came by choice. He set the uniform aside, shuttered the window tightly, and stretched out on the bed.

When hours passed without sleep, despite his exhaustion, he

335

climbed from the bed and huddled instead on the cold, familiar surface of the ground. Moments later, he was fast asleep.

#

For the first time in years, Shadow awoke from a night spent under a roof he could call his own. It took some time for him to come to terms with a few things that this new setting afforded him. He had long ago become accustomed to being unseen, and he was, at least, familiar with being scrutinized. This was the first place he had ever been where he was simply ignored. True, he felt a gaze turn to him from time to time, and in those moments, he saw distrust sometimes, or disgust. The glance seldom lasted more than a few moments, though, before turning back to conversation or study. And when it turned, it was not the swift motion of someone caught looking. It was simply that elsewhere had more interesting activities. He wasn't worth their attention at the moment, any more than a passing acquaintance might be. Despite this, more than once he caught himself stepping toward shadows or eying the low rooftops. To him, it was not natural, not *right* to move about in the open.

He walked the grounds, smelling the air and trying to steel himself against the burning anxiety that had until now been more than necessary to keep him safe. He found himself circling the long, roomy hut where the villagers met to eat. He paced for the better part of an hour before he realized that he was instinctively waiting for it to empty so that he could steal a morsel. With a deep breath, he stepped through the front door.

There were tables running the length of the building, and lattice windows lined the walls. A healthy cross-section of the residents were gathered at the tables. He stood to one side, his back to one of the supports between windows, and watched as the people of the village went about their meals. Each newcomer would approach a table perpendicular to the rest, situated at the far end of the hut. There they would take a spoon and empty bowl from a pile and present it to one of the villagers behind the table. The bowl would then be filled from a steaming cauldron and the hungry villager would take a seat. The hungriest among them would take a small loaf of coarse bread as well. It was just another thing that made this place eerily similar to the plantation. The only differences were the size of the portions and the presence of smiles.

He badly wished there was another way to find a meal—reenacting another scene from his youth was a stomach-turning proposition—but his belly was far too empty and the scent of the food far too appetizing to wait any longer.

He stepped forward, took a bowl, and placed it on the table. The villager manning the cauldron, a stout dwarf wearing an apron, dumped a ladle into the bowl. The food was a hearty stew, thick with vegetables and some sort of fish. The dwarf locked him in the same gruff stare that had greeted each of the other villagers and motioned with his head to move along. He took a spoon and some bread, sat at an unoccupied table, and nursed the meal, stretching it out as much as he could. When he was through, and the bowl had been licked clean, he stood to return it. It was twice the meal that he'd become accustomed to living on, but his stomach seemed to be aware that there was more to be had, and grumbled all the more ravenously. He stepped forward to place his emptied bowl with the others, but before he could, a fellow villager with a nearly empty bowl stepped up to the dwarf and presented it. Without comment, the server refilled the bowl.

Shadow looked to his own bowl, then to the server. Experimentally, he placed the empty bowl in front of the dwarf. Sure enough, the kitchen-worker dunked his ladle and filled the bowl again. The malthrope reached for another loaf of bread. No reprimand came. Without leaving the serving table, he downed the contents of the bowl and snapped up the bread in three bites, placing the bowl down for a third helping when he was finished. He took the freshly-filled bowl and a third loaf of bread back to the table and gorged himself further, as though if he ate enough now, he could wipe away half a lifetime of living near starvation.

"You know, the food will be here again tomorrow," stated a familiar voice. It was Leo, a grin on his face. Before Shadow could reply, he continued. "No need to explain. You're fairly fresh from the cave. I remember my trip through. Three years ago and sometimes it still feels like I'm picking bat bones out of my teeth."

"Your nose," the malthrope noted, when he'd swallowed his current mouthful.

"Mmm? Oh, yes," Leo said, touching the previously crooked and swollen flesh. It was now perfectly healthy, though only a night had passed. He didn't even have a black eye. "I finally gave in and let the white wizards have their fun. They do good work, don't they? Meanwhile, I see Master Weste has come to see you." He indicated the

Joseph R. Lallo

new clothes. "It will be enlightening to have you among us. With any luck, I'll get a chance to bloody *your* nose."

Shadow narrowed his eyes.

"Fair's fair," Leo said. "In a proper, vigorous training regimen, one must expect a few bumps and bruises . . . and, on one notable occasion, a few severed fingers." He spread his hand and admired it. "As I said, they do good work. You'd be surprised how little pain there is when you lose a body part."

"No. I wouldn't."

"Oh? Well, I'll trade my story for yours. Later, though. If you're through with your meal, and you're truly interested in earning that uniform, then you'll need to follow me. The day's instruction will begin shortly, and Master Weste requested I fetch you if you seemed interested in accepting his offer."

Shadow nodded, gulping down the remainder of his meal and placing the bowl with the others. Leo led the way south, and they began to weave their way through Warrior's Side. As they walked, Leo spoke.

"It will be a brief instruction today. Most days we do drills and learn techniques, but once or twice a week he gives us time to rest the body and work the mind instead. He calls it 'enrichment.' At first, it was the last thing I had any interest in, but there is an awful lot to do in this place. Getting a chance to sample a bit of it is a treat." Leo paused for a moment, likely hoping to inspire a reply from Shadow. When none came, he took a more direct approach. "So, from whereabouts in Tressor do you hail?"

"Why does that matter?"

"It doesn't. Chit-chat seldom does."

"Then why bother asking?"

He shrugged. "Curiosity. We'll trade, then. I tell you, you tell me. I come from a mixed family. Mother was from quite far south. Far enough that her home didn't have a name, because it was just a cluster of tents that moved from oasis to oasis. Father was from Kenvard. He was down south trying to find a source for some manner of dried herb or another. He met her and brought her home. Things got dicey once the war started, but that's another story. Now, I've given. What do I get in return?"

Shadow walked in silence for a moment. It was curious, but the vague obligation to reveal something of himself in return for what had

338

been revealed to him was simple yet powerful. Logically, he had no reason to do so. He hadn't agreed to anything, and it wasn't as though there had been any true transaction. Nevertheless, the feeling was very real. There was a pressure to restore the balance of information. He noted it for future use.

"My earliest memory is losing my mother and being sold into slavery, where I spent most of my life."

The perpetual grin slid from Leo's face as he processed the words. "Very . . . concise." He cleared his throat. "We'll, uh, set the rest of that aside for now. We've arrived."

The pair reached a patch of trees beyond the southern tip of the village, where the flat land between the mountain and seaward cliff was just beginning to narrow. It was hardly a forest, but there were enough trees that the gathering was hidden from view. A dozen or so villagers, dressed in the same strange uniform, stood in a stretch of clear land among the trees. The grass had been reduced to packed earth there, and a few weapon racks and training dummies were standing about, each very well-used. The group occupying the clearing was a varied lot, but most had a handful of features in common. They were all very lean. The heaviest among them was an older gentleman, and even in his case, there was no fat on his frame. They were in peak condition, and each had hair cropped short or gathered back. Each member also had a subtle awareness of their surroundings that was immediately apparent. Eyes were already glancing in the direction of the newcomers even before the first of them came into view.

At the approach of Leo, most gave a professional nod or a smile and wave. After a few moments of initial apprehension, the group formed a circle around the malthrope and looked him over. Some asked questions, though only one spoke Tresson.

"How far away can you smell something?" came the only question he understood. It was spoken by a young girl, barely in her teens.

He shifted uncomfortably, glancing to Leo. "It depends on the wind."

"So, like a dog, then. And you can track? Like hounds?" she asked.

The sound of snapping fingers twitched his ears, then drew his eyes. The culprit was the older man, a gap-toothed grin coming to his face as he made a comment in a thick dialect reminiscent of one of the tribesman from the plantation.

"He says the way you can point your ears at sounds is . . .

admirable," Leo explained.

"He didn't say admirable," the girl countered.

"That's enough, all of you," said Master Weste, who had managed to arrive unobserved by all. "You should each be uniquely aware of the discomfort caused by being the center of attention when that is something you wish to avoid. Let us do our newest student the courtesy of treating him as we would treat each other. Or, in your case," he said, indicating the girl, "treating him better than we would treat each other."

"What? I'm not wrong. He didn't say admirable, he said dishonest," she said, adding a muttered, "and that doesn't even make sense . . ."

"You will," the master interjected, *once again*, be working on decorum. You can't expect to infiltrate properly if you do not understand how to behave in a refined manner."

"I am *damn well* refined enough *already*," she objected, stomping away.

One by one, Weste handed out assignments as unusual as identifying different poisons by taste and as mundane as learning to tie knots. Finally, he came to Leo.

"You two seem to be getting along well enough, which is good, because starting one week from today and until I say otherwise, you will be partners. Leo, find out where he needs to catch up, then get him started catching up. Once he's started, get back to lock-picking. He'll have a week to learn the basics he should have had, then you'll start doing pairs drills."

"It shall be done, Master Weste," Leo said with a stiff bow. He turned to Shadow. "This way, my friend! I told you it would be brief today."

Leo paced off, Shadow once again in tow. The man who was now his partner looked to him.

"I admit to a certain lack of experience in reading the expressions of a face such as yours, but you look to me like you've once again got some questions. I've got a fair number of my own I'll need to ask, so you may wish to start."

Confusion swiftly overruled Shadow's distaste for conversation. "Why was that young girl there?"

"Deena? The same reason that you and I were there. To learn the ways of stealth and infiltration."

"She is a child."

"A young lady, yes, but you should see her with a stiletto."

"She came through the cave?"

"No, no. The young lady was born here. It earned her a few extra years of training, but cost her some lessons in how members of a civilized society comport themselves. Anything else?"

"She said the man called my ears . . ."

"Dishonest? I apologize for the deception. Dishonest isn't quite the best word either. He was suggesting that you had an unfair advantage. I assure you, he was indeed admiring the ability. Now, a few questions of my own. Your native language is Tresson and you know a bit of Crich and Varden, yes?"

"Yes."

"Well, you'll need to work on the northern languages. 'A bit' won't do. From there, you'll move on to the rest. Can you read in any of those languages?"

"No."

"You shall need to work on that as well. If you'll take my advice, I'd suggest beginning there, as it will take some time to master it. Find someone on Wizard's Side to teach you. That is more their specialty."

"I only wish to be a more skilled assassin. Why would I need to learn any of this?"

"Because whether your goal is assassination or espionage, or really any other worthwhile pursuit, the difference between success and failure is often information. Knowing weaknesses, knowing locations, knowing the truth when you are being lied to, these things are at least as important as knowing how to defend or attack when the time comes. And, unfortunately for you and I, we do not get to choose how that information comes to us. It may be spoken, it may be written, and it may be in any language. To be truly prepared, we must learn as much as we can. For you, that means tracking down a willing teacher and learning to read some Tresson, Crich, or Varden. However, combat *is* a part of it, so I must ask: what weapons do you prefer?"

"I've used a few blades."

"Swords? Daggers?"

"Whatever I could find."

"An opportunist, excellent. We'll take you to see Croyden Lumineblade, then. He's been working on something for me."

"I thought you said Croyden was the name of the man who made master-level weapons."

"He is, but he insists on seeing newcomers. He claims that there is no one better suited to determining what hand should be holding what blade."

It was only a short distance to the cluster of huts dedicated to the fabrication of the many, *many* weapons used by the denizens of Entwell. They were unique among the huts in their area, built a bit taller and with a greater proportion of stone than the rest. The huts dedicated to metalworking had stout chimneys poking out of their roofs, and from within there came the crackle of intense flames. The hammering of metal upon metal was now and again replaced by the hiss of water turning to steam, and from other huts came a chorus of sawing, chopping, creaking, and grinding. Taken as a whole, the half-dozen huts felt like the center of a thriving industry.

Leo led the way to a hut near the center of the cluster, situated between two similarly-equipped workshops. The one on the left was belching black smoke and had the distinctive sound of puffing bellows and grunting apprentices. At first, Shadow thought that the others were not in use, as there was no smoke or commotion, but there was certainly plenty of heat rolling out of the door, here and there the blow of a hammer.

The pair of assassins-in-training stepped inside to find it rather crowded and utterly stifling. Huddled around the furnace were three young men dressed in red tunics similar to the tiny outfit worn by Fiora. Each held a crystal, two with their bare hands and one at the end of a stone staff. Their eyes were shut tight and the staff-wielding one was quietly muttering arcane words. Presumably as a result of their combined efforts, a white glow too bright to look at pulsed within the clay dome of a quality furnace. Ducked low with his head turned aside and his teeth clenched was a dwarf of indeterminate age. He wore thick leather apron and pair of gloves and held a hefty set of tongs, maneuvering an iron rod within the glow. A wiry human with similar equipment was standing at the ready. Judging from the fact that he was looking anxious and was missing an eyebrow, he was probably a less experienced apprentice.

Supervising them was an elf. He had sharp, hawk-like nose, pointed ears, and a build close to the work-hardened elves Shadow had known from the plantation. His hair was dark, and his expression stern. One hand held a hammer, the other a pair of tongs, and he was watching with squinted eyes as the metal rod was heated.

342

"Master Croyden," said Leo.

The elf turned to the door, then recoiled somewhat at the site of his visitor. He made a comment in his native tongue that, though Shadow did not fully understand, seemed to have a passing familiarity. After a moment, he realized he'd heard Goldie and Blondie utter a similar phrase regularly. Presumably it was their own word for malthrope or, judging from his expression, "mally."

"He's been here for a few days, but we only discovered him yesterday."

This new information raised the weapon crafter's eyebrow. "Tresson?" he asked.

Shadow nodded.

"Go out back and wait," Croyden stated, before turning to his apprentices and delivering a long sequence of precise instructions in his own language.

Leo led the way to a courtyard of sorts. It was an open patch of ground behind the ring of crafting huts, and seemed to serve as a storage and testing area. Racks held weapons and armor of various types, and in all states of completion. The more complete pieces were kept in enclosed cabinets to keep the weather from them. There were painted signs indicating the contents—but for now, at least, those signs were meaningless to Shadow.

Croyden emerged after a minute or two and marched with purpose to one such cabinet. Inside were a few weapons that even to an untrained eye were magnificent. The metal was gleaming, the edges clean and precise. Most were swords of various shapes and sizes, though an ax and an assortment of daggers were on display as well. He selected a thin saber and swiped it through the air a few times. He then approached a rack with some weapons that, while quite well-made, certainly weren't to the same level of craftsmanship. Three identical swords were stored there. They were an odd shape, with double-edged blades only about as long as Shadow's forearm, and two-handed grips. It resulted in a weapon that was nearly as much hilt as blade and looked more like an oversized dagger than a proper sword.

Croyden selected one of them and, without a word of warning, heaved it toward Shadow. The malthrope managed to catch it by the grip with ease.

"Defend," Croyden stated.

Without another word, the elf launched himself forward, sword slicing through the air. Shadow managed to raise the sword to block the first attack, and after a second one nicked his ear he blocked the third and fourth. Croyden was unrelenting, almost manic in his assault. There was none of the grace or cunning one would have suspected from one of his kind. His attacks seemed almost random. The weapons clanged and clashed, no slash but the second managing to taste blood, but most coming close. Finally, the assault relented as quickly as it began. Shadow's eyes were wide and his teeth were bared. He was unsure if he was meant to return the attacks in kind.

"No skill," Croyden decreed, replacing his own blade, "but a fair amount of talent, and excellent reflexes. You are not ready for one of mine yet, but perhaps soon. Keep the trainer. That should do for now."

The elf then left the courtyard without further comment, leaving Shadow still confused and out of breath from the unprovoked attack. He looked to Leo, who grinned a bit wider and shrugged.

"By now it should be clear that such things are to be expected here. There is very little pretense. We have curiosities and we address them. It can be a bit off-putting at first, but once you are accustomed to it you'll see that it is quite liberating. At any rate, start working on those language skills, and become comfortable with that weapon. I'll check on you in a few days, but don't waste any time. After a week, you'll be thrust into the thick of it."

With that, Leo was off. Shadow stood for a time, bleeding from the ear and weapon in hand. He wasn't certain what was more unnerving to him: the fact that a villager had assaulted him without cause or warning and then walked away as though nothing had happened, or the fact that he was standing in the center of a community of warriors with a weapon in his hand and was not currently running for his life. Rather than press his luck, he decided to hurry to his hut and work out what needed to be done.

#

Shadow did his best to find a routine. Several years of having to scrape out a living for himself had left a deep impression upon him, and the reality of a place where food and water would always be available was slow to take root. Out of habit, he remained hidden through most of the day. He spent the time skulking in the shadows, watching warriors training and sparring. When night descended, he ventured out. Even at midnight, food was available in the designated hut, though in the form of lukewarm cauldrons of the day's leftovers.

344

Despite the fact that he at least appeared to be in no danger here, sleep continued to come in light and fitful dozes scattered throughout the daylight hours, as though if he ever let himself fall into a truly deep slumber he would awake surrounded by hunters.

This, at least, proved to be accurate.

To the other students of Weste, Shadow's considerable powers of detection were an irresistible challenge. Each made an attempt to get the better of him. Deena had been clinging to the rafters of his hut one night. The man who had dubbed his ears "untrustworthy" took to following him. None of the students managed to escape his notice for more than a few moments.

For many, the concept of being perpetually stalked by trained killers would have been a horrifying and debilitating distraction. For Shadow, it was the most familiar and comforting part of this entire experience in this place.

As dawn was nearing on the third day, Shadow was sitting at the edge of the village's lake near the seaside cliff. His sword was by his side and his eyes staring at the reflection of the moonlit clouds in the surface. In response to a tugging in the back of his mind, he twitched an ear, then turned his head to the south. A barely perceptible motion in the tall grass slowed and stopped.

"Leo," he said quietly.

"Confound it!" cursed Leo in a lighthearted fashion, "I've got half a mind to swing by the Wizard's Side and pick up some trinkets to give me the edge on you." He stood and walked toward the malthrope. Out of habit or training, he moved almost silently despite being discovered. "I've been asking around the village. It seems you've been remiss in your assignments."

"What do you mean?"

"You haven't approached anyone about teaching you anything."

"I've been watching and listening. I've learned a great deal of how to handle the blade."

"Watching and listening . . . no doubt you can learn quite a bit in that way, but if you step forward and *ask*, you shall be shown where to start and pointed in the right direction. All you need to do is ask."

"This is my way."

"Perhaps, but it is not the Entwell way. And what of reading and writing? Have you been watching people do that?"

"I don't see the need."

"Don't you?" Leo looked around, spotting a pair of blue-clad villagers from Wizard's Side making their way along the shore of the lake. "Well, let us see."

He ducked down and slid smoothly through the tall weeds until he was near enough to touch the students. They remained oblivious to his presence, even after he stepped out behind them and plucked something from each of them. In a few moments he was beside Shadow again, two parchments in hand.

"Tell me," he said, flipping the parchments open and glancing over them. "Who are those two, where are they going, and why?"

"They are dressed in blue. The water wizards seem to wear blue. I imagine they are going to train, since most people here start their day at dawn."

"Correct. But these parchments tell me that they are heading to the southernmost tip of Entwell, where they will meditate on a very powerful and very volatile spell. They are doing it under the instruction of a mid-level water mage named Narrel. They perform this task at dawn on alternating days, and report back to Narrel by noon. Other days they are to rest and collaborate with Narrel on the improvement of the spell."

"Nothing that I could not have determined by observing them for a few days."

"Certainly, but if you'd read these, you wouldn't have needed to. Three days of surveillance replaced by a few moments. Keep it in mind. I've got to return these."

Shadow thought for a moment before calling after him. "Can you teach me to use a sword?"

"I could, but I wouldn't be doing you any favors. It isn't my strongest subject," he called back. "And I haven't really got the patience for teaching, it shames me to say. There are plenty more able than me. Just ask!"

He vanished among the weeds, chasing after the wizards he had pick-pocketed. Shadow thought back to his attempts at bounty-hunting. In the larger cities, the bounty offices posted the descriptions they read each morning. Though the list of bounties were read only once, they were updated throughout the day. If he had been able to read them, he could have had hours of head-start over the other hunters. Other mistakes that might not have been made and opportunities that might not have been missed came to mind. He turned to the north, sniffed the air, and set off.

Following a scent on the breeze, he found his way to a tree on the opposite end of the village. Its bark was scorched here and there, and the whole of the trunk and many of the branches were wreathed in morning glories. The flowers on the vines were just beginning to open in the rising sun, and there was a clump of carefully arranged twigs, leaves, and woven vines over a crook between two branches that, to a trained eye, looked quite like a roof. From the darkness beneath came a slow, regular trill. He grasped a low branch and hoisted himself level with the nest.

Inside was the sleeping form of Fiora. Her head was toward the "entrance" of her little home, and the sound was evidently a fairy-sized snore.

"Fiora," he said.

The trilling stopped abruptly and the tiny head shifted upward. Its little eyes shot open and it released a startled chirp, darting backward and nearly demolishing its shelter with the flutter of its wings. After a moment the shock of coming eye to eye with a fierce creature many times her own size lurking inches from her door, she breathed a sigh of relief.

"Mr. Malthrope, sir," she said breathlessly. "You startled me."

"I apologize."

"No! It is fine." She straightened her tunic and drifted out of her home, allowing Shadow to drop back to the ground. "It was nearly dawn anyway. I would have had to wake up soon. How can I help you?"

"You said that you owed me a favor."

"I certainly do. Master Solomon complimented me on my initiative when I brought you to him! Do you know how difficult it is to get praise out of a dragon?" she said. "Why, did you have something in mind?"

"Can you read?"

She crossed her arms. "What sort of a wizard would I be if I couldn't read? I read every language I speak, plus two more besides."

"I need you to teach me."

She smirked and put her hands on her hips. "*That's* your favor? You don't know much about Entwell wizards, do you? You are giving me a chance to teach! Do you know how long I would have had to wait to get a student of *any* kind?" She clapped her hands in delight.

"This isn't returning the favor. Not *hardly.* I almost owe you *two* favors now. I *don't,* mind you, but almost. I've got a full day of my own studies ahead of me, but I can help you at sundown. I'll meet you at your hut, we'll go to the library, and we'll get started. For now, if you'll excuse me, I need some breakfast."

He watched as she fluttered up to the first fully-open flower and leaned into it, partaking of the nectar within.

One problem solved, Shadow made his way back toward Warrior's Side. He hefted the sword in his hand as he went, judging its shape and attempting to spot someone using a similar one. There were not very many. Croyden had referred to it as a "trainer." If it was truly a weapon intended for those just beginning their training, then it was possible that no one in the village was as fresh to swordcraft as he. There were plenty of masters instructing students, and plenty of people sparring or engaging in solo drills. Likely he could approach any one of them and request instruction, but every time he thought of reaching out to one of them, something inside of him recoiled. Even becoming comfortable with being seen by others was a steep hill to climb. Actually reaching out to them for help without something to offer in return seemed insurmountable. His frustration began to flare, both with the way this place worked and the fact that he couldn't adapt to it.

When he heard an unnatural shuffle of a foot and felt the familiar burning of observation, it was the last straw.

"Stop following me!" he snapped, spinning on his heel and pulling a black-clad figure from the shadows. It was the gap-toothed older man who had "admired" Shadow's ears. The man smiled and uttered a foreign remark that didn't sound like an apology. The raised voices drew the attention of the others in the area, but for now Shadow didn't care. "Do you speak Tresson?" The man nodded, grin still firmly in place, as though he was delighted with the situation. "Then *speak it!* I don't speak your language yet and I'm through relying on an interpreter."

"Hot temper on you. Makes sense," the man said, pulling out of his grip.

"What is your name?"

"Sama."

"Why do you keep following me?"

"You keep finding me, I keep following you. I need to find a way around those cheating ears. Same for all of us. What was my mistake?"

The Rise of the Red Shadow

Shadow growled, then looked to Sama's belt. There was a sword there. It wasn't the same sort, but close.

"Do you know how to use this sort of sword?" he asked, holding up the one he had been provided.

Sama nodded. "Simple."

"Show me! Use it!" he growled, brandishing his weapon. "If you are going to follow me and try to learn from me, then I expect the same. That's how things work here, isn't it?"

The crowd was growing as Sama paced out into the middle of the path. His sword was still in its scabbard. He hadn't even placed his hand on the grip.

"You want to know how to use your sword, eh?" the man remarked with a laugh.

In a flash, his hand went to his hilt and he drew the weapon. Shadow shifted his own to parry, but his foe subtly shifted the motion of his attack. His blade hooked around, clashed with Shadow's, and then continued in a tight loop. It was more than enough to wrench the sword from the malthrope's grip and send it flying. As the training sword clattered to the ground, Sama put the point of his weapon to Shadow's throat.

"Not like that," Sama said. "If you want a proper lesson, ask properly. Maybe you get on your knees. Maybe you beg." The grin finally left his face, his final words deadly serious. "Or maybe I take one of those cheating ears as a trophy, eh?"

Shadow looked Sama in the eye steadily. There wasn't fear or anxiety in his expression. To the contrary, this was the first time since his initial assessment outside the elder's hut that he was experiencing something for which he felt fully prepared. Sama was a brute, a bully. This was intimidation, or an attempt at it. He was trying to put Shadow in his place. He'd seen the same expressions, the same body language on Menri, then the slave-drivers, and a hundred hoods and scoundrels since. Somehow, knowing that such a person existed in Entwell helped the place seem real to him. The man was using an old tactic, one of which Shadow had had his fill.

"I ask you now, with all of the respect you deserve. Will you teach me how to use a sword?"

Sama narrowed his eyes. "You say you ask me with the respect I deserve, but you don't do as I say. That doesn't show much respect at all."

349

Joseph R. Lallo

Shadow sidestepped with blinding speed, ducking below a reflexive swipe of the sword and springing toward the crowd. In three strides, he was out of sight behind a hut. Sama followed close behind, but not close enough. He reached the opposite side of the hut to find the malthrope missing, then a hushed sound of surprise from the crowd drew his attention. He turned to find the malthrope face to face with him, sword in hand. Before he could react, the tip was to Sama's throat.

"You *earn* respect from me. And you have as much to learn from me as I do from you," Shadow growled.

A sequence of expressions crossed the older warrior's face in stages. First shock, then fury, and finally his default grin. "Over the roof, right? Over the roof, down to your sword, and behind me. I should have seen it coming. Silent and fast though. You are right. We have secrets to trade. This way."

Sama led the way further into Warrior's Side and directed shadow to one of the training areas. There were three rows of training dummies, little more than straw and burlap bound to wooden poles. There were crosspieces to approximate arms, hooks and straps to affix various weapons and armor, and a stuffed sack in place of a head. On the specific dummy Sama selected to be Shadow's opponent, someone had drawn an angry face with a bit of charcoal.

"This is your enemy," he said, slapping the dummy and causing the head to flop forward. "He is armed with a sword, here." He plucked a crude wooden prop sword and secured it to the right hand. "Now step back. Good. You are too far away to hit, but swing like you would swing if you wanted to hit this man."

Shadow cut a diagonal slice through the air. Like the first time he sampled the air under the tutelage of Sorrel, he had thought that this was so simple an action it could not be done incorrectly. Once again, he was quite wrong.

"No, no. Already I see three mistakes," his teacher said. The man approached. "It is not a club. It matters how you swing it. Align the blade with the line of the attack. Be exact, otherwise you waste the swing. You are left-handed, so this hand should be here, and this one here, for more power. And you grip too tightly, I can see from here. If you connect with something solid you will sting your hand. Now, again." Shadow tried another swing. "No, no. Still wrong." Shadow looked to Sama with skepticism. "You do not believe me? Go, try that swing on the dummy."

The Rise of the Red Shadow

The student stepped forward and executed what he believed to be a proper swing. The blade struck the wood and glanced off, taking an odd twist that wrenched one of his wrists and sending a sharp pain across both palms. The wood was barely splintered.

"There, you see? Maybe now you listen to your teacher. Now, swing again."

It was remarkable how much time and energy could be spent on a simple thing like swinging a blade. Sama drilled him on it continuously for most of the day. He was either a very patient, very precise teacher, or else he was reveling in the fact that in this area he was clearly and vastly the malthrope's superior. Regardless of the motivation behind his teachings, there was no doubt as to the truth behind them. Each time he was run through the sequence of diagonal, horizontal, and vertical slashes, he could feel both where he was wrong and where he was improving.

The unfamiliar motions quickly fatigued Shadow, but he pushed through until Sama abruptly decided he was through.

"That is all. We will learn more tomorrow. Now you must tell me, what is it that *I* did wrong?"

"I heard you. Your footsteps."

Sama rolled his eyes. "Yes, I know this, because of your cheating ears. But there were many people around. What about *my* footsteps told you that there was a man tracking you?"

"A man steps differently when he is trying not to be heard."

"Interesting," Sama said. He paused to consider the words. "I will see you tomorrow, when my training is done. Perhaps, though, you will *not* see me."

Shadow made his way to his hut to recover a bit. The unfamiliar and precise motion, simple though it was, had left his arms and back well beyond sore. It wasn't until the shadow of the mountain had shrouded the entire village that he could raise his arms again without difficulty. Not long after, the subdued buzzing of gossamer wings could be heard outside the door.

"Mr. Malthrope, sir?" came the tinkling voice, with a bit less enthusiasm than in prior instances. He opened the door to find Fiora fluttering at eye-level. Her posture had sagged a bit, fatigue apparent in expression. "Are you ready for your first lesson? The library is this way." She pivoted and led the way with a slow, bobbing flutter. "I apologize if I am not my usual self. It was a particularly taxing day of training. We fairies are really very adept at the little magic, but when it comes to stamina, it takes a *lot* of work to build it up. It is worth it, though. Magic is a big part of what we are. Working on our magic keeps us young. It's good for the soul."

She continued to chat in a one-sided manner about what exactly she'd been up to with Solomon and Duncan. Twice along the way, Shadow had been forced to irritably expose one of his fellow assassins in training as they endeavored with varying degrees of success to follow without being seen. After the second time, Fiora felt the need to comment.

"What is that all about?"

"They are using me to test their stealth."

"What fun! You warriors have such wonderful little games," she said. "Ah, here we are."

The library, perhaps tellingly, occupied the same central location in Wizard's Side that the smith's shops occupied in Warrior's Side. It was large, nearly a match for the dining cabin, but far less open. It was made from thick planks of wood that seemed older than most of the huts surrounding it. The roof was sloped and comparatively steep. Along the edges of the roof were eaves carved into a complex pattern of curves and points, and metal plates with etched runes were affixed to the outer walls at regular intervals. Between the plates were narrow, shuttered windows, except for along the eastern wall, where a series of long windows opened out to the seaward side of the village. Though no sun poured through the windows now, a few points of light within marked the seats of students eagerly studying from thick tomes. The overall effect was a combination of grandness and solemnity, as one might normally find in a place of worship.

Fiora fluttered apprehensively in front of the door, chewing her lip for a moment before turning to Shadow. "Do you mind if I ride on your shoulder? I'm attuned to flame magic, and they suppress flames inside the library to protect the books. It makes it very difficult to stay airborne, and I just don't think I have it in me right now."

Shadow nodded reluctantly.

"Many thanks!" She drifted over and alighted on his left shoulder. "Go right on inside and we'll try to find something for you to start reading."

He pushed open the door to find the inside quite dim, though there was light enough for his keen eyes to navigate. Ahead of him there were shelves upon shelves of books forming orderly rows. Each shelf reached easily twice his height toward the lofted ceiling, and stools and ladders were scattered about to help reach the less-accessible volumes. Apprentices paced the aisles, reading the hand-lettered spines of the books or flipping through the pages with reverence and care. To light their way, they held smooth crystals that cast a gentle glow of moonlight white. Beside the door was an older gentleman with a white beard and a black tunic seated at a podium. An ancient, leather-bound volume was open on the podium, and a coarse crystal was hanging in the air above it, glowing with a warmer yellow color than the others. When Shadow made ready to stride inside, Fiora stopped him.

"Not so quickly. First, this is Master Nozim. He's one of our black magic masters, and chief librarian. Master Nozim, sir, this is the newcomer."

The black wizard nodded.

"Next, maybe you can see in here, Mr. Malthrope, sir, but for me I'll need a light. Take one of those and hold it in your hand."

She indicated a netted bag of gems identical to those held by the others. He reached inside the bag to select one. Each gem that his fingers brushed against briefly took on a glow, tingling lightly where it touched him.

"I don't like magic," he reminded her.

The comment drew a glance from the librarian.

"It is just simple light, silly," she said. "Nothing at all to worry about."

Grudgingly, he pulled a small one from the bag. The glow within it steadily intensified, until it was more than enough to light their way.

Fiora raised her eyebrows. "That's pretty bright for a warrior. This way." She directed him along one side, toward the western wall. "These books were mostly written by the villagers. The rest were brought in from the outside. As they were brought by wizards and warriors expecting a battle, what we mostly have are grimoires—those would be spell books—and manuals of fighting techniques. There are a few histories and memoirs, too, but not much in the way of light reading, which is where you really ought to start. Those simply aren't the sort of things people carry with them into a cave. What we do have is over here." The pair reached a single bookcase with only two shelves filled. "Put your hand on the shelf, please."

Shadow obliged, and she trotted down his arm and onto the shelf.

Once there, she paced along looking up and down at the spines of books that were taller than she was.

"We're looking for something thin. You speak some Varden, right?"

"Some."

"I think we'll have to try that language first. It is an easier alphabet, and we have more books in that language. Here . . . try this one."

He pulled the indicated book, which was a slim volume, little more than a stack of pages bound together with thread. Rather than request to be picked up, Fiora snagged the edge and hitched a ride, climbing up the spine and looking over the top as he flipped it open. She smiled and made a fluttering hop from the book to his shoulder to whisper in his ear.

"You're holding it upside-down." She patted him on the back of the neck. "Come, we'll take it back to your hut. Just make sure you replace the crystal and let Nozim know you are taking the book. We don't care much when someone takes one of these."

Fiora rode on his shoulder all the way back to his hut, where he placed the book down on his table. She fluttered down to it, hefted the cover open, and paced out onto the page.

"Now, let's start with the title. This says *One Final March: A Play in Three Parts* . . ."

#

Over the next few days, his sessions with each of his tutors became a normal part of his routine . . . or, at least, as normal as a set of lessons can be when one teacher is standing on the page as she instructs and the other begins by attempting to creep undetected until he is within stabbing range.

The sword drills were swift to fall into place. He quickly understood what needed to be done, and with practice he found himself a bit closer each day. Learning to read was another thing entirely. It was unlike anything he'd had to do before. There was so much to remember, so many rules, and none of them truly made sense to him. It was raw knowledge, and very slow to take root, but Fiora was patient and calm, and with time the words on the page began to link themselves to the words in his head. He'd yet to assemble even the first sentence, though, when his first week was through, and the true training under Master Weste began.

#

His first lesson was to begin at dawn, and he arrived just as the sun was turning the sky golden. It is a unique and unnerving experience to be present when a class of stealth apprentices comes to session. First the training ground was empty, and then, gradually, it was not. There was little sound, little evidence of arrival at all, yet one by one new individuals appeared. Much to their chagrin, however, each was greeted by a purposeful glance from Shadow long before they would have chosen to reveal themselves.

"Almost got you! Almost!" said Deena, the last apprentice to arrive.

"Not nearly," Leo said in reply. "He was looking at you before you even entered the grove."

"As far as I'm concerned, I only need to get close enough to kill him," she countered. "I could have killed him from the edge of the grove if I needed to. I'm getting better with the blow gun."

"That's enough," came Weste's voice. Again, all eyes turned to the north side of the clearing to find their teacher having arrived without being observed by even the malthrope. "We will all get our opportunities to test ourselves against our newest apprentice in due time. Since he is new here, I will take a moment to explain how things will progress. I pair you together based on your strengths. Every few days, I will assign enrichment tasks to develop your mind and dexterity. The rest of the time, I will have you do drills and advise.

"Though your tasks all contribute in some way or another to the task of hunting another, I want to make it clear that both in Entwell and in the rest of the world, we are not simply killers. Life is precious, and it is valuable. We will not endanger the lives of our fellow students, and we will never take a life that does not *need* to be taken. Now, Deena, since you are so impressed with your blow gun progress, we shall start with you. The rest of you, pair up."

As the students began to align themselves beside their designated partners, Weste began pointing to them and uttering seemingly random phrases. Some, like "infiltration," at least made sense. Others were nonsensical. Sama and his partner were assigned "tandem fishing." As for Leo and Shadow, "courier."

"Excellent," Leo said, rubbing his hands together as the others went off to their tasks. "I enjoy courier."

"What is it?" Shadow asked.

"It is great fun," Leo said, making his way to a small wooden chest beside one of the weapon racks. From within, he selected two stones. They were smooth, like river rock, and were identical save for a unique symbol carved into one side. He gave one to Shadow. "We each have a stone. Now, we will head back to the center of Warrior's Side. We'll pick a courier. Your goal is to be sure that he is carrying your stone, and that *you* are carrying *my* stone. My goal is the same, but reversed. If the courier notices, the person responsible gets a mark against and we find a new courier. The game ends at sundown. It tests a host of different skills. You need to watch your target and your opponent. You need to track for long durations without being detected. You need to defend and strike, also without being detected. Picking pockets, planting things. Think of the sequence of it. If you plant your stone first, I have to steal it and plant mine. Then, to plant yours again you have to steal it back from me. It is truly challenging."

Shadow looked long and hard at the stone, memorizing the shape, then followed as Leo led the way to a crowded section of Warrior's Side. He pointed out a young man suited in heavy armor.

"That's Tavis. He is trying to build stamina, so he will be spending most of the day marching about in that armor. He's a good starting courier. The game starts now. Enjoy!"

With a deft and precise tap of his finger, Leo managed to dislodge the stone from Shadow's hand. He snapped his head down and tried to catch it, but found that Leo had managed to snatch it out of the air and was already just a few paces away from Tavis. With a smooth motion of his hand he flipped the edge of a thick leather messenger bag at Tavis's side up, lowered the stone in, and withdrew his hand. The armored student never noticed Leo's presence.

And so the game began.

Tracking was second nature to Shadow now. Finding either the courier or Leo was of little difficulty, and lingering near either without being noticed was almost an afterthought. Taking the stone, however, was exceedingly difficult. His first three attempts were devoted to taking his own stone back from Leo, as the other apprentice was typically out of sight, and thus failing to take the stone without being noticed wouldn't cost him anything but time. Leo, however, was measurably more alert than the courier, and he was expecting to have to protect his prize, so getting the stone away was no simple task.

He decided to switch tactics, instead following the courier, but while he could easily bring himself to within inches without being noticed, he lacked the practiced finesse that Leo had. Three times, Tavis's head jerked toward his bag a fraction of a second too slowly to see Shadow, and finally he stopped and bellowed something in Varden.

"Enough of this courier foolishness," he grunted, rummaging through his bag until he found the stone. "Choose another target."

"Ha-ha!" Leo piped triumphantly as he revealed himself from nearby. "That's one for me!"

Shadow gave Leo a hard look, then snatched both the stone in Tavis's hand and the one in a pouch on Leo's belt.

"Hah," Leo said, now with a bit less enthusiasm. "I must remember that speed of yours. Fine, then, you choose the next courier—but be careful. Now that we've been caught once, the herd will be spooked, so to speak."

The rest of the day played out much as it had begun. Picking pockets was a nuanced art, but one that Shadow had at least managed to begin to grasp by sundown. Planting the stone was another matter entirely. It could not simply be dropped into a sack or pocket, as doing so would alert the courier. Conversely, lowering it too slowly left one exposed for much longer. The trick was to let it slip smoothly from palm to fingers to pocket, a continuous motion that began as soon as the fingertips were in the pocket and ended with subtlety and speed. Despite dozens of attempts that day, he never once managed to do it successfully.

"So much for the claim that your kind are natural thieves," Leo said as walked beside Shadow toward his hut. The pair had filled some bowls in the dining hut and now it was nearly time for his reading lesson. "I'll tell you where you need to improve. You need to match their gait when picking the pockets or planting the stones. Same pace, same height, same sway, same rhythm. You've got to get that right, then you can go for the pocket. Also, strange as it sounds, once you've got the skill for it, you are less likely to be noticed with your hands in their pockets if you do your picking while they are moving. They are already jostling about, so they are likely to dismiss your work as just another shift. Now, as for me, I noticed I caught a flip of your ear every time I changed direction. Where precisely is my misstep?"

Shadow opened his mouth to answer, but paused for a moment. He had spent years learning the proper ways to avoid humans and the best ways to detect them, he was now telling them how to stalk *him*. He'd been helping Sama with such things, but compared to Leo, Sama was clumsy as an ox. The man with him now was as close to his own stealth as he'd ever encountered in a human. Nonetheless, Leo had been open and helpful with his own advice.

"You pivot with your toe on the ground. I can hear the grind of the dust."

"The grind of the dust . . . sharp ears, my friend. Sharp ears indeed."

"Mr. Malthrope, sir!" piped Fiora's tiny voice in the distance.

The fairy buzzed up, a good deal more chipper than usual for this time of day.

"Oh, hello, Stealth Apprentice Leo, sir," she said with a polite bob. "I was worried I was late. Master Solomon has adjusted my training. I will be doing my endurance training while I'm helping you. It will be a little bit of a blow to my dignity, but in the end it will help us both."

"I'll leave you to it, then," Leo said, nodding a goodbye to them both.

Fiora fluttered with excitement ahead of Shadow until they reached the hut. He opened the door and she pointed to the lamp that had provided their light each evening. It was a finely crafted piece, with a clear glass bulb to keep the flickering flame from throwing sparks onto the table. The bulb was shaped like a narrow flower vase, with a flared opening at the top, and attached to the polished brass fittings that secured it in place and held the reserve of lamp oil and the wick.

"Pull the bulb from the oil please, and set the oil aside," she said, a bit of unpleasant anticipation in her tone.

He did so, setting the oil on the far side of the table and laying the bulb and its metal base on its side. She flitted into the air, grasped the top of the bulb and, with some effort, slid it to beside the open book and stood it upright. Then, with as deep a sigh as her little body could muster, she squeezed through the opening at the top and dropped inside.

"I'll be providing the light to read by, but Master Nozim forbids naked flames near his books," she explained from inside the jar. "I'm not strong enough yet to summon a flame from afar for any length of time, so this is where that leaves us." She took a deep breath and released it shakily. "It just stirs up some bad memories, is all."

"What memories?"

"Well, out in the real world, there aren't an awful lot of fairies eager to take on the creature of the cave. It certainly wasn't *my* idea to come here. The cave is a dangerous place, and so some parties of adventurers used to catch little fairies and put them in cages or jars.

They would take us with them into the cave. We *hate* caves, and most of us are attuned to wind magic. It doesn't matter how far you take a fairy into a cave, we can feel from the wind which way leads out. They even have special cages with a string through the bottom so they can reel us back after we try to get away. We were their escape plans, stuffed into jars, thrown into bags. Small places . . . dark places . . ." She shook herself, then twirled, sparking a brilliant flame around herself. "But now there *aren't* any dark places if I don't want there to be. So . . . where were we?"

Chapter 26

The days rolled into weeks, then months, and his skill grew by leaps and bounds. Training drills like "courier" became genuine competitions, his picking and planting becoming nearly a match for Leo's. Slow but steady progress was made in building his language skills as well. He came to understand the proper usage of a sword, and quickly developed a knack for throwing knives. Every day brought more knowledge—but perhaps more important than the knowledge was the understanding of its value. Immersed as he was in languages that he had at first only half understood, he was beginning to catch words and sentences that would have been lost to him before. All around him, he was seeing markings that had before been meaningless patterns suddenly taking on meanings.

He found himself becoming ravenous for knowledge, almost desperate for it, and most were happy to oblige and pleased with his progress.

One area, though, seemed to fall short of expectations. Though he was an able combatant, his sparring matches did not turn out as well as he had imagined. At first, he gained some rapid victories, but as his opponents came to understand his tactics, the balance shifted in their favor. Each battle ended with critiques and advice, and thus the battles lasted longer and his victories caught up to his defeats, but he was, at best, a moderate student. For a typical apprentice, it was as it should be, and likely he would have been allowed to continue as he was.

Weste, however, did not feel the same way about Shadow.

The master was watching as he engaged in a battle with Leo, each student armed with a blunt wooden training sword. They most frequently faced each other, and as a result the sparring matches between the two were faster and more intense than either would have with another. Each knew his opponent's moves and habits and was quick to capitalize upon weaknesses and defend against strengths. It produced a heated and fluid display of martial prowess. This particular battle had been raging for some time, building steadily in speed and vigor. Shadow was doing well, his blows precise and relentless. There was the sense that something was building, that he was gaining momentum. Leo did his best to interrupt or counter, and sometimes he succeeded, but the assault was becoming more vicious with each strike.

Then, without any clear indication of why, Shadow hesitated and faltered. An opening appeared, Leo capitalized, and the battle was over, Shadow on his back and the mock blade pressing hard into his chin.

"A fine battle," Leo said breathlessly, as he reached down to pull Shadow to his feet. "But today victory is mine."

"No," growled Weste, appearing unobserved as always. "It was indeed a fine battle, and you did everything properly, Leo, but you did not win this battle—*he* lost it." He turned to Shadow. "You had that battle. It was *yours!* But you let it slip away. You held yourself back. Why? Why didn't you take the final step? Why didn't you finish?"

Shadow was silent.

"Do you know why I came to you, why I offered you my instruction? It wasn't because you were able to sneak into this place. That is impressive, but it is a trick that any of my students here could do if they'd been of a mind to try it. And it wasn't because of your senses or perception. Those are useful, even remarkable, but without a dedicated will to use them properly, I would have had no use for a creature that possessed them. I came for you because of a single instant. When you were being tested in front of the Elder's quarters, in the moment that you realized that Leo was sneaking up behind you, I saw something in your eyes. A spark, an intensity that cannot be passed from a teacher to a student. It must be there from birth. I saw it in you that day, and never again." He marched up to Shadow and looked him in the eye. "Today I mean to see it again."

Master Weste drew a sword from his belt. It was not a wooden training sword, but one of gleaming steel, likely one of Croyden's creations. It was long, with a narrow, single-edged blade.

"Give him a weapon. A proper one," Weste said.

The tone of the training ground changed. It was always serious. Even in its lightest moments, each of the students knew that the skills they learned and the methods they used were to be treated with respect and reverence, but now an intensity filled the air. Quietly, Shadow was handed his sword and a space opened around them.

Weste's stance as he prepared to battle was different from those of his students. He stood with his body angled aside. His sword arm was forward, weapon loosely in his grip and toe pointed to Shadow. The trailing foot and arm were each casually to the side. There was an air of disrespect to the stance, as though Shadow was not worth his full attention.

"Fight," he ordered.

Shadow held his weapon as he had been taught, but Weste did not change his stance to a properly defensive one.

"What are you waiting for?" Weste asked.

"I am waiting for you to raise your weapon."

"Well, I am waiting for you to give me a reason to."

A few more seconds passed, and Shadow finally decided to make his move. In a blur of steel and motion, Weste's weapon streaked through the air and knocked Shadow's from his hand. The master then flipped his sword back, cutting a deliberate nick on Shadow's snout.

"Now pick it up," Weste said, "and fight."

Shadow retrieved his sword and returned to his stance, blood trickling down the side of his nose. This time he didn't hesitate, slicing instantly, but once again, the merest motion of the master disarmed him and earned him another shallow cut, this one to the chin.

"Again," Weste said.

The other students watched silently as once more the newest among them retrieved his weapon and with the same humiliating simplicity had it stripped away. Shadow was bleeding from three superficial slashes now, and after collecting his weapon, he was hesitant to return to a combat stance.

"I'm waiting," Weste rumbled. Shadow did not react. His eyes were turned low, and his grip was loose. The master narrowed his eyes slightly. "You know something? My other apprentices, they call me master. I have not heard you do the same. Let me hear it now."

Shadow raised his eyes, locking Weste in a steely glare. "I will not call you master."

"And why not? It is what I am, is it not?"

"That word does not mean the same to you that it means to me."

"Oh? And why is that? Ah, yes. You were a slave, weren't you? A Tresson slave. Then those three stripes I've given you, they mean something else as well, don't they?" He raised his sword. "They mean you are worthless."

Shadow's grip tightened. He slashed fast and hard, his blade clashing with that of the master. This time the exchange lasted three blows each, and when the master finally knocked Shadow's blade aside, it did not leave his hand. Now Weste stepped to him, his stance serious.

"Did I say stop?"

They clashed again, more vigorously and viciously, but again it ended with Shadow's sword knocked aside and a fresh slash across his pelt. Anger was building in him. He did not wait to be goaded further, thrusting himself at his teacher with bared teeth and turned-back ears.

"There . . . I can see it under the surface," Weste said between strikes. "You still won't let it free." He began to sweep the sword in broad, powerful strokes, forcing Shadow back. "Show it to me! Show me the fire!" Now the apprentice was backed against a tree, growling. "Show it to me you filthy, worthless *mally!*"

When the final word struck his ears, what little control Shadow still had was thrust away. He dropped his sword and lunged forward, clawed fingers slashing. Weste managed to pull his head nearly clear, but still earned four shallow gashes on his cheek. The master wasn't fighting a student anymore. He was fighting a wild animal. Shadow was blinded with fury, jaws snapping and claws scraping. It was all that Weste could do to keep the beast from tearing his throat out, but what wit and breath could be spared was dedicated entirely to keeping the other students at bay.

"No!" he urged when they tried to step in, "keep your distance."

Weste abandoned his sword and the two began to circle each other, the master now staring into the eyes of a predator. Shadow was low to the ground, moving in quick, sudden attacks that often shredded the cloth and scored the skin of the instructor. Finally Shadow launched himself forward, jaws snapping short of Weste's throat by the width of a hair. The master seized the cloth of Shadow's shirt, continued the motion of the attack, and turned it into a roll. The two tumbled cross the ground and finally came to a rest with Weste straddling the maddened beast, holding him to the ground.

"This is it! This is the fire! This is what you have that sets you apart! It is raw, powerful. Single of purpose, but it is wild." Shadow struggled and roared. "You have no control over it, and that's why you are afraid of it. That's why you don't want to let it out." Slowly, the malthrope's wits were returning. "You've probably seen that part of you do some terrible things. You think if you can push it down, lock it away, then it won't hurt anyone again. You are wrong."

The intelligence had returned to Shadow's eyes now. Weste stood and helped him to his feet.

"You cannot defeat something like that by denying it. Cage a beast, try to starve it, and you'll only drive it into a desperate frenzy. You'll make it that much deadlier when it breaks free. And it *will* break free, because it is a part of you, and you can't change what you are. What you need to do is harness it. That intensity, that drive, forged by wisdom and training. It is the stuff of legend. Become its master and there is nothing in this world that will keep you from your goals."

"Master Weste, I think we should take you to the healer," Leo said. The apprentice had a look of concern on his face.

Weste wiped the blood from his cheek, but did not even bother to give the scattering of bloody gashes a second thought. "No healers. If a student can spill my blood, if he or she can take my life, then so be it. Such a thing is a victory, and I will not allow it to be taken away." He turned back to Shadow. "From this day forward, I want to see that same fire in everything you do. Remember that."

#

Combat drills and training became an entirely new task after his confrontation with Weste. For so long, he had fought to force down the part of him that had taken all of those lives when he escaped from the plantation. Now he was tasked with drawing it up and funneling it through the training and discipline he was learning. It felt like he was being asked to use a forest fire to cook a meal, harnessing so uncontrollable a force for so precise a purpose. It was a mercy, then, that combat was just one of the many aspects of his training. In the months that followed, he was subjected to drills of every type, each designed to force him to develop skills essential to the role of an assassin. For all of that time, though, he had never been assigned the task they called "tandem fishing."

Currently, he was learning how fortunate he had been to have avoided it.

The drill took them to the cliff that faced the ocean. He had often come to the place when he felt the need to spend some time away from the bustling activity of the village. The cliff was easily the least hospitable place in all of Entwell. It seemed to be the only part of the village that was aware that they were in the north, as the wind had an icy bite to it that was absent from the rest of the strange setting. The rocks were slick and dropped steeply to a sheer cliff that led down to the ocean, which was far enough below that the crashing waves couldn't be heard.

Tandem fishing brought him not only to the cliff, but over the edge.

He was linked to his partner—as always, Leo—and asked to climb down to the edge of the water. Once there, they would fetch a net of fish and haul it to the top. It was a frigid, dangerous task that forced them to bundle up in cumbersome clothes, then spend hours climbing across a surface that would have been difficult to navigate in the best conditions.

"Why would anyone do this?" piped a little, irritable voice.

Fiora, it was clear, had come to consider Shadow a friend. He was the first good friend she'd made on Warrior's Side, and, as such, she'd been using him as something of a window into how the other half of the village lived. To help Shadow practice his Crich or Varden, she asked him questions about what he'd been doing, and found herself fascinated by the answers.

Warriors, she decided, had much more enjoyable training than wizards, and she'd made it a point to tag along whenever she had the opportunity. Thus, she'd decided that "tandem fishing" would be just as fun as the rest, and navigating the cliff was little concern for a creature who could fly. It wasn't until she had been forced to endure the wind and cold for a few hours that she decided that she would rather slip into the warmth of Shadow's hood and wait for the ordeal to be over. When the duo reached the bottom, where a narrow gravel beach of sorts offered the first stable place to stand and work since they'd left the top, she'd taken the opportunity to squeeze out and watch as they worked. They were hauling slimy, half-frozen lines that were all too eager to get caught on jagged rocks.

"Did the devil on your shoulder say something?" Leo asked, shielding his face from the sea spray.

"She asked why anyone would do this."

"Oh, well, there's the reason it needs to be done, and the reason *we* need to do it," he said. "Here in Entwell, anything we can't grow needs to come from the sea or the lake. The wizards have rigged up these lines," he said, indicating a network of ropes and pulleys that led all the way back to the top of the cliff, "and with them—and probably a fair amount more magic than they would care to admit—they can haul up more than enough fish to keep us fed. Sometimes, though, the ropes break, or the pulleys jam, or whatever enchantments they use to help things along fail, and someone needs to come down to fix them. And so there must be climbers. Of course, that didn't happen this time. In our case, it is a part of our training because we must learn to infiltrate, and frequently the best way to infiltrate is to use an approach that would normally be considered impossible. A castle wall, for instance, or an icy and precarious ocean cliff. We are tethered together to keep each other from falling. Weste feels it helps build trust, which I think we can both agree continues to be an area of weakness for our malthrope friend."

"Well, it is the first bit besides the fighting that is no fun at all," Fiora decreed.

"I must agree," Leo said. "This is the second deadliest sort of training he's put together. I'm told half a dozen students have failed this particular test over the years."

"What's the deadliest?" she asked.

"Say again?" Leo said, joining Shadow in hauling up the last bit of line necessary to tug the fish net ashore.

"She asked what the deadliest training is."

"That would be the Lain Trial," Leo said. "It also has claimed six lives, but it has only happened three times."

"What is the Lain Trial," Shadow asked. He did so more for Fiora's benefit than his own, but the name of the trial stirred some memories.

"It is a final exam—or, perhaps more accurately, a high honor for those wishing to become assassins. To be quite frank, one of us must kill one of the others. In each of the three prior trials, both combatants have managed to kill the other. The Lain Trial is entirely optional, and it only happens when at least two people seek the title. Right now, Sama is the only one of us who has expressed any interest. But enough of that. We've got to get these back up there so that we can call it a day."

Contrary to expectations, the climb up was a good deal safer and easier than the climb down, if only because it was easier to see what was above than what was below. A few hours and they had reached the top again, tipping up the net of fish for it to be hauled away— mercifully, by others.

"I am not certain which is the more pressing need right now, a hot meal or a trip to the healers," Leo said, holding up hands. They were raw and skinned from the climb. "These are going to be rather painful when the feeling returns."

Shadow looked at his own hands, which were equally injured by the climb. Though it took a practiced eye to interpret the expressions on his usually stoic face, Fiora had managed to become an expert.

The Rise of the Red Shadow

"Something bothering you, Mr. Malthrope, sir?"

He looked to her, then to his hands again. "I shouldn't go to the healer."

"Why not?" Leo asked.

"Because when the time comes to leave this place, I won't be able to turn to healers."

"You're still thinking of what you'll do when you leave this place?" Leo said, with smile.

"Of course. I came here to learn how best to serve my purpose. When I'm through, I'll return to it."

"Well, I tip my hat to you. I honestly cannot remember the last time I thought about leaving this place."

"I don't know if I *ever* thought about leaving," Fiora added.

"That's a curious thing about Entwell," Leo said.

"Mmm," Fiora said. "Well, the mountain there—the one that the cave runs through—that's scattered through and through with fragments of casting stone, the crystal we use to focus magic. It makes it quite difficult to cast complex spells within the cave, and some of the other wizards suppose that it acts as a sort of dam, allowing mana to pool here in the village. Combined with the four major ley lines that meet here, it makes mystic manipulation very easy indeed. Perhaps that same quality has a focusing effect on the mind, increasing satisfaction and curiosity to the point that continuous study becomes an ideal for any who come here." She turned the riddle over in her head. "The high levels of mana also make this place attractive to spirits, and spirits in turn have an affinity to the very strong of mind and single of focus. Perhaps they influence us to stay. Or perhaps it is simply that the very particular set of qualities that lead a person safely to this place are the same qualities that *keep* a person in this place. It could even be . . . why are you both staring at me? Doesn't the subject interest you?"

"I don't have the wizardly need to unravel the mysteries of the world. I was quite content to leave it at 'that's a curious thing about Entwell.' Now, if you'll excuse me, the throbbing is beginning to show its ugly head, and so I've decided that healer precedes meal. Will you be joining me? Or will you rely on time?"

"You could always learn a few healing spells," Fiora suggested, "I understand it is one of the more frequent mystic disciplines that warriors like to add to their studies. And you *are* expected to add two

367

mystic disciplines."

"No."

"Well, I suppose there is always the—oh, what is it called?" Fiora said.

"The Warrior's Sleep?" Leo supplied over his shoulder as he made his way toward the village. "I wouldn't recommend it if you want to keep your mind in once piece."

"What is it?" Shadow asked.

"It is a sort of trance," Fiora explained. "If you learn it properly, you can bring yourself very close to death, a sleep deeper than sleep, though your senses stay alert. It is enormously recuperative to the body. It does the work of hours of sleep, but in minutes. It speeds healing, too. We count it as a mystic discipline, but there is no real magic to it at all."

Shadow considered her words for a moment. "Can you teach me?"

"Not me. You'd have to talk to Apprentice-to-the-Elder Ryala," Fiora said with a yawn. "Sundown is still a few hours away. I'm going to have something to eat. I'll see you later for your lesson."

As Fiora flitted away, Shadow hauled himself to his feet and coaxed his aching legs into taking him to the Elder's hut.

The inside of the hut, there was the same subdued chaos that always seemed to reign there. Today six heavily-armed warriors were in a very animated discussion. The Elder was listening quietly, leaving the keeping of order and civility in the hands of Ryala. She was speaking in a firm and authoritative voice, but things were quickly escalating. From what Shadow could determine with his growing understanding of the assortment of languages here, one of the masters of a very specific combat discipline had decided to pursue a new area of training; as such, his three top students would need to be assigned to a different master. The argument at hand was how precisely the hierarchy of apprentices would be adjusted. The current apprentices believed that the displaced ones should start at the bottom, while the displaced believed that they had earned top spots and should retain them. Presumably the discussion had begun with logic, but since then it had devolved through posturing, threats, and was now on the verge of violence.

"Warriors, you will comport yourself in a respectful and dignified manner, or you will forfeit the right to voice your grievance in the presence of the Elder," Ryala stated.

The Rise of the Red Shadow

The warning fell on deaf ears, and one by one the ring of steel could be heard, the two sets of apprentices taking up arms and selecting opponents. Their voices and weapons were raised. Ryala stepped between them, but they looked through her, eying their foes. With an almost imperceptible glance to her master, and a nod from him in return, she threw one hand to the side and opened her fingers. A beautifully ornamented quarterstaff launched itself from a stand beside the Elder's seat and planted itself firmly in her hand. With a graceful twirl of the staff, she delivered a jolting blow to the fingers of the most agitated of the warriors, prompting a cry of pain and knocking his weapon to the ground. Five more blows, strung effortlessly together, struck skillfully selected weak points of each of the disgruntled fighters, sending some of them sprawling and others into hunched over fits of profanity. In the space of a few heartbeats, she was the only one armed and upright.

"As you are behaving as first-day apprentices, you shall be treated as them. You shall all approach your master and request apprenticeship. All earned titles and honors are stripped from you until the Elder sees fit to restore them. His will is spoken. Now go," she decreed.

When the shock and sting of the attacks passed, the scolded apprentices filed out of the hut. Ryala huffed a breath and straightened her garb. Shadow approached her and received a respectful nod of acknowledgment.

"Do you require an audience with the Elder?" she asked, walking back to beside the Elder and replacing her staff, as though the previous act was of little concern.

"I was told you would be able to teach me something called the Warrior's Sleep."

One of her thin eyebrows arched. "You wish to learn the Warrior's Sleep? For what reason?"

He held up his ravaged hands.

"I would recommend you see our healers. The Sleep is not to be undertaken lightly."

"I will not always have healers. One day I will leave this place."

"Then become a healer yourself."

"I am told the Warrior's Sleep can refresh me more quickly than normal sleep, and without leaving me defenseless."

"That is true, but it does not come without a price."

"I am accustomed to paying a high price for the things I need."

369

Ryala drew in a slow breath. "Come with me," she said.

The stately elf excused herself from the Elder's presence and led Shadow out into the courtyard. They continued to walk with no clear destination. As they walked, she spoke.

"In the lives of all beings, there are moments, memories, feelings of which we wish we could rid ourselves. To live our lives, we push these things aside. We banish them to the darkest recesses of our mind and soul. For most of us, that is enough. These things may haunt us in our weakest moments, but they are suppressed. Controlled. The Warrior's Sleep works wonders, but in doing so, it drags the consciousness deep inside, to the shadows in which we exile our fears and sorrows. If you learn the Warrior's Sleep, you will be forced to face this part of yourself. You will see the unmasked truth within you. For many, it is more than their sanity can withstand."

"I am willing to face such a risk."

"Why? What about the mystic arts are so distasteful to you that you would sooner subject yourself to this trial by fire?"

"I don't want any more power. I don't want to rely upon things larger than myself. The outside is not like this place. I survive there only if I can vanish into the shadows. Power makes me more visible to people like you. To pull upon forces beyond me . . . it would be a curse, not a blessing. I must be able to rely upon myself alone."

Ryala considered the words. "It is an enlightened view. Come, to your hut, then. It helps to be someplace you feel most at ease."

The pair made their way to his home. In the time he had been in Entwell, he had done nothing to make it his. If not for the dismantled lamp that Fiora had been using in his education and the most recent book she'd been coaching him through, one scarcely would have known someone lived there at all. The only addition he had made was a small chest filled with a change of clothes and a rack containing the handful of weapons provided to him.

Ryala directed him to sit. He chose the floor. She sat in a chair behind him and spoke, her voice steady and deliberate. Over the course of many hours, she coached him, teaching him to clear his mind and withdraw it from the surface. He focused on the very most fundamental parts of himself—the rhythm of his heart, the coming and going of his breath. Session after session, she led him deeper, taught him to take control of these things, to slow them. Learning the sleep took time. It was no simple task.

Lessons became part of his routine, taking place after Fiora was through for the evening and lasting as long as Ryala was willing to remain. He pushed himself further each time, bringing his body closer to complete stillness, closer to death. As he did, he could feel the world around him drop away—yet, simultaneously, it became more vibrant and intense. He could hear every sound around him, smell every scent. He could feel the wind rustle his fur, and if he willed his eyes open, he could see as clearly as if he were fully awake.

In time, he began to feel the rejuvenation as well. The closer to death he pulled himself, the more quickly he felt the fatigue and injuries slip away. But, finally, there came the day that Ryala had warned about. He journeyed deep enough to find his demons.

Shadow had believed he was ready for what horrors might lurk in his mind when he was shut away deep within himself. He knew the images of his worst crimes. He had endured them in a dozen nightmares throughout his life. What awaited him, he reasoned, could not be worse. He was wrong. The sights, the sounds, the scents. They were all there for him, the horrid day on the plantation playing itself over . . . but with them came the feelings, the emotions that had been mercifully blotted from his mind by the intensity of the moment. He felt the anger, the hate at what had been done to him and those like him. But there was more. There was exhilaration, unbridled glee in delivering the justice so richly deserved.

He hadn't just performed these evils . . . he had enjoyed them.

When he pulled himself from the trance, Ryala was there with him. His eyes were wide, his breathing harsh. It felt as though his soul was on fire, his mind doused in scalding water. The Apprentice to the Elder looked into his eyes. With a knowing look, she placed a hand on his shoulder.

"I can see in your eyes that you have witnessed the worst of yourself. You are to be applauded for pulling yourself back from it. Many before you have been lost to such sights, ending themselves rather than enduring them. Are you prepared to face such things each time you choose to use the Warrior's Sleep?"

He looked down and slowly caught his breath. Outside, the sun had moved only slightly. Mere minutes had passed, but he felt more energized than he had upon first rising. Now he looked to his arm, where a poorly blocked blow with a training sword had left him swollen and bruised the day before. Now even the soreness was gone.

Finally, he looked to her.

"I cannot change what I am. But I can become more. Thank you."

"Do not thank me. I only hope you use it well, and you continue to rise above the things that it shows you."

Ryala stood. Her work was done, and so she took her leave. For Shadow, it was only the beginning.

Chapter 27

In the blink of an eye, Shadow's training had been in progress for four years. In that time, he studied under more than a dozen of the masters. Foregoing proper sleep entirely in favor of the Warrior's Sleep, he gained hours a day, but it was agonizing. Each time he used it, his mind seemed to dredge up a new horror, a new truth best left a mystery. The reward, though, was considerable. He worked from sunrise to sunset, developing his skills in every type of weapon and every style of combat he could. He earned praise from masters for his progress with weapons ranging from the bow and arrow to whips, from axes to clubs. He had no interest in titles or honors, maintaining each apprenticeship only long enough to fully grasp the key elements of the style or weapon, then continuing his studies on his own. He honed his body, adding as much strength as he could to his already considerable stamina. To fulfill his second mystic requirement, he had runes tattooed to give him a measure of resistance and learned to suppress and hide the "powerful soul" that the other wizards seemed so keen to praise.

He spent more and more of his time in or near his hut as the months crawled on, retreating from the others and isolating himself. He never socialized, and even after years in Entwell, he continued to take his meals at times when he could be assured he could do so alone.

The one discipline he never abandoned in favor of personal study was stealth. In their time working as partners, Shadow managed to become Leo's equal in nearly all aspects of the art. Likewise Leo had become one of only two people in all of Entwell who was ever able to sneak up on Shadow. The two climbed head and shoulders above their peers.

While the other masters had a small number of tactics and techniques, with their training focused on attaining perfection in these skills, Weste seemed to have an endless list of elements that he considered key to the stealth arts, parts of the art of assassination that had nothing to do with combat. He taught how to observe, to glimpse at a scene and learn every detail. He taught how to unlock doors, to use grappling hooks to scale walls.

Shadow excelled at most, but one continuously eluded him. It was a test that came rarely and suddenly, always with Weste uttering the same request.

"Show me Leo," Weste said.

Shadow snapped an eye toward him. At the sound of his name, Leo turned as well, and upon realizing what was occurring he marched over and smiled wide, crossing his arms.

"Yes, my friend, show us Leo," he said.

"I still fail to see the value that this skill could ever have to me," Shadow objected.

"It is very simple, but I will restate it if I must. In the world of a spy or assassin, there will inevitably come a time when simple observation will not provide you with all of the information you seek. When such a time comes, you must interact. No disguise you can apply, not even a great one, will withstand face to face scrutiny for very long. You must thus learn to disguise yourself from within. Adopt the mannerisms of someone deserving of trust and respect."

"Perhaps that is possible for a human, or even an elf. You and I both know that a glimpse is all it will ever take to label me a beast. This is a skill with no use to me."

Weste gave him a stern look. "There is no limit to the capacity of a person to see what they wish to see. If you show them something that they can trust, then they will trust it."

"In all fairness, Master Weste, the task is not equal," Leo said. "When I am asked to show you *him,* I need only become distant and taciturn." Leo adopted what could only be described as a foxy expression, then turned his head down and deepened his voice. "Speak quietly. Sparingly. Keep to myself. Do not look at people. Measure them instead."

His changes were subtle, but uncanny. The voice didn't sound much like Shadow's, but there was something in his posture, in the way that he moved his head and formed his words that made it unmistakable who he was intended to be. Most impressive of all, though, was that it did not seem unnatural. He didn't seem to be impersonating someone else, he seemed to *be* someone else. The first time Shadow had seen it, he'd felt strangely exposed, as though the skill with which Leo had been able to assume his own identity was evidence that he'd been too open, given too much of himself away.

"I'll ask you again. Regardless if you respect them or not, you do not have the luxury of deciding which of my teachings are worth your while. It is one of the only tests you've failed to show due dedication. Show me Leo," Weste said.

Shadow eyed his teacher savagely, breathing slow and deep.

"Then you are not ready," Weste said.

"No hard feelings, friend. We can't all have the dedication to perfect *every* skill," Leo said. "Have you eaten, Master Weste? I'd like to have a word with you, if I may . . ."

Master Weste and Leo walked away, Leo chatting idly about what weapon would be best suited for the next stage of his combat training. Weste nodded and paced along beside him, commenting where appropriate. Shadow followed. With each step, a gradual change came over him. It began at his feet. His ankles relaxed, dropping him down from his tense, coiled gait into a casual and easy one. His hunted and guarded posture became more leisurely, arms loose at his sides, thumbs hooked into the straps beside his belt. He slouched his shoulders and stepped with a bit more rhythm and sway. By the time Leo and the master were halfway to the dining hut, Leo had become visibly uneasy. He turned to find Shadow walking with his precise mannerisms. With a bemused look, Leo stopped and faced Shadow. The malthrope tipped his head, and looked up. On his face was an open, friendly grin.

Shadow spoke, and when he did it was with a warm, outgoing sincerity. "I am sorry to interrupt, Master Weste, but you were absolutely right. It has been nothing less than a pleasure to study under you for these past few years, and I would be doing myself a grave disservice if I were to disregard even a word of your sage advice. I trust that you will forgive my disrespect. I shall endeavor to devote the full measure of my focus and dedication to this task as I have all others, and it is my great hope that I will rise to meet your flattering expectations of me." All at once, like a veil dropping, his rigid and guarded features returned, complete with a smoldering glare. "Do not question my dedication."

Leo's eyebrow's raised and his mouth fell open. He offered a slow, genuine clap of his hands. "That was just this side of terrifying, my friend. I am honored by the performance."

Master Weste nodded. "Well done."

Shadow held the master in his gaze. "I've shown you everything you've asked. I've learned to the best of my ability, and matched the best the others could offer, in each new skill you've presented."

"You have."

"When you first came to me, you told me that I have a blind spot. It is one that you exploit without fail. In the years that I've been training under you, I've helped Leo to find that blind spot, and I've helped Sama come as close as I believe he is capable. I have found a matching blindness in countless others. You have never given me so much as a word of advice on how to eliminate my own. I am satisfied that I can fight, and I am satisfied that I can track. The warrior I am now is the one I hoped to become. Outside of this place, there is a task waiting to be done, but I will not feel prepared to take that task on again until you show me how to eliminate this weakness. I feel I've earned that."

Weste looked upon Shadow steadily. "You feel you've earned it, do you? You and Leo are my best students. There is no doubt. If there are any in Entwell worthy of knowing this final secret, you two are. But what you are asking is more than just a simple lesson. It is the final lesson. It is the keystone, the crown. I share that secret only with an honored few." His tone was solemn, even ominous.

"Master Weste . . . Do you mean to say . . ." Leo began, his voice hushed.

"What? What must I do?" Shadow asked.

"The Lain Trial. Pass the Lain Trial and you will have this final piece."

"But if he fails it, he dies," Leo said.

"What he's asking for is perfection. Perfection is the most precious thing in the world, and it brings with it a price to match."

"Tell me what I have to do," Shadow said, without hesitation.

"It is very simple. You will have one month to prepare. When the month is through, you will enter the crystal arena. There, you will find an unfamiliar city. Somewhere in that city, there will be your target: someone you must kill, and who must kill you. Sama has long been after the title of Lain. He will be your target, and you his. Nothing is disallowed. You will not be held responsible for anything that you do during the trial. There are no rules, save that the killing blow must be delivered by you. The trial ends when one of you succeeds. The survivor will be Lain."

"And if I do this, you will teach me what I need to know?"

"If you do this, you will know."

The Rise of the Red Shadow

It was a difficult decision, but Shadow had learned long ago that it didn't matter if a decision was difficult. If it was truly important, if it needed to be done, then there was only one option.

"I will do it."

#

A month to prepare was generous, but it was worthless if he didn't know what he was preparing for. His first course of action was to follow Sama to determine what he had in store. As much as each of them had grown and improved in the last few years, Shadow still had little trouble following Sama closely enough to overhear his whispers.

The older, more experienced warrior must have been planning for this moment for years, as he instantly plunged himself into the task of preparation as though he was working off of a carefully-kept list. He gathered weapons—and, more worrying than that, he gathered allies. One by one he approached friends and associates from among the stealth apprentices and the many other disciplines he'd studied in his years here. Many accepted. In the space of a few days, it became clear that Shadow would be facing an arsenal and a veritable army. Now he had to do what he could to balance the scale, and his options were limited.

#

"You are doing what!?" squealed Fiora.

"It is called the Lain Trial," Shadow said.

"And you *must* kill someone?"

"Or be killed."

"I don't—how could—" She darted around the clearing near her tree, her expression drenched in frantic anxiety. "Why would you do such a thing?"

"Weste requires me to pass the trial before he will teach me to overcome my blind spot, and I refuse to leave this place while I still have that weakness."

"You—*you're leaving, too!?*" she cried. "You can't leave! You're my first student! And my favorite student! And my friend! I—I can't—*ooh!*" She literally sizzled with anger, flames flaring up around her until finally she charged forward and slapped him on the nose with all of her might. It wasn't even enough to make him flinch, though the heat of it stung a bit.

After the outburst, she clenched her fists and pressed her arms tightly to her side. Her vicious breathing subsided, and she regained

377

her composure. "I'm sorry, but you deserved that. Now, what can I do to help? I won't help kill anyone, but anything I can do to help keep you safe I'll do gladly."

"I don't know yet, but—"

"We'll figure it out together, then. How long do you have?"

"A bit less than a month."

"I'll cancel all of my lessons until we can see this through. I wouldn't be able to focus on them anyway." She shook her head. "This is the last time I get myself mixed up with Warrior's Side madness."

With the fairy in tow, his next stop was the workshop of Croyden Lumineblade. The frequently crowded and bustling place was nearly empty, with only Croyden himself inside. On the work surface in front of him were six different whetstones, and in his hands was a curious weapon with a short, curved blade. He eyed the blade thoughtfully, then began working it against the third whetstone. It was a long moment before he noticed the pair at the door. When he did, he acknowledged them with a glance.

"What brings you here, malthrope?" he asked in his own tongue.

"I've agreed to take the Lain Trial."

"Have you? Against whom?"

"Sama."

"I've worked with Sama. A fine swordsman. If he uses one of my blades, and I've made a few for him, you *will* lose."

"That is why I came. I want to know if you will give me a proper blade, one that will match his."

Over the years, Croyden had offered up master-level weapons of various types for Shadow to use in his training, but they had thus far been weapons that were already part of the elf's collection. Never had he offered to produce one of his masterpieces specifically for the malthrope.

"What sort of blade?"

"A short sword of some kind."

"How much time do you have?"

"Three weeks."

Croyden shook his head. "That is not much time to make a proper blade."

"I will take anything you can give me," Shadow assured him. "I just need something that I can be certain will stop his attack if it comes my way."

"To ensure such a thing would require blade tempered by the same intensity of flame. I use flame mages for that sort of thing, and I doubt you will find enough of them willing to help you on such short notice."

"I will stoke the furnace personally," Fiora said.

"It takes three apprentices to keep it at the temperature I require."

"I'm no mere apprentice, Master Croyden, sir. I am a master in all but title, one of Master Solomon's most favored students! What's more, I am a fairy first and a flame mage second. My innate knowledge of wind combined with my well-practiced knowledge of flame makes me uniquely suited for this task. I'll do what you need. If this blade is going to be all that stands between my student and certain death, then I want to personally ensure it is properly made."

Croyden eyed the fairy uncertainly.

Fiora glanced to a clay pot hanging on a hinged arm in front of the forge, which was currently cold. She flitted up to find it filled with iron ore. "Do you want a demonstration? Fine!"

With a vigorous buzzing of her wings, she threw herself against the pot and swung it into the forge, then disappeared into the pot. An instant later there was a brilliant, piercing light from within, and wind began to rush in through the door, down through the chimney, and through any other hole it could find. The light and heat quickly reached painful levels. As swiftly as it began, it subsided, and a much less vigorous buzzing reverberated from within the forge. Out from within, on a hook still glowing, swung the clay pot. It was blackened, and the iron inside was a white-hot pool of liquid. She fluttered out from behind it and landed on the anvil, striding confidently across its surface with the sound of grease hitting a frying pan accompanying each step.

"I trust that convinces you?"

Croyden ventured a glimpse into the pot. The temperature was such that he couldn't get very close, but he didn't need to get close. A distant look came over his face as his eyes darted in thought. He turned to Shadow. "How long have you been here?"

"Just less than four years."

"Less than four years. And in that time I've seen you take on straight swords and curved. Short swords and long. Two-handed, one-handed, hand-and-a-half. I've seen you use axes, knives, daggers, and picks. Staffs, flails, clubs . . . In four years I've seen you handle nearly every weapon we've got. You haven't always been the best. You may not be the best at *any* of them, in fact. But I've never seen anyone use so many weapons with such dedication. I've been making weapons for the finest warriors this world has to offer for longer than most of the people here have been alive; in that time, I've rarely seen someone with the potential you have. I'll make your weapon for you, but only because I want you to live long enough to let that potential flourish. Go. You'll have it in three weeks. There is a technique I've been tinkering with for some time, and your fairy may just have the skills necessary to solve my lingering problems. I'll send for her when I need her."

"Thank you," Shadow said, turning to leave.

Fiora flitted out after him, the air around her still wavy with heat. "I think I need a cool drink of water," she said, noticing for the first time that the hem of her dress was smoldering. She brushed it out.

"I thought you had difficulty with endurance," Shadow said.

"When we first met, I did, but then you turned out to be a slow learner and I spent a lot of long nights as a lantern. It paid off," she said. "So what is next?"

"There is only one other person who might help me."

#

Shadow and Fiora found Leo in his own hut, which was nearer to the sea. He was sitting in a chair, eyes fixed on the horizon, with a dusty bottle of wine on the table beside him. Leo was nearly as austere and dedicated to his training as Shadow, but wine was the one luxury he allowed himself from time to time.

When he saw the others approaching, he greeted them with a swirl of his glass. It was a short, ball-shaped glass with a flat bottom, and on the table beside him was a second just like it.

"Welcome, friends. I only expected one visitor, or I would have fetched a third glass. Though I suppose that won't be necessary anyway." He looked to Shadow. "I don't imagine you'll be interested."

"No."

"I'll have some. I've never had wine before," Fiora said.

Leo tipped the bottle and poured a splash into the second glass. Fiora, having cooled enough by now to keep the liquid from sizzling into steam, carefully tipped the glass down on its side, so that the wine was pooled within the curve of the cup, and had a sip.

"It tastes like nectar that's been left a bit too long," she noted.

"Leo, I need your help," Shadow said.

"With the Lain Trial? Yes. I imagined you'd ask for it. Sama has been working quite diligently. He's recruited most of the rest of the apprentices."

"I don't understand why that is even allowed," Fiora muttered. "We don't get help when we have *our* final tests over on the Wizard's Side."

"Stealth isn't only about the kill, it about building networks of trust. Amassing allies is just another part of the role of a spy and assassin. If he can convince others to help him here, then Sama could have done just the same outside. He's even asked me to offer any insight I might have on how you are likely to operate."

"Did you answer him?"

"I did not." Leo sipped his drink. "You know something, my friend? In all of our time as partners, there really hasn't been much in the way of conversation. Not the sort that goes in both directions, at least. You never really asked me about my past."

"I don't have time for stories."

"Well, it is now or never. You see, I believe I told you, my father was from Kenvard. Mother, she was from far, far south. They met before the war. I was born a few years before the war started. When things started to worsen, and the people of the north started to look upon her with distrust, my mother decided her place should be with her people. She didn't have any money, and thus she felt that father would be the one best suited to provide for me. I was left with him. This face of mine didn't make any friends as the hostilities heated up. Just a little too much Tresson in the features. Father was wise, though. He realized one day that with a bit of help, I could pass as a northerner just fine. And with different help, I could pass for a Tresson.

"He took me to an academy. Military. They decided I could be put to good use as a spy. I took to it quickly, and I was sent on over a dozen missions in the first year. I was so successful, they decided that I should take a more active military role. Assassinations. I did one, two, three of them. And then it struck me that I was killing people who looked *just* like my mother. It turned my stomach first that I could do this, and second that Father could have encouraged it. I decided to change sides. Even the score, so to speak. I should have known that it wouldn't be long before I felt the same sort of shame for killing my other half."

He took a long swig and placed his glass down.

"Something that you realize quickly when you are a spy: your job is to lie. You are untrustworthy by your very nature. And thus even when you are faithful to a single country, the plans are always in place to eliminate you if you become a liability. I was *not* faithful. By the time I was working for the Tressons, I'd already betrayed a country once. They weren't going to wait for it to happen a second time. I had to vanish. I'd burned every bridge. Had no connections to anything. And everyone, *everyone* wanted to kill me. Sound familiar? At any rate, I didn't enter the Cave of the Beast because I was hoping to kill the thing. What would I do if I *did* kill it? Fame would be a death sentence. To be honest, I was fine with that. I'd earned a death sentence a few times over. But I was tired of being afraid of how it would happen. I wanted the creature to do it so that at the very least I wouldn't have to worry about being stabbed in the back."

He poured a bit more and took a sip.

"I'm through killing, and I'm through worrying about being killed. I love the art of the assassination, but I hate the act. Why do you suppose I never went after the Lain Trial myself? Call me a coward if you must, but I won't take a side again."

"You'd send him in there alone?" Fiora said.

"*I* am not sending him in there," Leo said.

"He's your friend and he needs your help," she said.

"Is a friend someone who rescues you when you get into trouble, or is it someone who helps you avoid the trouble in the first place?" Leo asked. "Not that it matters. Anyone who could remain dedicated to a lost cause on the other side of a mountain even after four years in a veritable paradise is far too stubborn to listen to good sense. So if you need help plotting, planning, training, or anything of the like, ask. But my allegiance to you ends at the border of the arena."

"That is your choice," Shadow said. A breath of wind drew his attention to the north, where shortly there came into sight his adversary in this task, Sama.

The man walked with the heavy, plodding footfalls of someone unconcerned with stealth. He was not even dressed in his uniform; instead, he wore the unremarkable tunic worn by those residents with no current focus to their training. It was a rare sight on anyone, and rarer still on Sama. He approached the group and stepped face to face with Shadow.

"I understand you have been as busy as I have these last few days. Preparing. Good. That's good. I'll leave you to it, but first I want to thank you. I have been waiting for a chance to earn this title for more than six years. I've got a host of other masteries, but this one has always eluded me. It will be good to have it behind me and try something new. Pity I'll have to kill you to do it, but obstacles exist to be overcome. Good luck to you. But better luck to me," he said.

With that Sama departed. Fiora watched him go.

"I'll admit I was a bit conflicted about helping you, since it meant I was working against someone else," she said. "I'm less conflicted now."

#

The month passed swiftly. Much of the time was spent collaborating with Leo to determine what strengths the others Sama had recruited might bring to the trial. After a week, Croyden delivered a "rough blank" of the weapon he was working on. It was the same length, weight, and balance as the planned piece. With it, Shadow could practice how best to use the weapon—but he did so sparingly. Sama and his allies were everywhere, and every moment spent practicing in full view of them was tantamount to revealing his strategy.

It wasn't until nightfall the day before the trial was to take place that Croyden sent for Shadow. The malthrope stepped inside the master's shop to find the completed sword laying on a cloth on his worktable. Fiora was with him, looking more than a little fatigued.

To call the piece exquisite would fall well short of doing it justice. It was a single-edged blade. The blunt edge was mostly straight, while the cutting edge swept with a minor curve toward a subtle wedge-shaped point three-quarters of the way along the arm-length blade, then curving back to a point. It had a single-handed grip, covered with braided leather and ending in a flat pommel. Most striking about it, though, was the finish. The whole of the blade and hilt was soot-black, not the slightest gleam or shine glinting on its surface.

"It is remarkable," Shadow said. "It doesn't even look like metal."

"It isn't!" Fiora said eagerly.

"What is it?"

Croyden waved his hand vaguely. "The nearest I could offer you by way of comparison is pottery."

"Won't it be brittle?"

"More brittle than iron or steel, perhaps, but with a harder, sharper edge. I've reinforced it where necessary. You asked me for a weapon that could match any that Sama might carry. This will do it, and without a shine to betray you in the darkness. An assassin's blade."

Shadow swiped it experimentally through the air. Sure enough, it performed just as the sample one had. He would be able to use it well. He looked over the almost featureless surface and discovered, barely visible at the base of the blade, two small marks. They were handprints, and below them was a trio of intricate lines of text. The first said "For Luck," and the others were a language he couldn't read.

"What is this?"

Fiora blushed slightly. "Oh, uh . . . I had to touch the blade to focus enough heat, and my hands left a mark. I decided to write you a little message, too. The last bit is a pair of spells of protection. Not much, but enough to knock away a fireball or two. I thought you might need them."

"I am not usually one for blade enchantments. Pending the effectiveness, perhaps I'll have to look into it," Croyden explained.

"I'm very proud of that, Mr. Malthrope, sir," Fiora said, "so take good care of it. And I hope it takes good care of you."

Shadow nodded, taking the peculiar open-backed scabbard that Croyden had designed to accommodate the unique shape of the blade and strapping it to his hip. The weapon held in place securely, but slid free without effort. It was, without a doubt, the finest weapon he had ever held, and the finest thing he had ever owned. The question was: would it be enough? In one day, he would know.

Chapter 28

At sunset, Shadow approached the edge of the very place that had given him his first real taste of what Entwell was truly like. Now he would step into it for what may be his last waking moments. Waiting for him were Master Weste and Sama. Though neither had been instructed to do so, each combatant arrived alone, and each was carrying his equipment in a pack rather than in plain sight. Though they were out of sight, the scent of the squad of recruits that Sama had assembled was heavy in the air, the one trick up his sleeve that he couldn't readily hide.

"You have both had the same time to prepare, and you are both well aware of the rules," Weste said. "Once you both step into the arena, the trial has begun and there can be no backing out. One of you will die; if history is any indication, we may lose you both. If you choose to step inside, you will be greeted by Azriel. She will share a few words with each of you alone, then conjure up the field of play. It will be entirely of her design, and no one else has any knowledge of it. You will each appear at opposite sides of the battlefield, and the trial will end when one of you finishes the other and leaves the arena. At any time during the trial others may enter. They all agree to the same terms and may render aid to either combatant, but to earn your title you *must* be the one to deliver the killing blow. Is that understood?"

Both combatants nodded.

"Very well. May the best of you emerge and be honored at trial's end."

The opponents shared a long, final glance before each stepped inside. Just as it had when he first made the mistake of stepping inside, the world vanished. Shadow stood in a featureless black void, the air around him cool. A patch of the darkness wafted away, and Azriel was standing before him.

"Welcome back. I had a feeling I would see you again. You've come a long way since the terrified, half-starved beast who entered this place not so long ago. Entwell has treated you well."

"It has."

"A blue moon has come and gone since you entered this place. I

385

don't suppose you were a part of the ceremony."

"I had not reached the proper level of mastery."

"Pity. I suspect we would have learned a great deal if you had. As the proctor of this exam, I am required to judge you without bias. However, I freely admit that of the two of you, I believe that you have more to offer us. Fight well, Shadow. More hangs in the balance than your title and your life."

Her words were still hanging in the air when she swept away and the battleground began to take shape. First came a gentle glow in the sky. It swirled and contracted until it formed a brilliant full moon. The light spilled across the endless black, painting highlights on the nothingness. The shapes of walls and streets began to emerge as though they had always been there. Gradually, a city emerged: tight, cramped streets framed out by buildings taller and narrower than anything Entwell had to offer. Everything was built of dark gray brick and stone, weathered and rounded with time. It reminded Shadow very much of the port town of Sarrin.

When the setting had asserted itself, the world around it began to come to life. Perfect stillness was replaced by a fierce, ripping wind that shifted constantly. Dense black clouds wreathed the moon, thickening into a threatening thunderhead and cracking the air with the roll of thunder. Rain began to hammer down upon the conjured city, and thus the scene was set. The battleground would be a deserted cityscape in the midst of a horrendous storm.

There was a brilliance and an insanity to it. Entwell seldom experienced anything but perfect weather, no doubt due to the influence of the many elemental wizards who called it home. As such, neither Shadow nor Sama had been trained under these conditions. Furthermore, the chaotic wind made tracking difficult, and the constant drumming of raindrops made hearing anything more subtle than a falling tree nearly impossible. In the unfamiliar setting and inclement conditions, any advantage provided by Sama's years of additional training was hampered just as surely as that provided by any of Shadow's keen senses. The playing field was leveled, leaving only raw talent to decide the victor.

Shadow drew in a breath. The rain and wind were confounding, but his nose had not been rendered completely useless. It told him enough for him to know that there wasn't anyone near enough to be a threat just yet. That meant he had time to ready the meager equipment that he had chosen to bring. He pulled open his satchel and revealed the tools he would use to preserve his own life and take that of his foe.

There were nine throwing daggers fitted into three short belts. He affixed one to his right arm and one to each leg. Next came a coil of strong, thin cord, and finally his blade. It wasn't much, but he knew that he was outnumbered and out-equipped. If he was going to survive, he would have to rely upon the speed and agility inherent to his kind, and that meant staying light.

It was the work of moments to fit his equipment, and then came the task of finding his foes. In the few moments that it had been falling, the rain had already coated the smooth stones of the architecture into a hazardous and slick deathtrap for a climber. It would be much safer and simpler to stay to the streets and alleys, and it was for that reason that Shadow knew he dare not do so. With care and speed, he found the safest handholds and scaled the face of the building, keeping to the hidden walls facing other buildings in cramped side streets and only climbing as far as the second or third floor. The moonlight was only strong enough to see with any clarity in the brief moments when a crack in the fast-moving clouds slid by, but to be standing tall upon a rooftop during such an instant might reveal his location to everyone in the city.

As he moved, silent and sure, he felt the tension and exhilaration begin to rise up in him. The thrill of the hunt mixed with the fear of being hunted. As he had been taught, and as he had trained himself to do, he took the best of the sensations and rejected the rest. His senses became sharper; he became more alert. The endless patter of rain began to settle into the background, and through it he could hear the stutter and shuffle of anxious steps along a narrow ledge.

He could hear, far below him, a girl chilled to the bone by the falling rain. Deena. She was close, much closer than he normally came when tracking, which meant he was in real danger of being seen or heard. He called to mind what he'd learned of her over the years. Like him, she favored "the high road," taking to the trees and rooftops to gain an advantage. In the early years, she'd focused on long, thin blades, but as their training began to entwine, she'd begun to shift her interest.

He slid forward toward the front of the building and for an instant he saw a black-clad figure clinging to the side of the building across the street. It was her, he was certain. Hers was the scent that seemed nearest, and her tiny frame was unmistakable. In a flick of motion she vanished from sight. It meant she had seen him. He didn't wait to react, sliding backward three long strides and reaching up to haul himself to the next level. Below him there was a light metallic plink, a dart striking the stone wall just below his heel. A fraction of a second slower and she would have struck him. He couldn't waste any time. The glimpse he'd earned of her told him precisely where she was, but the more time that passed, the less useful that information was. She would be moving, seeking a fresh vantage for another shot with her blowgun, or else hoping to flank him and put her blade to work.

Down the side of the building he slipped, bounding from one wall of the narrow alley to the other, dropping a floor each time, and finally to the street. He kept his ears turned to the shadows that had most recently hid the first of Sama's recruits. What little he could hear of her came in tiny clatters of stone or scuffs of shoe. It wasn't enough to target, but enough to know he was still on her trail, and that she was retreating. The jingle of metal scattering along the ground prompted him to leap to the sill of a window. The barest glint of light across the ground betrayed the handful of jagged metal caltrops Deena had scattered. Shadow didn't slow, now scrambling and springing from sill to sill, ledge to ledge, keeping the pressure on Deena to keep her from having a moment to ready her more potent weapons. There was the sharp crack of wood and suddenly the sounds he pursued disappeared. She'd slipped inside one of the buildings, smashing her way through the shutter of a window to do it. Shadow heaved himself toward the source of the sound and in a few moments spotted the broken window.

When pursuing a warrior of similar skill and training, moments like these were more often than not the difference between life and death. Deena had taken a calculated risk by entering the building. Breaking the window, she gave away her position and presented Shadow with a choice. He could follow her through the window, but that would mean that for a brief moment he would be framed in the window against the comparatively brighter moonlight—an easy target. He could break through another shutter, but that would alert her to his position. He could take the time to enter silently, but that meant delay, distraction, and the opening for a counter attack. As she was not the target, he could leave her and continue to pursue Sama, but that would leave a known threat active and nearby.

One could deliberate for hours on such a choice and still not make the proper one—yet, in this case, even a few seconds of thought would create a lethal delay.

Shadow drew one of the throwing blades from his leg and drove it into the crack between the shutters of the window beside the one she'd entered, using his own momentum to force the slatted wooden doors open with a violent slam. A dart hissed through the air, passing through the open window, but Shadow was not there. He'd continued forward, slipping in through her window. By the time she'd realized what he'd done, he was inside and hidden in the pitch-black. He crouched low to the ground. His lungs were screaming for air after the burst of activity, but he forced himself to breathe in slow, silent breaths. He knew that she was doing the same somewhere in the darkness.

Outside, the wind wailed and the rain poured. Inside, each kept stone-still, waiting and listening. His sharp eyes began to adjust, but the interior of the building was crowded with tables and chairs, cupboards and chests. It was a fully-furnished, though uninhabited home, and that meant there were countless places to hide. Training and discipline can hone a body in astounding ways, bringing to bear a thousand techniques to eliminate any trace of sound. Some things, though, cannot be helped. Each of them had been in the pounding rain moments before, soaked to the skin. Now they were inside a dark, sheltered building . . . and the rain was beginning to run off of them. He filtered out the sound of rain and focused. Beneath him he could hear the soft tap of drops falling on wood. To his left, just on the other side of an open doorway, he could hear the same noise.

He made his move, covering the space between them in a single dive. Deena had been ready, stiletto swiping through the air, but he rolled aside and caught her hand by the wrist. He held tight to it and circled around behind her, pulling the arm cross her chest and wrenching her wrist. The weapon slipped from her fingers—but, as if from thin air, she produced a second in her free hand and attempted to skewer his leg. The blade cut a deep slice across his thigh, but he managed to catch the wrist with his other hand and lever it up behind her back. She made a brief and concerted effort to shatter his feet with her heel, but he managed to sweep the legs from beneath her and take the pair of them to the ground, hard. The impact dazed her just long enough for Shadow to muscle her arms behind her and wrap a few loops of cord around them.

"What . . ." Deena said, the haze beginning to clear. "What is this?

What are you doing?"

Shadow didn't answer. He simply continued bind her hands, then moved on to her feet. When she was securely bound, he pulled the pouch from her belt. It contained her blow gun and three more darts. He sniffed the point of one. She'd tipped them with a potent sedative, something that would have put Shadow to sleep so that Sama could be the one to score the kill. Shadow secured it to his own belt and hauled her to her feet.

"Where is Sama and what is his plan?" he asked, voice low and stern.

"I am a *warrior.* I have pledged my aid to Sama. I will not betray him or endanger his mission," she declared in defiance.

"Would you die for him?"

"I would die for the honor of the mission. It is what I was trained for, and it is what I was born for. Do what you must. There is no shame in falling to a superior foe."

"This is not your battle. This is a trial. A test. You would die for a test?"

"It is a mission, regardless of the purpose. I would gladly die if it was the difference between success and failure. Kill me if you must. It is your right. I knew the risk when I agreed to help him."

Shadow looked out the window. "I have a better use for you."

\#

On the other side of the battleground, Sama was huddled with three of his fellow stealth apprentices in what he'd determined to be the most defensible position with the best vantage. It was the bell tower of what, if this had been a real place, might have been the town hall. It stood as a spire, sticking high above the rest of the city. Most of the streets led directly toward it, meaning that from the four main windows one would have been able to see along them to the very edge of the city if the darkness and rain hadn't made seeing more than a few streets away impossible.

Among those dedicated to silence, measures are taken to avoid verbal communication. Since they had arrived, Sama and his recruits had not spoken. The plan had been laid out days ago, and the instant the battleground had presented itself, they had each gone about their tasks. The first had been to find and secure the high ground. The second had been to dispatch scouts. One by one, they returned and sketched out a map of their section of the city. Each did quick, efficient work, and in the space of an hour, there was a fair approximation of most of the city sketched onto the floor of the bell tower in charcoal pencil. There was only one section that remained unknown, as there was one scout who did not return. Deena's absence provided the most important piece of information of all. It must be assumed that she had found and fallen to the enemy.

They knew where he was—or, at least, where he had been—and that meant that they knew where to start looking.

With little more than a nod, the stealth apprentices set out on the next stage of the mission. Communication of any kind would give away the position of one or more of them, so silence was maintained. Instead, they moved in waves.

The first pair of them sought out suitable vantages and made their way forward. Once there, they briefly held their position until they could see the shadows of movement signaling that they had been spotted by the second set, who then found positions of their own. In that way, the four stealth apprentices swept toward the unexplored section of the arena.

As they moved, the weather worsened. It was as though Azriel felt that if the final battle was to play out now, it deserved a suitably dramatic backdrop. Lightning danced from cloud to cloud and thunder rumbled across the city. The rain came down in sheets, cutting the visibility, and wind whipped it into a painful, stinging spray.

Their trained eyes quickly converted the city that unfolded before them into a network of nooks and crannies, each assigned a value and a risk. The best choice was selected and acquired just long enough to find the next. In their calculations, they determined where their partner would be, and moved forward only when each had seen the other. It was a dance, tightly choreographed and yet entirely improvised, spread across the whole of a street. Then, with a flash of lightning, the dance came to a stop, as all eyes turned to a single point. Ahead was a dangling form. Strung over the streets, midway down from the rooftops, was Deena. She was soaked to the bone and rocking in the wind. Vicious struggles revealed that she was bound, but still very much alive.

Sama and his men held their ground. They each came to the same conclusion. Deena was bait, strung there to prompt them to attempt a rescue. It was a foolish tactic, as each had received the same training, and thus each knew that the mission was paramount. There would be no rescue, nor any attempt. Each apprentice worked at the riddle of why this might have been done, and what to do about it. Some thought quickly, some more slowly. The slowest of them never reached the end of the line of thought, noticing first that his counterpart had moved on, second a brief hiss, and third a painful prick in his neck.

Sama watched from a considerably more secure hiding place as the weakest link in the chain stumbled forward from his perch and plummeted a mercifully short distance to the ground, one of Deena's darts protruding from his neck. Deena had not been bait—she'd been a distraction, and the blasted fool hadn't realized. Now odds had shrunk to three-to-one, but they had been given another clue. There were only a few places the dart could have come from, and fewer still were proper hiding places. Sama knew that his opponent must be in one of them.

He drew to mind what he'd seen of this stretch of street. The rooftops had been clear, but even if they hadn't, in this diabolical wind no dart would have stayed true to its course from that distance. The street was too dangerous, as it forfeited the high ground. There were five open windows near to the ledge the fool had chosen. Three were close enough to reliably make the shot that had been made, and all three were on the street-facing side of the same building. The malthrope could only have been hiding within it. The place was one of the larger structures on the street, four stories tall and perhaps five rooms wide. It was rectangular and simple. If not for the large, shuttered windows it might have resembled a prison or castle keep.

The member of Sama's team in the best position streaked along face of the building. He stayed low and tight against the face of the building. There it would be impossible for the malthrope to use the blow gun without revealing his position. Sama and the others moved to positions carefully hidden but properly situated to observe all three windows. From here, the sequence was simple. If the malthrope revealed himself from one of the windows to attack the approaching apprentice, Sama and his remaining partner would descend upon him and the test would be over. If the apprentice managed to enter the building, then the others would know that the entryway he selected was a safe one, they would each move inside, and the outnumbered malthrope would fall quickly thereafter.

They were the only two logical outcomes. The creature had allowed himself to be cornered, and thus would lose. It was at that moment that a third option presented itself. In a blur of shifting shadows—so brief only the trained eye of an assassin could have been swift enough to follow it—a figure launched from the alleyway, pounced upon Sama's infiltrating man, and bounded off. The stricken target staggered and clutched at another dart that had been driven into his neck by hand.

Sama and his one remaining ally launched after the fleeing form, neither willing to let their foe slip away. As they moved, Sama worked through what had happened. The scoundrel *had* been hiding on the street. He'd selected the weakest position, and he must have done so on purpose, knowing that it would have been dismissed. He was being deliberate, choosing the course of action not that he had been trained to choose, but that he had been trained to avoid. One of the surest ways to earn victory was to make one's enemy's choices for him. Normally this was achieved by creating a choke-point or concealing oneself someplace with a single entrance. This malthrope was using their own training against them.

But if the last two obvious courses of action had been traps . . .

The realization dawned a moment too late for his partner. His foot came down upon the very same caltrops dropped by Deena earlier, and the rush of pain was enough to give Shadow his chance to drive home yet another dart. The last of his allies having fallen, Sama knew he couldn't afford to waste another moment. He managed to grasp Shadow by his arm and pull him from the alleyway. The malthrope stumbled out into the open street and quickly regained his footing, drawing his black blade and facing Sama. The elder warrior drew his own weapon.

"So, here we are," Sama taunted, yelling over the howling wind. "Funny that a test of stealth would come down to a test of swords instead." He circled cautiously. "Funnier still that I taught you everything you know about swords." He grinned, glancing at the bloody remains of Deena's one successful attack. "You're already bleeding. The only times you've ever bested me with a blade came when you used your blasted speed. That hole in your leg will take that tactic away from you. I know you can't beat me, and you know it, too."

Sama launched himself forward, sword slashing with lethal skill. Shadow parried with his own blade. The clash of metal upon what seemed more like stone resulted in a flare of sparks. Three vicious attacks followed, but Shadow managed to just barely block each before retreating a few paces. He drew three throwing blades and released them with a single motion in a narrow arc. Sama deflected one with his sword and a second went wide, but the last bit into his thigh. He grunted in pain, refusing to take his eyes off of the malthrope even long enough to pull the dagger free.

"Now you are bleeding as well," Shadow said.

The swordsman replied with a growl, lurching forward and tangling again. The battle that followed was vicious. Blades clashed and sparks flew. It was clear that Sama was the better swordsman, but he was not nearly so firmly Shadow's superior as he believed. The balance shifted back and forth between them, and when blades were locked, neither was above using fists, feet, knees, and elbows to deliver punishment. Minutes of furious battle passed, and each was bloodied and bruised by the attacks of the other.

Sama was beginning to tire, the desperation of his attacks growing. A wild slash managed to catch Shadow across the arm, and a follow-up attack left the pair with swords crossed. Sama's downward slash was held barely at bay by Shadow's raised weapon. Shadow's injured arm was robbing his defense of strength. Sama pressed harder, bringing the blade of his weapon steadily closer.

Shadow's limbs were on the brink of collapse. He lacked the strength to break the attack with enough force to create an opening, and if he relented for even a moment, Sama's blade would come down. Either way, the battle would be over. His opponent leaned close, pressing down with all of his weight. Under the strain of holding off the attack, Sama's blade slid against his own, spitting a few weak sparks. Inspired, Shadow shifted his blade and dragged it in a swift swipe across the length of Sama's weapon. The darkness was suddenly a wash of brilliant white sparks. The flash was enough to momentarily blind and stagger Sama. He swung his blade viciously toward Shadow, and though the malthrope had managed to retreat somewhat, the attack caught his other arm and knocked the sword from his grip.

Rather than risk attempting to recover the weapon, Shadow fell back and disappeared into the shadows.

Sama recovered and swiveled his head madly about, eyes wild and teeth bared. "Well? Come on! Make your move! What have you got left? Those little throwing daggers?" Sama pulled three such weapons from a belt and held them at the ready in his free hand. "Do you believe you can score a blow that will kill me before I can return the favor? Let us see you try!"

In reply, five blades burst from the darkness. Hurled by the injured and fatigued malthrope, they lacked both the force and accuracy to finish Sama, but he nonetheless needed to dodge and deflect them, giving the creature a few precious heartbeats to charge out from his hiding place, coiling cord around his fists as he moved.

Sama sliced the air, but Shadow slid beneath the attack, springing to his feet behind his foe and throwing a loop of cord around his neck.

Training and discipline can go a long way to overruling one's instincts, but when something pulls taut around one's throat, it takes a tremendous amount of will to do anything but tear at the constriction in desperate hope of restoring air and blood flow. Sama made two attempts to stab at Shadow, but the awkward positioning made the sword nearly useless. By the time he was making a third attempt, his vision was already beginning to dim. He abandoned his weapons and clutched at the cord, struggling as his strength sapped away until finally he slumped into unconsciousness.

Shadow held tight for a few more moments, then rolled Sama aside and scrambled to where his sword had fallen. He collected it, then returned to the fallen foe and leaned low over him. Sama's heart was still beating, and his breath was weak but steady. The job was not yet done.

Shadow put his sword to the man's throat . . . but returned it instead to its sheath.

"No," Shadow said. He stood and proclaimed to an unseen overseer. "This man's life was mine to take. I have succeeded in this task. I have been taught not to take a life unnecessarily, and it is not necessary that I kill him to prove that I could."

He marched, cold rain pouring down around him, toward the edge of the city. As he walked, he cast a wary eye behind him every few strides. Though he was confident Sama would not be conscious again for several minutes, he knew better than to trust his confidence or Sama's mercy. The fallen opponent did not move. Shadow needed only to reach the edge of the arena again and it was over.

The edge of the false city was not more than a dozen strides away when something happened. Without knowing why, he found his hand flitting to the hilt of his weapon. He pivoted on his heel, shifted his weight, and twirled. In the same motion, he pulled his weapon free and angled it for a thrust. The blade sunk deep into a black-clad form that had been not two steps behind him. The figure stumbled backward, a blade dropping from its hand, and crumpled to the ground.

Shadow's attack had happened without thought, without a decision. He'd heard no sound of approach, smelled not a whiff of danger. He'd seen nothing, and even the peculiar burning of being watched had not alerted him. Yet he had acted. Had he not, the blade of his enemy would have been at his throat.

Shadow withdrew his weapon from the bloody wound it had caused and looked up for the first time to the face of this attacker. It was not Sama. Instead, it was a man hidden by a cloth mask and dark hood. Shadow tore the disguise away. Beneath, he found the aging face of the very man who had subjected him to this trial. It was Master Weste. He clutched at the wound, then lifted his fingers to his face to see them drenched in blood.

"A well-placed blow," he said shakily.

"What were you doing? What is this?"

The city was wiping away now. With it went the rain and wind, leaving Shadow and the stricken Weste alone in endless blackness, surrounded by deafening silence.

"I told you. If you passed the Lain Trial, you would know how to overcome your blind spot."

"But I didn't sense you. I didn't know you were there. I just . . . acted."

"And that is the answer," he said, his speech becoming labored. "No one . . . has perfect perception . . . there will always be something you cannot see . . . something you cannot hear . . . . Where vigilance fails, you must rely . . . upon instinct. And that comes only when it is needed . . . the danger had to be real. This test was never about killing your target . . . it didn't matter if you killed him or shook hands and agreed to go on your way . . . I would have been behind either of you as the moment of victory loomed . . . . That is why there has never been a Lain . . . until now . . . ."

As Weste spoke, Shadow uncoiled rope and tore away the sleeves of his uniform to fashion a bandage. As he tried to apply it, Weste pushed him away.

"No, no . . ." Weste said, voice weak and fading. "You are an assassin . . . embrace this. It was always . . . my intention . . . well . . . done . . ."

With those final words, he leaned back and released his last breath.

A moment later, Azriel coalesced beside him. Shadow turned to her.

"Can he be saved?"

"He did not wish to be," she stated simply. "He was a warrior. This was the end he chose for himself. You should be proud that you were able to provide it. Now, rise."

He did as he was told, standing before her.

"By the decree of Master Weste, and by my judgment, you have passed this trial. Congratulations, Lain."

Chapter 29

In the days and weeks to follow, all involved in the Lain Trial—save Master Weste—recovered. The former master's passing was mourned and honored in the manner befitting of a warrior whose time had come. Now dubbed Lain, the malthrope was similarly honored for his achievement. Deena and the others recruited by Sama regarded their defeat with respect—and even an air of pride. To each of them it was something of a privilege to have made Lain's ascension possible. Only Sama regarded the trial as a failure, but he bore no malice.

Lain's new title, combined with the many other disciplines he had studied, afforded him the rank of "Full Master of the Warrior's Arts." To attain such a title through so diverse an education was much admired, and the whispers regarding his skill, his race, and his mark began to flow.

Shortly after his recovery, representatives of the Wizard's Side began to approach him, requesting that he participate in the so-called "Ceremony of the Blue Moon." The next blue moon was just a bit more than four months away, but Lain had other plans. His purpose in the world beyond Entwell had waited far too long already. The very day the falls relented, he made ready to leave.

"Are you sure you won't stay just a bit longer?" asked Fiora, her voice wavering a bit with held-back tears. "You could be one of the Chosen! I could help bring back the Great Elemental!"

She was fluttering in the window of Lain's hut. He was busy loading what little clothing he had into a pack and strapping a few carefully-selected weapons to his belt. He was dressed for travel, a light but sturdy cloak about his shoulders. It was reversible, charcoal-gray on the inside and milky white on the outside.

"I entered this place hoping to become the warrior I needed to be. I've come far enough. I need to return to my purpose or it was all for nothing," he said, fitting the sword Fiora and Croyden had made for him onto his belt.

"But no one *ever* leaves! Why does the one warrior I get along with have to be the one warrior who leaves?" Fiora moaned, crossing her arms.

"I'm sorry to hear we don't get along," came Leo's voice as he approached.

"I didn't mean that, Stealth Apprentice Leo, sir. I only meant that . . ." Fiora paused, trying to work out how best to address her newly-promoted friend. "That *Lain* is my best friend among the warriors."

"I, for one, find it admirable that in four years of intense training he has not lost an ounce of his resolve. He does, however, leave me with a bit of a dilemma," Leo said.

"What?" Fiora asked.

"It was always assumed that, should anyone become Lain, he or she would take the master's place when he passed on. Now you are leaving. You will leave us without a master of stealth."

"You know as much as I do. And you remain the only one besides Master Weste who has ever been able to sneak up on me."

"Perhaps, but Sama will certainly be after the title for himself."

"I am confident you will defeat him."

"You could stay to find out!" Fiora offered.

Lain merely looked to her briefly.

"Please?" she offered, voice shaking a bit more.

"I'm sorry."

"Have you seen the Elder? Has he blessed your departure?" Leo asked.

"Ryala did. She wishes me well."

"You've brought food and water, I trust? And a lantern?"

"I have."

"Well then, no sense delaying any further," Leo said with a shrug.

The trio made their way to the base of the now-quiet falls. Fiora fought back tears heroically as she fluttered along, listing off things he might need as though she was a nervous mother sending her child off for his first journey alone.

"Will you be warm enough? It is awfully cold in the north this time of year. Do you have enough light? The journey can take a very long time and you can't make your own light like I can."

They reached the base of the falls.

"Well," said Leo, extending his hand for a shake. Lain returned the gesture. "Good journey to you. And if you ever decide to use that impression of me, be sure to be a gentleman. I'd hate for my name to be dragged through the mud."

Lain looked to Fiora. The little fairy tried to speak, but her voice failed her. Instead she darted forward, hugging his throat tightly for as long as she dared. She then flitted back, kissed him on the nose, and finally waved a teary goodbye. Not knowing how best to return such a sentiment for someone her size, Lain simply nodded to her, turned, and dropped down to the cave's mouth.

Chapter 30

Navigating the cave was infinitely simpler the second time. It was remarkable how swiftly his mind dredged up the skills learned during his months in the cave. The twists and turns of the place had etched themselves indelibly into his mind. Up this slope, through that tunnel, along this ledge. The endless cycle of flooding and draining had reshaped the path somewhat, but nevertheless, a months-long odyssey was traced backward in mere days. In no time at all, he saw the silvery light of a snowy forest and felt the icy chill of the north.

His pack was still heavy with supplies when he stepped back into the sun and felt the bite of the northern wind again. Without hesitation, he set off to the south, to Tressor. When he'd last walked this ground, he had been lost, defeated, injured, and hopeless. Now he was stronger, better trained, and better equipped than ever before. He moved swiftly, tirelessly. When he could go no farther, he found a dark corner, slipped into the Warrior's Sleep, and was on the move again in hours.

His time in Entwell had sharpened his mind—and, with it, his senses. Even things he'd done with ease before were made easier. Hunting was an afterthought. Stalking unseen through the places of man was of little concern. He saw how people moved, heard how they spoke, and knew where their eyes would turn and their steps would take them. For the first time, he felt prepared for the task at hand.

Now all that remained was to take care of unfinished business to the south.

#

On her porch in the still-deserted town of Millcrest, Maribelle was just finishing the daily litany of bounties. It was traditional to read the list at dawn, but, like most other aspects of her increasingly superficial title of bounty officer, she'd let that erode over the years. Lately she didn't even crawl out of bed until midday, and what few bounty hunters still showed to hear the list had grown accustomed to her lateness. It meant that she didn't turn in very many fugitives, and thus didn't get many new ones to announce, but that suited her just fine. For the better part of the last two years, most of the food was put on the table by a small stable of "black list" workers anyway. The bounty façade was just handy for explaining away the large amount of money on hand and the other more questionable behaviors associated with the enterprise.

"That's all you get, boys. I don't figure on getting any fresh ones before the end of the month, so don't bother coming back unless you like disappointment," she bellowed.

The three holdouts—who, for reasons all their own, had continued to endure her attitude—wandered off muttering to themselves. She yawned and watched them go. When she was satisfied they were far enough away, she barked to her pair of thugs.

"I'm going to go lay out the black list contracts for tonight. Can I trust you idiots to hold down the fort while I'm gone?"

The reply was a barely coherent grumble followed by a pair of inebriated laughs.

Maribelle made a sound of disgust. "I'll be quick about it then."

She stood and paced out into the city, jingling her ring of keys as she went. Keeping her black list jobs safe from people eager to cut her out as the middle man was one of her primary concerns, so her methods were constantly evolving. She stored the raw details of the jobs written out on parchment. Certain key information was kept abstract, a symbol or phrase of which only she knew the meaning. The buildings she used to store the more valuable contracts were purposely scattered, so that a dedicated searcher would need to pull apart half the city to find more than one or two of her best jobs. Unfortunately, that meant a great deal of walking. She made her way to the first building on her list and fumbled for the key. Absentmindedly, she pushed on the door before putting the key into the lock . . . and it opened.

"No," she muttered under her breath. "I locked the door. I know I did. I always lock the door."

She rushed inside, fearing that she would find the interior ransacked. In the dim light that filtered through the open door and between the boards covering the windows, everything appeared to be intact, not that there was much to see. The previous residents had taken all they could when they left. The three rooms were almost bare. A table, a few scattered chests, and the broken frame of a bed were all that remained. She heaved a chest aside and levered up the floorboard beneath it. There was a shallow hollow dug into the ground. It was where she'd hid the pending contacts and materials for at least a dozen jobs, big and small. She earned a cut of each job, and as such the mound of papers was worth a small fortune. Or it would have been, if it had still been there.

"How? How is that possible? There is no sign of a search! How could they have known where to look?"

At the sound of a short, sharp creak, Maribelle's head turned to the door. It slammed shut; in the relative darkness, only a vague form was visible. She cried out, a profanity-laden plea for help echoing off the rafters as she pulled a strange weapon from her belt. It was a pouch of leather, sagging as though stuffed with pebbles, and affixed to the end of a short stick. She raised the weapon and charged. There was clear skill and training behind her motions, and significant weight behind her attack, but before she could take a second step, a gloved hand closed around her wrist. A tug, twist, and sidestep spun her around. The full force of her charge sent her backward into the door. The air burst from her lungs and her head thumped hard against the wooden planks. Her weapon was ripped from her hand and its stout handle was pressed to her throat.

"Be silent," he instructed calmly.

The weapon was held lightly enough to allow her to breathe, but firmly enough to threaten a far more forceful application if needed. She struggled to catch her breath and wisely did as she was told.

"Your men are bound and gagged, and your hiding places have all been cleared."

Slowly it became apparent to her, once her eyes had adjusted, what it was that had so quickly bested her.

"A mally?" The weapon pressed harder. "Malthrope, malthrope," she hastily corrected. "You're the one, aren't you. The one Duule let get away. So he never caught you. What do you want?"

"First, answers."

"What do you want to know?"

"I want to know about these," he said, pulling a stack of pages from his belt and waving them. They were the briefings Maribelle had hidden. "I want to know why these people deserve to die."

"I . . . I don't remember all of them. Half of the time, the people making the offers don't even say."

He breathed a hissing breath. "Then tell me who made the offers."

"I can't tell you that. These people pay for discretion. I tell you their names today and tomorrow they find someone else to handle their jobs, and the first price is on *my* head."

Joseph R. Lallo

"Then you've got a choice to make." He leaned closer. "Today or tomorrow."

She breathed a few shaky breaths, eyes locked on his. Keeping the pressure on the weapon held to her throat, he smoothly stowed the pages and drew out thin dagger with a long, deliberate ring of its blade.

"You can't kill me. The contacts will be worthless to you if you do. You won't know who ordered them, so you won't be able to collect!"

"I am an animal, remember?" he said, angling the blade over her heart. "I can't be expected to understand such things."

Her breathing quickened as he pressed the blade slowly into the leather armor. The blade passed through it as though the armor wasn't there. When she felt the tip of the blade touch her skin, she gasped.

"Fine! Fine, I'll tell you! And I swear I won't tell anyone about you!"

"Yes," he said, withdrawing the blade. "You will. You'll tell everyone about me. An assassin needs a reputation. So you will tell about the man who works for you. You will tell how he wears the skull of a wolf as a helmet. You will tell that it is stained red with the blood of his victims. You will tell everyone who will listen that this assassin, the Red Shadow, has carved a bloody swath across Tressor for years. He is vicious, without remorse, and unmatched."

"You think people will believe that?"

"They will," he said with certainty.

She considered the words again. "They might, at that. But Duule is still alive, and more powerful than ever. When he catches wind of you, he will come after you. No one holds a grudge like Duule."

"Let him come. I will deal with him when he does," he stated. He sheathed the dagger and flipped through the pages at his belt with his free hand. He pulled three free and held them out. "Take them. Tell me who ordered them."

She shakily took the pages. Her eyes had adjusted enough to the darkness that she could just barely make out her own writing. They were three of the highest-priced jobs. She glanced at some markings she'd left on the corner of each and quickly offered up a name and description of each client. They were all wealthy, aristocratic scoundrels from nearby cities. He listened intently, then backed away, finally taking the weapon from her throat. Despite the fact she was no longer in immediate risk of harm, some mixture of wisdom and fear inspired her to keep still and keep quiet.

"In a few days, if these targets have earned their fate, then you will have your proof and I will have my payment."

"Payment! All of this just to do the job? Why? If you are after my money, why not just steal it when you took care of the boys? And why be so choosy about the job?"

"Because I am a hunter, not a scavenger. And because not everyone deserves to be hunted."

He stepped to the boarded up window and delivered a single swift kick. The blow dislodged the boards, bringing the light of day streaming in to viciously sting at Maribelle's eyes. By the time she had blinked away the tears, he was gone.

#

Locating the men responsible for ordering the kills was simple enough. By the time the sun had set on that same day, he had found the first of them. He was an elf living just outside of a port town. The place was Korr, and the man was Gorinil. Elves were common in the eastern ports, and wealth was common among the elves. Gold was the sort of thing that accumulated over time, and elves had more time than most. They often owned ships, sometimes dozens of them, and earned absurd sums for ferrying otherwise unattainable goods across the sea from South Crescent. Fine woods, rare gems, exotic creatures, spices, and all manner of other commodities had made whole families wealthy, and even those not fortunate enough to own the ships still made a tidy living working as sailors and on the docks.

Elf society tended to favor simple, elegant clothing and accessories, but Gorinil had fully embraced Tresson culture. He dressed in flowing, silken robes colored with priceless dyes and detailed with gold thread. His estate was massive and well-protected. Around the grounds, which were nearly as large as Jarrad's plantation in the early days, ran a tall and sturdy fence. There was a pair of ornate and mismatched carriages inside a coach house toward the back of the grounds. Six guards were stationed near the two fence gates. The manor at its center was three stories tall and had dozens of rooms. The roof had slate shingles, the doors had polished brass hinges, and the whole of the structure had been solidly built to withstand the harsh storms that scoured the shore region a few times a year. To a casual observer, it was an insurmountable task to slip inside such a place; before his time in Entwell, Lain would not have considered it. Now, though, he knew better than to take it at its appearance.

405

Gorinil's guards were little concern. Though they were well equipped, it was clear that more had been spent on the weapons than the men carrying them. The dead-eyed men stood their ground, staring without seeing. There was no patrol, and they seldom even took a glance around them. In moments, Lain had scaled the fence and found a dark crevice of the manor's outer wall to plot the next step. The sturdiness of the building would have made it difficult to force his way in, but with so many windows to take advantage of the view, finding one that wasn't properly secured was a certainty. In no time, he had scaled the wall and found his way to a small window leading into the attic. Once inside, the heavy construction of the mansion simply meant that sounds didn't travel very far. For his sensitive ears, it was little problem. Closing his eyes and keeping still, he focused on the voices from all over the house as they filtered through the thick walls to him.

There was a pair of carriages outside, which suggested that Gorinil had a visitor of similar wealth. This was fortunate. When the sort of wealthy man who would build a place such as this met a peer, each would boast. They would boast of their fortune, and power that such fortune brought. Nothing was a greater expression of power than the having the means and will to order the death of another. If he listened, before the night was out, the motivation would come spilling proudly from the scoundrel's mouth.

The attic was just as extravagant as the rest of the manor, entirely finished and more pleasant than most commoners' homes. Furniture and clothing that had fallen out of fashion cluttered the pitch-black space, draped with sheets and left to be eaten by moths. He navigated the space silently until he reached the chimney. Once there he put his ears to work again. The voices of the household were nearest: these spoke of chores to be done, those of the nearly finished evening meal.

When he found two voices speaking exclusively and reverently of business, he knew he'd found the master of the house. He tuned his sensitive hearing to their conversation and followed it through the rooms as the night progressed. At first, the conversation spoke in broad terms of schedules and volumes and prices. There was talk of this acquisition and that commodity. After they had eaten and retired to the study to smoke and sip brandy, though, the conversation turned to those troublesome rivals who were standing in the way. It was at this point that the name of the target was peppered into the conversation. To Gorinil's credit, he remained vague on the subject, but he couldn't resist remarking that this equally ruthless thorn in his side would cease to be a concern before long.

And so the reason was revealed. This man, with all of the greed of Marret and the savvy to feed it, had ordered the death of a counterpart in another town. Two predators competing for the same prey, and one deciding to eat the other along the way. It was all Lain needed to hear. He slipped out of the attic, over the fence. He would take this target and earn his bounty, and now was as good a time as any.

#

It was a short trip to the home of the target. Rather than at the center of a fenced-in estate, it was huddled on a busy street of a bustling port town. Even late into the night, the city around his home was alive with activity. Gorinil would likely have been furious to know that despite all of the time and money he had devoted to ensuring his own security, the home of his hated rival was far safer by simple virtue of the bystanders who gathered in the streets around it. An overly curious neighbor was worth ten guards, and no fence could match the security of being surrounded by occupied homes. If only the man had been modest enough to occupy a single floor rather than an entire building, it would have been truly challenging to reach him. Instead, he chose to flaunt his own wealth by making a home of the tallest building in town. It was a narrow building of painted wood and slate shingle that rose a full four floors over the street, and just as had been the case with the man who had ordered his death, a shuttered window near the roof was the weak point. It was hanging loosely ajar, and a flicker of lantern light revealed that there was nothing else to bar the way.

Even before Entwell, flitting unseen across the rooftops had been second nature to Lain. He made his way from the city gates to the walls of the doomed man's home without once touching the street. It was tempting to head straight for the window, but he knew that if there was light in the window, there was someone in the room beyond. Instead he pulled himself silently to the sloped roof and crouched low, senses sharp. From the sound of voices he could tell that there were three people inside. The potent scent of some sort of polish was wafting through the window, and the jingle of delicate metal could be heard beneath the conversation. There were servants, two women. They were engaging in what appeared to be the favored pastime of people in their walk of life: complaining in hushed voices about their

407

Joseph R. Lallo

employers.

"I tell you, I don't know why he has us clean the blasted silver. The way he eats, he may as well use a trough," muttered one of the women.

"He's having us polish the silver because if not for that, there would be nothing for us to do. He would have to let us take the night off, and perish the thought," remarked the other. "Now he gets to sleep off half a bottle of wine while we choke ourselves on the fumes of this horrid stuff."

There was the thump of feet on the stairs, prompting a sudden silence from the women.

"It is only me, ladies," came the voice of the man, evidently not the target of their frustrations. "And if I were you, I would not speak ill of the master of the house. If he hadn't had so much wine, it wouldn't be nearly so easy to convince him tomorrow that he *finished* the bottle."

There was the slosh of a purloined bottle and the trio slipped away from the window to one of their quarters to split the ill-gotten gains, taking the lantern to light the way. Like a breath of wind rustling the curtains, Lain nudged open the shutters and flipped down from the roof and into the window. He moved swiftly across the cluttered servants' floor, reaching the steps without so much as creaking a floorboard. Whereas the servants' quarters were packed with cupboards and cabinets, piles of rags and work to be done on every flat surface, the living space of the owner was immaculate and lavish. Elegant furniture was carefully arranged in each room. Stuffed chairs with lustrous horsehair upholstery sat awaiting guests. Tables draped with intricate lacework and carved chairs stood at the ready for meals most could only imagine. All of it was shrouded in darkness, but compared to the cave, it might as well have been the height of day. He wove between the finery, staying low to the floor rather than risk being seen by an unexpected stray servant.

After another such floor, he heard the heavy breathing of sleep. He moved with even more care now. The most critical tasks lay ahead. He needed to identify the target, find the proof that was required by the contract, and . . . perform the deed. The first part was easy enough, as the heavy breathing he heard was now turning to a rattling snore, and was coming from a room not far from the staircase. He found his way to it. There was a magnificent four-post bed, heaped with comforters. A man and woman were laying beneath them. The man was deeply asleep, erupting periodically with a fresh snore. The woman, presumably his wife, was sleeping fitfully.

Lain crouched low beside the bed and conjured to mind the papers he'd taken from Maribelle. The man carried a silver coin, the first payment he'd received for his first shipment many years ago. It had an engraving of some kind, and he wore it on a chain around his neck as a good luck charm. The assassin hunched with his eyes level with the bed. All but the man's head was beneath covers. The night was barely cool, the nearby sea adding a bit of clamminess to the air, but native Tressons often seemed to have a low tolerance for the cold, hence the layers. Keeping a watchful eye on both the man and woman, and keeping his ears pointed to the door, Lain slowly folded back the comforter. The man did not wake, so he put his fingers to the blanket to do the same.

The man released a sudden, grating outburst, a noise loud enough to stir his wife. Lain disappeared beneath the bed just in time for her to launch herself upright and elbow the man in the ribs.

"Ugh," he groaned, jostled from sleep. "What . . . why did . . ."

"You were snoring. Again!" she growled.

He muttered something unintelligible, then drifted back to sleep. She grumbled and climbed out of bed, fumbling her way out of the dark room. Soon Lain could hear glasses and pitchers rattling from a few rooms away. Lain slipped out from beneath the bed, more cautious now, and looked over his prey. His wife's abrupt departure had upset the covers, and tucked beneath the man's night shirt was a round shape. He tugged the chain until he could just see that it was indeed a silver coin. He was the man, it was certain now.

Lain looked to the doorway. The woman was likely in the kitchen getting a drink, but she would not be long. This needed to be done quickly and silently. He looked down to the man and made his decision. With sharp, precise movements he clamped his palm across the man's mouth and pinched his nostrils shut. Crouching down, he wrapped his arm around the man's head, reaching behind and grasping the side of his face. The target's eyes were only just beginning to open from sleep again when Lain twisted his head firmly. There was a snap, a few weak shudders, and it was done.

He removed his hand, straightened the man's head, and plucked the coin from his neck. The sound of his wife's returning footsteps prompted him to slip out through the other doorway. Just before he disappeared up the stairs and toward his exit on the upper floors, he

Joseph R. Lallo

heard the woman remark in relief that the man had finally stopped snoring.

Chapter 31

With his new skills, the jobs came and went quickly. In just a few months, Lain earned nearly enough gold to buy a small farm, but working so quickly and efficiently had unforeseen consequences. Maribelle, despite her best efforts, had never been anything more than a small player in the world of blades for hire. She had very few contacts, and even the most ruthless of scoundrels had only so many people who they want killed—or, at least, who they could afford to have killed. The largest of the jobs were wiped away quickly, and those that remained were a pittance compared to them. Nevertheless, until he could manage to find a new source for such work, he had little recourse.

This particular set of tasks took him to a small east coast town called Dravis. The town was home to two of the smaller jobs that Maribelle had been able to secure for him. The first and most valuable was an assassination. One of the lesser members of Duule's growing network of thugs and killers had decided that the next step on the ladder was long overdue for a vacancy. The other job, a much lower bounty from the more legitimate side of her business, had to do with a rash of poaching from private hunting grounds. A lord with vast land holdings had discovered that his private wild stock was being targeted. Maribelle had indicated that it was initially thought that the animals were falling to predators, but evidence had since found that it was likely a man or woman, as steps had been taken to hide the remains. The wealthy lord decided that such an injustice would not stand, and so a bounty was offered.

As it was both the most valuable and most time-sensitive of the tasks, Lain chose to pursue the assassination first. It was clear that the man he was after was well aware of his sensitive position. The information regarding his likely location and his routine was minimal. No matter. Criminals hadn't changed in the four years he'd spent in Entwell, and the things he'd learned under Weste had made finding and sifting through the clues even simpler. What's more, there were methods available to him that Weste would never have imagined. With a bit of concentration, he could hear at least a word or two from every person in every building in half a village, all without leaving his chosen vantage point. His nose could tell him things that even the finest tracking hound couldn't, such as which scent was common to two shady neighborhoods.

In the space of a few days, Lain was confident that he had narrowed the possible hiding places from half of the east coast to Dravis alone. He was circling the town wide, making his way downwind of the place. It was for his nose what getting a bird's-eye view would have been for his eyes. As always, he chose to travel by night, to more simply shield himself from witnesses and to increase the odds that his target would be stationary. On this night, the proper vantage turned out to be an overgrown field just outside of town. There, huddled among the bushes, he drew in a sample of the night breeze and began to unravel its secrets.

As always, the air carried a symphony of scents. A strong base of sea salt and fresh-turned earth enfolded the smoky scent of cooking fires, the potent aroma of the stables, and the unique scent of each of the town's residents. Weeding through the torrent of information could be swift if the event he sought was a familiar one, or the work of an entire night if the scent was still a puzzle. He had only just begun to sift through the first long breath when, woven in among the myriad of others, a scent asserted itself and seized his mind.

Without thinking, he found himself slipping from the field and toward the city. Every few moments, he would sample the air again. The scent was always there, stronger, more certain, and more maddening to him. The trail led him first to the city, where it traced a long and complex path through the back alleys and side streets. From there, it headed north and east, where it came to the stubbly grass of the seashore. It mixed with older traces of the same scent, the remnants of prior trails from recent days. He was getting close to a place it returned to frequently. As the scent led him to a craggy section of seaside cliffs, a sharp shift in the breeze brought a perfectly fresh whiff of that which he so eagerly sought.

He shifted from a stalk to a silent sprint toward a stretch of beach that had been turned into a veritable maze by great slabs of sloughed-off stone from the cliffs. Now he could hear footsteps, the quick, sure steps of an experienced runner well aware that they had been found. He gave chase, now following the echoing sounds among the wind-smoothed spires of stone. The pursuit circled back on itself, placing

Lain between the sea and his quarry. The instant the breeze was at his back, the steps ahead of him skidded to a stop just on the other side of a natural pillar of stone. At the sound, he, too, slowed, and after a few pounding heartbeats, a figure stepped into the open.

"Teyn?" came a voice heartbreaking in its familiarity.

It was her. The instant he had taken his first breath he had been certain. Smelling it had conjured to mind the same sandy gray eyes that now stared with tear-soaked disbelief into his own. In his mind, he'd seen the mahogany fur, the confident grin. There was no question that it had been her, and no question that he had to see her again. And now she was in front of him. He was lost in the moment, paralyzed. All he could do was stare at her and endure the torrent of emotions.

She crossed her arms and looked aside, sniffling and wiping her eyes. "It has been a long time, Teyn."

"A long time," he repeated.

The years had treated her well. She wasn't the scrawny, half-starved wretch who had stolen his meal seven years ago. Her build was still the lean, healthy one she'd enjoyed when they'd parted ways. In place of the light garb she'd worn in those days was a billowy tan shirt with long sleeves, matching trousers, and a thin robe. Her tail was hidden, tucked down one leg of the trousers, and hanging from her belt was a simple broad-brimmed hat of the sort worn by many of the field workers on the east side of Tressor. In short, she was in disguise, dressed as best she could to pass for human at a glance. The only thing about her wardrobe that remained unchanged was the jewelry, which dangled proudly from her ears and adorned both wrists and three fingers on each hand.

Sorrel wiped away the tears streaming from eyes that stubbornly refused to be as aloof as the rest of her. "You still look at me too much, Teyn."

"You are looking well," he said.

"And you are looking . . ." She glanced him up and down. "Different." Her eyes locked with his again, staring deep into them. After a few moments she narrowed her eyes slightly and gave her head a sorrowful shake. When she spoke again, her voice was hushed and distant. "What has happened to you, Teyn?"

"A great deal . . ."

"Too much, I think." She sniffed. "Why do you come here now?"

"I came because I'm tracking someone, and I caught your scent.

Why are you here? Why did you leave the Great Forest?"

"What does it matter to you?" she snapped. "You had this purpose. This thing so important to you. What does it matter what I am doing, or why I do it?"

In her anger, she jostled something that she was wearing around her neck, causing it to swing out from behind the robe. The motion drew Lain's eyes. Hanging from a worn, knotted rope was a stone, mirror-smooth and deep purple. When she realized what he had seen, she turned her back to him and crossed her arms. "I told you not to follow me."

Lain felt a tightness in his chest, an anxiety he'd not felt in years. He had faced certain death countless times and clashed with some of the best-trained warriors in the world, yet a few words from Sorrel took his voice away. He tightened his fists and fought the feelings under control.

"Sorrel, listen to me."

"Why should I listen to you?

"This is important."

"What is important to you is not important to me."

"I think you may be in danger."

"We are always in danger. I can take care of myself."

"Sorrel, *listen to me!*"

She turned her head to the side and glared at him over her shoulder, the sharpness of his voice catching her off-guard. He continued.

"Someone has been hunting in a stretch of wooded land to the south west. It is a private hunting ground, and the lord who owns it has discovered poaching. That is what brought me here. Perhaps you are the one doing the poaching, perhaps you are not, but there is a reward for anyone who brings back the person responsible. It will bring others. I know that you've lived your life avoiding people like this, but you must not take it lightly. I know these hunters. I am one of them now. There are those among them who have more than enough skill to find you. I followed your scent through the city. If they were to bring hounds to the hunting grounds, then bring them here, they would find you as surely as I did.

"You would not join me in my own quest because it was too dangerous, and I did not blame you. All I ask is that you understand that you are in the same danger now. If you are angry at me, if you hate me, that doesn't change the fact that I'm giving you a warning. We both know that such a thing is rare for a malthrope. I don't want you to die because you were too proud or stubborn heed my words. You are too important to me for that."

His voice was steady and firm, his words earnest. Sorrel simply turned her head away.

"Very well."

Lain turned and began to walk back the way he'd come. After a few steps, there came the sound of desperate, pounding footsteps. He turned just in time for her to tackle him into an embrace that nearly knocked them both to the ground. She held him tightly, her head hooked over his shoulder and her eyes shut tight. He returned the gesture, gently, as he felt her silently weep.

"I'm sorry," he whispered.

"No," she said, reluctantly loosening the embrace to look him in the eyes. "Do not tell me you are sorry. It hurt me what you said years ago. It hurt me the way you felt, but do not be sorry for it. I could not understand then because I did not understand what it was to have a purpose of my own. I do now. I look at these creatures and I know what it means to have something that you would give your life for without thinking twice. That is why I am here." She sniffled and wiped her eyes. "That is why I cannot go back to where it is safe."

"What is it?"

She continued to look into his eyes, then slowly released him from her arms. "Before I tell you, you must tell me something."

"What do you need to know?"

"When my leg was hurt, you told me that you were a killer. I looked in your eyes that day, and I was sure you were not." She took a deep breath to steady herself. "Why, when I look in your eyes today . . . am I no longer sure? What has happened to you, Teyn?"

Now it was Lain's turn to take a breath. In the past, he might have felt shame for the story he had to tell, but as he spoke of the lengths he had gone to and the things he had done, he found he felt nothing at all. It was as though the years of forcing away such thoughts had caused the part of his soul that burned and ached at such things to wither away. It was a simple record, spoken with such dispassion and detachment, he might as well have been speaking of a stranger rather than himself. When he was through, he looked back to Sorrel. The tears still trickled from her eyes, and her expression spoke volumes of the conflict within her. She reached out and touched him on the chest, then put her hand to his cheek.

"Is there anything left of you, Teyn? Is there anything of who you were?"

He considered her words, then slowly reached to his side. From within a pouch, he drew a small wad of cloth. It was beyond ragged, frayed at the ends and stained a dozen shades of brown and red.

"What is it?" Sorrel asked.

"The last thing you did for me before you left was tend to my wounds. You used this. It is the one thing I still carry with me from those days. It was with me in the cave, and it helped me to keep my wits about me. The only part of me that remains from those days . . . is you."

She looked at the swatch of cloth, then put her hand to the stone hung about her neck.

"Come," she said, taking his hand. "I will show you."

She turned and quickened to a run, dragging him beside her. Lain had forgotten just how fast his fellow malthrope could run. It was rare for him to encounter anyone who could match his speed. Staying beside her as she led the way through the maze of fallen stone and onward into the jagged cliffs took every bit of his agility. She led him along the seashore at the base of the cliffs until they reached a narrow crevice in the cliff side. Beside it was an alcove, sheltered somewhat from the sea spray.

"Wait there," she said.

Sorrel sidled through the crevice, and for a minute or two left Lain alone on the shore. The wind was blowing in a steady breeze off the sea, filling his nose with salt air. Any scent that might betray what lay within the cave was whipped up along the cliff. In time, there came the crunch of sand under foot. Then a voice.

"Teyn."

He looked up to see Sorrel stepping free from the crevice. A moment later, two other forms tumbled out . . . malthrope children. They were young, barely chest-high to Sorrel. If they'd been humans, they would have looked to be perhaps ten years old. As members of his own kind, he guessed their age to be five years. One was a male, his fur orange, but a shade darker than Lain's own. The other was female, her fur deep red, but lighter than Sorrel's. They were dressed in simple clothes, tanned and sewn hides no doubt prepared by Sorrel herself. At the sight of Lain, they huddled behind her.

Sorrel placed a hand on the boy's head, and the other on the girl's. "Wren, Reyna. This is Teyn. Say hello to him," Sorrel said to the children. They merely huddled closer. She sighed. "Go. Play. Stay where I can see."

This instruction they eagerly followed, chasing each other as they scampered off toward the sea.

"Your children," Lain said.

"Mine . . . yes. Twins. They are shy, as they must be. They have had no one but me."

Lain watched as the pair frolicked on the beach sand. They yelled and laughed. It seemed that they spoke well enough, their playful calls to each other coming in the intricate patterns of Crich speech. A question burned in Lain's mind. He looked to Sorrel. Her eyes seemed to implore him not to ask it. There was little reason to. Some things were better left unspoken.

"They seem healthy."

"Of course they are. They are my everything. I've provided for them better than I ever have for myself. And I couldn't have done it half as well if it had not been for you."

"Me?"

"I taught you all of the malthrope things you should have known from the start, but you taught me the useful things of men. Smoking the food. Making the clothes. There were times when we did not have much, but if not for the things you had taught, we would have had nothing. But . . ." She sighed. "The life I have lived, I do not regret. It has been enough for me. It is not enough for them. They deserve better. I need for them to have the life you and I could not have. And I know that I cannot find it here. Across the sea are North and South Crescent. There are few men there. I know this."

"South Crescent is home to elves, mostly. They feel the same about us as men do."

"I hear this, too. But there are not so many. There may be a place for us there. And North Crescent?"

"I do not know, but . . . I have met someone who has family that came from North Crescent. She seemed more accepting than the rest."

"It is more than we can hope for here."

"You do not know what you will find there. It could be a terrible place."

"*This* is a terrible place. If I find the same there, then nothing has

417

changed. But if there is something better . . . I owe it to them to give them the chance. That means I must find a way to get there. I sneak into the city when I can. I listen. I do not know how, but I will find a way to get them to that place." She stepped close and put a hand on his shoulder. "You say you've worked with men, and you spent time in this other place. Do you know a way? A way to get to the Crescents?"

Lain sat on a log of driftwood. Sorrel took a seat beside him. He looked to the sea and thought. How could such a thing be done? There was gold. There was always gold. But arranging even a simple sale of land or slaves had already proven treacherous and difficult, even with the money to do so. A journey to the Crescents? That would take months, and even if every member of the crew were bribed into compliance, all it would take was a single man having a second thought in that time and Sorrel and the children would be doomed. The only way that it could work would be if the people on the ship did not know what they were delivering . . .

A memory sifted to the surface, and with it came a glimmer of hope. It must have shown in his eyes, because Sorrel clutched his leg.

"You know something. You've thought of something!" She said with guarded excitement.

"There was an elf called Goldie. He and I were together on the plantation. He was one of the ones who escaped. One of the other slaves told me that he worked in Delti. His family smuggles goods and people to South Crescent. If what I was told can be believed, he may feel he owes a debt to me. Even if he doesn't . . . I've managed to gather some money."

"You think he can take us to the Crescents? You think you can trust him?"

"I don't know. I don't even know if it is true. But Delti is not far from here." He stood. "I can find out."

She stood and placed her hands on his shoulders, turning him to face her. "You can find out tomorrow. For now it has been too long since I have had anyone but the twins to talk to. Stay and listen for a while," she said, smiling. "For me."

He nodded and sat, listening for hours to the voice that he'd feared he'd lost forever.

#

In a city not far from the east coast of Tressor, the hunter and tracker named Dihsaad was just finishing the long trek the next in a string of bounty offices. He was a man of few needs, and his past association with Duule had provided him with more money than he was likely to spend for the rest of his days. Nonetheless, a man needs something to fill his time; since his collaboration with the criminal, he'd developed something of an obsession with the creature that had slipped through his fingers. Thus, when a message arrived from Duule suggesting that the malthrope may have returned, he threw himself into the task of finding it once more. Evidently Maribelle's business had sharply improved, and when Duule had her questioned about it, she spun a ridiculous yarn about a man with wolf skull for a helmet. When she was encouraged to be more forthcoming, she revealed that it was indeed the same creature.

So the hunt began anew. Duule had placed men in and around Maribelle's bounty office, but somehow the thing still managed to slip in and out without being caught—or even seen. If it was going to be found, it would have to be the old-fashioned way. A bounty office, one less crooked than Maribelle's, would hold the specifics of the crimes giving the local authorities the most trouble. The malthrope was both troublesome and a criminal, so the local offices were places as good as any to learn if he was back in the area.

Like most such places, this one was little more than a single room with a chest of dispatches and small lockbox inside of it and a crude signboard outside. Inside the cramped space was a burly, heavily-armed man with the task of preventing the lockbox filled with bounty payments from walking away. He was joined by an official of the kingdom, no doubt one who was rather disappointed with his current assignment. The official was responsible for reading out the daily bounties and meting out payments. In lieu of holding cells, a row of thick wooden posts lined the courtyard in front of the building. Holes had been drilled in the tops, and shackles had been threaded through them.

Dihsaad had been a frequent visitor to this particular office in his more active tracking days, so much so that the official and his guard didn't feel the need to offer any more than a nod when he arrived. He stepped into the dimly-lit bounty office, pulled the only unoccupied chair up to the dispatch chest, and began to sift through its contents, muttering to himself.

"Kidnapping. Not his style . . . arson, no . . . stolen jewelry, perhaps . . . poaching." He nodded. It was certainly a malthrope's prerogative to take advantage of a decent hunting ground. Dihsaad unrolled the scroll and began to read the details, skipping along vaguely. "By the order of . . . for the crime of . . . a sum of . . . ah, here. As evidenced by the discovery of bones stripped of their meat and," he smiled, "buried to conceal the crime."

He stood and presented the scroll to the official.

"Has this bounty been claimed?" he asked.

The official yawned, not bothering to look. "No bounty has been claimed at *this* office for eight months."

"Has anyone shown interest in this?"

Now the official snatched the scroll and reviewed it. "No. I cannot speak for the other offices, however. That one is offered in every office from here to the border."

"This one is mine, then."

"Very well," the official acknowledged with supreme disinterest. He dabbed a quill into a pot of ink and etched something onto a sheet of parchment. "Noted."

Dihsaad paced out the door and made his way to the only other building worthy of note in the tiny town, a sizable tavern named *Stone's Bottom*. It was an inexpensive place for travelers to fill their stomachs and wash the accumulated road dust from their mouths and throats before continuing on to more worthwhile destinations. As tended to be the case for such places, it attracted more than its share of the seedier sort of clientele. Far from interested in the swill they served, it was the riffraff in the back room who Dihsaad was after. Just as the bounty office was ostensibly the local representation of royal authority, the dim recesses of the tavern were an extension of Duule's influence. Notably, Duule's men were far more efficient and enthusiastic in their roles.

Waving off the understandably skittish bartender, Dihsaad shouldered his way through the door that separated the more mannerly patrons from the cutthroats and thugs. Inside the room, lit by a single soot-blackened lamp, the air was thick with stench, smoke, and profanity. As the command structure of a den of thieves was a rather fluid thing, Dihsaad addressed the room as a whole, keeping his message brief.

"Send a message to Duule. Dihsaad may have found his creature."

#

A message to Duule seldom took long to arrive. Barely three days

420

had passed before a messenger, thoroughly unprepared for the wildfire he was about to spark, arrived at a palatial mansion farther inland. Duule's influence had grown in leaps and bounds in Lain's absence. With it had grown his confidence. After a period of attempting to conduct his business in increasingly secure locations, the banishment of the one foe with the suicidal willingness to turn him in to the authorities gave him a feeling of security. He began to flaunt his wealth, moving in four years from one estate to another, each one larger and more opulent than the last. He conducted his business openly, flaunting his frightening influence upon the underbelly of Tressor with complete disregard to the far less resourceful and less organized authorities of Tressor.

Duule was on the porch of his current residence, sipping from a brandy glass when the messenger arrived on horseback. The young man, recruited chiefly because his downright emaciated frame would do little to slow a horse, marched up to Duule on wobbly legs and declared his cryptic message.

"I have a message for you, sir. Er. Dihsaad found your creature," he said, his insides not having settled from the ride.

Slowly lowering the brandy glass, Duule looked at his messenger. "Are you certain you have relayed that message properly?"

"Yes. Yes, sir. Dihsaad found your creature."

He stood. When he began speaking, it was with exaggerated enunciation, but each successive word grew in intensity. "I want you to go back to wherever you got that message. I want you to tell *everyone* you meet that Dihsaad shall have everyone and every*thing* he needs to find this creature. My forces are at his command. Fast horses, strong men, anything he needs. And tell him I'll be arriving *personally* in a few days, and when I do, I will be bringing a damned *army* to find this creature and watch as the heart is torn from that monster's chest. Understand?"

"I . . ."

"Understand!?"

"Yes, sir!" the messenger yelped.

"Then *move!*"

The messenger fairly leaped from the porch to his horse's back and rode off as though death itself was chasing him. Duule turned to the door of his home, stalking forward and knocking the brandy glass angrily to the ground.

"He dies this time. He dies!"

#

In days, the sum total of Duule's network was turned entirely to the task of finding Lain. Under the guidance of Dihsaad, they swept like flood waters across the land. Sorrel was skilled at hiding any trace of her presence, but with two young children to care for and a legion of highly-motivated individuals searching the land, evidence began to arise. Footprints here. More buried bones there. Dihsaad began to assemble the pieces. There were certainly malthropes. More than one, some of them children. They had spent time in a few different port areas.

Unbeknownst to Lain and Sorrel, the noose was tightening around their necks.

Chapter 32

In the city of Delti, two weeks later, an elf was seated at a desk in his small but respectable home. His name was Glinilos, but somehow the nickname of Goldie had managed to follow him through the years. Spread on the desk before him were maps depicting shipping routes, tables containing dates and values for shipments, and price lists for various services. Absent from any sheet was the name or address of any individuals associated with the shipments. For the most part, the shipments under his supervision were the sort of which the recipients would prefer no records linked them to the items in question. Business was doing well, thanks mostly to the deeply-entrenched war with the north.

With the coming of the war, many vital ores and minerals previously available almost exclusively from the north had suddenly needed to be sourced elsewhere. Things like iron and copper were in horribly short supply. What little supplies of these resources that Tressor could produce were earmarked for the war effort. For the rest of the kingdom, alternative sources needed to be found. Increasingly, those alternative sources had been in the mineral-rich Southern Crescent. Much of the imported ore found its way to the military as well, but people like Goldie could be coerced into providing a steady supply of anything one might find across the sea if the price was right.

Keeping track of such matters and maintaining the necessary network of connections, typically through bribery and partnerships, required a specialized set of skills. Goldie had proven phenomenally well-suited over the years. Though his unfortunate past had left him with a terrible limp and lingering pains, his mind was as sharp as ever. He was currently working long into the night, endeavoring to find room on one of his outgoing ships for a bundle of exquisitely woven rugs that had been purchased by one of his older brothers back on the South Crescent. He took great pains to keep his office private and isolated from his other affairs, and only worked on the most sensitive aspects of his job during those hours in which he was least likely to be disturbed. It was thus a nearly heart-stopping surprise when, without any warning, a voice spoke out from directly behind him.

"Goldie," Lain said. The elf snapped around and inhaled, ready to scream for help, but Lain was ready for that, seizing the back of Goldie's head with one hand and clamping his mouth with the other. "Do not scream. I come seeking information. Do you understand?"

He nodded. Lain slowly removed his hand.

"Do you remember me?" asked the malthrope.

"You are the mally from the slavery days," Goldie said.

"I have spoken to Gurruk and Menri in the past. They told me they felt that they owed me a life-debt. They said you would agree."

Goldie drew in and released an angry breath before grudgingly nodding. "I do."

"I am told that you are able to smuggle things to South Crescent, and people as well."

"I can."

"I want you to take three of my kind as far as you can toward North Crescent. It must be done secretly, and safely."

"Three malthropes . . ." Goldie said, his face twisting with disgust.

"An adult and two children."

"That is . . . that is a very difficult request."

"Can you do it?" Lain asked steadily. There was no threat in his tone, but there was the ring of bone-deep dedication to the task, the willingness to do anything to see it achieved.

"When I smuggle passengers, they travel in disguise. With malthropes, that will not do," He explained. "But . . . there may be a way."

He turned to his bundles of manifests and schedules and one by one drew out the tightly-rolled parchment. He flattened them against the table and ran his fingers along the carefully scribed lines.

"Yes . . . I have something that may do. It will not be comfortable."

"Comfort is not important. I require only safety and secrecy."

"Very well. There is a ship coming in twenty days. Just north of Delti, you will find a small inlet. Bring these malthropes of yours there an hour before dawn on that day. They will be brought as far as Qualia. It is near the northern tip of South Crescent. From there, your creatures can make their way north by land."

"And their safety is assured?"

"One does not remain the overseer of an enterprise such as this by losing cargo. For this matter, I will escort the cargo personally to its final destination."

Lain stepped back, reaching out to snuff the flame of the lantern. "Do this and your debt is paid. You will forever have my gratitude." He stepped back into the darkness. "Betray me . . . and I shall take what I am owed."

With that, he was gone.

#

Days with Sorrel passed quickly. At first, she was concerned that Goldie could not be trusted, but she was nothing if not practical. If she intended to wait until someone she could trust with certainty could take her across the sea, she would never see the Crescents. At Lain's behest, the group made a habit of moving to a new shelter every few nights, in case someone else had taken the bounty and was able to find her trail. Once a temporary home had been selected, the nights and days were theirs.

There were moments, precious and few, when it was as through the long years they had spent apart had never happened at all. Sorrel learned, to her delight, that Lain now spoke Crich fluently. It meant that he at least could share some tales with Reyna and Wren, each of whom knew only a few words of Tresson. Strangely, when she spoke to Lain alone, she insisted on using her broken Tresson. She said it felt better, familiar. It brought back the old days.

The twins were slow to warm to Lain, but they listened in fascination when he spoke, and when his back was turned, they crept near to investigate him. It was the same curiosity he dimly remembered from his youth. For their sake, he pretended not to notice them.

Too soon, the morning of the twentieth day had come. The inlet Goldie spoke of was shallow and marshy, little use for proper shipping or sailing, and thus empty and unused. The four malthropes crouched in a bushy patch of overgrowth and watched the water. A mist hung over its surface, and the deepening gold of the coming dawn was not enough to cut far through it.

"You are sure he will come?" Sorrel asked.

"He will come, or he will answer to me." Lain reached into his shirt and pulled out the swatch of cloth he'd held for so long. "Take this. When you reach the Crescents safely, give it to Goldie, and give him a message that could only come from you. I will wait for him to return. If he has it, I will know you are safe. If he does not . . ."

As if in response, a skiff emerged from the mists. It was small, barely enough to carry Goldie himself and the shoulder-high crate that took up the rest of its deck. He pushed the vessel along with a pole, and when he reached the sandy shore of the clearing, he looked around and hopped down.

"Well? Where are you hiding?"

Lain stood up and approached him.

"Ah," Goldie said. "There. Fetch your other malthropes. They shall ride in the crate."

"First tell me what you have planned."

Goldie sneered. "From time to time, I receive requests from those in my homeland to send a live specimen of an exotic beast native to these lands. Some friends of my family have a vast and varied menagerie, and they are ever eager to increase its stock. It is one of the more difficult tasks we are called upon to fulfill, but we've managed it with beasts large and small. We will load your malthropes into this crate, take them back to the ship, and load them into a special cage in the hold. Very close slats. No one should be able to see. The crew has been told we are transporting a basilisk. One gaze will turn them to stone. That should keep their curiosity at bay. When we reach Qualia, the cage will be transported to a forest north of the city and left with me for pickup. I will release your creatures and they will be on their way. Does that meet with your requirements?"

"How long will they be at sea?"

"Forty days, depending on weather."

"And they will be fed?"

"Salted meat and fresh water daily."

Lain turned to the bushes. Sorrel reluctantly revealed herself and took the twins by their hands. They pulled and tugged, unwilling to step out until Sorrel gathered one into her arms and beckoned Lain to do the same. The four of them walked past Goldie, who recoiled at the sight as though a swarm of rats had scurried by. Sorrel looked him the eye long and hard before loading Wren into the crate and dropping her pack in after him. Lain helped Reyna in, then took Sorrel's hand to help her in as well. She stood for a moment eying the elf warily.

"You are sure we can trust him?" she asked doubtfully.

"I will be near," Lain said.

She nodded once and finally ducked inside. Goldie closed and latched the lid, then turned to find Lain gone . . . gone from sight, at least. The elf stepped onto the skiff, put the pole to the water, and slowly pushed it back toward the harbor.

Lain was true to his word, stalking the craft as it made its way along the shore. He always kept himself hidden, but never let the skiff out of his sight. The port of Delti was less than an hour away. By the time dawn was finished breaking, the skiff was drifting along the deeper water of the harbor. It was a bustling place, a dozen ships at dock and hundreds of sailors and port workers yelling out orders to one another. Waves rolling in from the sea jostled the skiff, and within its heavy cargo, the twins began to whimper in fear from the strange noises and sudden motions.

Goldie rapped the top of the box, barking orders in a harsh whisper. "Keep them quiet. I don't imagine these folks know what a basilisk sounds like, but it certainly doesn't sound like a pair of mewling kits."

Inside the crate, striped by the light shining between the planks, Sorrel gathered the twins closer and hushed them. "Teyn will make sure we are safe." She repeated it, eyes shut. "He will make sure we are safe."

The skiff made its way to the rear of a ship marked *The Path of the Sun*. It was a grand vessel, narrow of hull and with vast triangular sails; a ship built for speed. The deck was already piled with crates, bundles, and bales, shielding the far side of the ship from view from the dock. It was there that the crew on the deck swung a pair of stout wooden struts over the side of the ship, lowering ropes that Goldie secured to the crate. Inside, Sorrel held her children tight as the crate was hauled up and onto the deck. She managed to keep the terrified little creatures quiet as workers nervously lifted the crate carried it below decks to the cargo hold. Goldie docked the skiff and made his way into the ship.

It was no small task to navigate the boat without being seen by its crew, but Lain did so with ease, lurking among the rows of cargo already loaded when Goldie met the workers at what appeared to be the rear wall of the hold. Once there, he pulled aside an inconspicuous plank and tugged at the ropes that it hid. The wall shuddered, and with a shove the workers managed to slide it aside. Within was the cage Goldie had mentioned. It was large, perhaps the size of a prison cell, and made from study wood. The slats were indeed very close, space enough for a finger to slip through between them if that. One whole wall of the cage swung aside, revealing a slatted floor with wider gaps. The floor was raised somewhat, and beneath it was a trio of loosely-fitted troughs with sloped bottoms. The lingering stench in the air left

427

little doubt what they were used for. A long, thin opening on one wall led to the open air outside, providing barely adequate ventilation and virtually no light. Inside the cage, a pair of smaller troughs aligned with two small hatches on the cage wall. The rest of the room was packed tight with the sort of goods that would never be allowed to leave Tressor if the authorities knew about them.

"Go," Goldie said to the workers. "The instructions are quite clear. I will transfer the beast according to the client's specifications. No sense risking too many members of the crew."

The men gratefully retreated. A moment later, Lain slipped into the hidden room, and Goldie clicked the passage shut behind. He opened the top to the crate and helped Sorrel and the twins out. She sniffed the air and peered in disgust at the surroundings. Goldie pointed first to the troughs on the floor of the cage, then the ones beneath.

"Food and water come in there. Leavings fall through there. Once a day, workers will leave one and take the other. The wood is good and thick. With this door shut, you can make a fair amount of noise without alerting anyone. It isn't luxury, but it will get you there alive, and without prying eyes," he said dispassionately.

"It is horrid," Sorrel growled.

"You don't have many options," Goldie said. "Now, move— quickly. This ship is to leave within the hour."

Sorrel stepped into the cage, her children hopping in to stay with her. She reached out to Lain. He took her hands. It was a solemn moment. In the short time since they had been reunited, Lain had already forgotten how he'd ever lived without her. He had hoped that when this time came, he would have the words to express his joy and sorrow and finding and losing her again so soon, emotions he'd thought had died long ago. No words came. He simply stared into her eyes, and she stared back. Finally, she spoke.

"Come with me," she said.

"I . . ." he began, unprepared for such a request.

"Do not tell me you do not want to. Do not tell me you can look at these children and say you do not feel the need to see them grow." Fresh tears were running down her face now.

"I do."

"Then come with me."

"I cannot. There are things here that need to be done."

"Things that need to be done," she muttered. "Always you are doing things because they need to be done, or they are right to do, or because other people want you to do them. You can find a way to serve your purpose in the new land, and maybe you can be happy there, too! For once in your life, do something because *you* want to do it!"

She stared with agonizing intensity into his eyes.

"Look, stay or go," Goldie barked. "I can smuggle four as easily as three, but make your decision! The longer we delay this ship, the more likely they'll hold it for a search."

When the words finally left Lain's mouth, they came directly from his heart, skipping his mind entirely. "I will go with you."

Sorrel rushed to him and squeezed him tight, openly sobbing as he squeezed her back.

"Fine, fine. Into the cage with you," Goldie said.

Lain stepped inside, the cage door was closed and latched, and the hidden door sealed. For a long while, there were no words. Just a tight, prolonged embrace, copious tears, and thoughts of the future.

#

Lain and Sorrel spoke for a long time. They spoke with hope and enthusiasm of things to come and lands awaiting them. The journey would be an unpleasant one, but they would be making it together. As the minutes rolled on, though the part of each creature that had become sensitive to bad omens and festering plans began to invade their sanctuary. Lain was forced to pull his mind from the bliss and back to reality.

"*Gohveen* . . . something is wrong," Sorrel stated.

"Yes. It has been well over an hour. The ship should have been on its way by now," he said.

She tightened her fists. "It is fine. It will be fine. They are still loading, something like that." She spoke hopefully, but there was doubt in her voice.

"We shall see."

Lain pulled his sword from its scabbard and passed the blade between the slats on the latch end of the cage door. It was a simple door, built to keep wild animals inside, and as such it was locked by way of a simple hinged brace that was easily lifted aside. Lain quietly pushed the cage door open enough to squeeze out. He closed the cage again and climbed on top, pressing his sensitive ear to the ceiling. Hearing nothing of specific concern above, he put his ear to the ventilation slit.

"What is it?" Sorrel asked.

He closed his eyes. "Raised voices. Someone on the deck of the next ship over is arguing."

"About what?"

"The captain of the ship is demanding to see an official proclamation of some kind. The other man says he doesn't need one . . . that voice."

"What? Who is it?"

Before Lain could answer, the sound of the hidden plank being pulled aside drew their attention.

"Mally!" hissed Goldie's voice, whispering through the opening. "We've got trouble. I don't know why, but the man responsible for half of my shipments is on the docks. He is demanding each ship let him personally inspect the hold. He is looking for malthropes!"

"Duule!"

"You know of him?"

"I claimed the bounty on him once."

"That was *you!?* Did you feel as though there weren't enough people who wanted you dead? No matter. This is a problem. He's got blood in his eyes, I can feel it. I hesitate to think of what will happen to me and my crew, let alone the lot of you, if he finds out we are hiding you."

"Take the ship away! Take it to sea! We can run!" Sorrel urged.

"The harbor patrol is in his pocket. They are holding us here, and he could easily close this harbor if he felt the need. Somehow he is convinced there is a malthrope on board one of these ships."

The hidden door slid open, and Goldie found himself face to face with Lain, startling the already frantic elf.

"The deal is off. You may have saved my life seven years ago, but it is no good to me if I lose it now. He won't rest until he finds a malthrope, and I'll be damned if I let him find it on one of *my* ships."

Lain lowered his head. "If he will not rest until he finds a malthrope, then we must give him one," he said. "I will make my way onto the ship he is trying to search now, and I will draw his men away."

"No!" Sorrel gasped.

"It . . . may work. I might be able to get this ship moving once Duule is off the docks, but you'll have to *keep* him off the docks until we pass the harbor buoys. If he suspects we've still got something to hide, a few rings of the harbor bells and we'll be stopped and brought back."

"Fine."

"No, Teyn, we will find another way!" Sorrel cried.

Lain pulled open the cage and held Sorrel one last time. "I am sorry. It has to be this way. Men like Duule are everywhere, and threats like this will always follow me. I can't go with you if it means I would bring that upon you. At least let me ensure that you have your chance."

Sorrel choked back tears and took his hand, pressing it to her cheek. "If ever I meet the gods, I will demand that they tell me what you could have done to anger them so." Finally, she turned to the twins, who were huddled fearfully in the corner. She called to them, her voice faltering. "Wren, Reyna. Come. Say goodbye to Teyn. Say thank you."

The little ones came reluctantly forward, and Lain crouched to meet them eye to eye. Though he doubted they understood what was happening, tears were in their eyes as well. He lowered his head, and the children lowered theirs, pressing their brows against his as he stroked their heads one last time. He held the moment for as long as he dared, then stood and looked to Sorrel.

"Live well," he said. He then pulled his hood up and darted through the cargo hold.

His heart was screaming in pain, and his vision was blurred with tears, but he forced it all aside. There was a job to do now, more important than he'd ever done before. His motions were fluid and flawless as he weaved his way to the decks. The eyes of the sailors were turned to the spectacle on the deck of the ship being boarded by Duule. *All* eyes were watching the escalation on its decks. It was that alone that kept him from view as he threaded among the canvas-strapped crates and bundles littering the deck and made his way to the edge of *The Path of the Sun*. Cutting along the railing and charging for the back of the ship, he spotted the loading arms that had hoisted Sorrel's crate to the ship. The ropes were still dangling from their ends.

His mind worked at the angles, and with a confident leap he hurled himself of the edge of the ship, catching the rope on the way down and swinging in a long arc over the water. He released the rope at a calculated moment and hurtled through the air, catching the anchor line of the ship currently under scrutiny. With ease, he scaled the line and the side of the ship, pulling himself onto the deck. The screaming of the captain and Duule was still enough to keep the monster among the crew from immediately gaining notice.

Duule was standing, flanked by towering henchmen. To his left was Dihsaad, the tracker's hand clutching at the leashes of three hounds with noses to the ground. Lain silently heaved open a chest on the deck. It was filled with coiled rope, but there was just enough space to conceal him. He slipped inside and waited to be discovered.

"Listen to me," Duule growled. "I don't care who you are or what rights you think you have. If you value your life, you will stand aside and let my men search your ship."

"This is an outrage! Why would I harbor a malthrope?" demanded the captain.

"It may have boarded your ship without your notice. This creature is wily," remarked Dihsaad.

The hounds began to bay and pull at their leashes.

"And what is this?" Duule fumed. He turned to his men. "I am through being civil. Clear the way."

His men descended on the assembled sailors, shoving the smaller men aside and threatening the larger ones. Voices began to rise and blades were drawn as Duule's men further intruded, but he commanded them forward. Finally, Dihsaad's hounds reached the chest, scratching at it and howling.

"Open it!" Duule ordered.

The nearest of the henchmen reached for the lid, but before he could touch it Lain burst from within. Chaos erupted. Duule and the captain alike screamed orders at their men. Lain sprinted across the deck, his own weapon still in its scabbard. Duule directed his men forward, charging after the beast. Dihsaad released his hounds, which eagerly made chase. By the time Lain made it to the streets, it seemed that half of Delti had converged there to see the cause of the commotion.

With one vaulting leap, he grasped the edge of a low roof and hauled himself up, springing from building to building in plain sight but out of reach.

#

Goldie reached the deck of *The Path of the Sun* just in time to see Lain vanish into the thick of the city, a veritable mob on his heels. He scanned the decks of the ship until he spotted the captain at the top of the gangplank.

"Ho there! What is keeping us in port? We are losing the day!"

432

Goldie called out.

A greasy-looking thug on the dock side of the gangplank answered. "I am keeping you here until Duule says otherwise."

"With all due respect, sir," Goldie began, marching over to Duule's lackey, "I would think by now that it was clear that Duule found what he was looking for."

"You don't leave until he says so."

"He was looking for a malthrope. He found it on the other ship. Do you honestly think he would find another one here? The filthy things aren't exactly a valued export."

"You stay."

Goldie looked desperately to the horizon, then back to the lackey. "You represent Duule's interests, right?"

"Yeah."

The elf stepped close, speaking so that only the man could hear. "The hull of this ship is stuffed with, among other things, a king's ransom of contraband being sold by Duule himself. Much of it is perishable, and all of it is worth more than your life or mine. Now, do you see that dark patch in the sky to the northeast? That is a storm. A storm we are hoping to beat. If you delay us any longer, we will sail through that patch of bad weather. Perhaps it will delay us, and half of our shipment will spoil. Perhaps it will sink us, and all of that precious cargo will be lost. Duule knows you are holding this boat, correct?"

The man nodded.

"Then he will know that it was your fault that it was delayed. Now, which do you think he would prefer: earning a fortune because you wisely let us go, or losing a fortune because you held us to allow him to search for something he'd already found?"

It did not take the man long to come to a decision.

"You're all right. Head out!"

"Wise decision," Goldie commended, signaling the captain.

#

Lain's retreat took him to the edge of the city. It was a tricky thing to keep far enough ahead to avoid capture but near enough to keep the pursuers on his tail. Some of Duule's men were armed with crossbows—and, unlike other times that he'd been pursued by similarly-equipped individuals, they were not shy about firing them when innocents might be caught in the crossfire. He quickened his pace, heading for a row of bluffs to the north of the city. There, at least,

433

stray shots would not find their way into a crowd. When this day was through, he would have enough blood on his hands without having to worry about people whose only crime was standing too near.

The city began to thin, and the roar of the crowd faded. Behind him, he now heard the pounding of hoofs. Duule and his men had taken to horses, and without the crowded streets to contend with, they were gaining ground. Since their prey had remained visible, they had managed to outrun their hounds. Lain pushed himself harder, leading them as far from the city as he could. The ground was sloping upward when the first bolts of a crossbow, fired wildly from horseback, began to streak past. He cast a glance over his shoulder. There were six horses. One carried Duule, lagging far behind. Two carried men with crossbows, now attempting to load and draw them while at full gallop. Dihsaad rode a fourth horse, and the remainder were ridden by swordsmen.

Lain looked to the sea now. Against the climbing sun, he could see the familiar sails of *The Path of the Sun* just beginning to pull away from the docks. He looked back to the path ahead. It was leading to a stretch of sandy ground overlooking the city. Behind him, the sound of rope cutting through the air buzzed to life. An instant later cords and weights wound themselves around his ankles, sending him hard to the ground. He pulled from his belt a pair of daggers and rolled to his back. With two deft motions, he let them fly. Each one buried itself in the throat of a crossbow-wielding thug. A few moments more was all it took for the other horses to surround him. He pulled a third dagger and severed the ropes binding his ankles. By the time he made it to his feet, the riders were dismounting. He pulled his sword and bared his teeth.

"Kill him! Kill him, kill him, kill him!" bellowed Duule.

The swordsmen descended upon him, battle-notched longswords at the ready. Lain raised the black blade in one hand and the dagger in the other. The clash began. The men he faced were strong, but slow. They heaved their weapons with all of their strength, and where they clashed with the black blade, sparks scattered and flew. Dihsaad dismounted and drew a whip from his belt, lashing at Lain whenever it seemed he would gain the upper hand, and attempting to entangle one or both of his weapons.

The battle raged for minutes, Lain's speed and skill keeping him just barely from harm. The stress of blocking such powerful blows, it seemed, was beginning to take its toll, as the blows came nearer to their marks with each moment. Finally, with a roar of effort, the malthrope swiped the sword through the air with blinding speed. There was a horrid screech and a blinding flash as his masterpiece of a weapon sheared through the blade of one of the longswords. Lain took advantage of the distraction to deliver a punishing kick to the fingers of the swordsman who was still armed, prompting a howl of pain as he dropped the weapon and clutched a clearly broken hand.

Dihsaad lashed his whip, finally meeting his mark. Lain's sword jerked from his fingers, the weapon entangled. The disarmed swordsman dove upon the malthrope and began to rain blows upon him. Lain deflected some, but more and more of them began to connect. He swiped with the dagger, but the enraged thug with the shattered hand seized the wrist with his healthy one and wrenched it hard, knocking the weapon from Lain's hand and leaving him unarmed.

"Restrain him!" Duule ordered.

The healthiest of the henchmen wrestled Lain's wrists behind his back. Duule smiled and dismounted. He leaned down and plucked the black blade from where it had fallen.

"Quite a weapon you've found," Duule said, admiring it. "You were gone for quite a while. What was it? Four years? Five maybe? See, any proper creature—any *thinking* creature—would have known to stay away. It would have known that I am not a man to be trifled with. I was actually banking on it. A rather powerful sorceress who seemed to hate you as much as I came to me after you'd been gone for a while. She wanted to know if you were dead. She made it very clear that she wanted to hear me say yes. I was glad to do so, assuming you'd either drowned or wised up. But not you. You're a blasted malthrope, so you come back. You fall into the old ways because you don't know anything else."

"I do not think you should take him so lightly, Duule. Finish him quickly," Dihsaad advised, kicking the fallen dagger away and then retreating to a safer distance.

"That is not how I conduct business, Dihsaad. You see, to me it is important that my enemies know precisely what mistakes they made before they die. Call it an act of charity. At least they may enter the afterlife a little wiser. Now, malthrope, what you need to understand is that you were never truly my match. You—*look me in the eye when I talk to you!*" He screamed, slapping Lain across the face.

Lain merely kept his eyes on the horizon. Watching . . . waiting . . .

435

"I am going to tell you one last time, malthrope. Look me in the eye when I speak to you, or I will make sure this death drags out for days."

Squinting his keen eyes against the sun and its glare on the sea, Lain watched as the sails of the ship carrying Sorrel crossed the line of buoys. His bloodied and bruised face pulled into a weak grin.

"What could you possibly have to smile about?" Duule growled.

"You are out of time. She's on her way."

Duule's brow furrowed in confusion. In a blur of motion, Lain's foot darted up, striking the pommel of the sword and sending it twirling out of Duule's grasp and skyward. The heel came down with punishing force on the foot of the man restraining him, allowing him to pull his right arm free and deliver a lightning strike to the throat of the other swordsman. He then brought the elbow back and drove it into the gut of the first swordsman. Freeing the other arm. He reached out and plucked the descending sword from the air and, with two well-placed swipes, ended the henchmen. Duule tried to run, but a quick thrust of the blade split his heart. Dihsaad made it a few more steps before Lain closed the gap and, in one strike, separated his head from his shoulders.

And so it ended. Not with a stirring speech or a thrilling duel. Such are the things of stories and legend, but this was an act ill-suited for such things. Such are the acts of heroes, but Lain was no hero. He ended it as he had been taught to end it, the way an assassin would: first with deception, then with efficiency. Taking lives, even vile ones, was not something to be enjoyed or savored. It was a task to be completed, and now it was done.

There was nothing left but to watch as the ship carried its precious cargo over the horizon. When the last glimpse of its mast had slipped from view, he turned his back to sea. He had to return to his purpose. It was all there was now.

Epilogue

With the death of Duule, his empire swiftly devoured itself. A hierarchy of scoundrels and thieves scrambled to seize what power it could. It was a profitable time for Lain, as men and women across Tressor suddenly found that those previously too fearful of Duule's wrath to take action were now only too eager to settle scores. In a few months he completed more than a dozen jobs, thinning the ranks of Tressor's underworld considerably before things finally settled into a new stability. It was enough to earn him a small fortune, and with it he managed to convince some of the slaves he'd freed in the past to purchase a whole plantation and everyone on it. Fittingly, he chose Jarrad's land.

Seeing the place that had at once been his home and prison freed of its yolk forever stirred something in Lain's soul. With Sorrel gone, this bit of land and the suffering it had brought were the last real connections he had to Tressor. Now he had destroyed it, broken its chains. What it symbolized was gone.

He thought about what he'd seen in his travels. He remembered the tight, isolated cities of the north, and the way the people dressed in heavy clothing. His purpose would be easier to pursue there. He could pass among the people of that land unrecognized, just another face hidden in the hood of a cloak. Yes. He would go north . . . but before he left, there was one thing that remained to be done.

He made his way back to Delti, to the home of Goldie. The elf was working at his desk as he always was, a single light illuminating the charts and lists. Lain slipped inside silently and spoke the elf's name. Goldie shuddered, but did not gasp or scream, as though he'd been expecting the interruption. He simply opened a drawer and pulled from it a small rag. Lain accepted it.

"She said she knew there was a question you wanted to ask," Goldie said, "and that the answer was yes. Any idea what that means?"

He nodded.

"Good. Is my debt paid?"

He nodded again. Without another word or even a sound, he slipped back into the shadows, and out into the street. He made his way west, to a hole in a mountain, its walls etched with patterns and its floor scattered with smoothed rocks. He placed the rag reverently beneath one of the stones. Sorrel was gone, but she was safe, and she was happy. His heart would always be with her. It was hers, and it was just as well. Without her, he had no need for it any longer.

His most cherished memory laid to rest in a fitting memorial, he stepped once more into the light and set off for the north. There were slaves to free. There were jobs to be done. There was a purpose to serve. Always.

###

ABOUT THE AUTHOR

A native of Bayonne, NJ—the fabled birthplace of George R. R. Martin—Joseph Lallo is an unlikely entry into the world of literature. After a childhood spent daydreaming and reading, he fully intended to pursue a career in the tech sector. He received a Master's Degree in Computer Engineering from NJIT and subsequently got a job working IT. Things changed when, in January 2010, his friends finally convinced him to publish the story that had accumulated over the course of a decade of spare time. That story, now known as the Book of Deacon Trilogy, was a surprise hit, and once he got a taste of the world of indie writing, he was hooked. Now he splits his time between crunching numbers, writing novels, and writing articles and reviews for BrainLazy.com, a group blog he helps run.

OTHER BOOKS
BY JOSEPH R. LALLO

The Book of Deacon Series
The Book of Deacon
The Great Convergence
The Battle of Verril
The D'Karon Apprentice
The Crescents

Book of Deacon Sidequests
Jade
The Redemption of Desmeres
The Adventures of Rustle and Eddy

The Big Sigma Series
Bypass Gemini
Unstable Prototypes
Artificial Evolution
Temporal Contingency

www.ingramcontent.com/pod-product-compliance
Lightning Source LLC
Chambersburg PA
CBHW070734120726
47910CB00001B/97